Orion and King Arthur

Orion
and
King Arthur

BEN BOVA

TOR®

A Tom Doherty Associates Book

New York

ORION AND KING ARTHUR

Copyright © 2011 by Ben Bova

Originally published as an audio book by Audible

A Tor Book
Published by Tom Doherty Associates, LLC
175 Fifth Avenue
New York, NY 10010

www.tor-forge.com

Tor® is a registered trademark of Tom Doherty Associates, LLC.

Library of Congress Cataloging-in-Publication Data

Bova, Ben, 1932–
    Orion and King Arthur / Ben Bova. — 1st ed.
        p. cm.
    "A Tom Doherty Associates book."
    ISBN 978-0-7653-3017-8 (hardcover)
    ISBN 978-1-4299-4752-7 (e-book)
 1. Orion (Fictitious character)—Fiction.   2. Time travel—Fiction.
3. Gods—Fiction.   I. Title.
    PS3552.O84O676 2012
    813'.54—dc23

                                                    2012011662

First Hardcover Edition: July 2012

Printed in the United States of America

0 9 8 7 6 5 4 3 2 1

To my tennis buddies: good friends and true

Nearly all men can stand adversity, but if you want to test a man's character, give him power.

—Abraham Lincoln

Orion and King Arthur

Prologue: Heorot

1

For the first time that bitterly cold winter, Heorot was bright again, ringing with song and a king's gratitude to the hero.

And then the beast roared, out in the icy darkness.

"But he's dead!" King Hrothgar bellowed, pointing to the shaggy monster's arm that now was affixed over the mead-hall's entrance doorway.

"I killed him," exclaimed Beowulf, "with these bare hands."

Hrothgar turned to his queen, Wealhtheow, sitting beside him on the dais between the royal torches. She was as beautiful as a starry spring night, her raven-dark hair tumbling past her shoulders, her lustrous gray eyes focused beyond the beyond.

Wealhtheow was a seer. Gripping the carved arms of her throne, shuddering under the spell of her magic, she pronounced in a hollow voice, "The monster is truly dead. Now its mother has come to claim vengeance upon us."

Hrothgar turned as white as his beard. His thanes, who had been sloshing mead and singing their old battle songs, fell into the silence of cold terror.

The captives from Britain huddled together in sudden fear in the far corner of the hall. I could see the dread on their faces. Hrothgar had sworn to sacrifice them to his gods if Beowulf had not killed the monster. For a few brief hours they had thought they would be freed. Now the horror had returned.

I turned to gaze upon the lovely Queen Wealhtheow. She was much younger than Hrothgar, yet her divine gray eyes seemed to hold the wisdom of eternity. And she was staring directly at me.

How and why I was in Heorot I had no idea. I could remember nothing beyond the day we had arrived on the Scylding shore, pulling on the oars of our longboat against the freezing spray of the tide.

My name is Orion, that much I knew. And I serve Beowulf, hero of the Geats, who had sailed here to Daneland to kill the monster that had turned timbered Heorot, the hall of the stag, from King Hrothgar's great pride to his great sorrow.

For months the monster had stalked Heorot, striking by night when the warriors had drunk themselves into mead-besotted dreams. At length none would enter the great hall, not even stubborn old Hrothgar himself. Until Beowulf arrived with the fourteen of us and loudly proclaimed that he would kill the beast that very night.

Beowulf was a huge warrior, two axe handles across the shoulders, with flaxen braids to his waist and eyes as clear blue as the icy waters of a fiord. Strength he had, and courage. Also, he was a boaster of unparalleled brashness.

The very night he came to Heorot with his fourteen companions he swaggered so hard that narrow-eyed Unferth, the most cunning of the Scylding thanes, tried to take him down a peg. Beowulf bested him in a bragging contest and won the roars of Hrothgar's mead-soaked companions.

After midnight Hrothgar and his Scyldings left the hall. The

torches were put out, the hearth fire sank to low, glowering embers. It was freezing cold; I could hear the wind moaning outside.
Beowulf and the rest of us stretched out to sleep. My shirt of
chain mail felt like ice against my skin. I dilated my peripheral
blood vessels and increased my heart rate to make myself warmer,
without even asking myself how I knew to do this.

I had volunteered to stay awake and keep watch. I could go for
days without sleep and the others were glad to let me do it. We
had all drunk many tankards of honey-sweetened mead, yet my
body burned away its effects almost immediately. I felt alert, aware,
strong.

Through the keening wind and bitter chill I could sense the
monster shambling about in the night outside, looking for more
victims to slaughter.

I sat up and grasped my sword an instant before the beast burst
through the massive double doors of the mead-hall, snarling and
slavering. The others scattered in every direction, shrieking, eyes
wide with fear.

I felt terror grip my heart, too. As I stared at the approaching
monster I recalled a giant cave bear, in another time, another life.
It had ripped me apart with its razor-sharp claws. It had crushed
my bones in its fanged jaws. It had killed me.

Beowulf leaped to his feet and charged straight at the monster.
It rose onto its hind legs, twice the height of a warrior, and knocked
Beowulf aside with a swat of one mighty paw. His sword went
flying out of his hand as he landed flat on his back with a thud
that shook the pounded-earth floor.

Everything seemed to slow down into a dreamy, sluggish
lethargy. I saw Beowulf scrambling to his feet, but slowly, lan-
guidly, as if he moved through a thick invisible quagmire. I could
see the beast's eyes moving in its head, globs of spittle forming

between its pointed teeth and dropping slowly, slowly to the earthen floor.

Beowulf charged again, bare-handed this time. The monster focused on him, spread its forelegs apart as if to embrace this pitiful fool and then crush him. I ducked beneath those sharp-clawed paws and rammed my sword into the beast's belly, up to the hilt, and then hacksawed upward.

Blood spurted over me. The monster bellowed with pain and fury and knocked me sideways across the hall. Beowulf leaped on its back, as leisurely as in a dream. The others were gathering their senses now, hacking at the beast with their swords. I got to my feet just as the brute dropped ponderously back onto all fours and started for the shattered door, my sword still jammed into its gut.

One of the men got too close and the monster snatched him in its jaws and crushed the life out of him. I shuddered at the memory, but I took up Beowulf's dropped sword and swung as hard as I could at the beast's shoulder. The blade hit bone and stuck. The beast howled again and tried to shake Beowulf off its back. He pitched forward, grabbed at the sword sticking in its shoulder, and wormed it through the tendons of the joint like a butcher carving a roast.

Howling, the monster shook free of him again, but Beowulf clutched its leg while the rest of us hacked away. Blood splattered everywhere, men roared and screamed.

And then the beast shambled for the door, with Beowulf still clutching its leg. The leg tore off and the monster stumbled out into the night, howling with pain, its life's blood spurting from its wounds.

That was why we feasted and sang at Heorot the following night. Until the beast's mother roared its cry of vengeance against us.

"I raid the coast of Britain," Hrothgar cried angrily, "and sack the cities of the Franks. Yet in my own hall I must cower like a weak woman!"

"Fear not, mighty king," Beowulf answered bravely. "Just as I killed the monster will I slay its mother. And this time I will do it alone!"

Absolute silence fell over Heorot.

Then the king spoke. "Do this and you can have your choice of reward. Anything in my kingdom will be yours!"

Before Beowulf could reply, sly Unferth spoke up. "You have no sword, mighty warrior."

"It was carried off by the dying monster," Beowulf said.

"Here then, take mine." Unferth unbuckled the sword at his waist and handed it to the hero.

The hall fell absolutely silent. Giving one's sword to another was a mark of the highest respect, even admiration. Unferth could pay Beowulf no higher honor. Yet it seemed to me that Unferth was dissembling. I saw hatred glittering in his cold reptilian eyes.

Beowulf pulled the blade from its scabbard and whistled it through the air. "A good blade and true. I will return it you, Unferth, with the monster's blood on it."

Everyone shouted approval, especially the British captives. There were an even dozen of them: eleven young boys and girls, none yet in their teens, and a wizened old man with big, staring eyes and a beard even whiter than Hrothgar's.

The monster roared outside again, and silenced the cheers.

Beowulf strode to the patched-up door of the mead-hall, Unferth's sword in his mighty right hand.

"Let no one follow me!" he cried.

No one did. We all stood stunned and silent as he marched out into the dark. I turned slightly and saw that Unferth was smiling cruelly, his lips forming a single word: "Fool."

2

"Orion." Queen Wealhtheow called my name.

She stepped down from the royal dais and walked through the crowd toward me. The others seemed frozen, like statues, staring sightlessly at the door. Hrothgar did not move, did not even breathe, as his queen approached me. The Scylding thanes, Beowulf's other companions, even the frightened British captives—none of them blinked or breathed or twitched.

"They are in stasis, Orion," Wealhtheow said as she came within arm's reach of me. "They can neither see nor hear us."

Those infinite gray eyes of hers seemed to show me worlds upon worlds, lifetimes I had led—we had led together—in other epochs, other worldlines.

"Do you remember me, Orion?"

"I love you," I whispered, knowing it was true. "I have loved you through all of spacetime."

"Yes, my love. What more do you remember?"

It was like clawing at a high smooth stone wall. I shook my head. "Nothing. I don't even know why I'm here—why you're here."

"You remember nothing of the Creators? Of your previous missions?"

"The Creators." Vaguely I recalled godlike men and women. "Aten."

"Yes," she said. "Aten."

Aten had created me and sent me through spacetime to do his bidding. Haughty and mad with power, he called me his tool, his hunter. More often I was an assassin for him.

"I remember . . . the snow, the time of eternal cold." But it was all like the misty tendrils of a dream, wafting away even as I reached for them.

"I was with you then," she said.

"The cave bear. It killed me." I could feel the pain of my ribs being crushed, hear my own screams drowned in spouting blood.

"You've lived many lives."

"And died many deaths."

"Yes, my poor darling. You have suffered much."

I remembered her name: Anya. She was one of the Creators, I realized. I loved a goddess. And she loved me. Yet we were destined to be torn away from each other, time and again, over the eons and light-years of the continuum.

"This beast that ravaged Heorot was not a natural animal," she told me. "It was engendered and controlled by one of the Creators."

"Which one? Aten?"

She shook her head. "It makes no difference. I am here to see that the beast does not succeed. You must help me."

Deep in my innermost memories I recalled that the Creators squabbled among themselves like spoiled children. They directed the course of human history and sent minions such as me to points in spacetime to carry out their whims. Many times I have killed for Aten, and many times have I died for him. Yet he brings me back, sneering at my pains and fears, and sends me out again.

I am powerless to resist his commands—he thinks. But more than once I have defied his wishes. At Troy I helped Odysseos and his Achaeans to triumph. Deep in interstellar space I led whole fleets into battle against him.

"Has Aten sent me here, or have you?" I asked her.

She smiled at me, a smile that could warm a glacier. "I have brought you here, Orion, to help Beowulf slay both monsters."

"Is Beowulf one of your creatures?"

She laughed. "That bragging oaf? No, my darling, he is as mortal as a blade of grass."

"But why is this important?" I asked. "Why has your enemy used these beasts to attack Heorot?"

"That I will explain after you have helped Beowulf to kill the second monster."

"If I live through the ordeal," I said, feeling sullen, resentful.

"My poor darling. I ask so much of you. If I could do this myself, I would."

Then she kissed me swiftly on the lips. I would have faced an entire continent filled with monsters for her.

3

The tingle of her lips on mine had not yet faded when the others around us stirred to life once again. And Wealhtheow was somehow back on her throne, on the dais beside her husband, aged Hrothgar.

Her husband. The thought burned in me. Then I realized that one of the men in this timbered mead-hall was one of the Creators, in disguise, controlling the monsters that killed Hrothgar's warriors. Why? What was the *purpose* of it all?

That was not for me to know. Not yet. My task was clear. The king and queen left the mead-hall, heading back to Hrothgar's fortress. The others milled about for a while, then started back through the frigid winter night also.

It was easy for me to slip away from them and start down the rocky trail that led to the sea. The moon scudded in and out of low dark clouds. In its fitful light I could clearly see the spoor of dark blood that the dying monster had left from the night before. This was the track Beowulf was following. I hurried along it.

The blood spoor ended at the sea, where the waves crashed against the craggy headland. Our longboat was still tucked up on the rocks, I saw, its mast stored along the deck. No one guarded it. There was no need. The boat was under Hrothgar's protection; no Scylding would dare touch it.

Bitter cold it was, with a wind coming off the sea that sliced through my chain mail shirt and chilled me to the bone despite my conscious control of my blood circulation.

The rocky cove stretched out to my left. In the moonlit shadows I thought I saw caves in among the rocks at the cove's far end. The den of the monster, perhaps.

A growling roar, like the rumble of distant thunder, came across the icy wind. I raced across the rocks toward the caves.

The second cave was the monster's den, half awash with the incoming tide, dimly lit by phosphorescent patches of lichen clinging to the rock walls.

Female this beast may be, but it was even bigger than its slain offspring, glowing faintly white in the dimly lit cave, snarling at Beowulf as it reared up on its hind legs. Even mighty Beowulf looked like a pitiful dwarf next to its enormous size.

He was already bleeding from shoulder to waist, his chain mail shirt in shreds from the beast's raking claws. He clutched Unferth's sword in both hands and swung mightily at the monster, to no avail. It was like hitting the brute with a tress of hair.

The monster knocked Beowulf to his knees with a blow that would have crushed a normal man. His sword blade snapped in half. And I realized that Unferth had given Beowulf a useless weapon. Crafty Unferth with his glittering snake's eyes was the other Creator among the Scyldings.

I ran toward the beast and again the world seemed to slow into dreamy, languid motion.

"Beowulf!" I shouted. "Here!"

I threw my own sword to him. It spun lazily through the air. He caught it in one massive hand and scrabbled away from the monster on his knees.

I circled around to the side away from Beowulf, trying to draw the brute's attention before it killed the hero of the Geats. Out of the corner of my eye I saw a gleaming horde of treasure: gold coins and jewels heaped on the dank cave floor. Swords and warriors' armor, spears and helmets were strewn in profusion. Whitened bones and gape-mouthed skulls littered the cave floor. The monsters had brought their kills here for many years.

The beast ignored the kneeling Beowulf and bellowed at me, dropping to all fours as it moved to protect its horde. But it moved slowly, as if in a dream. I dashed to the pile of weapons and pulled out the first sword I could reach.

Barely in time. The monster was almost on top of me. I slashed at its slavering jaws and it howled in pain and fury. I feinted sideways, then stepped back—and tripped on a helmet lying at my feet.

Off balance, I staggered backward. The beast swung at me; I could see those razor-sharp claws coming but there was nothing I could do to stop them. The blow knocked me onto my back. The monster's jaws reached for me, teeth like a row of swords. I clutched my own sword in both hands and rammed it upward into the beast's open mouth, but it did no good. Its teeth closed around me. I was going to be crushed to death, just as I had been all those long eons ago.

But the monster suddenly howled and dropped me. It turned

to face Beowulf, bleeding, battered, but hacking at the beast's flank with the fury of a berserker.

As the brute turned away from me, I scrambled to my feet and thrust my sword into its neck, angling it upward to find the brain or spine.

It collapsed so suddenly that it nearly smothered Beowulf. For long moments we both stood on tottering legs, gasping for breath, spattered with our own blood and the monster's, staring down at its enormous carcass.

Then Beowulf looked up and grinned at me. "Help me take off its head," he said.

<h1 style="text-align:center">4</h1>

It was pearly pink dawn when we staggered out of the cave. Beowulf carried the monster's gigantic shaggy head on his shoulder as lightly as if it were a bit of gossamer.

We blinked at the morning light. Icy waves lapped at our ankles.

Beowulf turned to me, his cocky grin gone. "Orion, I told Hrothgar before all his thanes that I would kill the monster myself, with no one's help."

I nodded, but said nothing.

Suddenly his broad, strong face took on the expression of a guilty little boy's. "Will you go on ahead and say that you searched for me, but could not find me? Then I can come later with the beast's head."

I glanced down at my bloody arms. "And my wounds?"

"Say you were set upon by wolves as you searched in the night for me."

I smiled at his stupid pride, but said, "Yes, I will do it."

"Good," Beowulf said. He dropped the monster's head and sat on a rock. "I will rest here for a while. I could use a little sleep."

So it was that I returned to Hrothgar's fortress and told the king that I had searched for Beowulf to no avail. All that long morning and well past noon we waited in growing gloom. Unferth said confidently that the monster had killed Beowulf.

He was considerably disheartened when the hero of the Geats finally arrived—with the monster's shaggy head on his wounded shoulder.

That night the feasting at Heorot was without stint. The torches flamed, the mead flowed, the thanes sang praises of Beowulf, and the women vied for his merest glance. Hrothgar's bard began to compose a saga. The king promised the British captives that they would be ransomed and returned to their dank, dreary island.

Only Unferth seemed unhappy, slinking in the shadows and glaring at me.

Queen Wealhtheow sat on her throne, smiling graciously at the uproarious celebration. Long past midnight, the king and queen left the mead-hall. Warriors and even churls paired off with women and strolled off into the darkness.

At last timbered Heorot fell silent. The torches were extinguished. The hearth fire burned low. I was left alone, so I stretched out on the earthen floor next to the fading embers and willed myself to sleep.

I dreamed, yet it was not a dream. I was standing in another place, perhaps a different universe altogether. There was no ground, no sky, only a silver glow like moonlight that pervaded everything. Wealhtheow stood before me, but now she wore a formfitting outfit of glittering silver metal. Anya, the warrior goddess, she was. In another time, a distant place, she was worshipped as Athena.

"You did well, Orion," she said in a low silken voice.

"Thank you."

"Your wounds?"

"They are already healing," I said.

"Yes, accelerated self-repair was built into you."

I wanted to reach out and take her in my arms, but I could not.

Instead, I asked, "Can we be together now?"

In the deepest recess of my memory I recalled a time, a lovely woodland filled with tame, graceful animals that we called Paradise, when we were together and happy. The other Creators, especially the jealous Aten, had torn her away from me.

"Not yet, my love," she said, with a sadness in her eyes that matched my own despair. "Not yet."

"At least, can I know why I was sent to Heorot? Why was it important to slay those beasts?"

"To save the British captives, of course."

That surprised me. "The captives? Those pimply-faced youngsters and that emaciated old man?"

She smiled knowingly. "One of those pimply-faced youngsters is the son of a Roman who stayed behind after the legions left Britain. His name is Artorius."

I shrugged. It made no sense to me.

"He will be important one day. A light against the darkness." She reached out her hand to me. "The sword you found in the cave. Please give it to me."

Puzzled, I detached the scabbarded sword from my belt and handed it to her. She slowly drew out the blade, examined the inscription on it, and smiled.

"Yes," she said in a whisper, "he will need this later on."

I read the one word inscribed on the matchless steel blade.

Excalibur.

BOOK I

Dux Bellorum

CHAPTER ONE

Amesbury Fort

1

"A Sarmatian, you say?" Sir Bors looked me up and down, sour disbelief plain on his scarred, bearded face. "And what is your name?"

"Orion," I replied. It was the one thing I was certain of. How I came to this time and place I knew not.

"And why are you here?" asked Sir Bors.

We were standing in the dingy courtyard of a hilltop fort named Amesbury, its walls nothing more than a rickety palisade of timber staves. These Britons had tried to build their forts in the way the Roman legions had, but their engineering skills were poor. They stared at the ruins of Roman aqueducts and monuments and thought that the stonework had been done by giants or magicians.

A few dozen men milled about the bare dirt courtyard, some leading horses, a few practicing swordplay with one another. The place smelled of dung and sweat. And fear.

"I came to serve King Arthur against the Saxons," I said.

Bors' eyes widened. "*King* Arthur? You've made him your king, have you?"

I felt confused. "I thought—"

Bors planted both fists on his hips and pushed his scarred face so close to mine that I could smell the stale wine on his breath.

"Ambrosius is our king, Sarmatian! Young Arthur may be his nephew, but the pup's still wet behind the ears. King indeed!"

I said nothing.

Bors grumbled, "His uncle's put him in charge of Amesbury fort here and sent Merlin to watch over him, but that doesn't make him anything more than an inexperienced babe in the woods."

"I . . . I'm sorry," I stammered. "I meant to say King Ambrosius."

Bors snorted with disdain.

My mind was spinning. I remembered Artorius as a skinny, pimply-faced boy, a captive of the Danes when I served Beowulf. I had saved him then, I dimly recalled.

Somewhere in my mind I knew he was to be king of the Britons, and he would lead these island people against the invading barbarians. Britain had been abandoned by the Roman Empire after centuries of their occupation. The legions had returned to Rome to fight against the hordes of Goths who were slashing into the empire's heartland. Britain was left to fend for itself, wide open to invasion by the barbarian Angles and Saxons.

Aten had put that knowledge into my mind. But why he had sent me through spacetime to Amesbury fort I did not know. Aten, the Golden One, is my master, my Creator, sneering and superior. I have died many times, in many strange and distant places, but always he brings me back, revives me to send me on still another task of pain and danger.

"You are my creature, Orion," he has told me often. "My hunter. I built you and you will do as I command."

I hate Aten and his mad dreams of controlling all of spacetime to suit his whims. There are other Creators, as well, haughty and demanding, toying with human history like children playing with dolls. Cruel gods and goddesses, all of them.

Except for Anya.

Anya of the gray eyes and supernal beauty. Anya is the only one among those Creators who cares at all for their creatures. Who cares for me. I love Anya and she loves me. Aten knows this and, vicious with implacable jealousy, sends me far from her, to serve him and die over and over again.

"Well, you're big enough," said Sir Bors, snapping me back to the moment. "Can you fight?"

I smiled tightly. I had led Odysseos' men over the high stone wall of Troy. I had made Mongol warriors gape at my battle prowess. I had helped Beowulf kill Grendel and its mother.

"I can fight," I said.

Sir Bors barely reached to my shoulder. He was thick and solid as a barrel, though, his arms heavy with muscle. He wore only a cracked and stained leather jerkin over his tattered knee-length tunic. But he had a long Celtic broadsword belted at his hip. I was in chain mail and linen tunic, my sword strapped to my back.

Drawing his sword from its leather scabbard, Bors said, "Let me see what you can do."

"Wait!" a young voice cried from behind me. "Let me test him."

I turned and saw a handsome tall nobleman walking toward us, so young that his beard hardly darkened his chin. His eyes were light and clear, flecked with gold, his shoulder-length hair a light sandy brown, almost blond. He was smiling warmly.

"My lord," Bors said, his tone several notches softer than it had been, "this Sarmatian—"

So this was Arthur. He had grown into a strong young man

since the time when he'd been a starveling captive of Hrothgar, king of the Scyldings, in Daneland.

"He's got good shoulders, Bors," said Arthur. Then, to me, he added, "Let us see if you know how to use your sword."

Bors objected, "But, my lord, you shouldn't engage yourself with a stranger. He might be an assassin, sent to kill you!"

Arthur laughed aloud. He had no fear of an assassin. He did not know that I had murdered men in other eras, at Aten's behest.

A squire, not much younger than Arthur himself, trudged up and handed him his helmet and a shield with a blood-red dragon painted on it. I drew my own sword, heard its steel tongue hiss as it came out into the sunlight. My fingers tightened on its leather-wrapped hilt.

"Where is your helmet, friend, your shield?" Arthur asked as he stood before me. His iron helmet covered his cheeks and had a nosepiece shaped like an upside-down cross.

"I won't need them," I said.

His smile turned down a little. "Pride goes before a fall, Sarmatian."

"Then I will fall," I replied.

Arthur shrugged, then put his shield up and advanced toward me, sword cocked in his right hand.

My senses went into overdrive, as they always do when I face battle. The world around me seemed to slow down, as if everything was happening in a dream. I could see Arthur's gold-flecked amber eyes blinking slowly over the rim of his shield. And Sir Bors stepping sideways to keep at my side. His sword was still in his hand, ready to strike me down if I endangered Arthur. I thought he was more worried that Arthur did not have the skill or experience to face a true fighting man than fearful that I was an assassin.

Arthur swung at me in lethargic slow motion, a powerful over-hand cut that would have sliced me down to the navel if I hadn't danced lightly out of harm's way. He grunted, frowned, and advanced upon me in sluggish slow motion.

I feinted once to the left, then slashed at his shield, splitting it in two with a loud cracking sound. My blade would have taken Arthur's arm off if I hadn't pulled back in time.

Arthur's eyes went wide with surprise. After only a moment's hesitation, he tossed away the broken shield and came at me again. He smashed another mighty overhand slash at me. I parried it easily and his blade shattered into several pieces with a brittle snap.

"Hold!" Bors shouted, sticking his sword between us.

I stepped back.

If Arthur had feared that I would kill him he gave no sign of it. Instead, he tossed away the broken stub of his sword and then reached out for mine.

"That's a fine piece of steel," he said admiringly as I handed the sword to him.

Without thinking of why, I answered, "I know where you can get one that's even better, my lord."

2

It took hours of arguing and cajoling, but at last Arthur and I set out for the distant lake in search of the sword I promised him. Sir Bors and the other knights were dead set against the king's nephew traveling alone with a stranger from a distant land. Bors complained that the fort might be attacked by Saxon raiders at any time, and Arthur's place was where his uncle had put him. But wizened old Merlin was on my side.

"The Sarmatian brings good fortune to Arthur," the old wizard said, stroking his long white beard as he spoke. The beard was knotted and filthy, his homespun robe even dirtier, but all the knights and squires stared at him with wide-eyed awe. They would not step closer than five paces to him; Merlin walked through the little fort's dung-dotted courtyard as if protected by a magical aura.

In truth, I saw a burning intelligence in the old man's narrowed eyes, a keen awareness that belied his wrinkled, ragged appearance. Beneath those shaggy gray brows his eyes were shrewd, sharp, penetrating. Was he one of the Creators in disguise?

To satisfy the suspicious knights, Merlin cast a spell to protect Arthur, nothing but hand-waving and muttering as far as I could see. But it seemed to satisfy Sir Bors and the others, at least enough to allow their young leader to leave the fort with me and no one else.

For two days we rode, and I got to know Arthur a little. He was burning for fame and glory. His highest hope was to one day be named Dux Bellorum: battle leader of his uncle's forces.

Yet, like many an untried youth, he doubted his own abilities.

"I can see it in the faces of Bors and the others," he told me as we camped for the night in a dark, dank forest. The huge, broad-boled trees grew so thickly that much of the day we had been forced to lead our horses afoot. "They would never follow someone so young."

"They will, my lord," I said, "once you prove yourself in battle."

He shook his head mournfully. "The curse of the Britons, friend Orion, is that they will not follow anyone for long."

"They will follow you, my lord. I'm sure of it."

In the darkness of the forest night I heard him make a sound that might have been a sigh. "No, Orion. Look at us! Ambrosius calls himself high king, but who follows him? A handful, that's all. You travel for two days in any direction and you pass through two or three different kingdoms. We have kings every few miles, each of them jealous of all the others."

"No wonder the Saxons can raid and plunder as they wish."

"Yes," he said grimly. "Our people shatter like the sword I used against you. One blow and they break."

He was silent for a moment. Then, "But if I *could* bring all the Britons together, unite all these petty kingdoms . . ."

"You could clear the land of the barbarian invaders," I finished his thought.

This time he sighed unmistakably. "It's a pretty dream, Orion. But only a dream."

The ambition was there. He had the dream. But he needed the courage to make it come true. I could sense that he was longing for the daring, the tenacity, the strength to become the true leader of all the Britons.

Again Arthur fell silent, this time for many moments. At length, he spoke up again.

"That sword of yours," he said, changing the subject because it was too painful for him to continue, "a sword such as that is a rare treasure, Orion. A man would travel to the ends of the earth to get such fine steel for himself."

Like so much else, the art of steel had been lost when the Romans departed. In centuries to come the Celts would learn the art of fine steel-making, but that time was far in the future of these dark years.

"You could have taken my sword from me," I said.

He laughed softly as he lay in his blankets. "I'd have to kill you for it, I wager."

Lying on the ground a few feet from him, with the dying embers of our tiny fire between us, I replied, "Not so, my lord; I would give it to you willingly."

It was too dark to see the expression on his face. The night wind keened above us like an evil spirit, cold and harsh, setting the trees to moaning.

"No," Arthur said at last. "If I am meant to drive the Saxons out of our island, I will not do it with another man's steel. I must have my own. Merlin prophesied that I would, when I was just a lad."

He was hardly more than a lad now, yet this young man wanted to drive off the Saxons and other barbarians who had seized most of the coast of what would one day be England.

3

I dreamed that night, but it was not a dream.

I found myself in an emptiness, a broad featureless plain without hill or tree or even a horizon: nothing but an endless flat plain covered with a softly billowing golden mist stretching out in every direction to infinity.

Vaguely, I remembered being there before, in other lives, other eras. And, just as I expected, I saw a tiny golden glow far off in the distance, like a candle's warm beckoning light, but steady, constant, without a flicker.

I began to walk toward it. I was clad as I had been when awake, in a simple tunic and chain mail. But my sword was gone. Except for the little dagger that Odysseos had given me during our siege of Troy, I was unarmed.

Something drew me to that beacon of light. Despite myself, I began to run toward it. Faster and faster I raced, legs churning through the ground mist, arms pumping, my lungs sucking in air. After what seemed like hours I was gasping, my throat raw, my legs aching from exertion. But I could not stop. I wanted to rest, but I was unable to stop. I was drawn to the light, like an insect obeying an inbuilt command.

The tiny distant glow became a golden sphere, a miniature sun, so bright and hot that I could not look directly at it. I raised my arms to shield my eyes from its glare, yet still I ran, racing toward it as if it were an oasis in a world-covering desert, a magnet pulling me with irresistible force.

At last I could run no more. Soaked with sweat, exhausted, panting as if my lungs would burst, I collapsed onto the strangely yielding ground, still blanketed with the perfumed golden mist.

"Are you tired, Orion?" a mocking voice asked. I knew who it was: Aten, the Golden One. My Creator.

The blazing bright golden sphere slowly dissolved to reveal him. He stood over me, strong and handsome: thick golden mane of hair, eyes tawny as a lion's, perfectly proportioned body encased in a formfitting suit of golden mail.

He sneered down at me. "What is this madness you are engaged in, Orion? Where are you leading that young pup?"

I blinked up at him. His radiance was so brilliant it made my eyes water. "I thought you wanted me to—"

Angrily, Aten snapped, "You are not supposed to think, creature! Your purpose is to do what I instruct you to do. Nothing more. And nothing less."

"But Arthur needs—"

"I will decide what Arthur needs, not you!" Aten snarled. "I want you to help him win a few battles, not take him on a foolish excursion through such dangerous territory."

I bowed my head, my eyes burning at the radiance streaming from him.

"Arthur's only purpose is to resist the Angles and Saxons well enough to force them to unite against the Britons. Then they will drive the Celtic oafs into the western sea and take the island for themselves."

"But what will happen to Arthur?"

"He will be killed."

"No!"

Aten's voice hardened. "All men die, Orion. Only my own creatures, such as yourself, are revived to serve me again."

"But Arthur . . ."

"He could make a nuisance of himself," Aten said. "He could become too powerful. For the time being, I allow him to live. But that time will end soon enough."

"And then?"

"Then the Angles and Saxons and other barbarian tribes will create a mighty empire, Orion. An empire that spans the globe and begins to reach out into space."

"But can't Arthur be permitted—"

"Stop pleading for him, Orion! Obey my commands. That is your destiny. Arthur's destiny is death and obscurity."

I wanted to argue with him. I wanted to tell him that I would not obey his commands, that I would help Arthur and save him.

But suddenly I was sitting on the ground at our forest camp again, soaked with sweat, breathing heavily. The first milky light of the coming dawn was just starting to filter through the tall trees. Arthur slept across the ashes of our dead campfire from me, as blissfully as a man without a care in the universe.

Should I turn back to Amesbury fort? Abandon this quest for a sword for young Arthur?

His eyes snapped open, bright and clear as the finest amber. He was awake instantly.

"How far are we from my sword, Orion?" he asked as he sat up, all youthful eagerness.

"Not far, my lord," I replied. "We will reach the lake today."

I couldn't turn back now. I couldn't disappoint Arthur. He trusted me, and I would not betray him, not even for Aten and all his haughty demands.

Yet I should have known that Aten would not willingly allow us to reach our goal.

4

The forest was like a maze of giant trees, their boles as massive as the pillars of a mighty cathedral, their thick leafy canopy so high above us that it was like a dark green roof that blotted out the sun. We had to walk our horses most of the morning, picking through the sturdy trees while birds whistled far overhead and tiny furred creatures chattered at us.

The ground sloped gradually downhill. We were nearing the lake, I realized, although how I knew about the lake and its location was beyond me. Something in my mind told me that we would find the sword for Arthur there; but just how and why—I had no idea.

The forest thinned out as we led the horses, but the underbrush became thicker between the trees. I saw a clearing up ahead, strong morning sunlight slanting through it, and smelled smoke. It was rising from a tiny thatched farmhouse.

Too much smoke. The farmhouse was afire.

"Saxons!" Arthur whispered, dropping to one knee as we peered through the underbrush at the scene in the clearing. I crouched down beside him.

A dozen men in long blond braids and steel-studded leather jerkins were laughing and whooping as two of their compatriots dragged a pair of screaming, struggling teenaged girls across the clearing toward them. A trio of bodies lay in their own blood before the burning farmhouse door: husband, wife, and baby.

Arthur stared, barely breathing.

"We've got to stop them," I whispered.

"Two against fourteen?"

"They'll murder those girls when they've finished with them."

Arthur wet his lips and shook his head. "Too many of them, Orion. It's useless."

He was no fool. Young he may be, but Arthur was not rash. He was loath to charge in against hopeless odds.

"Perhaps we can at least divert their attention," I whispered hastily, "long enough for the girls to get away."

Without waiting for his reply, I pushed through the screening foliage and stepped out into the clearing, keeping my sword in its scabbard upon my back. Although the Saxons' attention was centered on the struggling, pleading girls, one of them noticed me approaching and pointed toward me.

"What clan are you?" I called out in the Saxon tongue. It never occurred to me to wonder how I knew their language. Aten built such knowledge into me.

"Who are you?" demanded the biggest of the barbarians. They were armed with axes and short stabbing swords, I saw. A few steel-tipped spears lay on the ground at their feet.

The men who were holding the sobbing, shaking girls threw them to the ground and drew weapons. I smiled and kept walking slowly toward them.

"How did you get so far inland?" I asked, still approaching them at a leisurely gait.

"We got lost in those damnable woods," one of the Saxons admitted. "Do you know which way leads to the sea?"

I raised my hand and pointed toward the rising sun. "That way, I think."

Quicker than they could follow I reached behind my head for my sword and cut the nearest man in two before he could blink an eye. As his blood fountained over me, the others roared with rage and ran toward me. I saw their charge in slow motion, languid as a dream, as my senses speeded into overdrive.

Even so, thirteen against one could end only one way. One of them threw his axe at me; I dodged it easily as it spun lazily toward my head.

The first two that came within arm's reach of me I cut down like a scythe mows wheat. The others skidded to a stop and began to encircle me.

Then I heard the furious bellow of young Arthur as he charged on horseback into the fray. Out of the corner of my eye I saw him, helmeted and crouched in the saddle behind his red dragon shield, sword upraised, glinting in the morning sun.

Arthur had cleverly maneuvered to my right, so that his charge forced the Saxons to turn away from me to face him. I drove into their midst, slashing bone and sinew, shattering the blades they tried to use to protect themselves. Arthur cut a swath through them, then turned his steed and came back at them even while his first victims were sinking to the ground.

The remaining few broke and ran, screaming for their lives. Arthur galloped after them and cut them down before they could reach the trees. All except the one who dashed in the opposite direction. I hefted his discarded axe and threw it. Its sharp edge caught him between the shoulder blades and he went down face-first with a final shriek of death.

And then it was over. All fourteen Saxons lay dead or dying, and the two terrified girls knelt in the midst of the bloody carnage, by the stump of a felled tree, clutching each other in trembling fear.

Arthur sheathed his red-stained sword and lifted off his helmet, tossing his long sandy hair.

"Don't be afraid," he said softly to the girls. "No one will harm you."

They gaped up at him and the elaborate red dragon on his shield.

5

The girls led us to a village by the lake's edge, where they told everyone how Arthur had saved them from the Saxon raiders. I was taken to be Arthur's squire, a nonentity compared to the handsome young nobleman.

The whole village knelt at his feet and blessed him, but Arthur did not allow the villagers' adoration to affect him. When the village elders begged him to stay the night and take his pick of their women, Arthur replied gently:

"I cannot. I am on a quest that must not be delayed."

I wondered what would become of the two teenaged girls we had rescued. They were orphaned now, with no family to care for them.

But Arthur had already considered that. As he swung up onto his saddle, he pointed to them and pronounced solemnly, "Those maidens are under the protection of the High King. Send them to Cadbury castle in the spring and I will see that Ambrosius finds noble husbands for them."

The girls nearly swooned. The villagers raised a chorus of blessings. Yes, I thought, Arthur will make an excellent king—if he lives long enough.

6

As we rode slowly along the lake's edge that afternoon, Arthur grew somber.

"I've never seen Saxons this far inland before," he told me. "If we don't stop them soon, they will overrun all of Britain."

What could I answer? My Creator wanted the Saxons and their barbarian cousins to conquer Britain, to drive out the Celtic Britons and create an empire of their own.

"Well," I said, finding my tongue at last, "at least there are fourteen of them whose only part of this island is the ground they are buried in."

He grinned boyishly at me.

I thought that the Saxon raiders were Aten's attempt to turn me back from this quest for a sword for Arthur. Perhaps they were. My mistake was to believe that they would be Aten's *only* attempt to stop us.

We plodded along the lake's shore until nearly sunset, with Arthur asking every few minutes where his sword was, like an impatient boy.

There was a strange mixture of elements in him. He had been cautious about attacking the Saxon raiders, lacking in self-confidence. But once he saw me fighting alone against them he attacked with a wild frenzy rather than see me cut down. Then he showed the villagers the nobility of a truly great monarch. And now he was as impatient as a lad yearning to open his Christmas presents.

At last we had circled the lake completely. I reined my mount to a halt and stared out across the water, turned blood red by the setting sun.

"Well?" asked Arthur impatiently.

There was nothing I could say except, "Now we must wait, my lord."

We dismounted and tethered the horses loosely after removing their saddles and packs, so that they could graze for themselves.

"Wait for what?" Arthur asked. His impatience was beginning to show an edge of doubt.

"For the Lady of the Lake," I replied, without knowing the words until I heard them myself.

We ate a bit of the hard bread we had brought. No fire for cooking, although I could have eaten a rabbit raw, I was so hungry.

Surprisingly, Arthur stretched out on the ground. "I'm sleepy," he said, through a big yawn.

"Sleep then, my lord. I will stand watch."

"Just a little nap," he muttered. "Don't know . . . why I'm . . . so . . . sleepy . . ." His voice faded into a gentle snore.

The instant Arthur closed his eyes a soft silver glow began to surround me, as if I were bathed in moonlight. It was cool and glittering like the light of a million jewels twinkling all around me. And then, standing before me, beautiful Anya appeared.

She was in her warrior's suit of gleaming metallic silver, fitted snugly over her supple body. Her lustrous midnight-dark hair tumbled past her strong shoulders. Her silver-gray eyes regarded me solemnly. I could not move, could hardly speak, she was so exquisite and I yearned for her so.

"Orion," she said softly, "you play a dangerous game here."

"All I want is to be with you," I whispered, afraid to speak louder, afraid of breaking the spell of her appearance before me. Arthur lay soundly on the ground beside me, his eyes closed in sleep or a trance.

"Aten is furious that you are defying his command. He wants you to return Arthur to Amesbury. There is to be a Saxon attack upon Amesbury fort and he must be there to lead the garrison."

"To be killed, you mean," I replied.

Anya said nothing.

"Arthur needs a sword that will bring him victory," I said.

She smiled, a little sadly. "Do you really believe that a sword could make any difference?"

"It will give him the confidence he needs to fight against hopeless odds. And win."

"Aten does not want him to win," she said.

"But I do. I want—"

She silenced me with a finger upon my lips. "It's not that easy, my love. Aten controls this timeline. I can only interfere indirectly. You must do the hard work."

"What does Aten want?"

"Rome has collapsed," she answered. "He wants to build a new empire that stretches from the steppes beyond Muscovy to these British Isles."

"An empire of the barbarians," I growled.

"An empire that he can control and manipulate," Anya said.

"But why? To what end?"

She shrugged. "Who knows what plans are in his mind? He looks centuries ahead, millennia."

"He's crazy. No one can control all the forces of spacetime."

"He believes he can." Then she smiled again. "But he can't control you, can he?"

I felt an answering smile curve my lips. "He doesn't control you, either, does he?"

"But I have the power to work against him when I must. I can even get some of the other Creators to help resist his demands. I'm Aten's equal, not . . ." She stopped short.

"Not a mere creature," I finished for her.

"He could kill you horribly," Anya warned. "Final death, with no revival."

I remembered the horror of drowning in the tentacled grip of a gigantic sea monster. I recalled being flayed alive by the fireball of an exploding starship.

"Death is nothing new to me. If we can't be together, what is life except an endless wheel of pain?"

"I'm trying, Orion. I want to be with you, too, my dearest. But there are forces beyond your ken, forces that keep us apart."

"Forces manipulated by Aten," I said flatly.

She shook her head. "Forces that not even he can control, my darling."

I glanced down at the sleeping young Arthur. "And that young warlord plays a role in these forces."

"He might. I think there could be greatness in him. But Aten wants to remove him."

"Kill him, you mean."

"Yes."

"Then I want to protect him."

Anya said nothing. She merely regarded me with those somber gray eyes, eyes that held the depths of infinity in them.

"Will you help me?" I asked.

"Orion, you have no idea of the damage you do to the space-time fabric whenever you defy Aten."

"Will you help me?" I repeated.

She regarded me gravely. "I love you too much to allow Aten to destroy you."

"Then you must help Arthur, too."

She sighed. "Your young friend must help himself. Neither you nor I can put courage into his heart."

"It's not courage he needs, it's . . ."

But she was gone, vanished as if she had never been there at all, leaving me standing on the shore of the lake as the sky darkened and the moon rose, silver and cool and too far away for me to dream of touching.

7

Arthur awoke, sat up, and rubbed his eyes. "I had a dream," he said, his voice soft and puzzled. "About my sword."

As he climbed to his feet I looked out across the lake, silvered now by the rising full moon. It was as calm and flat as a mirror of polished steel. In its middle was an island that hadn't been there earlier. I realized that it was not an island at all, but an artifact, a structure of metal and glass still dripping because it had risen from the lake's depths only moments earlier.

Arthur followed my gaze. "Look!" he whispered. "A boat approaches!"

"The Lady of the Lake," I murmured. Anya was going to help us, after all.

Wordlessly we stepped down to the sandy edge of the shore, Arthur's eyes fixed on the boat that glided noiselessly across the placid waters.

It was Anya, of course, alone in the self-propelled boat. But now she was dressed in a flowing slivery robe and garlanded with flowers. In the moonlight she seemed to glow with an inner radiance. Her hair flowed long and smooth as a river of onyx down her back. Her face was calm, serene, utterly beautiful.

In her arms she cradled a sword in a jeweled scabbard. I recognized that scabbard.

The boat nudged its prow onto the sand before us and stopped. Anya rose to her feet and held the sword out in her two hands.

Arthur seemed frozen, transfixed by her appearance. His eyes were so wide I could see the white all around them, his breathing so heavy he was almost gasping.

"Take the sword," I coached him in a low whisper. "She's offering it to you."

Arthur swallowed hard, then summoned up his courage and stepped into the gently lapping wavelets to the side of the boat. His boots sank into the soft sand.

"Wield this sword for right and justice," Anya intoned, handing it to Arthur's trembling hands.

"I will, my lady," he said breathlessly. "Just as you command."

"Do so, and the others will follow you."

"I will, my lady," he repeated.

Without another word Anya sat on the boat's only bench once more and the vessel backed off the sand, made a stately, silent turn, and glided back to the "island" in the middle of the lake. We watched, Arthur dumbfounded and trembling, as the boat disappeared into an opening in the structure and then the entire mass slowly sank beneath the surface of the water.

It was not until the "island" was completely gone that Arthur blinked and shook himself, like a man coming out of a trance.

Then he pulled the sword out of its jeweled scabbard. I recognized the word *Excalibur* incised on its fine steel blade. It was the sword I had taken from Grendel's cave, the night Beowulf and I killed the monster's mother. Anya had held it all these years, protected it from Aten's knowledge, held it for the moment when Arthur needed it.

Arthur swished the blade through the night air, his grin bright enough to rival the full moon.

Then we heard the roar of the dragon.

8

It was a dinosaur, of course, a giant raptor fetched by Aten from its own time and translated across millions of years to kill Arthur.

It came crashing out of the woods, roaring like a steam locomotive, stepping nimbly on its two hind legs. Three times my own height, it had teeth lining its massive jaw that were the size of butcher's knives, sharp and serrated. The claws on its hind feet were the length of my forearm, curved like scimitars. Its forelegs were smaller, almost weak looking compared to the hind, but they, too, bore slashing claws.

I pulled my sword out as the monster's beady little eyes focused on us. Arthur turned and ran.

But only as far as our impromptu camp. The horses were bucking and neighing with terror. He slashed their tethers with one stroke of Excalibur, and they bolted away, galloping toward safety. Arthur picked up his shield and came back to stand at my side.

"We'll have a better chance if we can approach it from two sides," he said. His voice was calm and flat, as if he were discussing tactics over a map in the safety of his castle.

"We should do what the horses did," I said.

"Run?"

"As fast as we can," I replied fervently.

"No, Orion. If we don't kill this dragon it will ravage the countryside. It will kill the villagers and their livestock. We must protect them."

Two puny men armed only with swords against a twenty-ton killing machine.

But I nodded and edged off toward the water. Arthur sidled in the other direction, his eyes on the "dragon," his new sword held high in his right hand.

The dinosaur looked from him to me, swiveling its ponderous head slowly. It stepped toward me, hesitant, its tiny brain perhaps puzzled by the maneuvers of intelligent prey.

I dared not go so far out into the water that I could not move swiftly. I yelled at the dinosaur and waved my sword in the air, trying to hold its attention while Arthur moved stealthily behind it. It leaned down in my direction, as if to see me more clearly. I felt its breath, hot enough to make me almost think it could actually breathe fire.

I waited until those monstrous teeth were gaping just above me, then thrust my sword into the beast, into the base of its jaw, with all the power I could muster from both my arms.

The dinosaur howled and reared, lifting me completely off my feet. My sword was lodged in its jaw and I clung to the hilt with both hands, my legs dangling uselessly in midair.

Arthur dashed in and slashed at the beast's belly. Even in the pale moonlight I could see his blade redden.

The dinosaur bellowed and shook its head so viciously that I was dislodged and flung to the ground, my sword still wedged in its jaw. Stunned, I saw through a red haze of pain the dinosaur turn on Arthur, raking his shield with the powerful claws of one hind foot. Arthur tumbled onto his back and the beast bent over him, jaws gaping wide.

But Arthur still clutched Excalibur and slashed at the dinosaur's snout as he scrambled backward, trying to rise to his feet. The dinosaur yowled and tried to pin Arthur to the ground with one foot, but Arthur scrabbled out of the way once, twice . . .

I pulled myself to my feet and, avoiding the beast's heavy swinging tail, leaped upon its back. Like a monkey clambering up a tree I scaled along the dinosaur's spine, climbing toward its massive bony skull.

It must have felt me on its back, for it stopped trying to crush Arthur and reared up to its full height, nearly throwing me off. But I wrapped my legs around its neck and swiftly drew Odysseos' dagger. Plunging it into the back of its neck at the base of the thick skull, I hacksawed madly, searching for the spinal column.

Below me I saw Arthur, on his feet now, plunging Excalibur into the beast's exposed belly again and again, working madly, frenziedly, spattered with the dinosaur's dark blood again and again.

My blade found the spinal cord at last and cut it. The monster collapsed, nearly crushing Arthur as it fell.

I slid off its back and tumbled to the grassy ground, exhausted, gasping.

Arthur stood blinking at the dead carcass for a few moments, then raised both arms over his head and screamed an exultant victory cry at the distant moon. It was an eerie sight: the young warrior bathed in the beast's blood, holding his sword and shield aloft and shrieking like a banshee. Beside him the dead "dragon" lay, a mountain of scaly flesh, teeth, and claws.

"Did you see me, Orion?" he called triumphantly as he hurried over to where I lay. "Did you see me kill it?"

Slowly I pulled myself up to a sitting position. The dagger was still in my hand, but Arthur paid no notice to such a puny weapon.

He brandished Excalibur in the night air. "I must have struck its heart," he said, bubbling with excitement. "With this steel I can conquer anything!"

I smiled inwardly. Arthur had found his steel; not merely a sword, but the inner steel that would one day make him king of the Britons. If I could keep him alive that long.

I could sense Aten scowling angrily at me. He wanted Arthur removed from this timeline, and he would do all he could to work his will. And punish me for defying him.

All I really wanted was to spend the eternities with Anya. But for now, I was at Arthur's side, ready to battle men and gods to protect him.

CHAPTER TWO

The Bretwalda

1

Three days after we returned to Amesbury, with Excalibur belted at Arthur's side, a large band of Saxons made camp outside the fort. The next day they were joined by others. Day after day their numbers grew and we sat inside the fort. Arthur seemed uncertain of what he should do.

One evening I looked out over the parapet of the fort's flimsy palisade and watched the campfires of the Saxon invaders dotting the twilight landscape like a thousand angry red eyes. As far as the hilly horizon they stretched, more of them each night.

"They've never done this before," whispered Arthur, standing grimly beside me. I heard bewilderment and deep foreboding in his hushed voice.

"What are they waiting for?" grumbled Sir Bors, standing on Arthur's other side. "Why don't they attack?"

"Each night their numbers grow," Arthur murmured, staring transfixed at the Saxon campfires. "Their leader, Aelle, calls himself Bretwalda now—king of Britain."

"Hmph," Bors snorted.

"Other barbarian tribes are joining his host: South Saxons,

West Saxons, Jutes, Angles—they've all sworn their allegiance to Aelle."

We stayed hemmed up inside Amesbury fort for nearly two weeks. Usually the barbarians raided a village or farmstead and ran away before the British defenders could find them. But now they were camped outside this hilltop fort, with more and more of the raiders joining the besiegers every day. These were not mere raiders, they were a powerful army, under the leadership of Aelle, who obviously intended to destroy Amesbury fort and its defenders.

I looked up into the darkening sky. A fat gibbous moon grinned mockingly at me, while the Swan and the Eagle rode low off in the west. My namesake constellation of Orion was climbing above the eastern horizon. Autumn chill was in the air, yet the barbarian invaders showed no sign of heading back to their settlements on the coast and leaving Britain a season of peace and healing.

Wheezing old Merlin joined the three of us up on the parapet, climbing the creaking wooden stairs slowly, painfully. In the starlight his tattered white beard seemed to glow faintly. With his long robe he seemed to glide along the platform toward us, rather than walk.

"I have determined when the Saxons will attack," he pronounced in his quavering, thin voice.

"When?" Arthur and Bors asked as one.

"On the night of the full moon," said Merlin.

"A week from now."

Bors growled, "It makes sense. They know we're starving in here. They'll wait until they figure we're too weak to fight."

"Then we've got to do something," Arthur replied. "And soon."

"Yes," Bors agreed. "But what?"

Arthur had been put in charge of the hill fort's defense by his uncle, Ambrosius, who styled himself High King of the Celtic Britons. The Saxon barbarians had been raiding the coasts of Britain for years, decades, ever since the Roman legions had left the island. Now the Saxons and their brother tribes of barbarians were building permanent settlements in the coastal regions.

And moving inland. Amesbury was one of a string of hilltop forts that Ambrosius had hoped would stand against the Saxon tide. Some called it a castle, but it was nothing more than a wooden palisade enclosing a few huts and stables, with a single timbered tower, a rude wooden chapel, and a blacksmith's forge. Even so, it stood against the barbarians well enough. They knew nothing of siege warfare, had no knowledge of rock-throwing ballistae or any devices more complicated than a felled tree trunk for a battering ram.

Yet crafty old Aelle had decided to bring all their strength to Amesbury and destroy the fort. And afterward? I wondered. Would they methodically reduce each of Ambrosius' forts and leave the interior of Britain open to their ravages?

The dark night wind whispered to me and I looked up at the stars scattered across the black sky. I had seen the same stars at ancient Ilium, I remembered, in another life. I had built a siege tower there, under the watchful eye of wily Odysseos, and led my men over the high stone wall of mighty Troy.

In another life. I have lived many lives, and died many deaths. I have traveled among those far-flung stars bedecking the night sky. I have fought battles on distant worlds under strange suns.

My Creator Aten, the Golden One, has sent me to this place and time to serve Arthur until the moment comes when I must stand aside and let him be killed. Or perhaps the Golden One plans for me to murder Arthur. I have assassinated others for him, in other lifetimes. I knew that I must obey my Creator's commands, yet with every fiber of my being I wanted to defy those commands, to disregard his murderous orders and raise young Arthur to the power and authority that would save Britain from these barbarians.

Yet I stood helplessly in the gathering darkness beside Arthur, the son of an unknown father, adopted by Ambrosius and guided by Merlin. Barely old enough to begin growing a beard, Arthur had been marked by my Creator for a brief moment of glory—and then ignominious death.

To Bors and Merlin and all the others I was Arthur's squire, a servant, a nonentity. Arthur knew better, but we kept our friendship a secret between us. It was easier for me that way: I could remain at Arthur's side and provide him with advice and guidance—and help in the fighting, when it was necessary.

"Well, what do you want to do?" Bors asked again, gruffly. He was a blunt, hard-faced man, scarred from many battles, his thick beard already showing streaks of gray.

Without taking his eyes from the hundreds of Saxon campfires dotting the night, Arthur replied softly, "Instead of waiting for the barbarians to build enough strength to bring down this fort, we should sally out and attack them."

Bors said flatly, "There's too many of 'em already. We'd be massacred."

But some of Arthur's youthful enthusiasm was returning. "If a strong group of us charged out at them on horseback, we could do them great hurt."

"We could get ourselves killed and save the Saxons the trouble of scaling the walls," Bors snapped.

"Not if we surprised them," Arthur insisted. "Not if we attacked them tonight, after the moon sets, while most of them are sleeping."

"At night?" Bors frowned at the idea.

"Yes! Why not?" Eagerly, Arthur turned to Merlin. "What do you think, Merlin? What do you foresee?"

Merlin closed his eyes for several long moments, then wheezed, "Blood and carnage. The barbarians will fly before your sword, Arthur."

"You see?" Arthur said to Bors.

Bors glowered at the mystic. "Do you see the Saxons running away and heading back to their ships?"

Merlin shook his head slowly. "No . . . the mists of the future cloud my vision."

Bors grumbled with disdain.

But Arthur would not be denied. Bors had more battle experience, but Arthur had the fire of youthful vigor in him.

"Orion," he commanded, "get the horses saddled and fit. And ask all the knights which of them will honor me by joining in this sally against the enemy."

As a squire, of course, I went where my master went. Knights could offer excuses to remain safely inside the fort. There were no excuses allowed for squires.

Ϙ

It was well past midnight by the time we were armed and mounted, thirty-two knights and squires on snorting, snuffling horses that pawed impatiently on the packed earth of the courtyard. Arthur and the other knights were helmeted and wore chain mail and carried spears as well as their swords. The moon was down. Firelight glinted off the emblems painted on their shields: Arthur's red dragon, Bors' black hawk, the green serpent of Gawain, lions and bears and other totem symbols.

I was the only squire who wore a chain mail shirt. The others, mostly beardless youths, went into battle in their tunics, protected only by their helmets and shields. I carried neither helmet nor shield nor spear, only the sword strapped to my back, as I sat on my mount at Arthur's side.

Sir Bors, still grousing, nosed his horse up to Arthur's other side. "This is madness," he muttered. "They outnumber us a hundred to one."

Arthur smiled grimly in the starlight. "Their numbers will be smaller before the sun rises again."

"As will ours," Bors mumbled.

Arthur pointed with his spear and a pair of churls lifted the heavy timber bar from the palisade gates, then slowly swung the gates open. They creaked horribly in the stillness of the night. I thought that any chance of surprise was mostly lost already.

But Arthur bellowed, "Follow me!" and we charged out into the night, each man screaming his own battle cry.

The barbarians were truly surprised. We thundered down into their camp at the base of the hill, trampling the embers of their campfires and scattering the startled men like dry leaves before the wind. I stayed close behind Arthur, saw him transfix a running Saxon with his spear and lift the shrieking barbarian off his feet. Arthur was nearly knocked off his horse by the shock of the impact, and he had to let go of the spear. The barbarian warrior, clutching the shaft where it penetrated his chest, fell over backward, already dead.

I rode close behind Arthur, my sword in hand, ready to protect him against anything. Once more my senses went into overdrive and everything about me seemed to slow down into a sleepy, sluggish torpor. I saw a naked barbarian run in dreamlike slow motion at Arthur's left side, his long blond braids flying behind him. Arthur took his sword stroke on his shield and, while drawing Excalibur from its jeweled scabbard with his right hand, bashed the warrior's head with the edge of the shield. The man staggered back and Bors pinned him to the ground with his spear.

Another warrior hurled his axe at Arthur's unprotected right side. I saw it turning lazily through the flame-lit air and reached out with my sword to flick it harmlessly away. Then I drove my mount at the barbarian and slashed him from shoulder to navel with a stroke that nearly wrenched me out of my saddle.

Waving Excalibur on high, Arthur urged his mount forward against a gaggle of barbarian warriors who stood naked but armed with swords and axes. I pulled up alongside him and we sliced the lives out of those men, their blood spurting as they screamed their death agonies.

But still more were coming at us, roaring with anger and battle lust. The first shock of our surprise attack had quickly worn off and now they were hot for our blood. They seemed to grow out of the very ground, no matter how many we killed still more rose against us. We waded into them as they swarmed around us, pulling men off their mounts, pulling down the horses themselves. Men and beasts alike screamed as the barbarians hacked them to bloody pieces.

The knights fared better than the lightly armed squires, but even they were being hard pressed by the teeming, swarming barbarians. Arthur and I weaved a sphere of death with our swords. Anyone who dared to come within reach of our blades died swiftly.

But still more of the barbarians rushed at us, assailing us like swarms of wasps, surging like the tide of the sea.

"We've got to get back!" Bors shouted. "Their whole army is aroused now."

"Yes," Arthur agreed. "Sound the retreat."

The squire who served as bugler put his ram's horn to his lips and blew mightily. We turned back toward the fort, fighting and hacking our way through the maddened barbarians. The Saxons made no effort to climb the hill and get through the guarded gate; they were content to drive us out of their camp.

3

We were tired and dispirited as we alit from our mounts. Eleven of our number were gone, nine squires and two knights. Each of us was spattered with blood, mostly Saxon, although almost every one of us had been nicked or wounded.

Except for Arthur. He was untouched and still brimming with excitement.

"How many did we kill, do you think?" he asked.

"How many did we lose?" Bors countered.

Merlin watched us from the parapet as we dismounted wearily and helped the wounded off their horses. Several of the men groaned with pain. Many of the young squires were white faced with shock or loss of blood.

"Well, you had your moment of glory," Bors said sourly. "It didn't do us much good, did it?"

Arthur did not argue against him. Bors was an experienced fighter. Arthur had been named commander of this fort because he was the High King's adopted nephew, and he knew it. The

Saxons and their barbarian allies were still encamped around the base of the hill. There were fewer of them, yes, but still more than enough to take the fort when they finally decided to attack.

At last Arthur said, "We'd better get some sleep. No sense standing here until dawn."

Arthur and the others headed wearily for the timbered tower at the far end of the wall. I went to the stables, where my pallet of straw awaited me amidst the steaming, sweating horses. The heat of their bodies kept the wooden shelter warm despite the breeze that whistled through its slats. I automatically tuned down my sense of smell; the stables and horse grounds were not the most sweetly fragrant areas of the fort.

I stretched out on the pallet and thought of my beloved Anya. She had taken human form in many placetimes to be with me. She and I had faced the alien Set in the time of the dinosaurs. We had lived together for a brief interlude of happiness in the beautiful wooded glades of Paradise.

Always Aten pulled us apart, insanely jealous of her love for me. Yet time and again Anya had found me, helped me, loved me no matter where and when I had been sent by the Golden One.

I closed my eyes and pictured her perfect face, those fathomless silver-gray eyes that held all of eternity, her raven-black hair cascading like a river of onyx past her alabaster shoulders. She was a warrior goddess, a proud and courageous Athena, the only one of the Creators who dared to oppose Aten openly.

Suddenly a fireball of light blasted my senses, a glare of golden radiance so bright that I flung my arms across my eyes.

"I know your thoughts, creature."

I was no longer at Amesbury fort. I had been wrenched out of that point in spacetime, translated into a vastly different place, the ageless realm of the Creators.

I could *feel* the brilliance of his presence. Aten, the Golden One, the self-styled god who created me.

"Get up, Orion," the Golden One commanded. "Stand before your Creator."

Like an automaton I climbed slowly to my feet, my arms still covering my eyes, shielding them from his blazing splendor. The radiance burned my flesh, seared into the marrow of my bones.

"Put your hands down, Orion, and face the glory of your master," he said, his voice sneering at me.

I did as he commanded. I had no choice. It was as if I were a mere puppet and he controlled my limbs, my entire body, even the beating of my heart.

It was like staring into the sun. The glare was overpowering, a physical force that made my knees buckle and forced my eyes to squint painfully. After what seemed like an eternity the blinding radiance contracted, compressed itself, and took on human form. My eyes, watering with pain, beheld Aten, the Golden One who had created me.

He was glorious to look upon. Wearing splendid robes of gold and gleaming white, Aten looked every inch the god he pretended to be. To the ancient Greeks he was Apollo; to the first Egyptians he was Aten the sun god who gave them light and life. I first knew him as Ormazd, the fire god of Zoroaster in ancient Persia.

I loathed him. Aten or Apollo or whatever he chose to call himself, he was an egomaniac who schemed endlessly to control all of the spacetime continuum. But he is no more a god than I am. He—and the other Creators—are humans from the far future, or rather, what humans have evolved into: men and women of incredible knowledge and power, able to travel through time and space as easily as young Arthur rides a horse across a grassy meadow.

He had sent me to be with Arthur in the darkness of an era where a few brave men were trying to stem the tide of barbarism that was destroying civilization all across the old Roman world.

I looked into Aten's haughty leonine eyes, gleaming with vast plans for manipulating the spacetime continuum, glittering with what may have been madness.

"You hate me, Orion? Me, who created you? Who has revived you from death countless times? How ungrateful you are, creature. How unappreciative." He laughed at me.

"You can read my thoughts," I said tightly, "but you cannot control them."

"That makes no difference, worm. You will obey me, now and forever."

"Why should I?"

"You have no choice," he said.

I remembered differently. "I disobeyed you at Troy," I told him. "I refused to annihilate the Neandertals, back in the Ice Age."

His flawlessly handsome face set into a hard scowl. "Yes, and you came close to unraveling the entire fabric of spacetime. It cost me much labor to rebuild the continuum, Orion."

"And you have cost me much pain."

"That is nothing compared to the agonies you will suffer if you dare to resist my commands again. Final death, Orion. Death without revival. Oblivion. But much pain first. An infinity of pain."

"I will not murder Arthur," I said.

Almost he smiled. "That may not be necessary, creature. There are plenty of Saxons available for killing him. Your task is merely to stand aside and let it happen."

"I can't," I said. "I won't."

He laughed again. "Yes, you will, Orion. When the moment comes you will do as I command. Just as you assassinated the High Khan of the Mongols."

I blinked with the memory. Ogatai. He had befriended me, made me his companion, his trusted aide—just as young Arthur has.

"You can't make me—"

But I was in the darkness and stench of the stable again, alone in the night. The Golden One had played his little game with me and sent me back to Arthur's placetime.

Alone, I lay back on the brittle straw once again. Why had Aten sent me here? What schemes was he weaving about Arthur and these barbarian invaders of Britain?

Anya. She was the only one who could help me. She loved me, and I loved her with a passion that spanned the centuries and millennia, a love that reached out to the stars themselves.

Yet I could not find her that night, could not reach her. I called to her silently, searched out with my mind through the dark cold night. No response. Nothing but the aching emptiness of infinity, the lonely void of nothingness. It was as if she no longer existed, as if she never had existed and was merely a dream of my imagination.

No, I told myself. Anya is real. She loves me. If she doesn't answer my plea it's because Aten is blocking my efforts, keeping us apart.

I strove with every atom of my being to translate myself to the timeless refuge of the Creators, far in the future of Arthur's world. To no avail. I strained until perspiration soaked every inch of my body, but I remained in this smelly, dank, unlit stable.

Exhausted, I fell into sleep. And dreamed of Alexander.

4

The crown prince of Macedonia, son of doughty Philip II, Alexander was also young and impetuous when I knew him. Proud and ambitious, driven by his cruel mother, Olympias, young Alexander learned battle tactics—and the strategies of war—from his masterful father, Philip.

In my dream I was at Alexander's side once again as he led the cavalry at the epic battle of Chaeronea. We galloped across the field toward the Athenian foot soldiers, thrusting and slashing at their hoplites in a wild melee of dust and blood, screams of triumph and agony filling the air. I felt the horse beneath me pounding across the corpse-littered plain and strained mightily to rein him in, hold him back, as I slashed with my sword at the soldiers milling about us.

Alexander pushed ahead on old Ox-Head, his favorite steed, wading through the Athenian infantry, nearly sliding off his mount while jamming his spear into a screaming hoplite. Clutching my mount between my knees, I urged the horse on through the wildly surging tumult until I was beside Alexander, protecting his unshielded right side. Together we drove through the scattering Athenians, then began the grim task of riding down the fleeing hoplites and slaughtering them to the last man.

5

My eyes snapped open. It was still dark, well before dawn. Why did I dream of Alexander? Of all the lives I have led, of all the deaths that I have known, why did I dream this night of Alexander and the Macedonian cavalry?

"Find the answer, Sarmatian," whispered an invisible voice. A woman's voice. Anya!

I sat up on the pallet, ignoring the cold wind that sliced through the rickety slats of the stable, disregarding the smell and the snuffling of the drowsing horses.

Sarmatian. Anya called me a Sarmatian. I remembered that I had claimed to be a Sarmatian when I had first found myself at Amesbury, begging a skeptical Sir Bors for a place in Arthur's service.

Sarmatian.

I sat on the pallet wondering until daylight slanted through the cracks in the stable wall. I washed at the horse trough, drawing the usual laughs and jeers from the other squires and churls.

"You washed yesterday, Orion! Aren't you afraid you'll drown yourself?" laughed one of them.

"He washes every morning," called another, already at work shoveling in the manure pile. "He wants to smell pretty for the girls."

There were no women in Amesbury fort. All the women and children and old men of the region had been moved farther inland to be safe from the Saxons. If the fort fell, they would be defenseless.

"Don't you know that washing makes you weak, Orion? You're scrubbing all your strength away!"

They laughed uproariously. It was the only relief they had from the tension. We all knew that there was an army of Saxons and other invaders just outside our gate, a barbarian army that was growing with every passing day.

Ignoring their jibes, I walked across the dung-dotted courtyard to the timbered tower of the fort. The guard recognized me and let me pass unchallenged. Instead of going to Arthur's quarters, however, I climbed the creaking wooden stairs to Merlin's tower-top aerie.

There was no door at the top of the stairs. The entire top level of the tower was a single open area, roofed over with heavy beams of rough-hewn logs. It was a misty autumn morning, dank and chill. On a clear day, I knew, from up at this height you could see almost to the waters of the Solent and the Isle of Wight.

Merlin was standing at the low wall, staring out across the fog-shrouded camp of the barbarians, his back to me. His possessions were meager: a table that held several manuscript rolls, a few un-matched chairs, a couple of chests, a few blankets for a sleeping roll. Nothing more.

"What do you want, Orion?" he asked, without turning to look at me.

"How did you know it was me?" I asked.

He shrugged his frail shoulders. "Who else could it be?"

That puzzled me. He had a reputation as a wizard, a magician who could cast spells and foresee the future. Yet, as he finally turned to face me, all I saw was a wizened old man in a stained wrinkled robe of patched homespun with a long dirty white beard and thin, lank hair falling past his shoulders; both beard and hair were knotted and filthy.

"I need your help," I said.

"Yes, I know," he replied as he walked slowly, arthritically, toward his table.

"Then you know what I am about to ask."

"Naturally." He slowly sank his emaciated frame into the cushion-covered chair.

I stood before the table and folded my arms across my chest. I wore only a thin tunic, scant proof against the frosty autumn morning, but I have always been able to keep my body heat from radiating away and to step up my metabolic rate when I have to, burning off fat stored in the body's tissues to keep me warm.

"Sit down, Orion," said Merlin. "It hurts my neck to have to crane up to see your eyes."

As I sat, I said, "Can you help me, then?"

"Naturally," he repeated.

"Well, then?"

He stared at me for a long, uncomfortable moment. Old though he may have been, there was a gleam of intelligence, of curiosity, in his gray-green eyes.

Slowly, a smile spread across his wrinkled face. "You are playing a game with me, Orion."

"And you with me, sir," I answered.

"Must I ask you what your problem is?"

"You implied that you already knew."

His smile broadened. "Ah, yes. That is part of a wizard's kit, you see. Allow the supplicant to believe that you know everything, and the supplicant will believe whatever you tell him."

I grinned back at him and recalled, somehow, that psychiatrists in a future civilization would use the same trick on their patients.

"So tell me truly, Orion, why do you seek my help?"

"I can't remember my past," I said. "I can't remember anything from before the first day I came to Amesbury and met Arthur."

He leaned forward, all eager attention now. "Nothing at all?"

"Only my name, and the idea that I am a Sarmatian, whatever that is."

"You don't even know what a Sarmatian is?"

"No," I said. "I haven't the faintest idea."

Merlin steepled his fingers. They were long and bony, the backs of his hands veined in blue.

"The Sarmatians were a warrior tribe from far to the east, somewhere in Asia," Merlin told me. "Many of them joined the Roman legions, where they served as cavalry. They were great horsemen, great fighters."

"Were?" I probed.

"They left when the legions departed Britain. I had assumed that you were one of them who had stayed behind, deserted the legions."

"You thought me a deserter?"

"Bors did, as soon as you told him you were a Sarmatian. That is why he was so suspicious of you at first."

Nodding with newfound understanding, I asked, "Tell me more about the Sarmatians."

Merlin leaned his head back, raised his eyes to the beamed ceiling. "They were fine metalworkers. They claimed to have invented chain mail, and something else . . . I can't quite recall what it was."

"Chain mail is a great advantage."

"Yes, we have our smith working night and day to produce more."

"They came from Asia, you say?"

"So I remember."

Merlin spent much of the morning asking me questions about myself, questions I could not answer. Aten always erased my memories before sending me on a new mission. He said he provided me with only enough information to perform my task. Yet on more than one mission I fought through his mental blocks and recalled things he would have preferred I did not know.

But on that chill, foggy morning I could remember nothing beyond my first moments at Amesbury fort. A young serving boy brought up a tray of bread and a few scraps of cheese with thin, bitter beer for our breakfast. I realized that even with the fort besieged and our food supply dwindling, Merlin had better rations than the knights and squires down in the courtyard, despite his frail frame.

A horn blast ended our conversation. Arthur was calling all his men together. I got up from the chair before Merlin's table and took my leave as politely as I could.

As I got to the stairs leading down, the old man called out to me. "Orion! I remember the other thing that the Sarmatians are reputed to have invented."

"And what is that?" I asked.

"Some sort of footgear to help a man get up onto his horse. I believe they called it a stirrup."

Stirrups, I thought. Yes.

"Oh, and one thing more. A device that they fixed to the heels of their boots, to prick their mounts."

Spurs.

6

All that day I thought about stirrups and spurs, two simple and obvious-seeming inventions. Yet they were obvious only in hindsight, as most great inventions are.

Arthur and the other knights had neither stirrups nor spurs. When they rode into battle they had to rein in their horses or the first shock of impact with their spears would knock them out of their saddles. Often a knight went down with his victim when he forgot to slow his mount. Even in Alexander's day, I remembered, we had to be careful to stay on our mounts as we speared footmen. It was the same using our swords. A mounted warrior had to grip his steed tightly with his knees if he wanted to remain mounted while he slashed at the enemy with his sword.

But with stirrups a man could stay in the saddle despite a smashing impact. And with spurs he could goad his steed into a flat-out gallop. Instead of wading into the enemy so slowly that they could eventually swarm us under, we could charge into them like a thunderbolt, crash through their formation, then wheel around and charge again.

As the sun was setting I went to the blacksmith. He was a big, ham-fisted, hairy man with bulging muscles and little patience for what seemed like a harebrained idea.

"I've got all I can do to make the chain mail that my lord Arthur is demanding," he said in a loud, barking voice. Wiping sweat from his brow with a meaty forearm, he went on, "I don't have time to make some trinkets for you."

"Very well," I replied. "I'll make them for myself."

"Not until the dinner horn sounds," he said petulantly. "I've got to work this forge until then."

"I'll wait."

For the next few hours I watched the brawny blacksmith and his young apprentices forging chain mail links, heating the metal in their fire while two of the lads wearily pumped the bellows that kept the coals hot, hammering the links into shape, quenching them in a bucket of water with a steaming hiss. It was hot work, but it was simple enough for me to learn how to do it merely by watching them.

The dinner horn sounded at last and the blacksmith took his grudging leave.

"If you steal or break anything," he warned with a growl, "I'll snap your spine for you."

He was big enough to do it, if I let him.

I stripped off my tunic and, clad only in my drawers and the dagger that Odysseos had given me at Troy, strapped to my thigh, I began forging a pair of stirrups.

They were lopsided and certainly no things of beauty, but I admired them nonetheless. Forging a pair of spurs was easier, especially since I did not want them to be so sharp that they would draw blood. They were nothing elaborate, merely slightly curved spikes of iron.

When I went to my pallet that night I was physically tired from the hard labor but emotionally eager to try my new creations in the morning. I looked forward to a good night's sleep.

But no sooner had I closed my eyes than I found myself standing on the shore of a fog-shrouded lake. The moon ducked in and out of scudding clouds. I was wearing a full robe of chain mail with a light linen tunic over it, my sword buckled at my hip.

I remembered this lake. It was where I had brought Arthur so that Anya could give him Excalibur.

I looked out across the water, silvered by the moonlight, expecting to see the fortress of stainless metal arising from the lake's depths as it had then. Nothing. The waves lapped softly against the muddy shore, a nightingale sang its achingly sweet song somewhere back among the trees.

And then Anya's voice called low, "Orion."

Swiftly I turned and she was there standing within arm's reach, as beautiful as only a goddess can be, wearing a simple, supple robe of purest white silk that flowed to the ground. Her midnight-dark hair was bound up with coils of silver thread; links of silver adorned her throat and wrists.

We embraced and I kissed her with all the fervor of a thousand centuries of separation. For long moments neither of us said a word, we scarcely breathed, so happy to be in each other's arms again.

But at last Anya moved slightly away. Her hands still on my shoulders, she looked up into my face. Her silver-gray eyes were solemn, sorrowful.

"I can only remain a few moments, my love," she said in a near whisper, as if afraid someone would overhear us. "I've come to warn you."

"Against Aten?"

She shook her head slightly. "Not merely him. Several of the other Creators are working with him to help the Saxons and other invaders to conquer Arthur's Celts and make themselves masters of this entire island."

"But why?" I asked. "What purpose does it serve to tear down what little is left of civilization here?"

"It involves forces that reach across the entire galaxy, Orion. This point in spacetime is a nexus, a crucial focal point in the continuum."

Remembering the words Aten had spoken to me weeks earlier, I said to Anya, "He wants to build an empire of the barbarians that will reach from the steppes of Asia to these British Isles—all under his domination."

She hesitated a moment, then said, "It may be necessary, Orion. Aten's plan may be the only way to keep the continuum from shattering."

"I can't believe that."

She smiled, sadly. "You mean you don't want to believe it."

"It means that Arthur must be killed."

She nodded solemnly.

"No," I said. "I won't let that happen."

"You can't oppose Aten's will! He'll obliterate you!"

Anger was seething within me. "If I do what Aten wants, can we be together? Can we return to Paradise and live there in peace?"

Her lovely face became tragic. "I want to, my love. But it will be impossible."

"Because he'll keep us apart," I snapped.

"Because the work of saving the continuum, the task of keeping this worldline from collapsing and destroying everything we know, requires all my strength, all my energy."

"Forever?"

"For as long as it takes," she said. "My darling, I want to be with you for all the eternities. But how can we be together if the entire universe implodes? Everything will be gone, wiped away as if it never existed."

For many long, silent moments I stared into her beautiful eyes. I saw sorrow there, a melancholy that spanned centuries of yearning.

At last I found my voice. "And to save the universe, Arthur must be killed."

"That is Aten's plan. The barbarians are uniting among themselves now. There is no need for Arthur in this timeline anymore."

"Tell Aten to make another plan," I said. "As long as I live I will protect Arthur and help him to drive the barbarians out of Britain."

If I had thought half a second about my words, I would have expected Anya to be surprised, shocked perhaps, even angry.

Instead she smiled. "You would defy Aten, even at the risk of final death?"

I smiled back at her, grimly. "He promised me an especially painful final death."

Her smile faded. "He means to keep that promise."

"And I mean to stand by Arthur until my final breath."

"I won't be able to help you," Anya warned. "I have other tasks to do, far off among the star clouds."

I nodded, accepting that. "Tell Aten he'll have to save this timeline with Arthur in it. Let him build an empire of the Celts from this island to farthest reaches of Asia."

"You run great risks, Orion."

"What of it? If we can't be together, what good is living to me?"

She kissed me again, lightly this time, on the lips. "Protect Arthur, then. Help him all you can. But be warned: Aten is not alone in this. Others of the Creators will be working against Arthur."

"Thanks for the good news," I said.

"Farewell, my love," said Anya. "I will return to you as soon as I possibly can."

I wanted to say several million other things to her but she vanished, simply disappeared before my eyes, like a dream abruptly ending. I love you, Anya, I called silently. I'll find you again wherever and whenever you are, no matter if I have to cross the entire universe of spacetime. I'll find you and we'll be together for eternity.

But when I awoke I was back on my pallet in the dung-smelling stable, with the results of my ironwork lying on the straw beside me.

7

I washed as usual at the horse trough and took the usual jeering banter from the squires and churls. But once I sat on the bare dirt and started tying my crudely made spurs to my ankles, they howled with laugher.

"Are you going to a cockfight, Orion?"

"Maybe he'll put on wings next and fly out of the fort!"

They rolled on the ground, laughing.

Without a word to them, I went back into the stable and took one of the horses out into the courtyard. When I began to attach my lopsided, ill-formed stirrups to his saddle, they crowded around, curious and grinning.

"What are you doing, Orion?" one of them asked.

Instead of answering, I worked my sandaled foot into one of the stirrups and hoisted myself up into the saddle, careful not to touch the spurs to the horse's flank. Not yet.

"It's like a little step!"

"Orion, can't you swing up on a horse the regular way? Are you so weak from washing every morning that you need a step to help you up?"

They roared with laughter, slapping their thighs and pounding each other's backs. Wordlessly, I nudged my mount through them and cantered around the courtyard several times. The stirrups felt a little loose. I dismounted and tightened the thongs that held them to the saddle.

By now some of the knights had come out into the courtyard to see what was making the other men laugh so hard.

"What's that you've hooked your feet into?" Gawain called to me. He was several years older than Arthur, built more slightly, his dark hair curled into ringlets that fell past his shoulders.

"It's an old Sarmatian device," I answered, walking my horse to him. Better to tell them it's an old and well-tested idea; new ideas are always suspect. Besides, it was the truth.

Two more young knights joined Gawain, each of them looking just as puzzled as he.

"Why did the Sarmatians need help getting into their saddles?" Gawain asked.

I smiled tightly. "These are not for help in getting into the saddle," I replied. "Their purpose is to *keep* you in the saddle."

Gawain and the others were plainly baffled. Looking up, I saw Merlin peering over the edge of his tower at me. Arthur stood beside him.

Time for a demonstration. I trotted over to the corner of the courtyard where the spears stood stacked like sheaves of wheat, leaned over, and drew one from the stack. Turning my mount around, I centered my gaze upon one of the stout timbers that held the thatched roof over the blacksmith's open forge. The smith and his young apprentices were just starting up their fire, off to one side of their work area.

I spurred the horse and he took off as if a swarm of hornets were stinging him. I crouched forward in the saddle, my weight on the stirrups, leveled the spear as I galloped straight for that rough-hewn timber. Men and boys scattered out of the way as I raced forward with my spear jutting out ahead. The smith stood transfixed, staring with eyes so wide I could see white all around his pupils. His boys ran, wailing.

I rammed the spear into the timber. The spear shattered from the force of the impact but its point buried itself in the wood almost to the haft. I wheeled my mount around and trotted back to the center of the courtyard.

"I understand now," said Gawain, with a smirk on his handsome face. "That's the Sarmatian way of breaking a perfectly good spear."

Clod! I thought. But I had to remember that I was only a squire and had to be respectful to a knight.

"Not so, sir. With these stirrups I can drive a spear through an enemy at full gallop without being knocked out of my saddle."

"And what good is that if you break the spear?" Gawain sniffed.

He turned and walked away; the two younger knights went with him.

"Wait!" I called. When they turned back toward me I directed the young boys standing off by the woodpile to bring me the thickest, hardest log they could find.

It took two of the lads to carry the massive log to the center of the courtyard, their legs tottering under the load. As I directed them to stand it on end, I saw Sir Bors came up beside Gawain, a skeptical scowl on his scarred face.

I trotted my horse back to the main gate, then spurred him into an all-out charge, drawing my sword as the steed galloped madly across the packed dirt.

With one swing I split the log in half.

Gawain and the other knights seemed impressed—but only a little.

"You'd make a good woodcutter," Gawain joked as I got down from the horse.

"Don't you understand?" I said. "With the stirrups to hold you in the saddle you could charge into the enemy at full speed and hit with all the power of a thunderbolt."

"We've never used stirrups before," said Bors. "Don't see why we need 'em now."

"Because they can multiply the force of your attack!" I insisted, almost pleading with him to open his mind.

But Bors raised his thick-muscled right arm, crisscrossed with scars, and said, "This is all the force I need in battle. I've killed hundreds of Saxons, Jutes, Danes, Angles—all with this strong right arm. I don't need fancy contraptions to help keep me in my saddle."

"But—"

Gawain laughed gently. "Use your stirrups if you want to, Orion. If that's the Sarmatian way, then go right ahead. But we don't need such tricks."

I felt crushed. They didn't understand what I was offering them. I looked up toward Merlin's aerie, but neither the wizard nor Arthur was still watching me. I trotted the horse back to the stables and alit.

I handed the horse to a grinning stableboy, wondering what I could do to convince these men that stirrups would allow them to hit their enemies with the full force of a charging steed, instead of milling into battle slowly and hoping they could stay mounted by gripping the horse with their legs—while their enemies had plenty of time to fight back.

Out in the courtyard I saw Arthur standing by the blacksmith, talking. I went to him. The blacksmith shied away from me, anger and fear plain to see on his heavily bearded face.

Arthur was fingering the spear point still embedded deep in the timber.

"I thought you were going to kill yourself," he said to me, "racing across the courtyard like that."

I made myself grin ruefully. "I'm sure the smith thought I was going to kill him."

Arthur laughed lightly. "He did look petrified, didn't he?"

"My lord, what I'm trying to show—"

"I understand, Orion," said Arthur. "Those little things on your feet allowed you to stay in the saddle even when you hit hard enough to shatter your spear."

He was no fool, this young knight.

I replied, "It could turn your knights into a powerful battle force, my lord."

"If only they would listen to reason," he said.

"You are their appointed leader. Can't you make them accept this new idea?"

He shook his head slowly. "I am their leader, true: appointed by the High King to direct the defense of this fort. But I can't force them to do anything."

"But—"

"This isn't Rome, my friend," Arthur said quietly, sadly. "These knights are freeborn Celts. They don't bend to authority. They follow a leader only as long as they wish to. It's the curse of the Celts: they treasure freedom even in the face of disaster."

"Freedom is hardly a curse, my lord," I said.

"Yes, perhaps. But discipline is something that we sadly lack."

"If only one or two of them would *try* the stirrups," I said. "That would show the others what an advantage they are."

Arthur smiled at me, the warmth of true friendship in his eyes. "I will try them with you, friend Orion. We will sally out against the Saxons together and show them all what we can do."

8

"Absolutely not!" Bors thundered. "Your uncle would have my guts for his garters if I permitted it!"

"Then I'll go alone," Arthur said, "with no one beside me but my lowly squire." He nodded in my direction.

"You'll get yourself killed!"

We were standing in Arthur's chamber, nothing more than a small room made of rude logs at the bottom of the fort's lone tower. Its floor was packed earth, its ceiling of roughly planed timbers a bare few inches above my head.

Arthur did not argue with the surly Bors. He merely smiled his boyish smile and said gently, "But if you came with us, then you'd probably be killed along with me and you wouldn't have to face Ambrosius."

Bors went so red in the face that the scar along his cheek stood out like a white line. He was speechless.

"You will come with me," Arthur prodded, "won't you?"

With a great fuming gasp of exasperation, Bors growled, "You're determined to do this, are you?"

"Yes," said Arthur. "I am."

"Then I have no choice, do I?"

Arthur's face lit up with delight. "You'll come?"

Nodding sourly, Bors said, "I'll come with you."

"Fine!" Arthur exclaimed. "Now let's see how many of the others will come."

I worked all that night, going without sleep to make seven sets of stirrups and spurs. By the time the sun had climbed almost to its noontime high, Arthur gathered his knights around him in the courtyard and told them what he proposed to do.

Most of the men shook their heads warily, not trusting these Sarmatian innovations to be of any real use against the teeming hordes of barbarians outside the fort's walls.

"We sallied out against the Saxons three nights ago and it did little good," said Sir Peredur, his arm still wrapped in a blood-soaked bandage from that fight.

"But this will be different," Arthur urged. "We will strike them like avenging angels."

"I prefer to meet the barbarians from behind these stout walls,"

Sir Kay said, in his booming, bombastic voice. "Let them come to us."

The gathered knights nodded to one another and muttered their agreement.

Arthur turned to Gawain. "Sir knight, will you let Sir Bors and I ride into the Saxon midst alone?"

Gawain grinned like a man who knew he was being outwitted. "By God, never! Where you lead, Arthur, Gawain will follow. Right into the mouth of hell, if needs be!"

Arthur clasped his shoulder thankfully.

In the end, only five of the knights agreed to join Arthur's sally. I handed out six pairs of spurs and rigged seven horses with stirrups, plus my own, hoping we could find a seventh to join us.

One by one I led the horses out into the courtyard. One by one the knights mounted—some of them obviously with great reluctance. The seventh horse remained without a rider. I held the seventh pair of spurs in my hands, waiting.

"Is there no one here who will join us?" Arthur called out.

The knights and squires standing in the courtyard shuffled uneasily, guiltily, but none moved toward us.

Until one of the squires, a slightly built youth, pushed through the crowd and said, "I will go with you, sir, if you will have me."

Arthur smiled down at him. At first I thought Arthur would turn the lad away because he was so young, but then I realized that Arthur himself was barely more than a stripling.

Turning to Sir Kay, who still stood stubbornly off to one side, Arthur commanded, "Kay, find this squire chain mail, shield, and helmet." Then he leaned toward me and said, "Give him the last set of spurs."

In a few minutes the lad was mounted on the seventh horse, armed with coat of mail, a helmet that wobbled on his narrow shoulders, a dented, patched shield, a sword that seemed too big for his delicate hands, and a long spear.

I could no longer see Arthur's face, hidden by his helmet, but his voice rang out clearly: "Follow me, men, and we will drive the invaders back into the sea!"

9

The fort's gates creaked open, and the eight of us pricked our mounts into a thundering charge. For a brief instant I wondered what the Golden One was thinking. Was I playing into his hands and sending Arthur out to his death?

Not while I breathe, I swore to myself. I'll die before I'll let Arthur be killed.

As always in battle, the world around me seemed to slow down into a lethargic dreamy languor. My senses raced into overdrive, adrenaline flooding my arteries, everything around me seen in microscopically crisp detail.

The barbarian host had hurriedly formed a battle line as soon as they heard the fort's gates begin to creak. They were standing waiting for us as we charged down the hill, hard-muscled men bare to the waist gripping their swords and axes, round wooden shields on their arms, long blond braids running down their powerful chests.

I saw spittle form and drip in slow motion from the foaming mouth of Arthur's mount, at my left side. He was crouched forward in his saddle, spear leveled, weight on his stirrups. I picked out one of the Saxon warriors and aimed my spear at his chest.

The barbarian tactic for dealing with a cavalry charge was to absorb the impact with as many men as possible and then, once the horsemen had slowed down, to bring in more men from the flanks to swarm the riders under.

But this time we didn't slow down. Arthur was the first to strike, snapping a Saxon's head off his shoulders with the power of his thundering charger behind the point of his spear. I rammed my spear clear through my man's shield and hit him squarely in the chest, wrenched the spear free, and charged into the next rank. I could hear our seven men roaring as they drove through the barbarian battle line like a hot knife through butter, and the death screams of the invaders as those long spears crushed the life out of them.

We smashed through their battle line, wheeled, and charged into them again. This time they broke and scattered before us, wailing with sudden fear.

"Stay together!" Arthur bellowed, and we rode as one terrifying fist of death with seven long spears that smashed flesh and bone wherever they struck.

The barbarians were scurrying away from us like rats, running in every direction, desperately trying to avoid our bloody spear points. But no matter how fast they ran, our steeds were faster. Spears broke, and knights pulled out their shining swords with the hiss of metal on metal. Those blades licked out the life of every man they reached.

I was spattered with enemy blood up to my thighs; my sword was red and dripping.

"Look!" I called to Arthur. "Up on the ridge."

A small band of mounted warriors stood on the crest of the ridge, wearing helmets that bore horns and shone with gold and jewels.

"Aelle!" shouted Arthur. "He who styles himself king of Britain."

He spurred his mount up the slope toward the Saxon leader

and his band of picked guards. I charged up after him, leaving Gawain and Bors and the others to complete the rout of the terrified invaders.

I wondered how wise it was for Arthur to charge against nearly a dozen mounted warriors, but he was swinging Excalibur over his head, yelling wildly and spurring his steed up the slope. I charged after him.

For several eternally long moments we raced up toward the crest of the ridge. I could see, in slow motion, the troubled looks Aelle's men were giving each other. Their horses shifted and stamped, as if sensing the riders' unease. They all looked toward Aelle. The old man whom they had elected Bretwalda sat on his mount, wide-eyed with shock and sudden terror, stunned at what had happened to his warrior horde, shattered by the charge of a mere eight horsemen.

I expected them to charge downhill at us, eleven against two. Instead, Aelle abruptly yanked at his reins and turned away from us. He and his men disappeared behind the ridge's crest.

By the time Arthur and I reached the crest they were already halfway across the glade below, galloping for their lives.

Arthur reined in his mount. "No sense chasing after them, Orion," he said firmly. "Our mounts are tired, theirs fresh."

I turned back toward the plain before Amesbury fort. The invading barbarian army was gone, run away, scattered to the four winds. Arthur's knights were trotting their spent horses slowly up toward us.

"You've won a great victory, my lord," I said.

Arthur pulled the heavy helmet off his head and shook his thick sandy hair free.

"Thanks to you," he answered, smiling broadly, "and your Sarmatian tricks."

"It was your courage and leadership that won the battle, my lord. Without those qualities, my 'tricks' would have been mere scraps of iron."

Gawain was grinning widely as we walked our mounts back to the fort. "They won't be back," he predicted. "Not for a long time."

Arthur was also in a boyishly jovial mood. "Did you see old Aelle run away! One glimpse of Excalibur and he turned tail!"

Even Bors was pleased. "My lord," he said to Arthur, "you should note the bravery of this youngster." He pointed to the squire who had volunteered to join us. "He fought like Saint Michael the Archangel himself."

The lad drooped his chin timidly, hardly daring to look at Arthur.

"Don't be shy, youngster," said Arthur. "Praise from Sir Bors is as rare as snow in July."

Everyone laughed, except the youngster.

10

Once inside the fort, the knights began to hand their shields and weapons to their squires—while the knights who had remained behind watched in envious, shamefaced silence.

The youngster walked through the men to Arthur, and held out the spurs he had worn.

"Here, my lord. Thank you for allowing me to wear them."

"Keep them," Arthur said. "You went into battle a lowly squire, but your courage and skill demands better for you. Kneel."

Dumbfounded, the boy dropped to one knee.

Arthur drew out Excalibur, still caked with barbarian blood. Then he hesitated.

"I don't know your name," he said.

"Lancelot, my lord."

Arthur smiled and tapped him on each shoulder with the blade, leaving two dark red smudges.

"Rise, Sir Lancelot. And welcome to the company of knight-hood."

Lancelot's mouth hung open. He swallowed visibly before he could utter, "Bless you, my lord."

The other knights crowded around to congratulate the lad.

But that night, as I unrolled my sleeping blanket in the shadows of Amesbury's palisade, I thought I heard in the far-off echoes of my mind the Golden One laughing mockingly and saying, "The seed of destruction has been sown, Orion. Arthur's days are numbered."

Not while I live, I answered silently. Then I lay down to sleep. But as soon as I closed my eyes I felt a wave of utter cold take hold of me and I was falling, falling through a black infinity.

Interlude

I opened my eyes and saw clouds scudding past in a windswept sky above me. I was lying on the hard wet planks of the deck of a ship that was heaving up and down sickeningly. I smelled the salt tang of the sea and the stench of vomit and human sweat. Our little cockleshell bobbed in the choppy waters of the Channel so hard that we were all soaked to the skin from the spray coming over the gunwales.

"Up! Wake up!" a clear tenor voice called. "All hands to their stations!"

Scrambling to my feet, I saw my crewmates staring across the water at the awesome procession of Spanish men-of-war heading through the Channel for Gravelines, on the Belgian shore.

"There they are, lads," said our skipper, pointing. "Take a good look at the Pope-kissing bastards."

He was young to be a ship's captain, but then our ship was just an unarmed riverboat, wallowing in the swells of the heaving sea. As I looked around at the rest of us, I saw that they were all barely old enough to start their beards.

How or why I was here I didn't know. My last memory was of

Arthur and his victory over Aelle and his Saxon host at Amesbury fort. Somehow I was now aboard a small English merchant-
man, part of a pitiful little squadron of ships that had been sent
out to face the mighty Spanish Armada.

Britain was again threatened with invasion, and there was our
youthful skipper grinning defiantly at the enemy. He looked very
much like the Arthur I had known from a thousand years earlier:
broad of shoulder, handsome features with gold-flecked amber
eyes and the beginnings of a light brown beard.

It was near sunset. The sky was low and glowering red; a storm
was brewing to the west out in the wild Atlantic. The Spanish
fleet proceeded through the Channel in a stately line, big, square-
backed galleons leading the way, followed by smaller galleys,
their oars sweeping steadily, like rows of metronomes.

"Some o' them sweeps is Englishmen," said the sailor next to
me, his voice harder than his round, youthful face. "They caught
me brother off Jamaica last year, chained 'im to the oars."

"Do you think he might be aboard one of those galleys?" I
asked.

The youngster nodded grimly. "Could be. But if he is, drownin'
in th' Channel's better'n years as a bloody galley slave."

"Quit the chatter and look lively now!" the skipper commanded. "Get about your business, men, and best be quick about it!"

Our little *Minerva* was to be a fireship. We were to set her ablaze
and sail her into the Spanish ships when they tried to moor at Gravelines. The plan was to scatter the Armada so that Drake and
Frobisher and the other Seahawks could deal with the big Spanish
men-of-war individually.

We set about hauling the tinder and firewood up from below
deck, each of us casting uneasy glances at the rowboats we would
use to try to get away once we had lit the fires.

It was a desperate plan. Although the ramshackle collection of British ships sailing out from harbors all along the Channel actually outnumbered the Armada, the Spanish fleet was far superior in firepower and its ships were much bigger than ours. They were slower and less maneuverable than our tumble homes, and that could make all the difference in the tricky waters of the Channel.

"Smoothly, lads, smoothly," Arthur coaxed us as we worked. "We're going to give them hell."

I thought it might be the other way around. Our only hope was to be nimble enough to avoid their broadsides, and I knew we couldn't be lucky enough to escape them forever.

As if to prove my point, the nearest galleon fired a salvo at us. Even at the distance between us the roar of their guns shook the air. I heard the deep growling whistle of cannonballs swooping overhead, like evil meteors intent on smashing us to splinters. But instead they soared past us and splashed harmlessly into the sea, although one of them pocked through our topsail.

"They're just trying to warn us off," Arthur tried to reassure us. "Pay them no mind."

"Pay 'em no mind, eh?" grumbled the sailor hauling timbers next to me. "Not 'til they sink us, by damn."

All through the deepening twilight our skipper kept us on the edge of the galleons' cannon range while the sun sank below the horizon and darkness settled on the choppy waters. We could see the lights of Gravelines low on the horizon in the distance and the lanterns along the decks of the Armada's ships.

The hours stretched on. Arthur had us check the rowboats, make sure their oars were in place.

"Sir Francis and the other Seahawks will attack once the fireships have scattered the Spaniards," Arthur said confidently.

"Aye," whispered my grumpy fellow sailor, "and we'll be sittin' in the bloody dinghies, tryin' to row our way back t' Dover."

I smiled grimly at him. "That's better than being chained to a galley's oars, isn't it?"

It was too dark to see the expression on his face, but I heard his reply: "Bloody suicide job, that's what we've got."

Arthur must have heard him, because he said into the darkness, "We've a hard task, lads, true enough, but England needs our best and nothing less."

As the night wore on the wind freshened. "That storm coming in from the Atlantic," Arthur said, his voice brimming with youthful hope, "is going to blow our little fireball right into their midst. You'll see!"

"And we'll hafta row against the wind," my companion groused. "We'll be lucky if we make landfall in France."

Clouds were scudding across the face of the moon, making the night even darker. Stars winked out as the clouds built up.

"Get some rest, men," said Arthur, moving through the darkness among us. "Try to sleep for a while. I'll stand watch and when the time comes to light the fire, I'll wake you."

"That's for sure," my sour-voiced companion whispered hoarsely.

I stretched out on the wet planks of the deck and closed my eyes. And again felt the clutch of absolute cold, unfathomable darkness. I was hurtling through spacetime again as the universe shifted.

CHAPTER THREE

Spoils of War

1

I woke up back at Amesbury fort, wrapped in my bedroll at the base of the palisade. It was sunrise, a clear warm day was in prospect. I blinked in confusion. How did I get to the English Channel in 1588? Why? Who had sent me there?

It couldn't have been Aten, I thought. Or, if it was, why would he return me here to Amesbury, where I can protect Arthur? Was it Anya? I tried to contact her, reached out with my mind all that morning as I went through my usual ritual of bathing in the horse trough, to the usual jibes and jeers of the other squires.

Nothing. Not even a hint of her presence. Aten is blocking my effort to reach her, I told myself. He doesn't want me to be with her.

It didn't take long for the news of Arthur's victory over the Saxon host to spread beyond the fort's confines. The second day after he had scattered the barbarians, an itinerant Jewish merchant arrived at the gates of Amesbury fort in a creaking, lopsided wagon pulled by a pair of mangy mules.

His name was Isaac. He was short and wiry, all bones and tendons. His face was swarthy, as if permanently suntanned, and his lean jaw was covered with a luxuriant dark beard. His cheeks were hollow, but his deep-set brown eyes were alert and keenly intelligent.

Arthur sent Sir Kay, his chamberlain, to meet the visitor and look over his wares. Apparently the peddler had learned that we had taken a fair amount of booty from the Saxons that had been slain: weapons mostly, heavy swords and sharp-edged axes that the barbarians could throw like missiles. Dozens of helmets, many sporting polished horns. A few shields and several strange seashell pendants carved with curious runes. If they were meant to be magical amulets they had done little good to the men who wore them: they had been ripped from the corpses of the slain.

Merlin was curious about the visitor and whatever news he might have about the world beyond the stakes of Amesbury's palisade. Curious myself, I followed the white-haired wizard through the open gates of the fort and up to the merchant's top-heavy wagon.

"Greeting, oh wise one," said the peddler, bowing respectfully. "I am Isaac the Jew, a poor wandering merchant striving to eke out a living for my family. I have four children." Here Isaac paused and added, with a resigned shrug, "All daughters."

"I am Merlin," the wizard replied, "adviser to the High King, Ambrosius Aurelianus."

"Adviser to the High King? Indeed?"

A small crowd of inquisitive knights, squires, and footmen was gathering at the gate, ogling the pots and blankets and trinkets dangling from the sides of Isaac's overladen wagon.

I noticed Lancelot among them, and beside him stood brown-robed Friar Llunach, the fort's chaplain, his jowly face grim with dislike for the Jewish Isaac.

Pointing to the mound of spoils, Isaac said to Merlin, "You

have won a great victory here. News of it is spreading throughout the land."

Merlin nodded. "It will be a long time before Aelle tries to test young Arthur in battle again."

"Indeed," said Isaac. "Aelle will never again challenge Arthur or anyone else. The man is dead."

"Dead?" Merlin's eyes went wide. Everyone in the small knot of onlookers was startled by the news.

Isaac explained, "Some say he was slain by his own men, who felt shamed when their Bretwalda fled in panic from Arthur's charge."

"You must tell Arthur himself of this," Merlin said, gesturing toward the open gate.

"Hold!" cried Friar Llunach. "The Jew may not enter the fort."

"And why not?" Merlin snapped.

Frowning, the priest said, "He's a Jew! An unbeliever. One of Christ's murderers."

Many of the onlookers stepped back, as if afraid they would be polluted if they stayed near the merchant. Lancelot stood firm, though. As did I.

Merlin shook his head sadly. "This man is nothing more than an itinerant peddler. He no more murdered your Christ than you did yourself."

"Blasphemy!" hissed the friar.

For an instant I thought that Merlin was going to laugh in the priest's face. Instead, the old wizard drew himself up in his long, dingy robe and said merely, "This news must be told to Arthur."

Beckoning Isaac to follow him, Merlin went through the gate and into the fort, the little crowd parting like the Red Sea before the pair of them.

Friar Llunach stood there, radiating fury. Turning to young

Lancelot, he half whispered, "That old magician is no Christian. He still follows the old gods."

I smiled to myself. If I had it right, Merlin was himself one of the old gods. But was he aiding Aten or not? Would he one day assassinate Arthur or try to protect him from Aten's murderous plans, even as I was?

♌

"Aelle is dead?" Arthur blurted, delighted surprise wreathing his smiling face.

Isaac stood respectfully before the young commander, who sat in an ancient Roman camp chair behind the rough trestle table that took up much of his room. Sir Bors stood behind him, looking suspicious, as usual.

Merlin, standing beside the merchant, said, "Apparently he was killed by his own men, who were shamed by his flight at the battle."

Arthur leaned back in the creaking chair. Stroking his light beard, he muttered, "So much for the self-styled Bretwalda." Then he looked up at Isaac once again and asked, "Does my uncle know of this?"

"Your uncle, sir?"

"Ambrosius, the High King."

Isaac's eyes slid toward Merlin, then back to Arthur. "The High King is your uncle?"

"He is," said Arthur. "And he must be told of Aelle's death immediately."

As soon as Arthur asked his knights for a volunteer to carry the news to the High King, young Lancelot begged for the mission.

"It won't be easy," Arthur warned the youth. "You'll have to ride alone through deep woods and dark nights."

Lancelot was practically quivering with enthusiasm. "I can do it, lord! Please let me do it!"

Before the sun set, Lancelot galloped off for Cadbury on the fastest horse in our fort, trailing two other mounts behind him. Arthur, Bors, and I watched him disappear over the ridgeline from the parapet.

Bors shook his head. "That lad has more guts than brains," he muttered.

Isaac took his pick of the battle spoils, offering in return fine linen tunics, iron cook pots, blankets that looked newly weaved. The knights bargained with him day and night; Isaac never pressed them, he seemed content to accept whatever they demanded of him.

The evening before he was to leave, I went out to his wagon, where he was bundling the Saxon booty into rough burlap sacks.

"Are you satisfied with what you've gained?" I asked him.

Isaac shrugged in the gathering shadows. "Am I satisfied? Why not?"

"I think you could have bargained harder."

With a sardonic little smile, Isaac replied, "And make your fine knights angry with me? It's bad enough that the priest hates me. I'm not going to make enemies of men who carry swords."

I helped him lift a bundle and shove it into his cluttered wagon. "You're very cautious."

"I'm alive. Killing a Jew isn't a crime to these people, you know."

"These people? You don't think I'm one of them?"

The sun had dipped below the wooded hills, but I could see the crafty expression on Isaac's face. "You are taller than the rest of them. Your skin is almost as dark as mine. You're no Briton."

"You're very observant," I said.

"A Jew needs to be observant," he said, a tinge of bitterness in his voice. "And compliant. A Jew can't afford to make enemies. They already hate me."

"You follow a difficult path."

With a shrug, Isaac replied, "I manage to survive."

A sudden thought occurred to me. "You offered no coin for any of the spoils."

"Coin?" Isaac looked startled. "If they thought I carried coin with me they'd slit my throat on the spot and ransack my wagon."

Raising my hands, I said, "Sorry. Forget that I mentioned it."

"Just don't mention it to *them*," Isaac whispered.

Gold was so rare and precious among the Britons that it was the cause of murders, even among the Christians. Strange, I thought, how easily men forget their religion over gold, or anything else they covet.

By the time Isaac finished packing his wagon it was fully night, cloudy, moonless.

"Will you come into the fort for supper with me?" I asked him.

Shaking his head, he said, "I will stay here with my goods. I have a little bread and a few lentils."

"I don't think any of the men would pilfer your wagon," I told him. "Arthur wouldn't allow it."

With that sad little smile of his, Isaac replied, "Arthur I trust. But the others . . ." He waggled a hand.

So I stayed with the merchant, shared his bread and lentils— and a pair of ripe apples that he pulled out of a burlap sack—and slept the night on the ground beneath his wagon.

In the morning Isaac yoked his mules and drove off. But not before saying to me, "You are a good man, Orion. I will tell the others of my people that you can be trusted."

I thanked him and watched him drive the creaking wagon slowly away from Amesbury fort.

Five days later Lancelot came galloping back from Cadbury, covered with dust and grime, his mount lathered and heaving.

Even as he slid out of his saddle, Lancelot cried, "The High King wants to see Arthur! He wants Arthur to come to Cadbury castle! I've got to tell him!"

And he dashed past me, racing for the rough-hewn tower where Arthur stayed.

CHAPTER FOUR

Cadbury Castle

1

They attacked us while we were sleeping.

It was our second night on the hard journey from Amesbury to the High King's castle, and we were all weary, bone tired. That morning we had been forced to turn off the good Roman road that led arrow-straight to Salisbury and instead plunged into a thick, dark forest that seemed endless.

After hours of walking our horses through the lofty, thick-boled trees, hardly seeing the sun through their dense canopies, Arthur decided to make camp in a small clearing.

"We'll reach Cadbury castle tomorrow," he said, trying to cheer the twelve knights he had chosen to accompany him as they sat tiredly on the mossy ground.

Their squires—me included—were tending the horses while the half-dozen churls Arthur had brought with us were busy gathering firewood and preparing to cook the salted meat and dried beans that the packhorses carried.

The attack that night was meant to kill Arthur.

We were sleeping soundly, even I, who needs very little sleep normally. But the exertions of nearly constant battle and the long wearying days of painfully slow travel across the hilly, forested land had made even me drowsy.

I dreamed of Anya.

It was more than a dream. I was with her, the goddess whom I loved, the Creator who loved me. For only a few moments I stood in another world, another dimension, on a grassy hill warm with sunshine where flowers nodded happily in the gentle breeze coming in from the nearby sea. Soft puffs of clouds scudded across a brilliant blue sky. In the distance, where the hill sloped down to a wide sandy beach, there stood a magnificent city filled with gigantic monuments and graceful temples.

But the city was empty, lifeless. It was the city of the Creators, I knew, the beings who traveled through time to manipulate human history to suit their whims.

Anya: supernally beautiful with her lustrous sable-black hair and fathomless gray eyes. In other times she had been worshipped as Athena, Isis, Artemis. I had given my life for her, more than once.

She stood before me on that sun-dappled hillside, draped in a supple robe of silver threads. I reached out to her, but she raised a warning hand.

"Awake, Orion," she said, her voice urgent, her lovely face intent with alarm. "Arthur has been betrayed."

My eyes popped open. I was back in the clearing in the forest, hardly a moonbeam breaking through the dark canopy of the trees. Our fire was down to feeble embers. I didn't move a muscle. A chill wind sighed through the boughs so high above. An owl hooted once, then again.

It was no owl, I realized. Men were creeping around our little camp, signaling to each other as they surrounded us.

Furtively, I reached for the sword that lay at my side. My eyes adjusted to the dim light of our fire's embers and I could see the shadowy shapes of the attackers edging closer to Arthur's sleeping men.

"To arms!" I bellowed at the top of my voice, leaping to my feet, sword in hand. "Saxons!"

There were at least forty of them. I ran straight at the nearest ones, a trio of burly men gripping long two-handed swords. My senses went into overdrive; the action before me seemed to slow down, as if time itself had suddenly altered, stretching like taffy into a sluggish dreamlike pace.

Out of the corner of my eye I could see Arthur and his knights rousing themselves. Men were shouting, cursing, and someone screamed his death agony.

All this as the three before me braced themselves and raised their heavy two-handed swords against me. I dove headfirst into the nearest one, leaving my feet entirely in a leap that buried the point of my sword in his chest. We toppled to the ground together, his blood spurting as I yanked my sword out of him and rolled away from a mighty two-handed clout that would have cleaved me in two if it had landed on me.

Scrambling to my feet, I sliced the villain through his throat before he could swing at me again. He crumpled, gurgling blood, as I danced away from the powerful swing of his companion, then took off both his hands with a single blow to his wrists. He shrieked, wide-eyed with pain and terror, as his sword fell to the ground with both his hands still gripping it.

Leaving him, I turned to see that Arthur's knights were giving a good account of themselves. Without shields or helmets, without even their chain mail, they still were hacking through the attackers with grim efficiency.

I saw one of the attackers standing off, lurking beside the

massive bole of a rough-barked tree. Their leader, I thought, and raced toward him. He saw me and turned to flee.

I hefted my sword and threw it at him. It was a clumsy throw and the sword hit with the flat of the blade between his shoulders. The impact was enough to send him sprawling, but by the time I reached him he was scrambling to his feet, his own sword in his right hand and my sword in his left.

He grinned at me like a wolf. "Now you die, fool."

I reached for the dagger I always kept strapped to my thigh, the dagger that Odysseos had given me in the Greek camp on the shore of Ilium. Not much against two swords, but better than my bare hands.

Behind me I heard the din of battle: swords clanging, men screaming in pain, even the panicked horses neighing and stomping, trying to break their tethers and run away from this bloody mayhem.

He advanced upon me, waving his two swords as if trying to hypnotize me. I watched him, my supercharged senses studying every bunching of his muscles, every movement of his eyes. He was stalking me, still grinning confidently.

I flipped the dagger in my hand so that I held it by the point and, before he could think to move, hurled it into his chest. It hit him with a solid thunk and he staggered. The confident grin faded. His mouth filled with blood. He tried to step toward me, tried to reach me with the swords, but his legs had no strength in them. He collapsed face-first at my feet, driving my dagger even deeper into his chest.

By the time I had retrieved both my sword and dagger and cleaned them, Arthur, Bors, and Gawain had come up to join me.

"Your warning saved us," Arthur said, still breathing hard.

Gawain's chest was heaving, too. "A few of them ran off into the woods, but thirty or so of them will never leave this clearing."

I nodded. My senses had calmed down to normal. "Did we lose anyone?" I asked.

Bors answered gruffly, "Not a one. Two of the churls were cut down and several men are wounded, but that's all."

Obviously Sir Bors did not consider laborers to be worth counting as real men.

Arthur asked, "These knaves were not Saxons. They were Celts, as we are. Why attack us?"

"Robbers," said Gawain. "A band of robbers who thought they saw easy pickings."

"Attacking armed knights?" I asked. "And an equal number of squires? Robbers are not so bold."

"A dozen sleeping knights," Gawain countered.

Arthur added, with a smile, "And most squires are not fighters of your caliber, Orion."

Bors bent down to examine the dead man at our feet. "This one was no common robber, my lord," he said to Arthur.

"What makes you say that?" Gawain challenged.

"I know this face. He was a man-at-arms at Cadbury castle."

Arthur stared at Bors, dumbfounded. "He served my uncle Ambrosius?"

Bors nodded grimly. "Look here. He still wears the High King's crest on his tunic."

"Treachery," Gawain whispered.

With a shake of his head, Arthur said in a low, hollow voice, "I can't believe that my uncle would send these rogues upon us. Why would he do so?"

"Jealousy, my lord," answered Sir Bors. "Your victory at Amesbury gives the High King pause. He fears for his throne."

"But I would never . . ." Arthur seemed thoroughly shocked. "He knows I would never seek his crown."

"Does he, my lord?" Bors replied. "I wonder."

𝟤

The next day was sultry, the last touch of summer that we would see that year. Our little column of mounted knights and squires climbed the steep dusty road slowly, the horses tired, the men sweating and too weary even to grumble about the long journey or the hot sun blazing out of the cloudless sky.

I rode beside young Arthur, as a squire should. Usually Arthur was bright and eager, full of youthful enthusiasm, but this day he was quiet, thinking, worried about the treachery of the night before. The tunic he wore over his chain mail was covered with dust, stained with sweat. His light brown hair flowed past his shoulders, his amber eyes that usually sparkled with dreams of glory seemed to be focused elsewhere, looking for answers they could not find. Unconsciously he scratched at his bristly beard. It was coming in nicely, but it must have been itchy.

"I wish Merlin were with us," he said, with a sigh. "I miss his advice."

We had left the old wizard behind at Amesbury; too frail to make the trip with us, he would be coming later by wagon, together with the arms and other spoils from the battle Arthur had won.

"Merlin is very wise," I said.

"He prophesied I would win a great victory and he was right," Arthur said. He treated me more as a friend than a squire, and often unburdened his inner thoughts to me. "It was a great victory, wasn't it?" he said, smiling at the memory of it.

"Indeed it was, my lord."

"Thanks to you, Orion. And your Sarmatian stirrups."

"You led the charge, my lord," I said to Arthur. "It was your vision and courage that convinced the knights to accept the new ideas."

Arthur nodded, his face going somber. "Now I must convince the High King."

He had concocted a plan to drive the Saxons and all the other barbarian tribes completely out of Britain. Only three men knew of it, so far: Arthur, Merlin, and myself. It was a plan that could work, I thought, if Ambrosius was willing to accept it and was not already fearful that Arthur was threatening his position as High King.

There was one other obstacle in Arthur's path, as well: me. Aten had sent me to this time and place to prevent Arthur from defeating the barbarians who were invading Britain. To assassinate him if his enemies didn't kill him first.

"Look!" Arthur stood in his stirrups and pointed. "Cadbury castle!"

It stood at the crest of the steep hill we were tediously climbing. Cadbury was a real castle, built of stone, not one of the rude wooden hill forts that Ambrosius had strung along the countryside to contain the Saxon invasion.

"It must have been built by giants," he said, staring at the high stone wall and the towers rising above it.

"No," I said. "It was built by men."

"But Orion, mortal men could never lift such stones! Look at them! It's impossible."

I had scaled the beetling walls of Troy and helped to burn the fabled towers of Ilium. I had tried to defend triple-walled Byzantium against the ferocious Turks. Cadbury was nothing compared to them, but to this eager young knight it was the grandest architecture he had ever seen.

"Roman engineers built most of it," I told Arthur. "The High King's stonecrafters have added to it."

He refused to believe such a mundane explanation. Arthur was barely out of his teens, full of the naïveté and credulous innocence of wide-eyed youth.

"Not even the Romans could have built so high without the aid of the gods," he said. Then he crossed himself.

I held my tongue. If he knew what the gods truly were, he would weep in shocked disillusion.

"Look, Orion!" he shouted. "Ambrosius himself is at the parapet to welcome us!"

It was true. The bright blue-and-gold flags of the High King snapped briskly in the hot breeze up on the crenellations atop Cadbury's main gate. The drawbridge was down and through the open gate I could see that the castle's courtyard was thronged with people. If Ambrosius had truly sent those scoundrels to murder Arthur, why would he be waiting at his castle's main gate with pennants flying?

I thought I knew the answer. The would-be murderers had been sent by Aten, the Golden One. He knew I was resisting his commands to kill Arthur, so he arranged the previous night's attack. Even though it had failed, it had opened a wound of suspicion between the High King and his young adopted nephew.

Arthur spurred his mount lightly and trotted up the steep, dusty road, eager to reach the castle. I urged my horse forward, to be close enough to protect Arthur if the need arose. He had no idea that the gods he dreamed of wanted to kill him, no idea that I was defying those so-called gods to protect him.

"My uncle Ambrosius waits to greet us," Arthur said as I

pulled up beside him. His handsome face was wreathed in a delighted smile.

"You see? The word of your victory at Amesbury has pleased him," I said.

"Yes, perhaps so," Arthur agreed.

I glanced up at the flapping banners atop the open castle gate. I could see a group of men standing there, watching our approach. One of them must have been Ambrosius, Arthur's uncle, High King of the British Celts.

Arthur's eyes followed my gaze, but I heard him muttering, "We can drive the barbarians completely out of Britain, drive them away for good—if only Ambrosius will have faith in my plan."

"He will, my lord, I'm sure," I said.

Arthur nodded, but it was obvious that his thoughts had turned elsewhere. We rode along in silence up the switchbacks of the road, climbing the hill on which Cadbury castle was sited.

"What do you think of the castle, Orion?" Arthur asked at last. "Have you ever seen such mighty walls, such high towers?"

I smiled and kept the truth to myself. "It would be difficult to take by storm, my lord."

"Difficult!" He laughed, a youthful, boyish laugh. "I could defend Cadbury against all the barbarian hordes for a hundred years!"

No, I thought. You won't be allowed to live that long.

3

Ambrosius styled himself High King of the Britons, which meant that many of the petty kingdoms of the isles professed allegiance to him. He had earned that fealty by battling the Saxons and the other invading tribes for many years, building the string of hill-top forts such as Amesbury in the hope of holding the invading barbarians to their beachheads and not allowing them to penetrate into the heartland of Britain.

He had fought other Celts, as well. Celtic Britain was a patchwork of petty "kingdoms," each ruler jealous of his neighbors, suspicious of the kingdom over the next hill. When the Romans ruled Britain, the Celts had all bowed to Roman law. But once the legions were withdrawn, the very year that Rome itself was sacked by the Visigoths, the Celts swiftly reverted to their paltry rivalries.

Like his father before him, the Elder Ambrosius, this High King had won his shaky allegiances as much by the power of his sword over his fellow Celts as the need for all the Celts to unite against the invaders. The allegiances sworn to him were grudging, at best. Only a High King of inflexible will and exceptional power could keep the lesser kings loyal to him.

Now, as we assembled in the castle's great hall to have audience with the High King, I saw that Ambrosius Aurelianus—as he styled himself—was getting old. His lifelong struggles against the Saxons and his own Celtic neighbors had taken their toll. He had once been tall and stately, I could see, but the weight of responsibility had bent him and stooped his once-broad shoulders even though he tried to appear dignified in his royal fur-trimmed robes. His hair and beard were gray, nearly white, and thinning noticeably; his face had the pallor of approaching death already upon it.

In contrast, Arthur was strong and straight and vital, practically glowing with youth and bursting with confidence and enthusiasm about the future.

We had all washed off the dust of our journey from Amesbury before this audience with the High King. Sir Bors had teased me, as usual, in his rough way: "Pity the wash bowl isn't big enough for you to sit in, Orion," he had said, with mock seriousness. "We all know how you like to bathe yourself, like a fish."

The other knights had laughed uproariously. My cleanliness was a subject of much humor among them.

But we were all scrubbed, beards and hair trimmed neatly, and wearing our best tunics for Ambrosius. Even young Lancelot, his battle-earned knighthood scarcely a month old, had dressed in his finest Breton linen for this exalted moment.

The audience was largely ceremonial, however. Ambrosius received us in the great hall, with half the castle's inhabitants thronging the room. The women wore long gowns of rich fabrics, decked with gems and pearls. None of the men wore mail, although they each carried their favorite sword at the hip, many of the scabbards more heavily jeweled than the women.

"A pretty bunch of dandies," Sir Bors growled under his breath. "They'd be useless in a fight."

The hall itself was almost as large as Priam's court in old Troy. Long embroidered tapestries covered most of the rough stone walls, some of them not yet finished, their pictures of battles and hunts incomplete, lacking. Late afternoon sunlight streamed into the hall through the windows set high in the walls. It would take hundreds of candles to light this chamber at night, I thought.

The High King walked slowly, stiffly, through the bowing crowd. A woman walked beside him, dressed all in black and so heavily veiled that we could not see her face. She seemed youthfully slim beneath her floor-length skirts. She kept her gloved hands at her sides, she did not take Ambrosius' arm or touch him in any way. Indeed, he seemed to keep apart from her quite deliberately.

Ambrosius sat wearily upon his hard throne of carved dark wood. The mysterious woman remained standing off to one side. The High King welcomed his nephew and thanked Arthur in a thin, parched voice for driving the barbarians from Amesbury fort. Arthur knelt and kissed the High King's hand, then got to his feet.

"My lord," he said, in a clear tenor voice that carried across the room, "we can drive the Saxons completely out of Britain, if you will allow it."

I was well away from the throne, standing behind Bors and Gawain and the other knights, among the squires, but I could see Ambrosius' eyes shift momentarily toward the veiled woman.

"We will speak of this another time," Ambrosius said. "This day is to be given to feasting and celebration, and to prayers of thanks for your great victory."

Arthur wanted to insist. "But my lord—"

Ambrosius silenced him by lifting a hand.

"In addition," the High King said, "it is my wish to introduce you to another visitor to this court."

He turned toward the woman in black. She stepped forward, still veiled so heavily her face was impossible to see.

"This is the princess Morganna," said Ambrosius, "of the kingdom of Bernicia, far to the north."

Morganna reached up with both her gloved hands, lifted the veil from her face, and let it drop back over her shoulders. A sigh swept through the great hall. She was the most fabulously beautiful woman any of them had ever seen: hair as dark as a stormy midnight, eyes that glowed like sapphires, skin as white as alabaster.

I had seen her before. I knew who she was. Among the Creators she called herself Aphrodite.

4

For the next two days—and nights—Arthur spent every moment with Morganna. He was infatuated with her, besotted as only a young man can be.

"She's enchanted him, all right," said Sir Bors, chuckling.

I had sought Bors out, worried that Arthur was being cleverly turned away from speaking to the High King about his plan to drive the Saxons and all the other barbarians out of Britain for good. Bors had made himself at home in one of the castle's many private chambers, a room so near the stables that I could smell the horses. But to Bors it was almost sinfully luxurious, with a feather bed and serving wenches at his beck and call.

"And why not?" he added. "The lad's done well enough. Why shouldn't the High King give him a princess to wed? It makes political sense, Orion, tying Bernicia to Ambrosius' domains here in the south."

"But Arthur's plan . . ."

Bors grunted. "It'll keep. Winter's coming; there'll be no campaigning for months to come."

"The Saxons will use those months to fortify their bases," I said.

"Can't be helped. No man can outfight the weather." Bors hefted a flagon. "Relax, Orion. Enjoy the fruits of victory. Have some wine. Find yourself a wench or two."

It was tempting. Too tempting. Ambrosius was blunting Arthur's purpose with the luxuries of his castle. Wine, women, and winter were going to delay Arthur's plan, perhaps fatally. Or was this Aten's doing?

"Thank you, my lord," I replied to Bors. "Perhaps later."

He laughed and poured himself a mug. I bowed and took my leave of him.

"Find yourself a wench or two," Bors repeated as I stepped through the heavy oaken door of his chamber. I could hear his thick laughter even after I closed the door.

I thought of Anya, the goddess I loved. How could any mortal woman compare to her? Yet . . . the temptation was there.

5

That night, as I lay in the dark, narrow barracks on my straw pallet among the snores and stinks of the other squires, I tried to make contact with Anya. I needed her help, her guidance, her warmth and love. Squeezing my eyes shut, clenching my fists with the effort of it, I strained every atom of my being to translate myself into the realm of the Creators.

And found myself, instead, in the middle of the dark night out on a windy plain. I had not traveled all that far. Looming all around me were the giant megaliths of the stone circle of Salisbury.

I immediately recognized the place; in another lifetime I had helped the Stone Age tribes of this region to build this site. They were just beginning to turn from hunting to agriculture, and my goal had been to help them predict the seasons so they would know when to plant their crops. Ever since, though, Stonehenge was revered with awe as a religious site. The Druids had conducted human sacrifices here until the Romans stamped out the practice. I wondered if they had returned to their bloody ways, now that the Romans were gone.

Black clouds were boiling across the sky, blotting out the moon and stars. Forks of lightning flickered in the distance. A storm was coming, driven by the wind that scattered the dry leaves and set the trees to moaning. In the blue-white glare of a lightning strike I saw that two people were approaching the center of the ring, where I stood beside the sacrificial altar. A man and a woman. I could not make out their faces but I knew who they were.

"Orion, is that you?" Arthur's voice.

"Yes, my lord."

I could see now that the woman walking beside him was Morganna—Aphrodite, as I knew her.

He lifted both his arms and swung around, pointing at the immense stones rising all about us.

"Don't tell me that *this* was built by mortals," he said, his voice a mixture of awe and delight.

I said nothing. In centuries to come, I knew, men would claim that extraterrestrial visitors built Stonehenge. How little they believed in themselves!

"How did you get here?" Arthur asked.

"The same way you did," I replied, looking at Aphrodite.

Suddenly he seemed embarrassed, as sheepish as a lad caught in a misdeed.

"Morganna brings us here every night," he said, his voice dropping almost to a whisper against the gusting cold wind. "By magic."

Another lightning bolt cracked the black sky, etching her incredible face in cold white brilliance for a flash of a moment. I could see she was not pleased.

Even in fury she was matchlessly beautiful. Her eyes, which had been as richly blue as sapphires when I'd seen her at Ambrosius' court, were emerald green now. Instead of the heavy stiff gown she'd worn then she was clad now in a long white hooded robe that left her lovely arms bare. The hood was down, and her hair cascaded past her soft shoulders like a stream of flowing ebony.

"How dare you?" she spat.

I glanced at Arthur. He was standing absolutely still, frozen in time, as if he'd been turned into a statue. She had put him in stasis, I realized, so she could deal with me.

"You mean to murder him, don't you?" I accused.

"He will experience pleasure enough before he dies," Aphrodite said, gesturing to the dark stone altar. I saw that a groove had been chiselled into it, to carry away the blood of the sacrificial victims.

"I'm here to protect him," I said.

"Aten told me you've become troublesome," she said carelessly. "So be it. The Druids will have two victims this night."

I was unarmed, except for the dagger strapped to my thigh. I tried to reach for it, but found that I was frozen, too, unable to move a muscle.

Thunder rolled across the dark sky. Aphrodite laughed. "You would defy Aten, Orion? How foolish of you. Tonight you die the final death. There will be no revival for you."

I strained with every speck of energy I possessed, but could do nothing. I was imprisoned totally.

Smiling like a cobra, Aphrodite stepped to me and twined her bare arms around my neck. "I could make you very happy, Orion, if only you wouldn't resist me. Forget your Anya and love me, Orion, and you can live in rapture forever."

Only one word could force its way past my lips. "No."

Her smile turned cold. Beyond her, off in the hilly distance, I could make out a procession of torches heading toward us, their flames guttering in the blustery wind. The Druids, come for their sacrificial rite.

"You choose Anya over me?" Aphrodite hissed. "Then after you watch Arthur die, you yourself will be killed. Slowly. Very slowly."

She turned away from me. Arthur stirred to life.

"Where is Orion?" he asked, puzzled, looking right at me but not seeing me at all.

"Gone," Aphrodite said, with a shrug of her lovely shoulders. "Forget about him. Come with me, my love, now that we're alone."

She took his hand and led him toward the altar. I stood there, invisible to Arthur, unable to move, hardly able to breathe. I felt an icy chill creeping over my body, as if I were being submerged in a glacier. I recalled one of my deaths, deep in space, slowly freezing until my heart stopped beating.

And the torchlit procession of the Druids marched steadily closer.

Lightning flashed again and thunder boomed. Rain began to pelt down, but it didn't strike Arthur and Aphrodite; she was shielding them somehow.

A titanic crack of lightning struck the ground almost at my feet, blinding me for several moments. When I could see again, Anya stood at my side, dressed as she had been when she'd given Arthur his sword, Excalibur, in a flowing silver robe garlanded with flowers.

Arthur's eyes went wide. "Look, Morganna!" he cried. "It's the Lady of the Lake."

Aphrodite/Morganna whirled to face Anya, surprise and rage on her exquisite face. Two goddesses, each divinely beautiful but in very different ways. Aphrodite was all flame and passion, the embodiment of sexual allure. Anya, who had been worshipped as Athena in another age, was cool and calm, certain of her strength.

"It's time for you to leave," Anya said.

"Never!" spat Aphrodite. "He's mine! You can't have him."

"Arthur is under my protection. You cannot harm him."

"You think not?" Suddenly there was a slim dagger in Aphrodite's hand. "One scratch with this and the poison will turn his blood to molten fire. He'll die in agony."

Anya did not move. Arthur stood goggle-eyed, too close to Aphrodite and that poison-laden dagger to try to move away.

"You can't defy Aten's desires," Aphrodite said, smirking. "Not even you can get away with that."

"Can't I?" Anya replied.

Another lightning bolt crackled out of the black clouds and struck the dagger in Aphrodite's hand. She howled like the tormented souls in hell as for a flash of an instant she was outlined in ghastly blue light. Then she was gone. Vanished completely, except for the whimpering echo of her scream.

I felt warmth returning to my body. I could feel the rain pelting down on me, I could move my arms and legs again. Arthur stirred, too. He dropped to his knees before Anya.

"My lady," he said, in heartfelt gratitude, "you have saved my life."

"The witch has gone back to her own realm," Anya told him. "She is not dead. You will see her again. Be on your guard."

"I will, my lady," he said. "I will."

Turning toward me, Anya said, "Orion, escort your lord back to Cadbury castle."

With all my being I wanted to remain with her. But I bowed my head submissively. "Yes, my lady."

And in the blink of an eye I was back on my pallet in the squires' barracks. For a moment I thought it had all been a dream, but then I realized that I was dripping wet from the rainstorm that had struck Salisbury plain. Through the window set up near the barracks roof I could see a serene moon riding across pale, thin clouds. It had not rained at all here at Cadbury.

6

At first light I sought out Arthur. He was already risen and in the exercise yard, working out with a practice sword against a dummy target mounted on a swivel so that it pivoted when it was struck. Its two broomstick arms could swing around and strike a nasty blow to a man who was not quick enough to parry or at least duck.

I could see Latin graffiti carved into the dummy's wooden torso by long-departed Roman legionaries. Arthur was thumping and banging the poor thing as if it were all his frustrations gathered into one passive body.

He saw me approaching him and stepped away from the dummy, sweating and breathing hard. No one else was yet in the yard; morning sunlight had barely touched the upper turrets of the castle's towers.

"She's gone," Arthur said, his voice bewildered and sorrowful.

"She is a witch, my lord," I told him. "You are well rid of her."

He shook his head. "She certainly had me in her power. If it weren't for the Lady of the Lake I would be dead by now."

"Yes, truly."

"Why, Orion?" he asked, his voice suddenly pleading. "Why did she want to kill me?"

I didn't hesitate an instant. "To keep you from your rightful destiny, my lord. To prevent you from driving the Saxons out of Britain."

Arthur's brow furrowed. "Then was she serving my uncle? Is it he who wants to stop me?"

"I don't believe that," I answered. "The High King did not know Morganna's true nature, I'm sure. Ambrosius wanted a strategic marriage between his house and the kingdom of Bernicia, nothing more."

"I wish I could be certain of that."

He was deeply troubled, I could see. "There is a way to make certain of it," I said.

"How?"

"Obtain the High King's approval of your plan."

"How?" he asked again. I had no ready answer.

Other knights and squires were coming into the exercise yard now and began working out. Soon the yard was clanging with swords and shields under the watchful, impatient eye of Sir Bors. Young Lancelot, as usual, was a blur of zeal and frenzied action, knocking down one opponent after another. Even Gawain had a hard time against him.

Arthur and I practiced against one another for a while. I did my best to refrain from hitting him, and allowed him to whack me now and then.

Once we paused for a drink from the rain barrel, panting and sweaty, Sir Bors approached us.

"My lord," said the gruff old knight, "it's good to see you out in the sunlight once more."

Arthur nodded without enthusiasm. "Morganna is gone," he said simply. "She won't be back."

"Headed back to her northern realm, I expect," said Bors.

"I suppose so."

Gawain came up and banged Arthur on the back. "Good riddance to her!" he said, with a happy grin. "There are plenty of other women in this world."

"Not like her," said Arthur.

"That's what makes it all so wonderful," Gawain countered. "No two of them are alike!"

Bors broke into a hearty laugh and Gawain guffawed loudly. Even Arthur managed a slight smile.

He's going to be all right, I thought. He's going to be his old self again.

"My lord," I dared to interject. "We have much work to do."

Arthur shook his head, as if to clear away cobwebs. "Yes," he said, "I must seek an audience with Ambrosius immediately."

Yet the High King evaded Arthur's request for days on end, offering one excuse after another. Arthur began to worry that Ambrosius truly feared for his crown and had intended for Morganna to murder him. I stayed as close to Arthur as I could, fearing that Aten—or perhaps Ambrosius, after all—would send another assassin after him.

Autumn was drawing to its close. The air turned sharply colder, with a hint of snow in the gray clouds that covered the sky. Ambrosius ordered the last hunt of the season, and all the knights and squires rode out of the castle to run down the deer and other game that would provide meat through the coming winter.

"How can I convince him of my plan when he won't even see me?" Arthur complained as we rode several ranks behind the High King and his entourage.

"We need help, my lord," I said.

"Help? From whom?"

"Merlin."

7

Since his arrival at Cadbury some weeks earlier Merlin had remained closer to Ambrosius than Arthur. Yet when Arthur called for him, Merlin invited the young knight to his tower-top aerie that very night.

Arthur brought me along with him; together we climbed the winding stone stairs that circled endlessly up the lofty round tower. At last we reached the low doorway at the top. It was open, and the cold night wind whistled through the high chambers. I could see Merlin perched on a stool at a broad wooden table, wearing a frayed gray robe, poring over some parchment whose corners were held down with various weights, including a human skull. The wind made the lamp hanging above his table swing back and forth; it tousled his long white hair and plucked at his beard fitfully.

Arthur ducked through the doorway without knocking and walked up to his table. I stayed at the doorway, as a proper squire should.

The old man looked up from his parchment and smiled at Arthur. Through the wrinkles and the long, unkempt beard and hair I thought I saw a hard intelligence burning in his deep-set green-gray eyes. Again, I asked myself if Merlin could be one of the Creators in disguise. If so, which one: Sharp-witted Hermes? Self-assured Zeus? Surely he wasn't the burly, imperious Ares.

And if he is one of the Creators, whose side is he on? Is he working for Aten, as Aphrodite was? Or against the Golden One, as Anya and I were?

Merlin listened quietly as Arthur, pacing around the tower chamber, poured out his worries about Ambrosius. I stood by the open doorway, silent and unnoticed.

"Fear not," the old wizard said. "The High King bears you no ill will, of that I am sure."

"But why won't he listen to me?" Arthur demanded impatiently. "An army of knights equipped with stirrups and spurs could smash all the barbarian camps and drive the invaders out of Britain."

Reaching up to place a calming hand on Arthur's broad shoulder, Merlin explained, "Ambrosius is a proud man. Strong and intelligent."

"But he won't accept a new idea," Arthur grumbled.

"He will," Merlin explained, as he guided Arthur to a canvas chair. "He will accept your new idea . . . as soon as he becomes convinced it is *his* new idea."

Arthur glanced at me. We both knew that the stirrups and spurs that had led to Arthur's triumph at Amesbury had been my "inventions."

Turning back to Merlin, Arthur asked, "And how do we get Ambrosius to think it's his idea?"

Merlin pursed his lips for a moment and stared off into infinity, his eyes unfocused as if he were in a trance. Arthur gaped at him, wonder and hope written clearly on his young face.

At length, Merlin bent his gaze upon Arthur once more and smiled broadly.

"A tourney, Arthur. That is the way to fix the High King's attention."

"A tourney?"

Tugging at his knotted beard, Merlin nodded thoughtfully but said nothing for many long moments. At last he said, "Yes, a tourney will do the trick. Ambrosius likes tourneys. He takes a childish pleasure in seeing his knights bash each other."

8

Ambrosius was delighted with Arthur's suggestion of a contest: the knights from Amesbury pitted against the knights of his castle. In later centuries, when the so-called Middle Ages reached their zenith, knights wore complete suits of steel armor from head to toe, so heavy that they had to be hoisted up on their mounts. Even their horses were armored. Tournaments then were highly regulated affairs, a pair of knights entering the lists to thunder straight ahead at full gallop and try to unhorse each other with blunted lances.

That was all centuries in the future of Arthur's time. On that gray late November afternoon at Cadbury castle there was hardly any organization to the tourney. Ambrosius' mounted knights gathered at one end of the bare dirt field in their chain mail and helmets, their shields emblazoned with their individual emblems, armed with lances that were barely padded. There were forty-three of them, by my count. Arthur's knights, on their steeds at the opposite end of the dusty field, similarly clad and armed, were less than half that number.

Because the Cadbury castle knights so outnumbered Arthur's men, Ambrosius had graciously allowed ten squires to ride with Arthur. I was glad of that. Nosing my mount to Arthur's side, I intended to stay close by him, on the alert for treachery. It would not be difficult to "accidentally" murder Arthur once the melee started. Knights were often badly hurt in tourneys, sometimes even killed.

Lancelot was grinning broadly as he slipped his helmet over his head. I was uneasy about him: a teenager who could fight like a whirlwind, he had sprung up out of nowhere to win his spurs of knighthood at the Amesbury battle. He seemed eager for combat, perhaps too eager. Was he Aten's chosen assassin?

Gawain, for once, was serious. As we milled about, waiting for Ambrosius to start the fray, he rode up to the other side of Arthur's horse and muttered, "There's a lot more of them than there are of us."

I could not see Arthur's expression behind his steel helmet, but his voice sounded calm and even. "Yes, but we have stirrups and they do not."

"They're all experienced men," Gawain said.

Patting the neck of his nervous, snuffling mount, Arthur said, "Today they will experience something they've never seen before."

Off to one side of the field stood the crowd of onlookers from the castle and the town outside its walls, the women gaily arrayed in their brightest dresses; the elderly knights, too old even for mock combat, dressed in their finest, as well. Ambrosius was the only one seated; his servants had carted out a fine chair for him. Of course, many of the churls and yeomen and townspeople squatted on the grass at the edges of the field to watch the festivities.

A herald stepped self-importantly to the middle of the open field and made a long, rambling announcement of what everyone knew was to come. Then trumpets blared, drums rolled, and Ambrosius lifted his right hand above his head. He held it there for what seemed an hour, while we sweated with anticipation and our steeds pawed the ground impatiently.

Ambrosius let his hand drop at last and the two sets of knights—screaming their bloodthirsty battle cries—charged each other.

We prodded our horses into a full gallop and hurtled straight at the Cadbury knights, who were advancing at a noticeably slower pace because they did not have stirrups to keep them in their saddles. My senses went into overdrive; time seemed to stretch out into dreamy slow motion.

I galloped slightly behind Arthur, who was crouched low over his steed's mane, his lance pointed straight and true, the red dragon on his shield bright and gleaming, the red plume on his helmet streaming in the wind.

Arthur's men could charge at full tilt, and that is exactly what we did. We smashed into the Cadbury knights with a frightful roar and clang. Men went flying off their mounts; several of the horses themselves went down. Lances split and shivered.

Through the narrow eye slits of my helmet I saw a knight riding straight toward me, his helmeted head low over his shield, which bore the figure of a black raven. My own shield was plain and unpainted: as a squire I had no right to an emblem. I pointed my lance at his eyes, and when he unconsciously raised his shield slightly, I made the center of that black raven my true target.

I could see the padding on the point of his lance unraveling as the distance between us narrowed. I took the shock of its blow upon my shield, angling the shield enough to let the lance slide off harmlessly. Firmly mounted with my stirrups, I absorbed the impact easily enough. Not so for my opponent. My own lance struck his shield dead-on. He was jolted completely out of his saddle and went hurtling to the bare dusty ground with a painful thump.

Our compact formation drove straight through the Cadbury knights and wheeled around, ready for another charge. Half our opponents had been unhorsed; many of them were staggering off to the sidelines, dazed and bruised, some of them helped by their squires. Others lay on the dirt, too hurt to move. The crowd was roaring with bloodthirsty glee.

Two of our men were down, but Arthur seemed unscathed. Gawain had shattered his lance; roaring with fury and battle lust, he bent down from his saddle and grabbed another one from the spares stocked at the edge of the field.

Across the field, what was left of the Cadbury knights milled about in shocked confusion. Arthur raised his lance above his head and shouted, "Follow me!"

We drove at them again, but there was little fight left in our remaining opponents. It was all over in a few more moments. We knocked down almost all of them, and then Ambrosius jumped to his feet and waved both his arms. The heralds blew their trumpets and the tourney was abruptly ended.

I pulled off my helmet. From where I sat on my trembling, blowing steed, I could not tell if Ambrosius was pleased or not, exhilarated or furious.

9

He was more furious than exhilarated. At supper in his dining hall that evening, Ambrosius sat at the head of the long table, brooding and sulky. He barely glanced at Arthur, who was seated with his knights at the far end of the long table. The Cadbury knights were mostly a glum lot, bandaged and bruised, stiff and hurting. A few of them, though, asked Arthur and his men about the stirrups that had obviously made the difference in the afternoon's tourney.

Ambrosius did not. When he toasted the tourney's victors, as was customary, it was grudging and grumbling. He was not pleased with his nephew, not at all.

Even Merlin was unhappy with the High King. After dinner, when Arthur and I climbed up to his tower-top aerie, the old wizard shook his head cheerlessly.

"You have been too successful, Arthur," Merlin said sorrowfully. "Ambrosius sees his knights turning to you and away from him."

Arthur had seated himself before the wizard's heavy trestle table. From my post at the doorway I could see that his usually bright and eager face was a picture of gloom.

"My uncle fears more any danger to his own power than he does for the dangers of the Saxons."

And the Jutes, I added silently. And the Angles, the Danes, the Frisians, and all the other barbarians swarming into Britain. Aten wanted them to win, I knew. The Golden One wanted Arthur to go down in ignominious defeat and allow the barbarians to conquer this Celtic island just as they were conquering most of the old Roman Empire.

Merlin fiddled with his long, ratty beard. "I was so sure that a tourney would make him see the wisdom of your plan."

With a sigh, Arthur responded, "As you said, we succeeded too well."

"He truly fears you now, Arthur. He fears that you will take his throne."

"I don't want his throne!" Arthur burst out. "I want to fight the barbarians and drive them into the sea!"

Merlin got up from his elaborately carved chair and paced to the window. As he looked out into the dark cold night he muttered, "The curse of the Celts. I have warned you of it many times, Arthur."

"They will not unite, not even against the foe that threatens to destroy us all."

Turning back to face Arthur, Merlin shook his head wearily. "Ambrosius likes to think of himself as a Roman ruler. If only he would behave like a Roman!"

I knew what he meant. The Romans knew how to organize, how to delegate authority and responsibility, how to make a chain of command work. But despite his pretensions, Ambrosius knew nothing of such things. He was a Celtic king, possessive of his lofty position, unable to share his power.

Unless . . .

10

That midnight, as black clouds began to drop the year's first snow on Cadbury castle, I sought Anya once again.

Suddenly I found myself on that same sunny hillside, overlooking the Creators' city by the sea. The water glittered as gentle waves lapped onto the bright golden beach. The empty city itself seemed to shimmer in the warm sunshine. A protective dome of energy, I realized. Through its slight haze I could see the monuments that the Creators had collected from all the eras of human history, from the pyramids of Egypt to the levitated temples of the New Stellar Dominion, hovering in midair.

"Orion."

I turned and saw Anya standing slightly above me on the grassy, flower-strewn hillside. The sun behind her seemed to create a halo about her head. She wore a gleaming metallic uniform of pure silver.

"I need your help," I said.

"I know," Anya replied. "Come with me."

She reached out her hand. As I touched her fingers there was a moment of utter darkness and immeasurable, cryogenic cold. Before I could even blink, however, we were standing on the shore of the lake where Anya had given Arthur his sword, Excalibur. It was a calm, soft moonlit night. Anya was now the

Lady of the Lake once again, dressed in a long flowing robe, her hair decked with flowers, her graceful arms bare.

Ambrosius stood before us, knuckling his eyes from interrupted sleep, awkward and confused in a long wrinkled nightshirt, frayed and gray from many washings.

"Where am I?" he gasped. "Who are you?"

I realized that I was in the uniform of a Roman legionnaire; a tribune, no less, with a gleaming bronze cuirass sculpted like a beautifully muscled man's torso and a helmet crested with a crimson horsehair plume.

"I am the Lady of the Lake, protectress of your nephew, Arthur."

In the silver glow of the full moon I could see Ambrosius' eyes widen. "My lady!" he whispered.

"You are not pleased with your nephew," Anya intoned. "Tell me why."

Ambrosius dithered for a moment, but he could not avoid Anya's piercing gray eyes.

"The princess Morganna warned me against him," he said at last. "She said she would enthrall him and take him to her kingdom in the north, where he would no longer covet my throne."

"Arthur does not covet your throne, and you know that, no matter what lies the witch Morganna tells."

The High King winced at the word *witch.*

"You must tell me the entire truth," Anya demanded. "If you do not, I cannot help you."

Ambrosius stared at her in silence for many heartbeats. Finally he confessed, "I am old. He is young. His knights revere him. My own knights are beginning to show him more respect than they do me. How can I hold my throne if he gains more glory?"

Anya did not hesitate an instant. She replied, "Send him on a mission that will bring glory to you."

Ambrosius blinked with confusion. Such an idea was incomprehensible to him.

"As High King, you can command Arthur to sally forth against the barbarian encampments. Any glory that his victories win will be *your* glory, for Arthur will be obeying the commands of his lord."

"My glory? How can that be if—"

"Arthur will devote each of his victories to you," Anya said. "This I promise you."

"But if he is defeated? What then?"

"If Arthur is defeated it will be on his own head. If he is victorious, the High King will be praised for driving the invaders from Britain's shores."

Ambrosius stroked his beard, thinking hard, pondering these new ideas.

"It is what a Roman ruler would do," Anya urged. "You must think as a Roman. This is the way to glory. This is the way to win the obedience of all the kingdoms, throughout Britain. Then you will truly be the High King."

The old man's expression turned crafty. I knew what he was thinking: If Arthur is killed on his mission against the barbarian encampments, then his threat to Ambrosius' throne dies with him.

"Think as a Roman," Anya repeated. "That is the road to true power."

Before Ambrosius could reply, before he could even blink an eye, it all vanished and I was back in the squires' barracks at Cadbury castle, with the gentle snow sifting down through the silent, cold night.

11

That very morning Ambrosius held court in his audience hall. The entire castle turned out, thronging the cold, drafty hall with their colorful gowns and robes.

Ambrosius took his throne and gazed out on the crowd. All his knights were there, even those on crutches or bandaged from the tourney. Arthur and his knights had been invited to stand up close to the dais. I was behind them among the squires, off to one side by the unfinished tapestries that covered the icy stone wall.

I looked up and down the hall for Merlin, but the old wizard was nowhere in sight.

Once the crowd had settled down and the court's chief herald had gone through a long-winded introduction of the High King, complete with Latin honorifics, the hall fell totally silent. It was as if everyone held their breath, anticipating some momentous announcement from the High King.

They were not disappointed.

Using the royal pronoun, Ambrosius said in his deepest, most impressive voice:

"We have been pleased to observe that our nephew, Artorius, and his knights have indeed demonstrated an important new method of fighting. It is our wish that he teach our own knights, and all other knights who wish to join us, in this new method."

The crowd sighed with relief. Tension over a possible break between the High King and his nephew had crept all through the castle, I realized.

Ambrosius was not finished, however.

"Moreover, once the knights have been properly equipped and

trained, it is our command that Arthur lead them out into the land to attack the barbarian invaders in their camps and drive them from the shores of Britain."

Arthur broke into a boyish grin. Gawain and Bors, standing on either side of him, looked equally happy.

"To accept this responsibility is a heavy burden," Ambrosius went on. "We know that our nephew will gladly obey this command of his High King, but to aid him in his new duties we have decided to revive a title from the old Roman days."

Anya's advice, I knew.

"Henceforth Arthur will be Dux Bellorum, our battle leader across the length and breadth of Britain."

The crowd broke into spontaneous applause. Ambrosius let them cheer for a few moments, then raised a hand to silence them.

Looking directly at Arthur, the High King asked, "Nephew, do you accept this responsibility?"

"Gladly, my lord!"

"Then carry the title of Dux Bellorum from this day forward."

Again the crowd cheered. I could see on Arthur's face the eager anticipation he was feeling. Yet I knew that as the High King's Dux Bellorum he had many months of hard fighting ahead of him. Ambrosius had placed himself in a clever position, thanks to Anya and me. With every victory Arthur wins, the High King's power and prestige will grow. And if Arthur is killed in battle, a threat to Ambrosius' future is removed.

I looked through the crowd, wondering which of them might be Arthur's assassin. Would Merlin turn against him? Lancelot? Any of the other knights?

Then I remembered that Morganna—Aphrodite—was waiting in her kingdom in the northlands, planning her revenge against Arthur. And our campaign against the barbarian encampments would lead us northward, just as surely as the sun rose each day.

CHAPTER FIVE

Power and Glory

1

"My God," breathed Lancelot, "they *do* look like angels."

Sir Bors, mounted between Lancelot and Arthur, shifted uneasily in his saddle, making the leather creak. "Never seen angels bearing axes before, have you? Or spears."

"Or swords, either," said Arthur.

"They swarm like flies on a dung heap," Bors growled.

Lancelot laughed. "The more we kill, the more the bards will sing of us."

I was astride my horse just behind Arthur, ready to ride into battle with him even though I was a mere squire. Arthur's army was pitifully small compared to the host of Angles who were trudging toward us like a restless golden-haired tide advancing across the flat below. We were hardly a hundred knights with their squires and a few dozen footmen recruited grudgingly from nearby villages.

Arthur had maneuvered his mounted knights to the top of the ridge, pinning the tribe of Angles between us and the bend of the river that glittered in the bright sunshine of this beautiful summer morning. The footmen, farm boys for the most part, stood uneasily behind us, already looking frightened. They would run off at the first sign of trouble, I thought.

"Those look like Roman swords, some of them," Arthur said, totally focused on the approaching warrior throng.

"They've looted this region quite thoroughly," Bors agreed.

We had seen the consequences of the barbarian invasion of this eastern shore of Britain: burned-out homes, ravaged villages, fields given to the torch, crops ruined. Arthur had camped the night before in the crumbling remains of an old Roman villa. Once it had been the home of a prosperous Celtic landowner, a lord whose family had followed Roman ways even after the legions had left Britain. Now it was abandoned, blackened by fire, gutted by barbarian pillagers, the family who once lived in it nothing but rotting bones that the "angels" had not even bothered to bury.

Ever since the Roman legions had abandoned Britain, the barbarian tribes had been invading the island: Saxons in the south, Angles and Jutes along the east coast, even Scots from the far north had crossed the old wall of Hadrian to devastate the northern kingdoms.

"They're counting our numbers," Bors muttered.

Arthur leaned forward slightly to pat the neck of his trembling steed. "Hardly any need for that," he said, his clear tenor voice firm, unafraid. "They can easily see that they outnumber us ten to one."

"What matter?" said Lancelot, impatiently. "The more there are of them, the more glory for us!"

Arthur smiled at the young knight, so eager for action that he fairly radiated energy. Battle-scarred Bors shook his head in disapproval.

We all have our dreams. Young Lancelot dreamed of glory.

Arthur of victory. Ambrosius of power. Me? My dream was to be reunited with Anya, the goddess whom I love, the eternally beautiful immortal from the far future who loves me.

"My helmet, Orion," Arthur commanded.

I nudged my horse to his side and handed him the plain steel helmet with the nosepiece that projected down from the brows. I had seen much better helms at Philippi and even at Troy, more than two thousand years earlier. But Arthur disdained fancy plumed helmets and elaborate armor. No, that's not entirely right. He simply never thought about such things. Dux Bellorum he might be, and a natural leader of the volatile, independent-minded Celts. But there was not a shred of vanity in him. Not much out of his teens, scarcely older than glory-driven Lancelot, Arthur went into battle with nothing to distinguish him from the other knights except the bright red dragon emblazoned on his shield.

He slid the helmet over his sandy brown hair. All along the thin line of chain mail–clad horsemen, the other knights donned their helmets, adjusted the straps on their shields, took lances from their squires. Their steeds snuffled and pawed the ground nervously, sensing that bloodshed was near. Down the grassy slope, the horde of Angles were forming up into a battle line. I saw the golden-haired men hefting spears, staring grimly up at us.

One of the bare-chested warriors stepped out in front of the others, bearing a huge axe in one meaty fist and a thick-shafted spear in the other.

"Come on, you dung-eating cowards!" he shouted. "We will chop you to pieces and feast on your livers! I am Alan Axe-Wielder, son of Alan the Bold, grandson of mighty Hengist himself . . ."

Lancelot asked, "Hengist was a Saxon, wasn't he? Not an Angle."

Smiling from under his steel helmet, Arthur said gently, "They all claim to be descended from Hengist."

"With a bit of luck," muttered Sir Bors, "the Axe-Wielder will be sitting in hell with old Hengist before the sun goes down."

The barbarian leader ranted for a long time, working himself and his men into battle fury, boasting of their victories and invincibility, demeaning the prowess and even the masculinity of the Celtic knights.

When at last he drew a long breath, Bors bellowed, "Fools! You face Arthur and his knights, not some poor unarmed farmers and defenseless women. Prepare your souls to meet their maker!"

With that Arthur lifted his lance in his right arm and sang out a single word: "Charge!"

A hundred lances snapped down to point straight at the enemy. A hundred powerful steeds sprang into the gallop, with me and the rest of the squires close behind. Down the grassy slope we thundered like a spearhead of steel hurtling toward the vast surging sea of waiting barbarians.

Small though our numbers, we had an advantage the barbarians did not suspect: the stirrups and spurs that allowed the knights to charge into battle at full tilt and smash into the enemy without slowing down. These Angles had a lethal surprise ahead of them.

They were brave men, though. As we hurtled downslope toward them they gave ground slowly, instinctively backing away from our onrushing horses. But only a few grudging steps. Then they raised their weapons and stood their ground, waiting until we surged into their midst so they could surround us, swarm over us, bring down horse and rider, and hack us to pieces.

It was not to be.

Leaning close to his horse's mane, his weight on his stirrups, his spear pointed straight at the boastful Alan Axe-Wielder, Arthur led the charge into the host of Angles. I raced behind him, sword in hand, to protect his back. The world seemed to shift into slow motion, time itself stretched so that everything around me appeared to move in sluggish, dreamlike lethargy. I saw the horses pounding down the grassy slope as if they were drifting through a soup of thick, clear molasses, clods of earth thrown up by their hooves floating languorously through the air.

The charging knights took on a wedge-shaped formation, Arthur at its apex, Lancelot and Bors at his sides. They struck the barbarians at full gallop. Arthur's lance took the Axe-Wielder full in the chest, shattering his shield, lifting him completely off his feet. He looked terribly surprised as his rib cage caved in and his life's blood spurted out of him.

Wrenching his lance free without slowing down a fraction, Arthur drove his steed through the shocked barbarian line, bowling over warriors too slow to get out of his way. Following close behind him, I hacked left and right at any man foolhardy enough to try to get at Arthur from behind.

The knights had blasted right through the heart of the barbarian formation. Where the Axe-Wielder and his best men had stood a moment ago, there was now no man standing, nothing but shattered bodies littering the blood-soaked grass. The two wings of the barbarian host stood in shocked disbelief, separated, stunned, too amazed to either charge or run away.

Arthur wheeled his mounted knights to the left and we charged into that crowd of milling, dazed warriors. In truth, they seemed petrified, disorganized, the heart torn out of them.

Yet they stood and fought, though little good it did them. The knights smashed into them, a hurtling wave of steel dealing death with lance and sword. Before the stunned, disheartened warriors on the other side of the field could make up their minds to rush at the mounted knights, their brethren were smashed, disemboweled, scattered like dandelion seeds in a gale. Those that still could ran, dropping shields and spears and racing away as fast as their legs could carry them, howling with terror, splashing into the river, tripping, falling, floundering in the cold water, mad to escape onrushing death.

Lancelot drove after them, his sword licking the lives from the fleeing warriors. No, they were no longer warriors; they were terrified men trying to run away, desperate to save their lives.

With a sudden roar, our footmen came running down the ridge, armed with swords, sickles, clubs, knives. The river began to run red as they hurled themselves, bellowing with pent-up fury, on the men who had looted their homes, killing and raping and burning.

"Come back!" Arthur shouted after Lancelot. "Regroup!"

But Lancelot was chasing down the hapless barbarians, his steed splashing into the river alongside the vengeance-maddened footmen. Arthur wheeled his knights around to face the remaining barbarian warriors who were starting a ragged charge on foot toward us.

"Get back here!" bellowed Sir Bors, in a voice that could be heard across eternity.

Lancelot reined in his horse, turned around, and cantered back toward Arthur. His squire trotted to him and handed him a fresh lance. The belly of Lancelot's horse was red with barbarian blood; the knight's legs were spattered with blood up to his thighs. Even the golden eagle emblem on his shield was barely visible, covered with blood and dripping mud.

Once Arthur got his formation turned to face the remainder of the once-boastful Angles, the onrushing warriors slowed and then stopped altogether. From my vantage point slightly behind

Arthur I could see the consternation and fear on their faces. For a long moment they simply stood there, mouths open in shocked disbelief, eyes staring wildly. Arthur and his knights sat on their snorting, blowing mounts. Neither side moved, except for a few of the barbarians in the rear of their undisciplined mass, who slowly, silently backed away and then began to slink toward the river and the thick woods beyond.

Lancelot trotted up and, without stopping, spurred his horse into a charge.

"Wait!" shouted Arthur. But Lancelot was already galloping at the barbarians.

In truth, their host was no longer an army, it was a cowed, beaten mob. They were melting away; one by one at first, then by the twos and threes, by the fives and tens, they fled for their lives as Lancelot charged at them, alone. Yet there were still dozens of armed warriors standing their ground, many scores of men who were not running away.

"Damned fool!" Bors groused. "One man alone, they'll swarm all over him."

Arthur looked grim, watching Lancelot's solitary charge. The other knights seemed just as stunned as the barbarians; they all turned to Arthur for his command. Drawing Excalibur from its sheath, he shouted, "Charge!" once more.

Again we thundered into action. Seeing us all galloping after Lancelot, the remaining barbarians lost what was left of their nerve. They bolted and ran, scattering everywhere like mice trying to flee a hungry cat. Little good it did them. We caught them at the river's edge and slaughtered them. Blood and bones and severed arms, heads, bodies split from shoulder to crotch littered the grass and turned the river into a charnel stream.

At last Arthur shouted, "Enough! Enough!"

Lancelot was in the river again, up to his horse's belly, hacking away at any man left standing. Arthur had to splash in alongside him and grip his sword arm.

"I said enough," Arthur repeated.

For a long moment Lancelot simply stared at his commander. Then he sheathed his reddened sword and swept off his helmet. He was grinning, white teeth showing, eyes asparkle.

There were no barbarians left standing. The few who had escaped were fleeing into the woods on the other side of the river. Our footmen, ferocious in victory, were merrily slitting the throats of the wounded and picking their carcasses clean of weapons, helmets, boots, even their leather trousers.

"The crows will feast 'til they burst," said Bors, surveying the bloody scene.

"A great victory!" Lancelot shouted as he and Arthur rode side by side out of the river. "A wonderful victory! The barbarians will run all the way back to their own country, over the sea!"

Arthur was more thoughtful. "You mustn't go dashing off on your own. You could have been killed."

"But I wasn't!"

Bors interjected, "Only because we came up behind you, lad. You've got to keep your head in battle—or lose it."

Lancelot laughed and trotted away.

"He's going to be trouble," Bors said to Arthur.

Without taking his eyes from Lancelot's retreating back, Arthur said softly, "He's young. He'll learn better."

"Or he won't get much older," groused Sir Bors.

♈

That night we camped in a clearing in the forest across the river, upwind from the battlefield. Arthur sent a dozen mounted scouts to find where the remnants of the barbarian army had fled.

"Their main camps are close by the coast," he told us, over the dying embers of the campfire. "Their warriors must have headed that way."

"Probably along the old Roman road," said Gawain. "It's the straightest route to the coast." Gawain was one of the few knights who'd been wounded in the fight. His thigh had been sliced slightly by a spear. Laughingly, he claimed he'd taken the spear thrust to protect his horse.

Lancelot was still glowing with excitement. "Right now, the few barbarian survivors are probably telling their fellows how we crushed them. By tomorrow they'll be climbing into their boats and leaving Britain forever."

Arthur smiled tiredly at the young knight. "I wish it would be so," he said.

It was not.

I stretched out on my blanket, close to Arthur, my sword at my side, and closed my eyes to sleep.

Instead, I found myself standing on a windswept hilltop bathed in the cold silver glow of a gibbous moon.

Anya, I thought, my pulse racing. She's come to meet me here.

"Not your precious Anya," said the haughty voice I knew only too well. I turned and saw Aten stepping out of the shadows of the sighing, wind-tossed trees.

He styles himself the Golden One and, truly, he is magnificent to look upon. Even in this moonlit night he radiated light and strength. Golden hair, tawny eyes, the body of a Greek god,

Aten was dressed in a military uniform of purest white, with gold epaulets and trim.

"You continue in your pitiful efforts to thwart me, Orion," he said, a contemptuous smile on his lips that was half a sneer.

"I protect Arthur as best I can," I replied.

With a condescending shake of his head, Aten went on, "How little you understand the forces you are dealing with. But then, how could you understand? I did not build such knowledge into you."

"Teach me, then. You claim to be my Creator: educate your creature."

He laughed in my face. "Teach you? Can a mule be taught space-time mechanics? Can a flatworm learn how to manipulate the continuum?"

I said nothing. I longed to smash in his smug, gloating face, but I was powerless to move against him.

"The game grows more interesting, Orion, but it can end in only one way. Arthur and his Celts must be defeated by the invaders. That is what must be."

"Because you want it that way."

"Yes! That is my desire. I will not allow you or anyone else to stand against me."

"Others of the Creators do not agree with you," I pointed out.

"That is none of your affair," he snapped.

"Anya is against you."

He bristled. "Anya is far from here, Orion, devoting her misguided energies to another aspect of the continuum, another nexus that must be resolved properly."

"Another part of your game."

"It is hardly a game," Aten said sharply. "Because of you and your oafish stubbornness, this nexus here in Britain is in danger of unraveling. If it does, the entire continuum will be shaken to its foundations, whole worldlines will crumble—"

"And you will lose your power," I interrupted. One glance at his face, though, told me what he dared not say. "You will lose your *existence*!" I realized.

"So will Anya," he answered. "So will all we Creators be banished from existence. The Earth, the human race, everything will disappear totally and forever, wiped clean from the continuum as if we had never existed in the first place."

I stared at him. Then I heard myself say, "I don't believe you."

"Believe, Orion," Aten replied, totally serious. "You claim to love Anya. If you continue to protect Arthur you will be killing her, just as if you drove your dagger through her heart."

"But—"

He laughed bitterly. "No arguments, Orion. No matter what you do, it hardly matters. I have another assassin ready to kill Arthur, and the jest is that he hasn't the faintest inkling that he is an assassin."

"What do you mean?"

But Aten was no longer there. He winked out, like a light suddenly turned off. Like a hologram projection, I thought. Yet his sardonic laughter echoed in my mind.

Could it be true? By protecting Arthur, was I destroying Anya, the goddess I love, the only member of the Creators who showed the slightest concern for the human race?

And someone else was going to murder Arthur? Someone who doesn't even know that he will kill the Dux Bellorum?

I paced slowly along the crest of the hill as the moon edged lower in the night sky, trying to sort it all out, trying to decide what was true, what my course of action should be. At one point, Aten had seemed almost to be pleading with me. Was he lying?

Was he trying to manipulate me, using my love for Anya as a way of controlling me?

The Creators had godlike powers, but they were actually humans from the distant future, humans who had learned to wield the forces of spacetime to travel at will across the continuum. They had interfered in human affairs all through history and even earlier, always trying to bend the worldlines to suit their whims. Aten had created me and others, he claimed, to do his bidding at placetimes where the continuum comes to a focal point, a nexus that would determine the worldlines for eons to come.

Like spoiled children, the Creators often bickered among themselves. Their disagreements brought wars and disasters to humankind, their disputes were settled by our blood.

It was a cosmic irony. These so-called Creators were the descendants of ordinary humans such as Arthur and the men and women of this age. We had created them, in truth. They are our distant progeny. Yet they reached back through time to try to control us.

For hours I walked along that grassy hilltop as the wind from the sea tossed the leafy boughs of the trees and set them to groaning plaintively. The moon went down and I could see the spangled glory of the heavens, stars glittering like jewels, the Great Bear and its smaller brother, the Chained Princess and Perseus the Hero and the majestic stream of the Milky Way. The constellation of Orion was not in sight, though. And Anya was far away, beyond my reach, perhaps forever.

Then different lights caught my eye. Down on the seashore below the hill, fires were burning. Campfires. This was one of the places where the barbarians had built a settlement for themselves. I could see their boats pulled up on the beach, black against the starlit sand. Huts and larger buildings thatched with straw dotted the shore. The barbarians had built a village for themselves, a town for their families and flocks. There were even fields of food crops within easy walking distance of the huts.

The barbarians were not piling into the boats, as Lancelot had predicted. They were nowhere near the boats. They had built this village to live in permanently, and they had no intention of leaving. As I peered down at the starlit scene below me, I saw that they were digging a huge ditch across the old Roman road that led to their settlement.

They were preparing to fight.

3

I woke with a start, back at Arthur's camp. The first hazy gray hint of dawn was beginning to lighten the eastern sky. Venus hung in the west like a gleaming diamond.

What I had seen during the night had been no dream, I knew. Aten had translated me to the coastal base of the Angles. Why, I did not understand. But it was clear to me that the barbarians had no intention of fleeing Britain. They were digging in, preparing to fight against Arthur's advancing army.

After I had eaten with the other squires I sought out Arthur. He was sitting under a massive oak tree, alone, looking lost in thought.

"May I speak to you, lord?" I asked.

Arthur smiled boyishly at me and patted the mossy ground. "Sit here, Orion, and don't be so formal. We are all companions here."

"It's about the enemy," I said, sitting beside him.

"The scouts all report that they are fleeing along the Roman road toward the coast."

"True enough," I agreed. "The few survivors from yesterday's battle are retreating. But their brethren are digging defensive works along that road."

"Digging?"

"Trenches and earthworks. To stop you."

He looked puzzled. "How do you know this?"

"I saw it last night."

His perplexed frown deepened. "But you were here in camp with us last night."

I thought quickly. "The Lady of the Lake showed it to me." It wasn't much of a lie. Anya had appeared to us both in the past; under the guise of the Lady of the Lake she had given Arthur his sword Excalibur.

"She was here?" Arthur gasped. "In this camp?" He looked all around at the forest surrounding our clearing. Even though it was full morning, the woods were deep and shadowy, thick with brush, dark and mysterious enough to imagine all kinds of spirits and supernatural beings lurking nearby, enchantments and wizards and magic spells.

"She took me to the Angles' settlement on the coast," I said, trying to skirt my half-truth.

"You saw them digging trenches," Arthur said, sounding dismayed.

"Yes," I answered. "They were not loading their boats and preparing to leave."

He smiled grimly. "Lancelot will be disappointed."

"I imagine so."

"On the other hand, Lancelot will probably be glad for another chance for glory." His smile faded completely.

4

Lancelot was delighted that his prediction had failed to come true. All during our march along the old Roman road he chattered happily about the coming battle.

"We'll crush them like eggshells," he said. "The bards will sing of Arthur and his knights for a thousand years."

He was right about the fame that he and Arthur would win. Poets chronicled the deeds of Arthur and his knights for much more than a mere thousand years, I knew, although the heart of their romances dealt with Lancelot's falling in love with Arthur's queen. As we rode along toward the next battle, though, I began to realize that if Aten had his way Arthur would soon be killed and his story snuffed out. No bard would sing of the deeds of a young Dux Bellorum killed in battle before he was old enough to grow a full beard. Arthur would be forgotten, his bones and his legend decayed into dust.

Worse yet, Arthur might be assassinated, murdered by one of his own people. Would Lancelot be Aten's killer? Certainly I would not. What about crafty old Merlin, still back at Cadbury castle with Ambrosius? The High King had agreed to keep the Saxons along Britain's southern shores in check while Arthur flung his knights against the Angles and Jutes in the east. Might Ambrosius allow the new Saxon leader to bring his host up behind us, surrounding Arthur's knights between his Saxons and the Angles and Jutes?

No, I thought, Ambrosius wanted Arthur to succeed. Arthur was now the right arm of the High King; it would be criminally stupid for Ambrosius to work against Arthur.

And yet . . . the thought nagged at me. Merlin was more than a wizened old faker, I was sure of that. There was an intelligence and purpose in those shaggy-browed eyes of his. I wondered, again, if he might be one of the Creators in disguise. Not Aten, of course. But one of the others, come to this placetime to manipulate this nexus in the continuum.

My mind swirled with the possibilities as we rode along the paving stones of the old Roman road. Straight as a ramrod it ran, through forest thick with huge oaks and yews and elms. To these uneducated Britons the straight, paved roads and solid stone buildings of the Romans seemed like the works of gods. They did not know how to accomplish such engineering feats so they assumed the structures were beyond human capabilities. What foolishness, I thought. The Creators played on that credulity, just as I hoaxed Arthur into believing the Lady of the Lake had transported me to the Angles' settlement in the night.

The Creators enjoyed being worshipped by their primitive ancestors. If these humans knew what their so-called gods really were, it would make them sick with disgust and shame.

The thick woods on either side of the road made excellent cover for an ambush, I thought. Yet Arthur led his knights along the road without a worry. They rode two or three abreast, each knight dutifully followed by his squire, the whole procession plodding slowly along the paving stones. Our baggage train and footmen followed in the rear.

We had gained dozens more footmen. Those who had been with us in yesterday's battle now carried swords stripped from the barbarian dead. Some wore helmets and almost all of them had boots or some sort of footgear, probably for the first time in their lives. News of our victory had almost doubled their number. Most of them were Christians, although a few still clung to the older Celtic religion. Christian or not, they talked among themselves of slaughtering the enemy, dreamed of looting the barbarians and raping their women just as the barbarians had done to their own.

We trailed along the road all through the long, hot day. The lofty trees shaded us most of the time. I kept peering into the underbrush, worried about ambush. Dimly I remembered another life, in a distant jungle where every bend in the trail was a danger. I tried to laugh my worries away. At least the enemy doesn't have land mines and explosive booby traps in this age.

5

Midway through the second day we were halted by an entrenchment. The barbarians had torn up the road and dug a six-foot-deep ditch across it. Beyond the ditch was an earthen mound about six feet high, studded with spearheads. It reminded me of the trench and earthwork rampart that Agamemnon and his Achaeans had thrown up to protect their camp on the shore of Troy. These barbarians had no better military craft than the Greeks and Trojans of some two millennia earlier.

Arthur brought our column to a halt and summoned me with a beckoning hand.

"You said their trench was near their settlement on the coast," he muttered.

Nodding, I replied, "They were building one there in great haste, my lord. This must be another."

His youthful face knotted into a frown. "No telling how many such fortifications they've built along the road."

Gawain, at Arthur's other side, suggested, "We could send scouts through the woods to spy out how many of these ditches they've dug."

"That would take days," Arthur said. "We'd have to camp here and do nothing while they could slip through the forest and surround us."

"Let them attack us," Gawain replied. "It will be easier to kill them in the open than to try to charge against that ditch and wall."

Bors pushed his horse between Arthur and me. "There's forage enough here for the mounts. We can wait a day or two. Give the steeds a needed rest."

Lancelot joined the conference, his face eager. But he was too young to speak his mind in the presence of veterans such as Bors and Gawain. Yet it was clear that he was bursting to have his say.

"I don't like to wait," Arthur said. "Every day we sit idle is a day that the barbarians can use to strengthen their defenses."

"Then let's charge them!" Lancelot blurted. "One strong charge and we'll be over their earthen mound before they know what hit them!"

Bors shook his head. "The horses can't jump that ditch. And they won't charge those spear points. They've got too much sense for that."

"Then charge them on foot," Lancelot said, without an instant's hesitation.

Bors gave him a withering stare. "The horses are smarter than you are, lad."

Lancelot was totally unfazed. Turning to Arthur, he said, "I will lead a foot charge, my lord, if you will permit it."

"No," Arthur replied immediately. Then he added, "Not yet."

He spent the rest of the day studying the earthwork. We saw barbarian warriors poking their helmeted heads up above the rampart now and then. Once in a while they called to us, taunting us to charge against them. At one point, when Arthur rode slowly along the edge of the trench, a bowman popped up from behind the rampart and fired an arrow at him. I was afoot behind Arthur's horse, holding a brace of spears for him. My senses instantly went into overdrive. I saw the arrow gliding lazily toward Arthur, flexing slightly as it flew. Hefting one of the spears, I threw it at the arrow, grazing it just enough to deflect it away from Arthur.

It thudded into the ground at the horse's feet, making the mount rear and whinny in alarm. Arthur held his seat, barely. I imagine if he didn't have stirrups he would have been thrown. The bowman was still standing atop the parapet, knocking another arrow. I threw the other spear at him with all the force I could muster. As he looked up it caught him in the face. He screamed hideously and disappeared behind the earthwork.

Arthur had his steed under control by then. He stared at me, wide-eyed.

"You . . ." He glanced at the arrow embedded in the ground at his mount's hooves and then at the barbarians' earthen parapet, gauging the distance.

"We should call you Orion Strong-Arm," Arthur said, clear astonishment in his voice.

I shrugged modestly, trotted to the first spear and picked it up, then followed Arthur back to our camp, safely out of bow range from the barbarian entrenchment.

As the sun dipped westward, throwing long shadows through the forest, Arthur called his most senior knights together at his cook fire. Footmen had scouted through the woods on either side of the road. Their reports were not encouraging. There were hundreds of Angles behind the entrenchment and more coming up the road from the coast.

"We could go around it," Arthur suggested, "through the forest, and attack them from the flanks."

Sir Bors pointed out, "Those woods are too thick for horses. We'd have to attack them on foot."

"Their numbers would overwhelm us," said Sir Kay, gloomily.

"That young hothead Lancelot wants to charge them straight on," Bors complained.

"On foot?" Kay looked aghast.

Around and around the discussion went, while the sun set and a deep moonless dark fell over the woods. I heard an owl hoot, and a moaning wind began tossing the leafy branches of the trees. It was easy to understand how these people could believe deep forests such as this to be haunted.

The conference broke up with nothing decided. Arthur walked slowly away from the campfire. I followed him at a respectful distance.

"Orion," he called to me without turning around.

I came up to his side.

"I must decide, Orion. We must find a way to beat these barbarians. My mission is to drive them out of Britain. We can't retreat and leave them here unharmed."

"Then we must fight them," I said.

"On foot? They'll slaughter us."

We were standing in the middle of the paved road, looking up toward the enemy's position. They had lit big bonfires on either end of their earthwork, so sneaking across the ditch and up the rampart for a surprise attack was out of the question.

"Let me scout their position," I suggested. "Perhaps I can find a weakness that the footmen overlooked."

Bleakly, he nodded. Then he murmured, "I wish Merlin were here. He'd know what to do."

Perhaps, I thought. Or perhaps Merlin would lead you on to your death.

6

I slipped into the woods, armed with nothing but a sword and the dagger that Odysseos had given me at Troy, strapped to my thigh. The underbrush was thick, the going slow and difficult. It would be impossible to sneak up on the barbarians in silence.

Unless . . . I crouched in the deepest shadows of the bushes and squeezed my eyes shut, willing myself to another vantage point. If Aten and his so-called Creators can move across space and time at their whim, why can't I?

It was useless. No matter how I strained, no matter how hard I concentrated, I did not budge from my spot in the underbrush. If only Anya were near enough to contact, I thought. She could help me.

"I will help you, my darling Orion," her silvery voice whispered.

"Anya!"

"I am far away, far distant in time and space," she told me, her voice so faint I wondered if I were imagining it. "I cannot maintain contact for very long, beloved."

Just to hear her voice was more joy than I had known in ages.

"Close your eyes, Orion," she commanded gently. "Close your eyes and see."

I pressed my eyes shut once again. And suddenly I was high above the forest, looking down as a hawk would, as an eagle soaring among the clouds. I saw the thin straight line of the Roman road, the barbarians' ditch with Arthur's camp on one side of it and the enemy's on the other. Higher and higher I rose. There were three more trenches dug across the road, with several miles' distance between each one. The final trench was just before the Angles' village on the coast.

Barbarians they might be, but they understood the value of a defense in depth. Arthur and his knights might fight their way past one of those barriers, perhaps even two of them. But at what cost? How many knights would Arthur have left after two such assaults? How many footmen would remain loyal to him after such bloodlettings?

I opened my eyes and was back in the underbrush.

"Anya, what can I do?" I asked, hardly voicing the words.

There was no answer. Anya was gone. She had given me all the help she could; now the contact between us was broken. Instead I heard in my mind the scornful laughter of Aten, telling me without words that Arthur's quest to drive the barbarians out of Britain was doomed to dismal failure.

7

But Arthur did not think so. He listened grimly as I described the series of fortifications that the barbarians had dug along the road leading to the Angles' coastal base. When he asked how I could have seen so much in a single night, I told him that the Lady of the Lake showed it to me. That was not far from the truth.

The two of us walked alone through the deep woods that morning. The rest of Arthur's army lolled in camp, content to rest for the day. The Angles were not resting, though; they were digging, deepening their entrenchments, strengthening their defenses.

After my report Arthur walked slowly through the woods for what seemed like hours, silent, thinking, weighing the possibilities. It was cool in the deep shadows of the forest. The trees formed an almost continuous green canopy high above us, making it difficult to tell how far the sun had moved. The underbrush was so thick that we had to walk slowly. Horsemen could never charge through here.

At length, Arthur asked me, "Where are their fighting men, Orion?"

I blinked, trying to remember what I had seen. "There were many more campfires at this first barrier than at any of the others—except for the last one, near their village."

He nodded. "Most of their fighting men are here, then, ready to face us. If we break through their defenses, they will fall back along the road to the next barrier."

"That makes sense. The other trenches are held only weakly at present. The people digging near their village must be old men, boys, perhaps even women."

"Their defenses are of no use if they have no warriors to man them," Arthur said.

I looked at his youthful face with new respect. He understood the fundamental truth of war: destroy the enemy's army.

"It will be a costly battle, my lord," I warned. "It could be a Pyrrhic victory."

His brows rose questioningly.

"Pyrrhus was a Greek king who fought the Roman republic in southern Italy. He won many battles, but always his own casualties were enormous. Once, when an aide congratulated him on beating the Romans again, he said, 'Another victory like this one and I'll have no army left.'"

Arthur smiled. "Yes, I see. Still, it must be done."

I agreed. "If we must attack them, then it must be in a manner that prevents them from retreating to their next fortification."

"That's the problem. How can we accomplish that?"

I remembered another battle, at a place called Cannae. I had served the doomed Hannibal in that era.

8

It took the rest of the day to get the knights to agree to the plan that Arthur and I had hatched.

Bors was dead set against the plan, of course. "Divide your forces? Depend on the footmen? It's insane!"

Gawain was doubtful. "How can we get through those woods? They're impassable."

Patiently, Arthur said, "You walk your horse through the underbrush. It can be done."

"Walk?" Gawain looked shocked. "I'm a knight, not a footman."

Arthur laughed. "You'll fight on horseback, never fear."

Once again I marveled that these impulsive, individualistic Celtic knights could agree on anything. Dux Bellorum was Arthur's title, but it meant nothing by itself. None of the knights felt the slightest compulsion to accept authority or follow orders that he did not like. Arthur had to win them over to his view; he could not command them, he had to persuade them. Even the footmen could melt away, leaving the army and trudging on back to their farmsteads or villages whenever they decided to.

Lancelot was the only one who agreed without argument. He was avid for battle.

"Let me be in the forefront of the attack!" he pleaded. "On foot or ahorse, I'll make those barbarians feel the sharpness of my sword!"

In truth, it was Lancelot who won Arthur's argument for him. He was so eager, so willing to plunge into battle, that he shamed Gawain and the older men into a sullen agreement.

It was late in the day by the time all the knights, one by one, gave the grudging nod to Arthur's plan.

"Very well, then," said Arthur at last. "We spend this night preparing for an attack at dawn."

One by one, he clasped each of them by the shoulders, knowing that they might never see each other again. The last one he embraced was young Lancelot.

"Please let me lead the frontal assault," Lancelot begged.

"That's the most dangerous job," Arthur said gently. "There's a very good chance that you'll be killed."

"But it brings the most glory! What does it matter if I'm killed? My deeds will live forever!"

Achilles had felt that way, I remembered. Until an arrow crippled him.

Arthur looked the youth in the eye. "Leading the frontal assault is my task, my responsibility."

Before the crestfallen Lancelot could reply, he added, "But you can be at my right hand, my friend."

I thought Lancelot would explode with joy.

9

All that night the men deployed, most of the knights and all of the footmen moving off into the dark, scary forest as quietly as they could. The one brown-robed friar we had with us, a spindly, lean-faced priest named Samson, blessed kneeling men until his arm grew stiff with fatigue. Others knelt in the underbrush and prayed silently before they set off. Many of the knights held their longswords before them as they prayed, the sword's hilt serving as a makeshift crucifix for them. A strange sort of symbol for the Prince of Peace, I thought. But these were savage times, and these men were fighting for their homes and families.

So are the barbarians, said a voice in my mind. They have made their homes here in Britain.

I tried to get some sleep as I stretched out on the mossy ground near the dying embers of a campfire. Much of Arthur's plan—my plan, really—depended on the knights and footmen being in their proper places when the sun came up. Would they be in place?

An owl hooted somewhere in the woods. The totem of Athena, I recalled from another life, although in many cultures the owl was seen as a symbol of death. The night was still, hardly a breeze. A wolf snarled out there in the darkness. Fireflies danced to and fro in the underbrush. Even though I knew better, I almost thought the woods to be haunted, the habitat of elves and fairies and darker, more dangerous spirits.

I drifted off to sleep, only to find myself suspended in a featureless golden glow, floating as if in a weightless limbo.

"The end is near for Arthur," said Aten's haughty voice.

I turned, spun around weightlessly, but could see nothing except the glowing golden radiance that surrounded me.

"Show yourself," I said.

"Giving commands to your Creator?" He laughed. "Really, Orion, I ought to let you die with Arthur."

"Neither of us will die," I said.

"Arthur will. And once he does, your usefulness in this place-time comes to an end."

"I won't murder him for you."

Aten's golden form took shape out of the glowing mist. Now he wore a formfitting uniform of golden mesh.

"You won't have to assassinate Arthur," said Aten. "Young Lancelot will do your job for you."

"Lancelot?" I couldn't believe it. "He'd never kill Arthur. He adores the ground Arthur walks on."

"Yes, of course he does. And to show how much he adores Arthur he will be more daring than any knight. He will charge against the barbarians' spears, all courage and no fear. And Arthur will have to rush in beside him, won't he? Arthur would never stand back and watch the young hothead get himself killed in his foolish recklessness."

I saw it in my mind's eye: Lancelot charging blindly, Arthur rushing in to protect him, the barbarians swarming around them.

"Not while I live," I muttered. "As long as I have breath in me, I will protect Arthur."

Aten smirked. "Then you'll have to die, too."

I wanted to reach out and throttle him, but before I could lift a finger I found myself back in Arthur's camp in the gray misty light of early dawn. Already I could hear the woodsmen's axes chunking into thick-boled trees.

10

The tree trunks were rough and heavy. There was no time to split them or smooth them off. The barbarians must have heard the trees being felled and were wondering what we were up to; it was far too much chopping to be simply for firewood.

Arthur had kept only two dozen knights for this frontal assault on the entrenchment. The others were sifting through the woods, hoping to cut off the enemy's retreat.

If the enemy retreated. A dozen knights plus their squires and a few teenaged footmen was hardly an overwhelming force to pit against the entrenched Angles.

I was gripping one side of a massive tree trunk as we lugged it straight up the road toward the ditch and embankment behind it.

I could see barbarian warriors watching us, their horned helmets bobbing up and down behind their earthwork. They must be laughing, I thought, as I sweated with the heavy load. It was too heavy for us to run with it. We trudged up the road, our arms feeling as if they would be pulled out of their sockets by the weight of the trunk.

The knights walked beside us, protecting us a little with their shields. No one said a word. Not even the birds or mammals of the woods made a sound. All I could hear was the steady labored trudging of our boots and the heaving, weary grunts from the squires and footmen toting the tree trunk.

"Come on!" shouted a golden-braided warrior, climbing to the top of the embankment. He waved to us. "Come on to your certain deaths! We welcome you."

Arthur, walking beside me, drew Excalibur from its sheath with a silvery hiss. On the other side of the trunk Lancelot pulled his sword and behind me I heard the other knights drawing theirs.

We were within arrow range of the trench. Barbarian bowmen began pelting us. My senses went into overdrive and I could see the arrows soaring lazily toward us. One thunked into the trunk inches from me. Arthur extended his shield to cover me, exposing himself to their fire.

Is this how he will die, I asked myself, trying to protect me? How Aten will laugh if it happens that way.

Now they were throwing spears. I saw everything in slow motion, but although I could easily see arrows and spears coming my way, I could not dodge them. Not unless I dropped the tree trunk. Arthur caught an arrow on his shield. A spear hit the ground at his feet and clattered off the Roman paving stones.

We were within a few paces of the ditch's edge. I heard a man scream with sudden pain, and the trunk nearly twisted out of my grip.

"Now!" Arthur bellowed.

With every atom of strength in me, I ran down into the ditch, lugging the trunk with me. The other squires followed my lead, although two more of them went down with arrows through their bodies.

We rammed the tree trunk against the embankment. Most of the squires ducked under it for protection as the knights clambered atop it and rushed straight across the ditch to the top of the embankment. I drew my sword and climbed up the sloping earthwork to be with Arthur.

Lancelot dashed forward, straight onto the crest of the embankment, where the barbarian warriors waited with their axes and swords. Arthur was rushing up behind him. He caught an axe thrust on his shield and took off the arm of the axe-wielder with a stroke from Excalibur. The man shrieked as he fountained blood.

I dove in beside him as the other knights rushed into the fight, slashing and killing with the maddened fury that rises when blood begins to flow. Sir Emrys took a spear in his gut but sliced out his killer's throat before he died. The knights were forming a wedge of steel, slowly pushing the barbarians back, down the rear slope of their embankment. We were outnumbered by perhaps a hundred to one, but the knights—protected by their chain mail and shields—were weaving a web of death with their dripping swords.

Lancelot pushed deeper into the swarming mass of barbarian warriors, his sword a blur, men screaming and stumbling as he stroked the life out of them. Arthur struggled to keep up with him, wielding Excalibur like a bloody buzz saw that took off arms, heads, split bare-chested warriors from shoulder to navel.

I tried to stay close behind Arthur but he and Lancelot were driving deeper into the mass of roaring, screaming warriors and I had my hands full keeping barbarians off their backs. More and more of them came swarming up the embankment, eager to get to the handful of knights. The whole barbarian army seemed to be surging toward us.

Lancelot's squire went down, an axe buried in his skull, and Arthur stumbled over the body.

I saw it all in agonizing slow motion: Arthur falling forward, thrusting his shield out in front of him to support himself as he went down. A huge barbarian, blond braids flying as he swung his axe in a mighty two-handed chop at Arthur's unprotected back. Lancelot not more than three feet away, but with his back turned to Arthur, hacking other barbarians to pieces. And me, separated from Arthur now by a good five yards, with half a dozen bloodied fighters between us.

"Arthur!" I screamed, driving through a flailing wall of fighting men.

Lancelot turned at the sound of my shout. Without an instant's hesitation he swung his shield toward the descending axe. I cut down two men trying to stand before me and pushed on toward Arthur, knowing I could not get to him in time. Lancelot caught the axeman's forearm with the edge of his shield, knocking the blow away from Arthur. His axe thudded harmlessly into the ground as Lancelot split his skull, helmet and all, with a tremendous slash of his sword.

Arthur got to one knee as I reached him. A spearman tried to get Arthur, but I yanked the spear out of his hands and drove my sword into his belly.

At the top of the earthwork we could see the entire mass of the barbarian army, hundreds of them rushing up the dirt slope to get at us, eager to wipe out our small force of knights and squires. There were far too many of them for us to have any hope of surviving.

It was like fighting against a tidal wave. We stood at the crest of the rampart and fought for what seemed like hours. No matter how many we killed, more warriors charged up the slope at us. Knights and squires went down as the barbarians shrieked their battle cries and surged up at us with their spears and axes and swords.

We were only a handful to begin with. Our numbers were being whittled away. We slew three, four, seven men for every one we lost. But for every barbarian who went down, ten more charged up the earthen ramp at us. It was only a matter of time before we all were killed, like the Spartans at Thermopylae, three hundred men against an army. And we were far fewer than three hundred.

Then it happened. A trumpet blast came up from the woods and with a bellowing roar the bulk of Arthur's knights and footmen charged out from the trees on both sides of the road, into the flanks of the surging torrent of barbarians. The knights were afoot, but I recognized them by the emblems on their shields: Sir Brian's red badger, young Tristram's Celtic cross, and the black hawk of Sir Bors, who was hacking through the surprised barbarians like the angel of death himself.

All through history, troops that have withstood withering frontal assaults have broken and run when assailed from their flank or rear. Humans are made to look directly ahead; attacks from the side or from behind unnerve even the most battle-hardened soldiers.

Suddenly assaulted on both flanks, the barbarians broke and tried to run. They knew that a few miles down the Roman road was another defensive ditch, another entrenchment that could shelter them from these sword-wielding Celtic knights pouring out of the woods.

They still outnumbered us greatly, but they were shattered by surprise and sudden fear. From the top of the earthen rampart I saw them break and flee down the road.

But not far. Galloping up the road toward us came the rest of Arthur's knights, on their charging steeds, Gawain in the lead. They lowered their spears and smashed into the broken, disheartened barbarians.

It was soon finished. The paving stones were littered with bodies, slick with blood. A few of the barbarians had managed to slip away through the woods, but very few. The heart of their army lay dead and dying at the feet of Arthur's victorious men.

Victorious, but battered. Sir Bors was limping badly, his hip bleeding from an axe blow. Most of the other knights who had fought on foot were also wounded. To my surprise I found that I had taken a spear thrust in my side. I hadn't noticed it in the heat of battle. Now I automatically clamped down the blood vessels to stop the bleeding and lowered the pain signals along my nerves to a tolerable level.

I smiled tiredly as I watched the men patching each other's wounds. No need to bind my side; I could control my body well enough, and accelerated healing processes had been built into me.

Arthur slumped down beside me, resting his back against a tree, looking weary and grim. He was nicked here and there. Blood trickled from a slice along his right forearm.

"It's only a scratch," he said, when he noticed me staring at the wound.

Lancelot came up, all brightness and zeal. He was totally unharmed, untouched, his tunic not even muddied. Only the dents in his shield revealed that he had been in battle.

He squatted down beside Arthur. "We can gallop down the road and catch the few who got away."

Arthur shook his head.

"Why not?" Lancelot asked, surprised. He almost looked hurt. "It's not much past noon. We have plenty of time to dispatch them."

"They have another entrenchment up the road," Arthur said. "And still another after that."

That dimmed Lancelot's enthusiasm for less than a second. "What of it? We took this one, didn't we? We made great slaughter of them! Let's go on!"

"No," Arthur said, his voice low. "The cost was too high."

"But—"

Arthur reached out and put a hand on Lancelot's shoulder. "We have gutted their army. They won't be raiding our villages and farmsteads now. We've taught them a lesson that they will remember for a long time."

"But we haven't driven them into the sea!"

"No, and we're not going to. Not now. We've lost too many men. We need to rest a bit and recruit more men. Then we move north against the Jutes."

Lancelot looked shocked. "And leave the Angles in their villages? Without driving them into the sea?"

"We don't have the strength to drive them into the sea. Not yet."

Shaking his head in disappointment, Lancelot murmured, "That's not the path to glory, my lord. Leaving them chastened isn't the same as a glorious victory."

With a tired smile, Arthur said, "I'm not interested in glory, my young friend. I'm interested in power."

It was clear that Lancelot did not understand, but I thought I did. The Angles would huddle behind their defensive earthworks and stay in their villages, the cream of their manhood killed. It would be a long time before they ventured out again to raid Celtic farms and settlements. Arthur would use that time to draw new recruits to his army, to march north and defeat the Jutes there, to drive the Scots back behind Hadrian's Wall and secure the northern kingdoms.

He would win great power for Ambrosius Aurelianus, making the old man a true High King among the Celts. And perhaps, I thought, Arthur himself would in the end become the High King. He was certainly showing that he understood the workings of power.

Aten wanted him dead, but it seemed to me that Arthur was actually on his way to uniting the fractious Celts. Maybe he would one day truly drive the barbarian invaders out of Britain. I vowed anew to help him all I could.

Then I thought of Lancelot, so eager for glory. Aten had meant for Lancelot to lead Arthur to his death in the battle. Instead, Lancelot had saved Arthur's life. I felt glad about that.

Yet I thought I heard, in the far recesses of my mind, Aten's cynical laughter. Lancelot will still be the agent of Arthur's death, the Golden One seemed to be saying. Wait and see. Wait and see.

CHAPTER SIX

Bernicia

1

Arthur wasted no time marching northward.

He and his knights had fought all summer long, battling the invading barbarians in a bitter campaign that had started far to the south and now had brought us to the border of the Scottish lands. The aging Ambrosius Aurelianus, who styled himself High King of all the Celts, remained in his fine castle at Cadbury, ready to move against the Saxons dwelling on Britain's southern shore if they tried to push inland.

"It's the wrong time of year for campaigning," Sir Bors groused, peering up at the gray sky as we rode slowly along the old Roman road. "We should be heading back south."

"Aye," Sir Gawain agreed. "It's cold up here. And there are too few wenches."

Arthur shook his head stubbornly. "We'll turn back once we've driven the Picts and Scots back behind Hadrian's Wall."

There had been too few knights for Arthur to drive the barbarians entirely out of southern Britain. But he crushed their military power, annihilated the flower of their fighting manhood. Thoroughly cowed, they retreated to their fortified villages along the coast, but they would not be bringing fire and sword to the Celtic villages farther inland. Not until a new generation of boys grew to fighting age.

Meantime the wild and fearsome Scots and Picts had swarmed across the unguarded length of Hadrian's Wall to spread death and terror through the northern lands. Now we rode against them. They had thought the old crumbling wall was meant to keep them out of Britain's northern reaches. Arthur intended to show them that the Wall had other uses.

It was a terrible day, raining hard. Once we turned off the Roman road the ground beneath our horses' hooves was a sea of cloying, slippery mud. At last we found the enemy, half naked in the cold pelting rain, a huge mass of barbarians drawing themselves into a ragged battle line once they saw us approaching.

Sir Bors wanted to wait until the rain stopped and the field dried, but Arthur feared that the barbarians would escape across the Wall by then. So we charged through the rain and mud into the wild, disorganized mass of frenzied barbarians. Soon the mud was churned into an ocean of blood.

I rode behind Arthur, his faithful squire, protecting his back. He divided the knights into two divisions, one headed by Bors, the other by himself. We charged from opposite directions, catching the freezing, rain-soaked barbarian warriors between us. They fought bravely at first, but no man on foot can stand up to the charge of knights protected by chain mail, shield, and helmet, driving home an iron-tipped lance with all the power of a mighty steed at full gallop behind it.

As Arthur had planned, the Wall became a trap. Pinned against it, the barbarians could not flee when Arthur's knights rode down on them.

They crumbled after that first charge. The battle became a melee, with enemy warriors scrambling madly up the overgrown old stones of the Wall, made slippery by the incessant rain, slicker still by their own blood.

Arthur wielded Excalibur, stroking to the right and left, slashing the life from every warrior he could reach. Lancelot was at his left hand, his own sword a blur of swift death. I stayed on Arthur's right, alert for treachery.

The battle ended at last; Arthur was barely touched during the fighting. The blood-soaked mud was littered with the bodies of the dead.

"The crows will feast tomorrow," Bors said grimly.

"And the wolves tonight," added Sir Kay, limping from a slash in his right leg as he led his panting, lathered horse away from the carnage.

Night fell and the knights huddled around fitful campfires, sheltering beneath the flat-sided tents erected by their churls. But repose was not for me. I followed a summons implanted in my mind and headed off to the distant graveyard.

Like an automaton, like a puppet pulled by invisible strings, I walked through the pelting, freezing rain. The night was black and cold. I reached the scant shelter of a crumbling archway, its ancient stones dripping and slimy with green moss. Icy mist rose from the graveyard beyond the arch like ghostly spirits rising from the dead. It was easy to see how the people of this era believed in their supernatural terrors. Ignorance and superstition always go hand in hand.

I was soaked to the skin, despite the heavy woolen cloak I had draped over my tunic and chain mail. My body automatically clamped down my peripheral blood vessels, to keep as much body heat within me as possible.

The rain was turning into sleet. Back south where Ambrosius

ruled as High King in Cadbury castle it was harvest time with bright golden days and a smiling orange full moon. Here along Hadrian's Wall it was almost winter; snow was on the way. Arthur's long campaign against the barbarians was grinding to a halt.

I waited in the freezing rain beneath the dripping stones of the ancient archway. I half expected Aten or one of the other Creators to rise out of the mists in the graveyard. Instead, I saw the cloaked and hooded figure of a monk making his way around the perimeter of the cemetery, head bent and shoulders stooped against the pelting rain.

He carried a lantern that flickered fitfully against the miserable night. Once he reached me, he lifted it high enough to see my face.

"You are Orion?" he asked, in a voice thick with age and rheumy congestion.

"I am," I said. "And you?"

"I am but a humble messenger sent to fetch you. Follow me."

Coughing fitfully, he led me around the edge of the graveyard, not daring to cut through it toward his destination. Dark bare trees stood along the muddy path, their empty arms clacking fitfully against the cloud-covered sky. At last we reached a small dome made of stones. A monk's desolate cell, I realized. A place built for solitary prayer and penitence. A place, I thought, for hunger and pneumonia. Through the rain-soaked darkness I could hear waves crashing against a craggy cliff. The sea was not far off.

I had to duck low to get through the cell's entrance, and once inside I could stand straight only in the center of the cramped little dome. It was a relief to get out of the rain, although the stones of the cell's interior were slimy with mold and dripping water. The beehive-shaped cell was empty. In the dim light of the monk's lamp I could see that there was no chair, no hearth, not even a blanket to sleep upon. Nothing but a few tufts of straw thrown on the muddy ground.

"Wait here," wheezed the monk.

Before I could reply or ask a question, he stepped outside into the icy rain and disappeared in the darkness.

"Orion."

I turned to see Merlin. The old wizard stood before me in a circle of light, his dark robe reaching to the ground, his ash-white hair neatly combed and tied back, his long beard trim and clean, rather than in its usual knotted filthy state. He had stayed behind at Cadbury castle, many weeks' travel from this place; yet he was here.

"My lord Merlin," I said, as befitted a squire addressing his master's mentor, a man reputed to be a mighty wizard.

He smiled wanly. "No need for obsequies, Orion. We can speak frankly to one another."

"As you wish," I said cautiously.

He gazed at me for a long, silent moment, those piercing eyes beneath the shaggy brows inspecting me like X-ray lasers.

"You are one of Aten's creatures, obviously."

"And which of the Creators are you?" I countered.

"Why are you resisting Aten's commands?"

I was cold, wet, tired from the long day's fighting, weary of being Aten's pawn. This wizened old man, so shriveled and frail I could snap his spine like a dry twig, was toying with me and I resented it.

"Aten hasn't told you?" I asked. "Why don't you look into my mind and find out for yourself?"

He shook his head. "Aten has built blocks into your mind. Limitations. Do you recall when you first met Arthur?"

"At Amesbury fort, last spring," I said.

Again he shook his head. "No. Years before that. Arthur was merely a lad then."

I tried to remember. I could feel my face wrinkling into a frown of concentration.

"Do you remember Grendel and the cave where you found Excalibur?"

"Anya," I said, as the memory of her matchless beauty surfaced in my consciousness. "She is the Lady of the Lake; she gave Excalibur to Arthur."

"But you remember nothing of Grendel and Heorot?"

"Not much," I admitted.

"You see? Aten has blocked your mind. He allows you to know only enough to accomplish your mission."

"Who are you?" I asked.

"One of the Creators, as you guessed."

"Which one?"

He tugged at his beard for a moment, then smiled in a scornful, mocking way. "Do you really want to know, Orion?"

"Yes," I answered.

"Very well."

The light bathing him intensified, brightened until it was almost too dazzling to look at. It turned red, slowly at first, but then its color deepened, redder than fire, redder than hot molten rubies fresh from the Earth's fiery core. I felt its heat radiating against me, burning me, forcing me to squeeze my eyes shut.

"Don't be afraid, Orion. You may look upon me now."

We were no longer in the monk's cold, dank cell. We stood in a long columned hall, thick stone pillars so tall their tops were lost in shadow. Torches burned in sconces between the pillars, throwing baleful ruby light across the hard polished stone floor. Before me stood a man in the full splendor of youthful adulthood, magnificently garbed in a sculpted uniform of gleaming jet-black armor inlaid with intricate traceries of blood red. His hair and beard were dark, his eyes even darker, blazing like chips of onyx in the flickering light of the torches.

"You may call me Hades," he said.

Hades. The Creators took pleasure in appearing to mere mortals as gods and goddesses. The Creator who commanded me styled himself Aten, an ancient sun god. To the classical Greeks he was Apollo, to the Incas he was Inti, to the Persians of Zoroaster's time he called himself Ormazd, the god of light.

How many wars through the long millennia had been started by their petty jealousies and rivalries? How many millions of humans had been sacrificed to their obsessions and hates?

This one styled himself Hades. In Greek mythology Hades was the brother of Zeus, lord of the underworld. Death was his domain.

"Where is Anya?" I asked.

"Far from here," said Hades, his face grown serious. "Aten knows that she opposes his desires concerning Arthur and he has stirred a disruption of the worldlines that she is striving to repair."

"She saved my life when Morganna was ready to kill me," I remembered.

"She won't be able to help you when next you meet the bewitching Morganna."

"Morganna seeks Arthur's destruction," I said.

Hades nodded solemnly. "She supports Aten in this. Anya and a few of the other Creators oppose them."

"And you?"

Hades smiled again, a coldly calculating smile. "I haven't decided which way I will go. As Merlin, I have helped young

Arthur. He could become a powerful force in human history. He just might be able to make Britain into a peaceful, prosperous island, a haven of civilization in a world darkened by the collapse of Rome. But I doubt that he ever will. His time may already be past."

, "Aten wants Arthur out of the way so that the barbarians can engulf Britain," I said. "He wants to see a barbarian empire covering all of the Old World, from Hibernia to the islands of Japan, all of them worshipping him."

"There is much to be said for such a plan," Hades said slowly. "It will bring about a millennium or so of disruption, but—"

"A thousand years of ignorance and war, of disease and death," I said.

"What's a thousand years?" he quipped, shrugging.

"What's a few tens of millions of lives?" I retorted sarcastically.

"Orion, you bleed too much for these mortals."

"I will not let Aten murder Arthur."

His dark brows knit. "Bold talk for a creature. If Aten wills it, you will do whatever he wants."

"No," I insisted. "I'm not a robot or a puppet."

"He'll let you die, then. Very painfully. And you will not be revived."

If I can't be with Anya, I thought to myself, I might as well die forever.

"And he'll send another creature to carry out his commands. You'll suffer great pain and final oblivion—for nothing."

"I will not assassinate Arthur," I repeated stubbornly. "As long as I live, I will protect him."

Hades stroked his beard thoughtfully, staring at me for a long, silent moment. "It will be interesting to see how long you can carry out your resolve. Aten will destroy you sooner or later, of course, but I wonder just how long you can get away with defying him."

"You find this amusing?"

"Very," he admitted casually. "You know, I came to this place-time and took on the guise of Merlin to help Arthur through his childhood. Aten wanted Arthur to succeed only far enough to force the barbarians to combine against him."

"I understand that. Then Arthur is to be killed."

"Thanks to you, Arthur is trouncing the barbarians, shattering their power. Aten wants him stopped. So does Morganna."

"He doesn't deserve to be murdered."

"Perhaps, perhaps not," Hades mused. "Aten has been after me to join his side in this. But you . . . you and your ridiculous insistence on defying him . . . I wonder how far you can carry it out?"

"Help me, then," I blurted. "With your help Arthur can make Britain a beacon of civilization."

He laughed. "Aten would be furious."

"What of it? Is he more powerful than you?"

His laughter cut off. "I'll go this far, Orion. I will not help Aten. Neither will I join the other side. I will watch how far you can go. It will be an amusing game."

That's all that mortal misery and death meant to these Creators. We were a game to amuse them.

Then I recalled what he had said earlier. "Arthur will meet Morganna again?"

"Yes, and soon. You are on the edge of her domain now."

"Bernicia."

"Already she is laying her plans for him."

"What plans?" I asked eagerly.

Instead of answering, Hades disappeared. The torch-lit columned hall vanished. I was back in the cold, dripping monk's cell again. Alone.

2

"I dreamed of Merlin last night," Arthur told me when I met him the following morning.

I suppressed a smile and replied, "So did I, my lord."

The rain had stopped at last. The clouds had cleared away. A pale northern sun shone out of a crisp blue sky. It wasn't warm, but compared to the miserable weather of the past few days, it seemed like midsummer to us.

The long summer's fighting had toughened Arthur, matured him. To the casual eye he was still a very young man in his early twenties, broad of shoulder and strongly muscled. His sandy light brown hair fell to his shoulders; his beard was neatly trimmed. His gold-flecked light brown eyes were clear and sparkling with energy.

We were breaking camp that morning. Arthur had decided to take his knights across Hadrian's Wall into the land of the Scots, not so much to fight the tattered remains of their army as to show them that they had no refuge from his power. Ambrosius' power, actually. Ambrosius, Arthur's aging uncle, was the High King and Arthur his Dux Bellorum, fighting beneath his banner.

"It was a troubling dream," he said as we walked slowly toward the makeshift corral where our horses awaited. Unfortunately, the wind was in our faces.

If the smell and the flies bothered Arthur, however, he gave no sign of it. He talked about his dream.

"It was very strange, Orion. Merlin appeared to me with a very lovely young girl at his side. An enchantress, it seemed to me."

"Morganna?" I asked.

He shook his head. "No, not her, thank God." He crossed himself.

"Then who was she?"

"I don't know. But she certainly seemed to have Merlin in her spell. He told me he was going away with her and I wouldn't see him anymore."

I could see that Arthur was clearly perplexed.

"You don't think that Merlin would leave me, do you? He's been like a father to me. I can't remember a time when he wasn't there, helping me, showing me what I should do."

"Perhaps," I said, "you are old enough now to make your own decisions. Perhaps you no longer need Merlin."

He looked alarmed at that thought. "I've sent a messenger to Cadbury castle. I want to make certain that Merlin is still there. That he's all right. Perhaps this dream was a warning that he's sick. He's very old, you know."

Older than you can understand, I replied silently.

We rode that day through one of the gates in the wall built by the Romans nearly four centuries earlier. Even though Arthur's knights numbered scarcely two hundred, it took all day for them and their squires and the footmen and churls and camp followers to get through that single unguarded gate.

On the far side of the Wall the land stretched out before us in rolling green hills that led to misty blue mountains in the distance. We rode slowly along a broad dale covered with clover, with the footmen trudging behind us. Thick forest climbed up the hillsides on either side of us.

Sir Bors rode up to Arthur's side, a rare smile on his doughty, battle-scarred face.

"North of the Wall," he said proudly. "No civilized troops have been on this side of the Wall since the legions left."

Arthur smiled back at him, but said, "Detail some of the knights to ride ahead and along our flanks. Those woods could hide an army of ambushers easily."

Bors nodded. Thick forests were poor territory for mounted knights. We dealt best with our enemies in open ground, where we could charge them.

Young Lancelot, who always rode within earshot of Arthur, eagerly volunteered for the picket duty. Bors distrusted Lancelot's ardent quest for glory; he thought the young knight's fearless courage was little short of foolhardy. But on this day even tough old Bors nodded laughingly and sent Lancelot on his way.

It must be the good weather, I thought.

Then Bors turned back to Arthur. "We'll be in the enchantress' domain soon."

Arthur nodded and muttered, "Morganna."

He had been truly enchanted by Morganna, back at Cadbury castle a year earlier. Aphrodite had besotted him, and then tried to assassinate him. Only Anya's interference had saved Arthur's life.

"My uncle Ambrosius wants an alliance with Bernicia. It could be an effective buffer against the Scots and Picts."

"An alliance with the witch?" Bors grumbled.

Arthur smiled at the older knight, but it was cheerless, bitter. "The High King wants it."

That ended Bors' smiles for the rest of the day.

3

The next morning we reached castle Bernicia. It was an impressive citadel, standing high on a crag by the relentless sea, three of its sides protected by the sheer cliff. The only way to approach it was by the winding uphill path we rode. Unlike most of the fortresses I had seen, which were little more than grimy stockades with wooden palisades around them, Bernicia was protected by stone walls with turrets at each corner. A steep ditch ran in front of the main gate. Its drawbridge was pulled up.

Sir Gawain, freshly washed and his long dark locks shining with oil, whistled with appreciation as he looked over the battlements.

"No wonder the barbarians have never been able to take this castle," he said.

"What are you so prettied up for?" Bors jibed at him.

Gawain flashed his bright smile. "Where there's a castle there are wenches." He turned to Arthur. "You may have the princess, my lord, but you can't have *all* the women."

We stopped before the ditch and leather-lunged Bors hailed the castle.

"Who goes there?" came the time-honored challenge from the battlements above the main gate.

"Sir Arthur, Dux Bellorum of Ambrosius Aurelianus, High King of all the Celts, has come to see the princess Morganna."

Morganna's father had died some years ago, we knew, and she ruled Bernicia. By witchcraft, according to the fearful tales told of her. By the powers of the Creators, I knew. It amounted to almost the same thing.

"*Queen* Morganna will decide if she wishes to receive you," the sentinel responded.

"She styles herself a queen now," Bors said to Arthur.

"Perhaps she's married," Gawain suggested.

Arthur looked relieved at that thought. Then he wondered, "If she has married, it must be to a king. Who could it be?"

"Who would have her?" Bors muttered.

At length, the drawbridge came clattering down and we rode over it into the courtyard, our horses' hooves booming on the stout timbers, the footmen following close behind. The courtyard was a large square of packed dirt; all the exits out of it were firmly shut with spiked iron gates. Men-at-arms stood up on the rooftops all around us. I felt uneasy. We could be slaughtered here, penned like cattle.

Then one of the gates screeched open and Morganna stepped into the sunlight to greet Arthur. She was truly Aphrodite, the most incredibly beautiful woman on earth: hair as dark and lustrous as polished ebony, skin as white as alabaster. Her richly embroidered gown clung to every curve of her body. I glanced at Gawain; his eyes were popping. We all stared at her. I myself felt the desire she raised in every man: powerful, alluring.

At her side stood a tall, broad-shouldered man with long white hair falling past his shoulders. His beard was white also, and his face was lined and spiderwebbed with age, yet he stood straight as a forest pine, unbent by his years.

At Arthur's command we dismounted from our steeds. He walked slowly toward Morganna and her husband. The rest of us stood stock-still. I saw Bors, beside me, nervously eying the rooftops and the men posted there.

"Arthur," said Morganna, smiling. "How good to see you again."

"Queen Morganna," Arthur replied, bowing somewhat stiffly. "I bring you greetings from Ambrosius Aurelianus."

Still smiling, she turned slightly and said, "This is my husband, King Ogier."

"Ogier the Dane," Bors whispered, shocked. "She's sold out to
the barbarians."

4

Arthur accompanied Morganna and her husband, while the rest
of us were led to the quarters she had allotted to us. The knights
were taken to one of the towers, while we squires were sent to the
stables, of course. The footmen and churls were told to find corners of the courtyard where they could spread their blankets.

I didn't see Arthur again until dinner, in the castle's main hall.
It wasn't big enough to hold all of Arthur's knights; only a picked
dozen were invited to sit at the long feasting table by the huge
fireplace. Their squires sat on mean planks down on the packed-
earth floor.

The dinner was pleasant enough, although very little laughter
issued from the head table. Afterward, Arthur motioned for me
to accompany him to his quarters in the tower.

When I stepped into his room, I saw that Bors and Gawain
were already there, looking very gloomy indeed. Lancelot slipped
in behind me, before I could shut the heavy oaken door. Bors
frowned at the young knight, but Arthur merely smiled and waved
him to one of the beautifully carved chairs by the bedstead.

"Ogier the Dane," Bors said bitterly. "She's sold her kingdom
to a barbarian king."

Arthur spoke more softly. "It must be very difficult for a woman
to rule a kingdom. Especially here in the northlands, with the
wild tribes constantly raiding."

"It's said she rules through witchcraft," Gawain offered. "Why then would she need a barbarian warrior to be her husband?"

I saw the expression on Arthur's face. He had witnessed Morganna's witchcraft with his own eyes. He had been seduced by her charms, and then nearly murdered by her.

"She bears you no goodwill," Bors said. "That much is clear, despite her royal reception."

"We are as much her prisoners here as her guests," Lancelot said. "I fear that we have stepped into a trap."

Bors looked surprised and impressed with Lancelot's sound sense.

"Why has she married the Dane?" Arthur wondered aloud. "Does Ogier intend to bring his people across the sea to settle here? Must we add the Danes to our list of enemies?"

I decided to find out for myself.

5

Late that night, long after our meeting in Arthur's quarters had broken up in just as much puzzlement and uncertainty as it had begun, I got up from my pallet of straw in the stables. The other squires were asleep, snoring and muttering in their dreams. We had posted two guards, and they stood dutifully—if drowsily—by the stable doors.

I told them I couldn't sleep, and walked past them out into the courtyard before they could ask me to take the guard duty and let them rest. It was a cold, clear night. The stars were hard, sharp pinpoints glittering in the black moonless sky. I saw a meteor streak across, silently hurrying as if it had an appointment to keep in the heavens.

Dressed only in my thin linen tunic, wearing no sword nor any weapon except the dagger that Odysseos had given me, strapped to my thigh, I walked along the shadow of the wall, stepping carefully over the sleeping bodies of Arthur's footmen and camp workers.

Morganna and her husband slept high in the castle's keep, a solid tower that rose at the rear of the courtyard, next to the wall that overlooked the sea. I knew the guards would not grant me entrance; I had no intention of asking them to let me pass.

Keeping to the deep shadow of the wall, I climbed the rough stones of the tower, maneuvering slowly to the seaward side once I got up above the level of the castle wall. There were no guards patrolling the wall on this side, with nothing below except the rocky crag and the restless, heaving sea far below. The wind tugged at me and my fingers grew numb with cold despite my conscious efforts to control my body's internal heat. Still I climbed.

Just below the timbers of the tower's roof was a single window. Not a skinny arrow slit, as would be on the other towers facing potential enemy approaches, but a square window open to the beautiful view of the sea. I hauled myself across its ledge, pushing aside the thick drapes that covered it.

My eyes had long since adapted to the moonless night, but the interior of the room was even darker. I crouched by the window, peering into the shadows. This seemed to be a sitting room, well furnished but empty of people. Rich tapestries hung on its cold stone walls. Its fireplace, across the straw-covered floor, stood empty and dark.

A door led to a bedroom. I pushed it open slowly, slowly, so that it would not creak. The sullen red embers of a dying fire glowed in the fireplace. I could make out a bulky white-headed body asleep in the bed, one sizable foot sticking out from the blankets: Ogier, alone. Morganna was nowhere in sight.

I concentrated all my willpower on Ogier's sleeping form, praying silently for Anya to help me. Whether she heard me or whether I did it for myself I could not know, but I felt a flash of infinite cold and suddenly I was standing on a grassy hillside in bright warm sunshine, the golden city of the Creators standing beneath its protective bubble of energy down where the hill melted into the sandy beach that fringed the wide, placid, glittering sea.

Ogier was lying on the grass, looking slightly ridiculous in a nightshirt that had ridden up on his rump, exposing his skinny, bony shanks. He sat up abruptly, wide awake, eyes staring with shock and fright.

"Where am I?" he shouted. "Who are you? What has happened to me?"

"No need to fear, my lord," I said calmly. "You are perfectly safe."

He scrambled to his feet, towering over me. "Witchcraft!" he squealed, his voice high with terror.

"You are no stranger to witchcraft," I replied. "You married an enchantress."

Ogier stared at me, his chest heaving. He spun around, then fixed his gaze on me again. Seeing that I was apparently unarmed, he seemed to calm himself somewhat.

"Who are you? What have you done?"

"I want to know why a Danish king has married a British sorceress," I said.

"You're going to break the spell?"

"What spell?"

"She . . ." He hesitated, eyes darting back and forth as if he expected to see someone nearby.

"Morganna?" I prompted.

Suddenly he leaped at me, hands reaching for my throat. He was a big man, and quite strong despite his years. Yet I was stronger. I had been built for violence, designed not merely to fight but to take joy in fighting. A surge of malevolent pleasure raced through me as I ripped his hands from my throat and twisted his arms until he was forced to kneel.

"The witch can't protect you from me," I said sharply. "Now tell me why you have come to Bernicia."

He collapsed, sobbing, onto the grass. I waited for him to gain control of himself.

At last he said, haltingly, "I am old . . . older than you know. I saw the face of death. He warned me that he would come for me soon. Then Morganna came to me . . . she told me she would give me the gift of life . . . she said I could live forever."

"So do the Christians say," I told him.

He grimaced. "Nay, they offer eternity after death, in another world. I mistrust those who say you can live forever, but only after you die."

He was a man who believed only what he could see with his own eyes.

"Morganna told me I could live forever, *here,* on Earth. And I could be become master of all Britain."

That perked up my ears.

"What did she ask of you in return?" I demanded.

"That I marry her and come to Bernicia. That I bring my Danes with me and conquer this island."

"And what of Arthur?"

He looked embarrassed and turned away from me. Staring at the ground, he mumbled, "She said that Arthur would come to castle Bernicia, but he would not leave it. Not alive."

"You dare to interfere, Orion?"

I turned at the sound of her voice. It was Aphrodite, no longer pretending to be a mortal, dressed in a softly draped robe so sheer that she might as well have been naked. She was magnificent, physically perfect, utterly desirable. Even though I yearned for Anya, the presence of Aphrodite was enough to make me forget my lost love, almost.

Ogier got slowly to his feet, gaping at her. "Morganna, he forced me to tell—"

Aphrodite raised one hand and pointed a finger at him. He fell into silence, frozen like a statue, his mouth still open to form words that could not issue from his throat.

"He won't bother us now," she said, a cruel smile twisting her perfect lips. "And neither will you, anymore."

"You used Hades to frighten him, didn't you?" I accused.

Her smile widened slightly. "Hades put the fear of death into the old man. I offered him the gift of life. He took it willingly."

"Eternal life? For a mortal?"

Now she actually laughed. "Hardly eternal, Orion. He'll live long enough to conquer Britain. That's enough."

"I'll stop you," I said.

"You? Pitiful little creature, stop me? Remember that Aten is on my side in this."

"I'll stop you both."

Suddenly a star seemed to blaze out of the clear blue sky. Brighter and brighter it shone, turning the whole sky into molten copper, hotter and hotter until its glare forced me to throw my arms over my eyes and sink to my knees in agony.

"That's the proper attitude for my creature," said a voice I knew only too well. "You may look upon me, Orion."

I looked up, my eyes watering painfully. There stood Aten, in a splendid gold uniform, his thick mane of golden hair shining like a halo, his tawny eyes gazing down at me in amusement.

"You believe that you can stop me, Orion. Me, who created you? Who built you from atoms of dust and molecules of slime? Every bit of knowledge in your brain was put there by me. Every breath you take is taken only because I allow it."

Slowly I got to my feet, hatred burning deep within me at his sneering, haughty demeanor.

"Yet I fight against you," I said.

He smirked at me. "Not very well, I'm afraid. You've stepped into this trap easily enough."

"Trap?"

"Of course. How else do you think you were able to transport yourself and this mortal here? I brought you here, into the trap I've prepared for you."

"You're lying."

"You'll find out that I'm telling the truth. And once I've put you out of the way, I'll get the other Creators to join me in eliminating Arthur."

"Hades has agreed to stand aside and be neutral," I said hotly. "Anya and others of the Creators oppose you."

"Your precious Anya is far from here," Aten replied. "As for Hades, I don't need him for the moment. He'll return to my side soon enough."

"Destroy this one," Aphrodite hissed. "Eliminate him for all time."

Aten nodded. "I'm afraid she's right, Orion. You've become too difficult to control. It's sad to destroy the work of one's own hands, but . . ." He sighed. "Good-bye, Orion."

I was plunged into darkness, falling, falling in a black pit of doom, hurtling through a void where not even starlight could appear. I felt the cold of interstellar space seeping into my body, pain so deep it was like a thousand sharp blades flaying the flesh from my bones, a cryogenic cold freezing my limbs, my mind. My body was being twisted horribly, torn beyond the limits of pain, stretched into agony as if I were on a torturer's rack.

This is the end, I thought, my mind spinning. This is the final oblivion. A black hole is pulling me apart.

My last thought was of Anya. I would never see her, never again hold her. Death did not matter. Pain was meaningless. But being without her, not even able to say a final farewell, that was the ultimate torture.

My body died. The pain overwhelmed me. My bones were snapping, crumbling to dust. The last spark of my being flickered as it was engulfed by the darkness.

Yet I lived. Like an out-of-body experience, I somehow looked back and saw the poor suffering entity that was me being torn into bloody gobbets of flesh, crushed between invisible hands, torn apart on the merciless rack of the black hole's titanic gravitational power.

Your mind still lives, I heard somehow. The information that is *you* still flows through the cosmic spacetime, Orion.

Is this what death truly is? A bodiless, nonphysical existence, a shadow world of memories and desires, the same dreams and terrors endlessly repeating, echoing across the universes? Yet even as I wondered such thoughts, I could feel my bodiless mind fading, dwindling, dissolving into the final nothingness of ultimate oblivion.

"Focus," a voice said urgently. "Focus before your information pattern thins so much that it is drowned in the meaningless noise of the stars."

Anya's voice! I was certain of it. Perhaps I was insane, grasping at the last shred of hope like a drowning man thrashing for a piece of flotsam to buoy him up. But I was certain that it was Anya speaking to me.

"As long as the energy is there, matter can be formed. The pattern exists, and the body can be shaped from it."

"Anya!" I cried out into the lightless void.

"I am with you, my darling," she answered. "Even from the other side of the universe, from so distant in space and time that numbers lose all meaning, I am with you."

"I love you," I said. With all my being, I meant it.

"There's little I can do to help you, Orion," she said, "except to tell you what must be done. You must save yourself, you must find the strength to overcome the doom that faces you."

"Tell me," I said. "Tell me and I'll do it."

"The pattern of your consciousness is fading, Orion, wafting into the cosmic void like smoke drifting from a snuffed candle. You must focus that pattern, focus your consciousness, your being. You must use your energy to spark the candle into new flame."

I tried, but nothing happened. I concentrated, sought with every scrap of my remaining existence to focus the dying pattern of energy that was my being. But nothing happened. I could feel myself growing weaker.

"You're fading!" Anya's voice warned. "Dying."

Her voice. Her being. She was reaching across a universe of spacetime to try to save me, to try to bring me back from final death. She loved me that much. Enough to defy Aten and the other Creators. Enough to risk her own existence in an effort to save me.

I would not let her strive in vain. "I love you, Anya," I called across the light-years. "I will never stop loving you."

The vision of her, her courage, her loveliness, her love for me, brought new strength to my resolve. I could feel energy sharpening my consciousness, as if the streams of spacetime were flowing into me. I became a nexus, a protostar, pulling in energy and matter, growing, gaining strength.

"You're doing it!" Anya called from far away. "You're succeeding!"

Orion the hunter, I thought. Orion the warrior. All those abilities that Aten had built into me, all those powers of stamina and tenacity I used now to bring myself back from the oblivion into which he had thrown me.

I am not a toy, not a puppet to be tossed aside when it no longer pleases its master. I am Orion, and I live to do as *I* will, as *I* must. I live to find Anya and be with her for eternity.

I blinked my eyes and found myself in the stable at castle Bernicia, alive and whole. I laughed aloud and actually savored the stinks and snores that surrounded me. I was alive, and it felt sweet to be so.

6

"Where have you been, Orion?" Arthur demanded.

He looked more worried than angry. I had risen with the dawn and washed in nearly frozen water at the horse trough in the castle courtyard. Arthur, Bors, and Gawain came out of the tower where they had slept as I finished donning my tunic.

Bors' left arm was cradled in a rude sling. He limped noticeably. Gawain's head was wrapped in a bloodstained bandage.

"Orion's been wenching, I'll wager," Gawain said. His usual bright smile was gone. He seemed to wince at the sunlight, as if his head ached terribly.

"When you should be here, with your master," snarled the wounded Bors.

Before I could reply, Arthur said tiredly, "Orion, as my squire you must be at my call always. If you want to go away for a day or two, you must ask me first."

I had been missing for three days, they told me. That surprised me a little, but I was truly shocked to see how battered Bors and Gawain were.

Arthur seemed more relieved to see me again than angry that I had disappeared. He didn't really want an explanation; he wanted to make certain that I wouldn't disappear again unless I first asked his leave. Worse, though, he seemed tired, dispirited, exhausted as though he hadn't slept for days.

I apologized profusely, then asked, "My lord, are you ill? You seem . . . not well."

Arthur shook his head wearily. "How could I be, with all that's happened these past three dismal days."

"Witchcraft," Bors muttered darkly. "There's evil afoot in this castle."

"Is that what happened to you, Sir Bors?" I asked. "And to you, Sir Gawain?"

"No," said Arthur. "What you see is the devilish handiwork of King Ogier."

I gaped at the two wounded knights. "The Dane did this to you?"

Bors gave me a look that would have curdled cream. Gawain looked downright embarrassed.

Arthur explained, "I've been trying to find a way to get Ogier to join us. I invited him to become an ally of the High King. I told him that Ambrosius would support him in battles against the Scots and Picts."

Ogier had laughed in Arthur's face, he told me, and declared that he had no need of help from Ambrosius or anyone else. He intended to bring his own Danes from across the sea and march south to take as much of Britain as he wished.

Arthur had patiently explained that such a move would make them enemies, forcing his knights to go to war against the invading Danish army.

"We have beaten every foe we have faced, from the Saxons in the south to the Picts and Scots here north of the Wall," Arthur had told him. "We will defeat your Danes, as well."

"Conquer my Danes!" Ogier roared with laughter and offered a challenge to Arthur.

"Pick three of your finest, strongest knights. Old man that I am, I will fight them, I myself. If any one of them bests me, I will leave this land and return to Denmark forever."

Arthur immediately accepted the challenge himself, but Ogier declined to fight him.

"Nay, you are too young, little more than a callow youth. Pick three of your best knights. I will fight each of them. After I have defeated them, if you still dare to accept my challenge, then I will fight you—and your enchanted sword. It won't protect you against me," Ogier boasted.

So it was agreed: King Ogier the Dane would face three of Arthur's finest knights, on foot in the castle courtyard. If he defeated all three of them, then Arthur would face the Dane.

Sir Bors had been the first, and tough old Ogier had drubbed him thoroughly. After he was helped off the field of contest, Bors complained of feeling slow, weary, as if sick.

"You certainly looked it," Gawain had quipped as he helped carry the bleeding Bors.

It was Gawain's turn next. The next morning they met in the courtyard again. Gawain looked pale, unsure of himself.

"In a lesser man I would have thought he was frightened," Arthur said as we climbed the tower stairs to the room Morganna had given to young Lancelot.

"I wasn't frightened," Gawain maintained stoutly. "I felt sick. Weak. Feverish, almost."

Still, Gawain had put on his helmet and gone out to meet Ogier, sword in hand. The Dane, swift and powerful as a man half his years, cracked Gawain's head so hard that Arthur thought he would die.

"Not so," said Gawain as we entered Lancelot's room. "My skull's too thick, even for Ogier's great strength."

Lancelot was Arthur's last hope. If the challenge of facing Ogier worried the youngster, he didn't show it as he dressed for the contest.

"I won't fail you, Arthur," Lancelot said, smiling eagerly. He actually seemed to be looking forward to the fight as he draped his chain mail over his tunic.

His shield with the golden eagle emblem rested by the table in the center of the room. Atop the table lay Lancelot's sword and his helmet, a steel cylinder that covered the entire head, padded along its bottom rim where it rested on his shoulders.

"How do you feel?" Arthur asked.

Lancelot tried to smile, but it was shaky. "Butterflies in my stomach," he said lightly.

Arthur frowned worriedly. "Both Gawain and Bors felt sick when they faced Ogier."

"Witchcraft," Bors muttered again. "I tell you the witch has put a spell on us all."

Arthur did not contradict him. "I haven't felt all that well myself these past few days," he admitted.

Lancelot took a deep breath. "I feel good enough to face the

Dane," he said. Yet I thought that some of his usual vigor and enthusiasm was lacking.

I went to the window and looked down at the courtyard. Ogier was already there, bareheaded, taking practice swings with a mighty broadsword.

Someone knocked at the door. I hurried to open it.

Morganna stood there, midnight-dark hair tumbling past her shoulders, a warm disarming smile on her lustrous lips. She bore a silver tray of apples and roasted chestnuts in her hands.

If she was surprised to see that I still lived, she gave no sign of it. Stepping past me as if I didn't really exist, she carried the laden tray straight to Arthur.

"To show that I bear no ill will toward you, Arthur," she said sweetly, handing him the tray.

He had been totally infatuated with her, a year earlier. It was clear to see that she still held a powerful attraction for him.

Arthur had to swallow before he could find his voice. "Thank you, Morganna."

She looked up at him. "I'm sorry that it's come to this, Arthur. Once my husband bests your boy, there, you'll have to face him yourself. He might kill you, Arthur."

"That's in God's hands, Morganna," said Arthur quietly.

"Is it?" she replied.

Gawain chuckled. "Suppose Ogier gets himself killed, my lady? Then you'd be a widow."

She looked at Gawain the way a snake looks at a baby rabbit. "Would you come to console me, then?"

"Aye, that I would," said Gawain, reaching for one of the shining apples on the tray. He crunched into it with his strong white teeth. "I would indeed."

Morganna smiled at him. "Very well then. Should I be forced

to put on a widow's black weeds, you may come to beguile me of my grief."

With that she turned and swept out of the room, leaving Arthur holding the tray of fruit and Gawain munching thoughtfully on the apple.

Lancelot picked up one of the apples. "A bite or two might help calm my stomach," he said.

Bors stared hard at the closed door. "Witch," he growled. "She put a spell on me. On us all."

"No," said Arthur, putting the fruit tray on the table. "But she might win Gawain's heart."

Gawain said, "It's not my heart that—"

He stopped, his face going pale. His legs buckled. I raced to him and caught him before he collapsed to the floor.

"I'm . . . sick . . . ," Gawain moaned.

Lancelot suddenly clutched at his stomach and lurched toward the window. He made it only as far as the corner of the bed, then collapsed and puked up his guts onto the floor.

"The apples!" said Arthur. "They're poisoned."

Without an instant's hesitation I pried Gawain's mouth open and stuck two fingers down his throat. He gagged, then retched. It was a mess, but it probably saved his life. The remains of the apple came up, together with the breakfast Gawain had gobbled earlier.

We laid the two of them side by side on Lancelot's bed while his squire ran for a maid or two to clean up the vomit.

Gawain groaned, but the color came back to his face. "The witch . . . poisoned me."

"It was meant for me," Arthur said. "She still hates me, despite her smiles."

Lancelot was unconscious, pale as death.

"Lancelot's in no shape to fight Ogier," Bors said. "And if he doesn't show up, the Dane will claim a forfeit."

"Then he'll demand to face me," Arthur said. He, too, looked pale, unwell.

I knew what was racing through Arthur's mind: If Ogier wins his challenge he will bring his army of Danes to Bernicia. From there they will invade southward, bringing a whole new flood of enemies to spread fire and death across Britain.

But I saw a different scene. Morganna had been subtly poisoning the knights' food for days now. Bors and Gawain had both been too ill to fight well. Morganna's poisoned apples were meant to make certain that Lancelot could not even make it to the field of contest. Arthur would be forced to fight Ogier and the Dane was going to kill him. Morganna/Aphrodite had hatched this scheme to assassinate Arthur.

I looked into Arthur's eyes. "I'll go in Lancelot's place, my lord."

"You?" Bors snapped. "You're only a squire. That Dane out there will cleave you in half."

"I can fight him," I insisted. "In Lancelot's armor, so no one will know that Lancelot didn't show up."

"It would never work," Bors grumbled.

But Arthur said, "Can you best Ogier, do you think?"

I realized that Morganna had given the old Dane more than an extended life span. Aphrodite and Aten must have enhanced his body, augmented his muscular strength, amplified his reflexes. I recalled fighting for Odysseos before the walls of Epeiros, a thousand years before Alexander the Great conquered the Persian Empire. I faced Aten himself, in mortal guise, swifter and stronger than any mere human could be. The best I could do was a draw: we killed each other.

"I will beat him, my lord," I said firmly. Then I had to add, "Or die trying."

Arthur nodded, his mouth a grim tight line. "No one could ask you to do more."

So I put on Lancelot's coat of chain mail. It was a bit short for me, but we hoped no one would notice. I hefted his heavy shield with the golden eagle painted on it.

"I'll give you Excalibur . . ." Arthur began.

"No need, my lord," I said as Lancelot's squire buckled his sword around my waist. "Excalibur is meant for you alone."

We left Lancelot and Gawain in the tower room with their squires. Arthur commanded the youngsters to open the door to no one except himself. Down the long spiral of stone stairs we went, until we reached the ground level. Then I pulled Lancelot's helmet over my head. It covered my face completely. The world shrank to what I could see through the narrow eye slit in the steel helm.

Ogier stood waiting at the far end of the courtyard, tall, his shoulders as wide as two axe handles, twirling a two-handed broadsword in his right hand as if it were a toy. The courtyard was thronged with people who had come to watch the match, buzzing and chattering with excitement. Only the center of the packed-earth courtyard was open for our contest. Almost everyone in the castle must have been there—except, I noticed, for the men-at-arms stationed on the rooftops, armed with stout bows.

Morganna stood beside her husband. Even through the narrow eye slits of the helmet I could see that she was surprised that Lancelot had made it down to the courtyard. She stared hard at me, her incredibly beautiful face twisted into a puzzled frown.

Ogier wore a long coat of chain mail over his tunic, as did I. A squire stood beside him holding his long shield; it bore the emblem of a stag, in black. Its tapered bottom end rested on the dirt, its square top reached to the lad's eyes. Ogier handed his sword to another squire, and took his helmet from a third. The helmet bore steel prongs, like a stag's antlers, and a gold circlet of a crown affixed to it. Ogier would do battle with a king's crown on his head—or at least, on his helmet.

"He is very fast and very strong," Arthur warned me. "Be on your guard."

I nodded inside my helmet. "Wish me luck, my lord."

"May the gods be with you," Arthur said, lapsing back to his Roman heritage. Probably he unconsciously thought that the Christian God was too meek to be of help in battle.

I stepped out into the open space as the crowd hushed expectantly. Ogier's helmet covered his cheeks and had a flat piece between the eyes to protect his nose. The bottom half of his face was uncovered; his snow-white beard fell halfway down his chest.

"So, lad, you, too, have come to feel the bite of my blade," he said in a loud, strong voice.

I said nothing as I advanced slowly, warily toward him.

"Come then," Ogier said cheerfully. "Let us see who is the better man."

My senses went into overdrive again. Everything around me slowed down, as if time itself was stretching out into a languid, sluggish flow. A good thing, too, for Ogier was every bit as swift as a lightning bolt.

He swung a mighty overhand blow, meant to cleave my skull, helmet and all. I jumped backward and his swing cut empty air, instead. Without an instant's pause he swung backhand at me, advancing swiftly as I backed away.

"Stand and fight," he growled. "This isn't a dancing contest."

I was content to dance, at least until I could gauge the speed of his reflexes. I circled around the courtyard, Ogier pursuing me, as the crowd shifted and melted away from us. For several minutes the only sounds were the hissing swishes of his blade cutting through the air and the crowd's gasps as I backpedaled lithely. Not once did our swords clash.

He showed no signs of slowing, only a growing impatience with my retreating tactic.

"Coward!" he snapped. "Face me like a man, you spineless cur."

I had no intention of walking into that buzz saw he was wielding. Not until I was ready.

Around the courtyard we went, Ogier charging and me retreating. I nearly stumbled once, when I got close to where Morganna was standing. Did she somehow trip me? I couldn't tell. But I could see Arthur's face as he watched the match. He looked aghast, ashamed of what I was doing. Better to wade in manfully and be chopped to bloody bits, in his eyes, than to appear to be afraid of your enemy.

Ogier showed no sign of slowing down or becoming winded. If anything, he pursued me harder, swinging his blade so fast it was a blur against the clear blue sky even to my hypersensitized eyes.

After three times around the courtyard I thought I had his swing timed well enough. I suddenly stopped my retreat, and lunged toward Ogier, raising my shield to take his thrust while I swung at his midsection.

His blow shattered my shield. It simply cracked apart, half of it flying off into the crowd, the other half hanging useless from my arm. The force of the blow staggered me; my whole arm went numb. My own swing bounced harmlessly off his shield.

"Ha!" he roared, rushing toward me as I stumbled back.

I ducked beneath his swing and wedged my sword against the inside of his shield. Then I jabbed the point of the blade into his ribs. There was little force in my thrust, and the blade slid harmlessly against his chain mail.

But for the first time in our fight, Ogier backed up. The crowd went "Ooh!"

For a moment we stood facing each other, chests heaving, arms heavy. I tossed away the remnant of my shield. Past Ogier's imposing form I could see Morganna smiling.

"So you're ready to fight now?" he taunted me.

I said nothing, waiting for his next attack.

He sprang at me with another powerful overhand swing. I gripped my sword in both hands and parried his blade with a mighty clang that rang off the courtyard walls. The force of his blow buckled my knees, but I managed to back away and regain my balance.

Ogier came forward with still another overhand cut. This time I dodged it and swung two-handed at the haft of his blade, close to the hilt. My blow ripped the sword from his hand; it went spinning through the air and landed on the ground a good ten feet from where we stood.

The courtyard fell absolutely silent. Ogier stood for an instant, staring down at his sword on the dusty ground. Then he looked at me. I saw what was in his eyes. He realized that I could have just as easily taken off his hand, severed it at the wrist.

I stepped back and allowed him to pick up his sword. He hefted it, as if testing to see if it were still whole and sharp. Then he advanced upon me again, but not so wildly this time. Now he was grimly determined to finish me off.

Holding his shield before him, Ogier moved warily toward me, swishing his sword in swift circles over his head. The shield covered him from knees to eyes. He was taking no chances against me now.

I backed away for several steps, thinking rapidly, trying to find a weakness, an opening. From another life I remembered a martial arts instructor urging me, "Your enemy cannot strike without exposing himself to a counterstrike. Be alert. Be prepared. Use your enemy's strength to conquer him."

Suddenly Ogier roared like a bull and charged at me, ready to use his shield as a battering ram. I dropped to the ground and took his legs out from under him with a rolling block. He fell like a giant oak tree, landing facedown on his shield.

I planted one foot on his sword arm and knelt my other leg on the small of his back. Ripping off his golden-crowned helmet, I pointed my sword at the nape of his neck.

"Yield, my lord," I shouted, "or I shall be obliged to cut off your head."

Ogier had no desire to lose his head. "I yield," he said, his voice quavering.

7

We were not completely out of danger. That night Ogier feasted us, and Lancelot had to accept the plaudits of one and all as an invincible champion. He looked embarrassed, which everyone took to be humility, the kind of modesty that becomes a true knight.

We dared not eat anything except the sizzling meat of the boar that we saw being roasted on a huge spit in the great hall's fireplace. Nor would any of Arthur's men drink anything except water, by his command. He'd had enough of poison.

Ogier ate and drank mightily, but he seemed to have aged twenty years since the morning. He looked thinner, slower, his eyes red-rimmed and watery. Have Aten and Aphrodite already removed whatever it was that made the old Dane so youthful? I wondered.

He agreed good-naturedly that he would return to Denmark and never darken Britain's shores again.

"If you have knights like young Lancelot in your service," he said to Arthur as they sat side by side at the long dining table, "then I will keep my army in Denmark and harry the Frisians and Saxons there."

Arthur smiled graciously. I thought that Ogier's harrying would only lead to more Frisians and Saxons crossing the sea to Britain, but I was satisfied that the Danes would not invade.

Morganna sat at Ogier's other side, smiling mysteriously through the entire evening. That worried me. She did not appear to be angry or frustrated that her plot to kill Arthur had failed. She smiled like the Sphinx, like someone who is willing to wait for long ages to accomplish her goal.

The next morning, as we were ready to saddle up and leave Bernicia for the long trek back to Cadbury castle, Morganna came into the sun-drenched courtyard to say farewell to Arthur. Several of her ladies accompanied her.

"Will you go to Denmark with your husband?" Arthur asked bluntly.

Again that Sphinx-like smile. "No, I will stay here. This is my home, not some rude swamp across the sea."

"But what of Ogier, then?"

"What of him?" she replied carelessly. "He is old and will die soon. He serves me no purpose anymore."

Arthur shook his head. Then he fixed Morganna with a hard stare. "You wanted to see me killed."

"I will dance on your grave one day, Arthur."

He seemed more saddened than alarmed. "What have I done to earn such hatred?"

Morganna smiled again and beckoned to one of her waiting ladies. The woman bore an infant, asleep in a bundle of swaddling clothes.

"This is what you've done," said Morganna, taking the baby in her arms.

Arthur gaped at the child.

"He is your son, Arthur. I will raise him to hate you as much as I do."

"But Morganna," he pleaded, "you mustn't—"

"I will, Arthur. He will know that you are his father and he will hate you with every fiber of his being."

Arthur simply stared at her, uncomprehending, bewildered.

"I've named him Modred," she said, her smile turning truly evil. "He will be the instrument of your doom."

Yes, I thought. Aphrodite and Aten and the other Creators would not rest until they had destroyed Arthur. They had all the time they needed to put their hateful plans into action. Could I protect Arthur all through those long years?

I vowed that I would.

CHAPTER SEVEN

Wroxeter and Cameliard

1

As we left Bernicia and threaded our way back through Hadrian's Wall, a messenger from Cadbury castle galloped breathlessly to us. The news from the south was not good. The High King, Ambrosius Aurelianus, had fallen ill. And Merlin had disappeared.

After trouncing the wild tribes of the north and staving off an invasion threatened by the Danes in Bernicia, we were heading south again, seeking to escape the worst of the long, cold, wet, and dreary northern winter.

Arthur seemed more upset about Merlin's disappearance than Ambrosius' illness.

"He told me in my dream that he was leaving me," Arthur muttered as the two of us clopped along the Roman road, well ahead of all the others.

I rode alongside him, and saw the worry that etched his youthful face.

"I need him, Orion," he said. "How can I get along without his advice, his guidance?"

Knowing that Merlin was actually one of the Creators, meddling in the affairs of mortals in this placetime, I replied, "Perhaps, my lord, he knows that you are now able to make your own decisions, that you no longer need his guidance."

"But—"

"Perhaps this is Merlin's way of telling you that you can stand on your own feet now."

Arthur shook his head. "I wish I could believe that, Orion."

"Believe it, my lord," I said, "because it is true."

Southward we plodded: knights, squires, footmen, churls, and camp followers, long lines of men mounted and afoot, of horses and oxcarts, slowly winding our way through the bare trees and brown hills of the empty countryside toward the warmer clime of the south and Ambrosius' great stone castle at Cadbury.

Twice we were attacked, not by invading barbarians but by our own Celtic people, brigands who fell upon small groups of our men when they were foraging or hunting, isolated from the main column.

Lancelot was leading a small hunting party, scouring the hilly countryside for game to bring back to the cook pots, when bandits tried to ambush us. Arthur had commanded me to go with Lancelot because I had gained a reputation as a good hunter. My namesake, Orion, was famed as a hunter. We were afoot, looking for signs of deer, when they came screaming fiercely out of the woods, armed with swords and staves.

One of the squires went down while the others ran back toward Lancelot, who already had his sword in hand. The youngest of Arthur's knights, barely old enough to have the wisp of a beard starting on his chin, Lancelot must have looked like an inexperienced boy to the bandits. What a mistake!

He stood his ground, without shield or helmet, as the squires ran back toward him. I stood at his side, grasping my own sword, every nerve in my body tingling with the anticipation of battle. I had been created to be a warrior, and my senses speeded up whenever needed for the fight.

But there was no need for that this day. Lancelot waited until the bandits were almost upon him, then drove forward like a hurricane of death. Almost faster than my eyes could follow he cut down the first two brigands that reached him. His sword was a blur as he hacked the life out of two more. Four of them tried to circle behind him, but I slashed the arm off one of them and the others turned and ran.

It was all finished in a few heartbeats. Lancelot stood among the corpses, his sword dripping blood, not even breathing hard.

Arthur was not happy with our report.

"Britons attacked you?" he asked Lancelot.

"Aye, my lord. Hungry men, from the looks of them. God knows this countryside has been picked bare. There isn't a deer or even a boar anywhere around here."

Arthur rubbed his bearded chin. "If they're starving they'll attack again. We'll have to be on our guard each step of the way."

♌

Lean, gray-faced Friar Samson rode beside Arthur each morning, praising his victories as God's will and urging Arthur to cleanse the land of the pagan invaders. Arthur listened respectfully, even though Samson could become pompous in his pronouncements. On the morning after still another bandit attack, after patiently listening to Samson's droning lecture, Arthur asked the priest to see to the souls of the footmen trudging along the trail behind us.

The friar's gaunt face flashed anger for a moment, then he

meekly bowed his tonsured head and turn his horse back away from the knights. Samson looked nothing like his namesake: he was almost painfully thin, and his withered body was as bent and twisted as a man twice his age.

Gawain trotted up beside Arthur. "Had enough of piety for one cold morning, eh?"

Arthur said nothing.

"Why so downcast?" asked Gawain, riding alongside Arthur. "Those bandits were nothing more than a pack of knaves, Britons or no."

"Hungry knaves," Arthur replied glumly. "Look at the land around us."

I could see what he meant. For many days we had ridden through devastation. Since the Romans had abandoned Britain, barbaric invaders from across the seas had invaded the island, burning, raping, looting, killing. Towns that had once been peaceful and prosperous were now blackened with fire, abandoned, their people flown or dead. Farm fields stood bleak and fallow, abandoned by peasant and lord alike. The land lay gray and barren, crushed by the endless raiding and looting.

The countryside was so bare that Arthur had to split his army into four separate columns as we worked our way southward, so that we could find some fodder for our mounts. The foragers came back to camp each night with meager pickings; many days they found nothing at all. Even I, mighty hunter that I had been created to be, could find only an occasional half-starved rabbit. Deer and larger game had long since been devoured.

What was even worse than the invading Saxons and Jutes and Angles was the fact that each petty Celtic king made war against the kings around him. Where once they had given at least a nominal obeisance to Ambrosius Aurelianus as High King, now they fought each other while the invading barbarians established their own kingdoms along the coasts.

"I had thought to drive out the barbarians," Arthur said so softly that I—riding behind him as a squire should—could barely hear his somber voice.

"We will," said Gawain lightly. "Next spring, once the weather clears."

"And who will till the fields?" Arthur asked bitterly. "Who will build new houses? Who will make the land green and prosperous again?"

Gawain laughed. "That's peasants' work, not fit for a knight to dirty his hands with."

Gawain spurred his mount and trotted up ahead, to where Lancelot was riding point, alert now for ambushers along the trail, leaving Arthur to plod along in somber silence.

"I wish Merlin were here," he muttered, more to himself than me.

"You don't need Merlin anymore, my lord," I said, nosing my mount to trot alongside him on his right, the side that would be unprotected by his shield in battle.

"Perhaps not," he said, with a rueful smile. "But I'd feel better if he were here."

We would not beat the winter, I realized. Later in the day it began to snow softly, quietly, as the pale sun dipped low behind the silver-gray clouds that had blanketed the sky all afternoon. Silently the wet flakes drifted down through the calm, cold air, frigid as death. I have never liked snow, not since I had been killed by a cave bear in the bone-cracking cold of the Ice Age, many lifetimes ago.

"We'll have to camp up there," Arthur said, standing in his stirrups and pointing to a grove of deeply green yews off to the side of the trail. The woods climbed up the slope of the hills. A good place for an ambush, I thought.

That evening we were attacked again. Most of the knights and squires were dismounted, huddled around meager fires, shivering in their jerkins and cloaks as they waited for the evening meal.

"Where's the cook wagons?" Sir Bors growled. "They should be here by now."

Arthur turned to me. "Find them and hurry them here, Orion."

With an obedient nod I replied, "Yes, my lord."

Yet I did not like to leave Arthur's side. I knew that Aten and others among the Creators were plotting his death, and I had vowed to protect the young Dux Bellorum.

Ambrosius was dying, if the word from the south could be believed. Many among the knights were already muttering among themselves that Arthur should be the next king. That is why Aten wanted him killed.

I rode my tired steed through the dark, snowy evening, searching for the kitchen train that should have caught up with the main body of our column an hour ago.

I saw the flicker of flames through the black boles of the leafless trees. Urging my mount forward, I began to hear the shouts and curses of men fighting. And dying.

The kitchen wagons were strung along the trail, two of them ablaze, churls and cooks desperately trying to defend themselves against men attacking from both sides of the trail. Most of the kitchen workers were huddled beneath the wagons, a few on their roofs, fighting with knives and meat hooks, swinging heavy iron pots like clubs, using whatever they could lay their hands on as weapons.

My senses shifting into overdrive, I drew my sword and spurred my horse into a charge. I saw that the attackers were hardly better armed than their victims. They looked to be young men, boys even, fighting with staves and hunting knives for the most part. A few of them had bows, and they were standing off to the far side of the trail, trying to pick off the men fighting from atop the wagons.

With the loudest, most ferocious yell I could muster I charged the bowmen. They whirled to face me. To my hyperalert senses their movements seemed sluggish, listless, like men moving through molasses. In the lurid light of the flaming wagons I saw their eyes widen as I charged at them. Two of them pulled arrows from the quivers at their hips and began to pull their bow strings back.

They both got off their shots before I could reach them. I saw the arrows floating lazily through the snowy air, spinning as they flew. I had neither shield nor helmet with me, even my coat of chain mail lay bundled in the pack behind my saddle. The first arrow I flicked away with my sword but the second hit my horse in the neck. I felt him stumble as I swung one leg over the saddle and leaped to the ground a scant few feet in front of the bowmen.

They were all nocking arrows, but they were far too slow to save themselves. I slashed into them, my sword ripping the nearest one into a geysering fountain of blood. The next one fell, his head severed from his shoulders, and the others dropped their bows and ran.

I turned to the footmen battling the kitchen help hand to hand. They were totally unprepared for a swordsman, and I was no ordinary fighter. Within minutes they were running, howling, into the snow-filled night.

The men who had ducked under the wagons scrambled out now and got to their feet. Friar Samson was among them, his rough homespun robe caked with snow and dirt.

"God has sent us a deliverer!" he cried. Despite his frail body he spoke with a voice powerful enough to fill a cathedral. "On your knees, all of you, and give thanks!"

I said nothing, but I thought of Aten and the other self-styled gods. If Samson knew that they were deciding his fate, playing with the human race the way mortals play at chess, I wonder what he would think of his God?

Once up from their knees, the kitchen men turned into fierce warriors now that the enemy was beaten, and began to cheerfully slit the throats of the poor fools who lay in the snow wounded and too weak to defend themselves. Friar Samson ignored the slaughter, but I stopped them, yanking one of the butchers off the back of a screaming, crying boy who could have been no more than twelve or thirteen.

"We'll march these prisoners back to Arthur," I commanded. "Let him decide their fate."

Reluctantly, they allowed me to take the two youths who were still alive and able to walk. I walked with them, after giving my downed horse a merciful thrust through the heart.

3

The knights and squires roared with approval when the kitchen wagons creaked into camp. Arthur, though, sat grimly on a fallen log as I explained to him what happened. Bors, standing to one side with his burly arms folded across his chest, looked ready to hang both prisoners.

At last Arthur turned to the two wounded youths. One of them had been stabbed in the arm, the other's face was swollen on one side, where a kitchen churl had banged him with a skillet.

The youths sank to their knees before Arthur. He wore only a plain rough tunic over his chain mail, but Excalibur gleamed in its jeweled scabbard by his side, and it was clear to them that this young warrior with the soft brown beard and sad amber eyes was a man of authority, even though Arthur was not that many years older than they.

"Why do you attack us?" Arthur demanded. "We are fighting the invaders to protect you. Is this the thanks you give?"

"Hunger, my lord," answered the smaller of the two. His voice cracked, whether from puberty or fear I could not tell.

"Our village is in ruins," the older one said, a smoldering trace of resentment in his deeper voice. "You have much; we have nothing."

"You have a dozen dead friends," Bors growled, "if Orion's story is to be believed."

"Two of them were our brothers," replied the younger one, his face downcast.

Arthur shook his head. "Orion, find Kay. Tell him to send these two back to their village, or what's left of it. Let each of them take as much food as they can carry."

Bors' eyes popped. He started to object, but Arthur forestalled him with an upraised hand.

"We are not your enemies," he told the youths. "War has ravaged the land. We are trying to drive out the invaders so that we can all live in peace once again."

I took the prisoners to Kay and explained Arthur's decision. Kay looked dubious, reluctant, but he piled both youths' arms with food from the nearest wagon. The boys scampered away, despite their wounds, staggering slightly under their loads.

As I watched them disappear into the snowy darkness, I thought that Arthur knew how to be a king. If he lived long enough, he might indeed bring peace to this troubled land.

4

I wrapped myself in a thick, rough blanket and leaned my back against one of the yew trees. I had volunteered to stand watch because I need little sleep. Another of the superior abilities that Aten had given me. He had built me to be a warrior, with all the strength and bloodlust that a killer requires. Yet I was sick of killing, tired of the endless wheel of death and blood.

The piercing cold of the winter night began to seep through the blanket. Without consciously thinking of it, I clamped down on the blood vessels close to my skin, to keep my body's interior warmth from escaping. Still, the bitter cold and the wet flakes of snow chilled me. I unbuckled my sword and leaned it against the trunk of the tree. I could feel the dagger that Odysseos had given me, ages ago at Troy, pressing iron cold against my thigh where I kept it strapped beneath my tunic.

All I really cared for was Anya, the gray-eyed goddess whom the ancient Greeks knew as Athena. She was the only one among the Creators who truly cared for the human beings that her fellow Creators used as puppets. I loved Anya, a desperate, foolish passion that roused the jealousy of Aten, that egomaniac. She loved me, too. As impossible as it seems, this goddess, this Creator, loved me just as I loved her. Time after time, in the frozen wastes of the Ice Age and the temperate Paradise of the Neolithic, in the Macedonia of Alexander the Great and the far-flung interstellar empire of the Fourth Millennium, Anya had loved me and tried to protect me from the cruel whims of Aten and the other Creators.

As I sat in the cold, snowy woods, with the campfires dying down to smoldering ashes, I thought of Anya. Aten and the other Creators tried to keep us apart, but she had come to me here, in

Arthur's time. She had helped me. Arthur called her the Lady of the Lake. I knew her to be my love.

I saw a glow deep in the woods, just a tiny pinpoint of light but it didn't flicker as a fire would. It was as steady as a shining star. And growing brighter.

I jumped to my feet, the blanket falling from my shoulders. Snow was still sifting silently through the night; the green branches of yews were decked with white, bending under the growing weight of the snow.

And the light was getting brighter, coming closer.

Anya! I hoped. Could it be her?

"Not your precious Anya," called a deeply resonant male voice. "She has no time for you now."

He stepped out from the trees and I could see that it was the Creator who called himself Hades. He was tall and broad of shoulder, cloaked in a magnificent mantle as black as infinite space, threaded with finest traceries of blood red. His hair and close-cropped beard were dark, his eyes darker still, like polished onyx.

"I understand that Arthur misses his old mentor, Merlin," said Hades.

Merlin was in reality Hades, appearing in disguise to guide Arthur in his youth. Aten and most of the other Creators wanted Arthur killed, so he could not interfere with their grandiose plans for a barbarian empire that would keep humankind enslaved for millennia. Hades had opposed them originally, but now was moving toward their camp.

"You swore that you wouldn't interfere."

Hades smiled cruelly. "A promise made to a creature? How will you keep me to it, Orion? You can't even move your fingertips."

It was true. I stood frozen like a block of ice, totally under his control.

"But you can feel pain," Hades said.

Suddenly my chest constricted in white-hot agony. I couldn't cry out, couldn't even breathe. My legs were too weak to hold me up. I toppled like a felled tree onto the cold snowy ground.

Hades bent low and whispered to me. "Merlin will see Arthur one more time, Orion, whether you like it or not. At the castle of his foster father, Ector. Make certain that Arthur goes there, Orion. Elsewise, this little pang I've given you will feel like a love tap."

The pain ebbed. I lay gasping on the snowy ground as Hades drew himself up to his full height and turned away, laughing softly to himself.

Rage filled me. Despite the lingering pain I lunged at his retreating back, whipping out Odysseos' dagger as I leaped. I hit his body with a satisfying thud and we both fell to the ground. Before he could think I had the dagger's point under his chin. His eyes went wide as I pressed it deep enough to draw blood.

"Once you take human form you, too, can feel pain," I snarled. "You can feel death."

And then he was gone. Vanished. I lay alone on the wet cold snow, my dagger in hand, my anger melting into helpless frustration. I drove the dagger into the snow hard enough to penetrate the frozen ground beneath.

"That was foolhardy, Orion."

I turned over onto my back and Anya stood above me, splendid in white fur that reached to her booted feet. A hint of a smile curved her beautiful lips slightly. Her gray eyes were serious, though, almost solemn.

"You cannot kill a Creator, Orion," she said calmly. "You know that."

Scrambling to my feet, I replied, "I can frighten him, though. The terror in his eyes was worth the pain he inflicted on me."

Anya shook her head like a schoolteacher disappointed with her pupil. "Orion, my love, no matter how they provoke you, you must remember that many lives are at stake here. You must think of Arthur and all the others you have sworn to help and protect."

I nodded meekly. "Hades intends to see Arthur in his guise as Merlin."

"At Ector's castle, I know," she replied.

"Is it a trap?" I asked. "Do they intend to assassinate Arthur there?"

"No," Anya replied. "But it will be a test. Both you and Arthur will face a test that will be crucial to the unfolding of this line of spacetime."

"At Ector's castle."

"Yes. In Wales. Up in the mountains."

"But we're heading south, for Cadbury. The High King is ill. Dying."

"You must bring Arthur to Wales, Orion. To the country where he grew up as a boy."

"And the High King?"

"Trust me, Orion." Anya's image was fading, flickering in the dim light of the fading campfires.

"Don't leave me!"

"I must, my darling. I don't want to, but I must." She became as dim and misty as a ghost.

"Wait! Please!"

"There is too much for me to do, Orion. I cannot stay."

She faded into nothingness, leaving me standing in the snow with my dagger in one hand and my heart as empty as the distant-most stretches of outer space.

Why? I raged to myself. Why can't we be together? The Creators manipulate space and time as easily as you or I walk across a room. Why can't Anya be with me? How can she truly love me when we're kept apart?

Then, in the deepest cavern of my mind I heard Aten's sneering laughter. It is he who keeps us apart, I realized. Him and his fellow Creators. My fists clenched and I longed for the day when I would destroy them all.

5

It wasn't difficult to get Arthur to move into the mountains of Wales. Obviously we were not going to outrun the winter; snow and biting gales swept over us, day after day.

"We used to go sledding down these hills, Kay and I," Arthur was saying, smiling happily for the first time in many weeks. "We'd steal shields from the armory hall and ride them in the snow."

It was a bright, clear morning when we saw Ector's castle standing atop a steep hill, its watchtower silhouetted against the crisp blue sky. The storms had moved away, the air was bitingly cold but as clear as polished crystal. Arthur trotted up ahead, Lancelot and Arthur's foster brother, Kay, at his side, men and horses puffing steamy clouds of breath into the cold morning. I stayed slightly behind them, as a properly humble squire should. But I scanned the woods on either side of the climbing trail, alert for danger.

Ector was Arthur's foster father. Merlin had brought the infant to him, and Ector had raised Arthur to be the strong young man he was now, with his own son, Kay, as Arthur's playmate and brother. None of us knew who Arthur's true father was, although

Ambrosius had accepted the youth as his own nephew, knighted him, and made him his Dux Bellorum, battle leader.

All the scheming politics and blood-soaked battles seemed far from Arthur's mind as he spurred his mount up the final turn of the trail that ended at the castle gate. Like many of the castles of this dark age, Ector's castle Wroxeter stood near the ruins of a Roman city, Viroconium. We had passed the city, down in the valley below: its crumbling dark stone walls had awed Arthur's knights, even frightened some of them.

"No human hands could have built such walls," I heard some-one mutter behind me. "This must have been the work of giants."

"Or wizards," half whispered another voice.

I merely shook my head. Ordinary men had built those stone walls. Other ordinary men had put the town to the torch, gutted its stately homes and public edifices, hauled away many of the stones for their own buildings.

Part of Ector's castle was stone, I saw. The base of its outer wall was a haphazard collection of stones scavenged from the Roman town. Atop it was a stout wooden palisade, with a slightly tilting wooden watchtower flanking the main gate. Very few castles were entirely built of stone at this time. Morganna's keep in Berenicia was stone, although the other buildings inside its walls were wood and even wattle. The High King's headquarters at Cadbury was the wonder of its age: walls, buildings, towers, even the stables were solid stone.

As Arthur and his retinue came up to the castle gate, a hel-meted head appeared at the tower top and called, "Who approaches the castle of Sir Ector?"

Sir Kay stood in his stirrups and proclaimed, "His son, Sir Kay, with his foster brother, Arthur, Dux Bellorum to the High King."

It took no small time, but eventually a wizened, white-bearded face appeared at the tower's top. "Kay? And Arthur? Have my boys truly come home?"

"Yes, Father!" Arthur shouted happily. "I've come home."

6

Ector appeared overjoyed to see his son and foster son once again. He welcomed us personally as we rode through the castle gate and dismounted onto the snow-covered packed earth of the courtyard. Arthur towered over the old man, but he stooped down and embraced his foster father with all the warmth of a son's love.

Friar Samson insisted on offering a mass of thanksgiving for our safe arrival at Wroxeter castle; we had little choice but to participate there in the cold morning, heads bowed in pious respect. All the other knights knelt on the snowy ground, together with most of the squires. I stood to one side, watching to make certain no one knifed Arthur while he prayed.

At last the knights were shown to quarters in the stoutly timbered, largest structure of the castle, each attended by one squire. Arthur chose me to accompany him, for which I was grateful. All the others of the army had to camp outside the castle's main wall.

As soon as we were settled a page appeared at Arthur's open door and announced that Sir Ector would receive Arthur and his knights in the great hall, downstairs.

Ector's great hall was not as big as I had expected, although it was well timbered and its earthen floor pounded smooth and swept clean. The old man sat in a high-backed wooden chair next to the enormous fireplace that covered one entire wall of the room. Big enough for half a dozen men to sit in, the fireplace had only a meager fire crackling in it, sending gray smoke up the wide stone chimney.

Ector's wrinkled, white-bearded face was wreathed in smiles. "Tonight we will feast," he said in a high, piping voice as Arthur strode up to him. "But now, I have a surprise for you!"

He turned in his chair toward a curtained doorway. Merlin stepped through.

He appeared older than Ector, with a beard the color of ashes that ran all the way down to his belt and long white hair that flowed past his shoulders. He looked newly scrubbed and combed; often enough I had seen him as mangy as a bedraggled alley cat. This day he wore a handsome long robe of midnight blue decked with glittering stars that fell in soft folds down to the floor. Its hem was richly trimmed with fur, as was its collar and the cuffs of the wide sleeves. Despite his seeming years he stood erect and walked with a purposeful stride to stand beside Ector's chair. I could see his eyes clearly beneath their shaggy gray brows: they were the eyes of Hades, black and glittering like two chips of flint.

"Merlin!" Arthur exclaimed, sheer joy on his face. "They told me you had disappeared."

In a soft, quavering voice that matched his graybeard's disguise, Merlin replied, "I left Cadbury castle to meet you here, Arthur."

"You must have flown like the hawk of your namesake," Arthur said, awed.

Merlin replied archly, "I did not walk that long distance, true enough."

"But how did you know I'd be here?" Arthur gaped. "I didn't decide to come here myself until—" Then he stopped, grinning foolishly. "Oh. Of course. You knew it all along, didn't you?"

Merlin/Hades smiled benignly. But his eyes remained cold, remorseless. He glanced at me, and my blood turned to ice.

Is he here to assassinate Arthur? I wondered. And if he is, how could I possibly stop him?

7

That night Ector feasted Arthur and his knights. Sir Kay sat at one side of the old man, Arthur on the other. The wine was thin and slightly sour, but nobody seemed to mind. Mead and beer were there in abundance. Soon the men were throwing chunks of meat and even whole chickens across the table, laughing uproariously with each greasy-fingered toss, each spill of a mug across the planks of the long table.

I sat down among the other squires, far from the roaring blaze in the fireplace and the noisy, brawling men. I could never get drunk. My metabolism burned off alcohol almost as quickly as I could swallow the stuff. It made me warm enough to perspire heavily, though, despite my distance from the fireplace.

I noticed that Lancelot touched nothing but water, although he ate as heartily as any of the others. Gawain, Bors, and even Kay got uproariously drunk. I could have knifed all of them, I thought, before any of them realized what was happening. Arthur, though, remained sober enough. And so did Ector, although he laughed wheezingly at the knights' antics so hard I thought he would choke.

Merlin did not attend the feast. I thought I knew why. The rowdy merriment of mere mortals probably disgusted him. So be it, I thought, noticing that pinch-faced Friar Samson also was not present, and probably for much the same reason.

By the time the fire had gone down to smoldering, smoky ashes and most of the knights were snoring, their heads lolling on their shoulders or resting peacefully on the beer-soaked planks of the long table, Ector turned to Arthur and whispered something in his ear. He glanced smilingly at his son Kay, snoring loudly at his other side. Ector got up from his chair and Arthur got to his feet and followed his foster father out of the hall.

I moved silently behind them, intent on protecting Arthur from any attempt on his life.

Ector led Arthur up a stairway and into what appeared to be his private quarters. It was a low-ceilinged room with a single window, closed with wooden shutters against the night winds. A large canopied bed stood to one side, mussed and unmade. Across the room was a trestle table and several chairs.

I stood in the doorway as Ector gestured Arthur to one of the chairs.

The old man glanced at me, then said, "Arthur, what I have to tell you is for your ears only."

"Orion is more than my squire, Father," replied Arthur. "I have no secrets from him."

Ector's white brows rose, but he shrugged and said to me, "Shut the door, then, and stand there."

"Yes, my lord," I said.

But no sooner had I shut it than I heard a scratching on the other side of the door. Not a knock. Scratching. Just as the ancient Egyptians and Trojans did.

Despite his years, Ector's hearing was still keen. "That would be Merlin. Let him in, squire."

Sure enough, it was Merlin, still in his star-flecked robe, although now he had a woolen skullcap pulled down over his ears.

I smiled inwardly. Taking human form brings human frailties with it. Hades felt cold.

Arthur got to his feet, a tall broad-shouldered young man among two wizened elders.

"Tell him the news," Ector said to Merlin.

The wizard paced slowly across the room to join Arthur and his foster father, never so much as glancing at me.

"Ambrosius is dying," Merlin said. "He will not survive the winter."

Arthur bowed his head. "My uncle has been very good to me. It's sad to lose him."

"Sad for Britain," said Ector. "Without a High King, every petty king in the land will make war on his neighbors."

"They are already doing so. The curse of the Celts," Arthur murmured, "unable to stand together against the invaders."

"The land needs a High King," said Merlin. "One who can bring all the Britons together."

Arthur asked, "Yes, but who?"

"You."

Arthur gaped at the wizard. "Me? That's impossible! The other kings would never accept it. I'm hardly twenty, and a bastard, as well."

"About your age," said Merlin, "nothing can be done. But about the circumstances of your birth . . ." He turned to Ector.

"You know who my true father is?" Arthur blurted out.

The old man nodded and reached a hand up to Arthur's shoulder. "My boy, your father was Uther Pendragon, he who was king over much of this land. He who kept the Saxons in check by making a truce with them. He who was betrayed by Vortigen and died fighting the truce-breaker."

Arthur sank down onto the wooden chair. "Uther Pendragon was my father?"

"Why else would I give you the red dragon as your emblem?" Ector asked kindly.

Merlin said, "Uther was your father and Igraine, his queen, your mother. But they were not yet married when you were conceived."

"So Uther asked me to raise you as my own son," Ector continued. "He promised to make your birth known and proclaim you as his son and heir once you had grown to manhood."

"But he died before he could do so. And your mother, also," Merlin added.

Arthur sat in stunned silence.

"You must return to Cadbury at once and claim your inheritance," said Ector.

"You must become the next High King," Merlin agreed.

I watched and listened in growing confusion. Which side is Hades on? I asked myself. Aten wants Arthur killed. Now Hades is telling Arthur he should be High King? That's exactly the opposite of what Aten desires. Or is this another of their subtle plots? Arthur claims the kingship and he's assassinated by one of the others who want the title. Is that their ploy?

"You are the only man in the realm who can bring the petty kingdoms together, Arthur," Ector was telling him. "Unless you make yourself High King, Britain will tear itself apart."

"And leave the pickings to the Saxons and the other barbarians," Merlin said.

I could see the anguish in Arthur's eyes. It was one thing to be the High King's battle leader and thrash the invading barbarians up and down the land. But to be High King himself! The possibility had never entered Arthur's mind before this very moment.

Even when Bors and the others had told Arthur that Ambrosius feared for his throne, Arthur had flatly proclaimed his loyalty to the High King.

Slowly, hesitantly, Arthur muttered, "I never thought . . . this is more than I . . . anyone . . ."

"You must," said Merlin.

Ector smiled down at him. "You can do it, my lad. No one else in the entire land of Britain can."

Still Arthur sat, blinking in doubt, uncertainty.

Still standing by the door, I spoke out. "Why else do you think the Lady of the Lake gave you Excalibur, my lord?"

The two old men glared at me. But Arthur clasped the jeweled hilt of the sword at his side and slowly got to his feet.

"She knew?"

"She knows that you can be a great king," I said. "It is your destiny."

He stood straighter, squared his shoulders. "Then . . . I suppose it must be."

Ector clapped his hands in glee. And froze there, his wrinkled face smiling so widely I could see the rotted stumps of his teeth, like an uneven picket fence. Arthur stood immobilized, too, his hand on Excalibur's hilt, his face set in grim anticipation.

Merlin turned to me. "Congratulations, Orion. You've convinced him he should be High King."

"You're the one who convinced him," I said, knowing that neither Ector nor Arthur could see or hear anything.

"I told you I'd be neutral in this matter," Merlin said, in Hades' rich baritone voice. "I've set him on the road to Cadbury. Now his fate is in the lap of the gods." He laughed at his little joke.

"And the gods want him dead," I said.

"Most of them do. They agree with Aten. Only Anya and a few of the others want Arthur to succeed."

"As I do."

He laughed again, louder and more bitterly. "You? You're not even a mortal, Orion. You're a creature, one of Aten's constructions. What difference does your opinion make?"

"We'll see," I said.

"Yes, indeed we will."

With that, Merlin/Hades disappeared. He winked out of existence, as if he'd never been there.

Arthur and Ector stirred out of their stasis.

"Where's Merlin?" Arthur asked, bewildered.

"Gone," I said.

"But how could he—"

Ector shrugged his frail shoulders. "He's a mighty wizard, Arthur. His comings and goings are pure magic."

I remembered from somewhere in another lifetime the words of a very wise man: any sufficiently advanced technology is indistinguishable from magic.

8

The following morning Arthur was in a sweat to get started for Cadbury. The sky was a cloudless bright blue, but the land lay under a thick blanket of snow. With only a handful of his best knights—and their squires—Arthur left castle Wroxeter and headed south. Friar Samson accompanied us, wrapped in a thick black hooded robe, offering prayers and blessings as we left.

Ector insisted on coming along, despite the frailty of his years.

"I'll go only as far as castle Cameliard," he said, "to make certain that King Leodegrance makes you welcome."

Despite the numbing cold the weather was beautiful: the drifts of snow glittered beneath the crystal sky. Our horses floundered through the deep drifts as we rode slowly, painfully southward. And I wondered what awaited us at castle Cameliard.

9

If Leodegrance styled himself a king, I thought, he must be a very meager one. Cameliard was a ramshackle set of thatch-roofed buildings set on a hilltop and surrounded by a palisade of lopsided, sagging staves; their tops once has been sharpened to points but now they looked weathered, blunted, sadly neglected.

The castle's chamberlain recognized Sir Ector and quickly invited us to spend the night. Our horses' hooves boomed on the warped planks of the sagging drawbridge that covered the moat, which was filled with reeking putrid garbage instead of water. The chamberlain saw us safely quartered in one wing of the main building, then ushered Arthur and Ector to an audience with the king. I went with them, Arthur's squire, as unnoticed as a fly on the wall.

Leodegrance sat on a throne of age-dulled oak. He was iron gray: his beard had obviously not felt a brush in weeks, his untrimmed hair fell lank and greasy below his shoulders, his face was square and blocky, his eyes the color of a steel blade. His tunic looked new and clean, however. He smiled at Arthur as he and Ector approached the throne and made courteous bows, but I thought his smile had little warmth in it. To me his smile didn't seem forced, merely insincere. I remained at the doorway with Kay, who served as his father's squire this day.

Once Ector introduced Arthur and explained that he was going to Cadbury to claim his right as the son of Uther Pendragon
to be High King, Leodegrance's smile went even colder, crafty.
Something was being calculated behind those iron-gray eyes, I
knew.

Throwing aside the usual diplomatic niceties, Ector asked
bluntly if Leodegrance would support Arthur's claim.

To my surprise the king answered, "The son of Uther Pendragon? Of course you have my support."

Before Arthur could utter a word of thanks, though, Leodegrance's perpetual smile widened slyly and he added, "Under one
condition."

Ector said, "A condition?"

"A High King requires a wife, so that he can have legitimate
heirs who will carry on his line," said Leodegrance.

"True," Ector agreed. "But Arthur is scarcely twenty. There is
plenty of time for him to find a wife."

Ector did not know, of course, that Arthur had already sired a
son, Modred, by the witch Morganna. She was raising him in her
castle in Bernicia, beyond Hadrian's Wall, raising him to hate his
father.

"No need to search any farther for your wife, young Arthur,"
Leodegrance said, smiling with all his teeth now. "I have a daughter, Guinevere. You will meet her tonight at dinner."

Arthur looked as if someone had poleaxed him.

10

Guinevere turned out to be pretty and very young, slim and
sprightly as an elf, with long chestnut hair that tumbled down

her back and sparkling brown eyes. All through dinner she chattered away nervously, sitting between Arthur and her father. Arthur picked at the slab of beef set before him; Guinevere ate heartily, tearing into the roast with both hands, talking every minute. From my seat across the room, crowded in with the other squires and the slavering shaggy hounds, I thought she seemed jumpy, almost frightened. And down at the end of the high table sat Friar Samson, his brows knit into a scowl, hardly touching the meat set before him.

At the other end of the high table sat young Lancelot. His eyes never left Guinevere, not for a moment.

Is this the test that Anya warned me about? I asked myself. Arthur certainly looks uncomfortable, sitting next to her. Does Leodegrance plan to assassinate Arthur and claim the High Kingship for himself? Is Guinevere part of his plan?

I wished I could be up at the high table beside Arthur to taste his food and drink. My body absorbs most poisons and breaks them down into harmless ingredients. I have been bitten by venomous snakes without ill effect.

Despite my fears, Arthur got through the dinner with nothing more harmful than his discomfort at being placed beside the elfin Guinevere. At last the dinner ended. There was an awkward moment when the king pushed away the last bowl of apples and rose slowly and somewhat unsteadily to his feet. Everyone else stood, of course. Guinevere turned toward Arthur expectantly, but he simply stood beside her, his arms at his sides. After a few heartbeats she spun around and clutched at her father's arm. They walked off together, leaving Arthur standing there, looking befuddled.

Ector, Kay, and Friar Samson went with Arthur to the corner bedchamber that Leodegrance had given him. I went, too, determined to stand outside his door all night to guard against any possible treachery.

"Well," Ector asked, beaming, "what do you think of her, my boy?"

"Guinevere?" Arthur asked.

"Who else?"

Kay sat on the bed, bouncing slightly to test it. "She's a pretty little thing," he said, with a grin, patting the bedcover suggestively.

Arthur said nothing. I remembered how Morganna had enchanted him. Aphrodite, she styled herself: goddess of love and beauty. I myself had felt the power of her allure. It was clear to me that Arthur was still under her spell, at least a little.

"Guinevere will make a fine queen for you," Ector prompted. "You can be married here and bring her to Cadbury with you."

"No!" cried Friar Samson.

We all turned to him.

"This girl is a pagan," he said, his lean face hard and frowning. "She follows the old gods. She's not even been baptized!"

"Half the people of Britain have not been baptized," Ector said, frowning. "More than half."

"The High King must have a Christian wife," Samson insisted. "The example must be set."

"I'm a Christian," said Arthur. "Isn't that enough?"

The friar looked shocked. "How could you even think of taking a pagan for your wife?"

Arthur stared down at his boots for a moment, then said in a low voice, "I don't want her for my wife. I don't want to be married at all. Not now. Not yet."

Ector went to his side, took Arthur by the elbow, and guided him to the Roman-style wooden chair in the corner of the room.

Once Arthur was seated with Ector standing beside him, I realized that he and the old man were nearly eye-to-eye.

"Arthur, you have been like a true son to me."

"And you have been a good father to me," Arthur replied.

"Often I have given you advice. Has it ever been false or harmful?"

"No, never."

"Then heed me now, my boy. A king need not like his wife. Kings marry for political reasons, not for romance. A king can always find plenty of women to bed."

"That's sinful!" gasped Samson.

Ector ignored him. "You needn't like your queen. You only have to have a son by her."

Arthur looked torn, pained. "But my father—my actual father—he loved my mother, didn't he?"

Ector heaved a great sigh. "Ah, that was something else, my boy. Uther's passion for Igraine led him to go to war so he could possess her."

"Sin," hissed the friar. Arthur glared at him and he said no more.

"Marry Guinevere," Ector urged, "and you will gain Leodegrance's support. It would be foolish to make an enemy of him."

"Besides," Kay chimed in, still sitting on the bed, "she might be a lot of fun."

"But she's a pagan," Samson complained. "So is her father."

Ector was not deterred. "By marrying a pagan, Arthur, you show the people that you intend to be High King for everyone, not merely the Christians."

Samson looked horrified.

Quickly Ector added, "You can always baptize her after you're married. She'd have no choice but to obey you, then."

Arthur's head sank. "I've got to think about this," he muttered. "Please leave me now, all of you."

Reluctantly, Ector, Kay, and the friar left; Samson the most loath of all to leave before winning Arthur to his point of view. I went with them and stood outside Arthur's door in the drafty hallway as I watched them go to their bedchambers. Resting my back against the wooden wall, I listened to the wind moaning outside, intent on standing guard until daylight. The only light in the hallway came from a torch set into a sconce down by the stairway that led to Leodegrance's great hall. As the hours crept slowly by, it guttered and died, leaving me in darkness.

I need very little sleep, but I confess that I was drifting as I stood guard, my eyes heavy, my head sinking to my chest.

A sound snapped me to full attention. The creak of a floorboard; the padding of running feet. Someone was hurrying down the dark hallway, making no effort to be silent about it. I can see like a cat, and I quickly discerned the approaching figure of a man, sword unsheathed.

I pulled out my sword and the figure stopped abruptly.

"Who's there? Orion, is that you?" Lancelot's voice, high and tense with anxiety.

"What are you doing, prowling about at night?" I whispered.

"Guinevere!" he said urgently. "She's being abducted!"

"What?"

"I saw them, out in the courtyard. A band of hooded men, all in white. Six or more. They have her with them!"

Kidnapping Arthur's intended bride? Why? Who? A thousand questions raced through my mind. I wondered if I should leave Arthur asleep and unguarded. Perhaps this was a ruse to draw me away from his door.

"Stay here and guard Arthur," I said to Lancelot. "I'll go after them."

"No! One man can't fight them all."

"But—" It was too late. He was already running down the hallway toward the stairs that led down to the courtyard, shouting, "To arms! Rise! Awake! To arms!"

I had no choice but to follow him. He was right: one man could not face a half-dozen armed enemies, not even Lancelot. Behind me I could hear grumbles and curses as Arthur's knights stumbled out of their beds.

Down the wooden stairs Lancelot bounded and out into the numbing cold of the courtyard, with me two steps behind him. The stars were like hard gleaming diamonds in the freezing black sky. Lancelot had a cloak over his shoulders, but it flew open as he ran.

Lancelot hesitated a heartbeat, looked around, then pointed his sword toward the postern gate.

"That's the way they were taking her!"

"How did you come to see them?" I puffed as I hurried after him.

"I was up in the tower, keeping watch," he called back over his shoulder.

"We should wait for Arthur and the others."

"No time! God knows what they could do to her if we don't reach them quickly!"

My mind kept warning me that this could be a trap, but I couldn't imagine Lancelot betraying Arthur. The young knight worshipped Arthur, followed him like a puppy.

The postern gate was ajar. "They're in a hurry," I said as we ducked through it.

Beyond the snow-covered ground at the castle wall's base, a pair of logs had been lain across the refuse-filled ditch of the moat. They stood out dark and bare against the snow. Guinevere's captors had laid them there to speed their escape. Did they know Lancelot and I were pursuing them?

I could see no sign of horses in the dim starlight. They were on foot. There was a rough trail through the snow that led into the woods made by more than six pairs of boots, I saw.

Lancelot plunged into the woods as if he were chasing a single helpless foe. I pushed on after him as he followed the trail through the banks of snow. Up ahead, through the black boles of the trees, I saw a light. It flickered fitfully; not one of the Creators, I reasoned. It looked more like a bonfire.

Lancelot was plunging ahead, hell-bent to reach the kidnappers. I grabbed him by the shoulder and forced him to thump heavily down in the snow.

"Wait!" I whispered. "See how many we face before you go dashing in."

"They might harm her!" he whispered back. "Kill her!"

"Getting yourself killed won't help her," I said.

He shook free of my grip and crawled through the snow toward the firelight, his sword glinting in his right hand. I looked back along the trail we had come. No sign of any of the knights, neither could I hear anyone coming along after us.

Setting my teeth, I pushed through the snowdrifts, following Lancelot. He had dropped to one knee, eying the scene before him like a lion sizing up its prey.

In a small clearing a dozen white-robed figures were standing hand in hand, forming a ring around a blazing bonfire taller than a full-grown man. And Guinevere was standing with them, wearing nothing but a gossamer shift, her chestnut hair tumbling down below her waist, holding hands with the men on her right and left.

"Druids!" Lancelot whispered.

"They've been outlawed since the Romans ruled Britain," I said.

"But now they've returned to their ancient rites."

Human sacrifice was part of their ancient rites, I knew.

Lancelot tensed to spring into their midst. The Druids did not seem to be carrying arms of any kind, yet who knew what lay hidden beneath the folds of their robes?

Again I grasped Lancelot's shoulder, holding him down. He tried to wrench free, but I whispered into his ear, "They don't seem to be harming her."

As I spoke, they began to dance. Somewhere out of the darkness came the eerie wail of a wooden flute, and the Druids—with Guinevere among them—began a stately, slow dance circling around the crackling, sparking fire.

I stood up and Lancelot rose beside me. Together we walked out of the shadows of the trees, into the clearing, toward Guinevere. The Druids stopped, froze into immobility. I could see the shock on their long-bearded faces as the two of us advanced on them with drawn swords.

"Stop!" Guinevere commanded, holding out both hands to us.

"We've come to rescue you," said Lancelot.

"Rescue me? These are my friends."

"Friends? Bloody Druids?"

The Druids seemed thoroughly frightened of us. They were slowly backing away from us and our shining sharp-edged blades.

"We thought they were abducting you," I said.

Slight as a sparrow, Guinevere stepped toward me, no trace of fear in her demeanor. "They are helping me to escape."

"Escape?" Lancelot asked. "From what?"

"From Arthur. From marriage. He doesn't want me for a bride and I don't want to be married to anyone. Especially not to him!"

Lancelot looked as if she had clouted him between the eyes with a quarterstaff.

Through the dark woods I heard the shouts of angry men. Arthur's knights were approaching, probably with Arthur at their lead.

The Druids heard them, too. Without word among them, they bolted in the opposite direction and disappeared into the woods.

"So much for your friends," I said to Guinevere.

Her brown eyes snapped angrily at me. "What can they expect at the hands of Friar Samson and his like? Your holy man would burn my friends at the stake."

Yes, I thought, and sow the seeds of bitter enmity between Arthur and the pagans still living in Britain. A civil war of the most brutal kind would be the result.

At that moment, Bors and Kay burst into the clearing, swords in their hands. Leodegrance and Arthur were right behind him, the king of Cameliard looking more than a little ridiculous in his night shift, with a shield on one arm and a heavy battle-mace in the other. He was not smiling now. Arthur had thrown on his chain mail. Excalibur gleamed in the firelight.

"It's all right, sire," I said, thinking as fast as I could. "A band of cutthroats abducted the princess, but Lancelot drove them off single-handedly."

Lancelot's jaw fell open at that, but he said nothing.

"They intended to hold Guinevere for ransom, sire," I went on, "knowing that she is to be your bride."

Arthur looked me in the eye, then nodded as if he knew what was going on. Sheathing his sword, he turned away from me and grasped Lancelot by both shoulders.

"Thank you," he said. "You have saved the honor of my bride-to-be."

Lancelot stammered, "It . . . that is . . . I was glad to do it, sire."

For an awkward moment we all stood there next to the roaring bonfire, feeling slightly foolish. Then Arthur said, "Back to the castle, everyone."

Lancelot took off his cloak and draped it around Guinevere's slight shoulders. She smiled at him, then stepped to Arthur's side and allowed him to take her hand.

As the others started back toward the castle, Lancelot stood there in the clearing, looking downcast.

I said to him, low enough so that only he could hear it, "Arthur owes you a great debt, although he'll never know of it. You may have saved the kingdom this night."

Lancelot said nothing. His eyes were following Guinevere as she allowed Arthur to lead her back to the castle, back to their wedding. But she glanced back at Lancelot and smiled sadly.

In my mind, I heard Anya whisper, "*You* saved Arthur's realm from bloody civil war, Orion. Well done."

Before I could bask in the glow of her approval, though, Aten's smug voice intruded into my thoughts. "Very well done, indeed, Arthur. The seeds of Arthur's destruction took root tonight."

And he laughed his sneering, hateful laugh in the cold, dark winter night.

BOOK II

King of the Britons

CHAPTER EIGHT

The Sword of Kingship

1

Leaving Guinevere at castle Cameliard, Arthur, Bors, and Gawain—accompanied only by their squires—galloped south toward Cadbury castle and the dying Ambrosius Aurelianus. Guinevere and her father, King Leodegrance, were to follow us at a slower pace, escorted by Arthur's foster brother, Kay, and the rest of his knights—including Lancelot.

In truth, I thought that Arthur was glad to leave Guinevere and all thoughts of marriage behind him as we speeded toward Cadbury and his dying uncle.

By the time we finally reached Cadbury castle, its high main gate was draped in black. Ambrosius was dead.

His body lay in state in the castle's great hall, lying on a high catafalque with four armed knights standing at its corners, their heads bowed in grief. Ambrosius was decked in his finest mail and helm, his two-handed broadsword clutched in his mail-gloved hands. Its pommel was at his chin, the tip of its scabbard reached below his knees.

Even though the hall was wide and its ceiling so high it was lost in shadows, we could smell the sour-sweet odor of decay as soon as we entered, despite the heaps of sage, rosemary, and thyme that had been laid all around the bier. Arthur, Gawain, and Bors approached the body respectfully, while I stood by the entrance to the tapestry-covered stone hall, as a squire should. Even at that distance, though, I could see that Ambosius' cheeks were sunken beneath the heavy steel helmet that had been placed on his gray-bearded head.

Once we left the hall, Ambrosius' chamberlain led the knights to their quarters in the high stone keep of the castle. I followed at a respectful distance, alert as always for possible treachery.

The chamberlain seemed harmless enough, though. He was a man in his late thirties, I judged, his severely trimmed dark hair just beginning to show touches of gray. He was wire thin and fairly quivering with nervous energy. As chamberlain he must have eaten well, but it seemed to me that he burned off whatever he ate; he would never get fat.

"Kings and knights from all over the land are hastening to Cadbury," he said, in a clear tenor voice that sounded totally free of grief. "I don't know where we'll be able to put them all."

Arthur nodded solemnly. "They'll want to elect a new High King once Ambrosius is buried."

Walking behind them, I couldn't see the chamberlain's face, but I heard the surprise in his voice. "A new High King? Not likely! Who could replace Ambrosius Aurelianus?"

Gawain said, "He died without leaving an heir, I understand."

"He has no acknowledged sons," the chamberlain replied tactfully.

"Then someone must be named to take possession of this fine castle," Gawain said.

"I suppose there will be battles fought over it, yes," said the chamberlain, his tone now rueful.

Bors said, "Arthur is his nearest living relative. Arthur should have the castle and all its lands."

The chamberlain was silent for many paces along the stone-floored corridor. At last he said, "Perhaps so. But there will be others to contest his claim."

"No," Arthur snapped. "We must not fight among ourselves."

Bors shook his doughty head. "There's no other way, my boy. You'll have to fight for your rightful inheritance."

♌

The chamberlain was right. Knights and self-styled kings from all the corners of Britain descended upon Cadbury castle. Ostensibly, they came to pay their last respects to the High King. Actually, they were looking for a way to gain possession of Ambrosius' estate. And title.

Through the next several days, while the old man's body rotted so badly that all the sweet-smelling herbs in the kingdom could not disguise the odor of decaying flesh, the growing number of noblemen quarreled and squabbled over Ambrosius' inheritance. Good-natured practice bouts in the courtyard often turned into bruising fights that drew blood.

Arthur stayed clear of such engagements.

"I wish Merlin were here," he sighed as we watched a pair of self-styled kings thwacking each other with wooden staves.

Standing beside him in the chilly courtyard, Bors said, "The wizard has gone. Who knows when he will return? If ever."

"But I need him!" Arthur said. "We've got to find a way to settle this inheritance peacefully."

I told him, "You'll have to find the way for yourself, my lord."

He looked at me doubtfully.

"You can do it," I encouraged. "I'm sure you can. And by doing it, you will prove your right to be High King."

Arthur shook his head dejectedly and turned to pace the snow-covered castle courtyard in the bone-numbing cold of early morning, with Bors and I on either side of him.

"We've got to get the body into the ground before he stinks up the whole castle," Bors grumbled.

The sun had barely risen and the sky was a wintry dull gray, oppressive and dismal with the threat of more snow. The two battlers stopped their thwacking, breaths puffing steam in the cold air. Immediately their squires threw heavy fur-trimmed robes over their heaving shoulders.

Nodding to Bors, Arthur said, "I'll speak to the chamberlain. I know that Friar Samson has been making arrangements for the funeral with the bishop, from the cathedral."

The cathedral was little more than a stout stone church off in one corner of the courtyard, built more like a Roman fort than a place of worship.

"Kay should be bringing your bride and her father soon," Gawain said, almost smirking when Arthur visibly winced. "You can hold the wedding right after the funeral." With a laugh, he added, "Any leftovers from the funeral feast you can use for the wedding banquet!"

Arthur looked at his friend and companion for a long solemn moment. Finally he said, "There will be no wedding until we settle who gets Cadbury castle for his own."

Gawain laughed even more heartily. "I see. You want it for a wedding gift to Guinevere."

Arthur looked as if he could have throttled Gawain at that particular moment.

3

The funeral could wait no longer. Arthur asked Bishop Bron to conduct the ceremony. Stooped with age though he was, the bishop looked magnificent in his finest gold-threaded robes as he led the funeral mass. The dark thick-walled cathedral was so packed with the nobles who had come to Cadbury that mere squires were not admitted inside the church. I fretted out in the wind and snow, fearful that someone would try to assassinate Arthur during the funeral.

The mass ended without incident, though, and the bishop led the long procession through the beginnings of a snowstorm to the burial grounds outside the castle walls. Ambrosius' broadsword was placed atop his grave, fastened to the stone slab by rivets hammered in by a pair of beefy blacksmiths.

Once the bishop gave his final blessing to the kneeling knights, King Mark of Cornwall got to his feet and asked in a powerful voice, "Well, who gets the castle?"

Not be outdone, Bors bellowed, "Who will be the next High King?"

"We have no need of a High King!" said Mark. He was a powerfully built man: not tall, but wide in the shoulders and with a body shaped like a barrel. Dark of hair and eye, his face was pockmarked, his beard thin and lank.

"Yes we do!" Arthur shouted. "We must be united if we expect to drive out the barbarian invaders."

"Easy enough for you to say, lad," King Mark said. "Old Ambrosius favored you, everybody knows."

"He is Ambrosius' nephew," said another. "Of course the old man favored him."

"In truth, Arthur is not really Abrosius' nephew," Friar Samson pointed out. "The lad is a bastard." Turning to Arthur, the emaciated friar said more softly, "No offense, my lord, but the truth must be spoken."

Arthur stared at the friar and the older men surrounding him, bewilderment clearly written on his youthful face. I wished that I could push my way through the crowd to be closer to him. If this argument grew worse, blood could be drawn and Arthur struck down easily enough.

At last Arthur said calmly, "I am the son of Uther Pendragon,"

"Indeed!" King Mark scoffed.

"My foster father, Sir Ector, will vouch for that once he arrives here," Arthur insisted. "Merlin will tell you!"

"The old wizard?" one of the knights countered. "Why should we believe him?"

"A pagan," said Friar Samson.

"Where is he, anyway?" another voice demanded. "Why has he disappeared?"

Why indeed, I wondered. Apparently Hades had withdrawn from the contest, leaving this nexus in spacetime for Aten to handle as he sees fit. Anya would have few allies among the Creators, if any. But I vowed to myself all over again that I would defy Aten and protect young Arthur to my last breath.

Bishop Bron raised both his hands, silencing the noblemen. In a surprisingly strong voice he said, "This is not a matter to be decided in the snow and cold. Let us return to the castle and discuss it by a good warm fire."

A few chuckles rose from the assembled nobles. Heads nodded. Someone said, "The good bishop has more sense than we do."

Thus we returned to Cadbury castle.

Despite the blaze crackling in its huge fireplace, the great hall was scarcely warmer than the graveyard outside and still smelled faintly of decay.

The nobles asked the bishop to mediate their argument. They all remained standing, crowding around the bishop, who was still decked in his fine robes spun with gold thread. All of the nobles were armed with swords at their sides, all of them eager to have their say in the matter. The talk went on for hours, some of the knights insisting that a new High King must be named, most of them refusing to accept the need for a High King. Arthur's seemed to be the only voice raised that called for a united campaign against the Saxons and other invaders.

"You're the Dux Bellorum," said King Mark. "You raise an army and fight the barbarians. But stay out of Cornwall! I can handle the invaders by myself."

"None of the barbarians has landed on Cornwall's shores," a knight pointed out.

Mark smirked at him. "That's because the pagans know that I am king in Cornwall, and will deal with them sharply."

"Or perhaps," Gawain suggested, with a chuckle, "they know that Cornwall's so bleak it's not worth raiding."

Everyone laughed. Except King Mark.

At length even the bishop gave up and suggested that they have dinner and continue the discussion later in the evening.

"Discussion," Bors muttered as the knights and petty kings broke into small groups and headed for their quarters. "This isn't going to be settled by talk, Arthur. You're going to have to fight for what is rightfully yours."

Arthur shook his head. "We mustn't fight among ourselves. We've got to settle this peacefully."

Gawain clasped Arthur's shoulder. "Not among these men, my friend. Ambition and greed always outweigh common sense."

Before we could get out of the hall a serving boy scurried up to Arthur and, after bowing low, announced, "King Leodegrance and his daughter have arrived, my lord! The king asks for you, sir."

With the expression almost of a martyr, Arthur followed the boy out of the hall, heading toward the courtyard. I followed close behind.

4

A gentle snow was sifting through the chill air as we stepped into the courtyard to greet Arthur's future bride and her father, together with the knights who had escorted them from Cameliard castle.

Leodegrance looked tired from his journey, his gray beard bedraggled, his perpetual smile drooping. Guinevere seemed bright and pert as ever, although she hardly glanced at Arthur as she descended from their wagon.

Even Lancelot, normally eager and energetic, appeared drained and weary. "I've brought your bride safely to you, my lord," said Lancelot, avoiding Arthur's direct gaze.

Glancing at his foster brother, Kay, Arthur smiled at the younger knight. "I thought that Sir Kay was in charge of your journey."

Lancelot's youthful face flamed red. "Yes, of course, my lord. I simply meant . . ." His voice trailed off into an embarrassed silence.

Grasping Lancelot's shoulder, Arthur said, "Good work, sir knight. I thank you."

As the other knights dismounted from their steeds and the wag-ons creaked through the castle's open gate, Arthur offered Guine-vere his arm, to lead her inside the castle. She took her father's instead. Without saying a word, Arthur turned and led them to-ward the doorway, where the overwrought chamberlain stood in the stone doorway, out of the falling snow, his hands on his hips and his face clearly showing dismay as Arthur's knights filled the courtyard.

"Where am I going to put them all?" he wailed. "The castle is already filled to bursting."

Arthur said, almost apologetically, "These men have followed me the length and breadth of Britain. They have dealt the Saxons and other barbarians many heavy blows."

"But there isn't any room for them!" the chamberlain com-plained. "Where can I put them? How can I feed them?"

Lancelot said bravely, "We are accustomed to sleeping in the open. Find quarters in the castle for King Leodegrance and his daughter. The rest of us will camp in our tents here in the court-yard."

"Not in the courtyard!" the chamberlain exclaimed. "There are too many of you!"

"Outside the walls, then," said Sir Kay, with an irritated edge in his voice. "We wouldn't want to cause you any problems."

The chamberlain didn't feel his sarcasm. "And how can I feed such a host?"

"We'll hunt for game!" Lancelot replied eagerly. "We'll orga-nize a gigantic hunt."

Before the chamberlain could reply, Arthur said, "Well spoken, Lancelot." Turning to the fussing chamberlain, he added, "You see? My men can take care of themselves."

5

Despite the chamberlain's grumblings, Arthur saw to it that fully a dozen of his knights were invited inside the castle to have dinner with all the others in Cadbury's great hall.

I waited patiently in Arthur's quarters, watching as he changed into a fresh white tunic for dinner, wishing that I could sit beside him, fearing that among his rivals for Ambrosius' inheritance there was probably an assassin. Or perhaps more than one. Bors and the others were in rooms nearby, also preparing for dinner—and the debate about kingship that was to follow.

But just as Arthur was ready to leave his room for dinner, King Leodegrance rapped once on his door and entered, uninvited.

Without so much as a greeting, Leodegrance said bluntly, "I've been talking with the other nobles, Arthur. Many of them are unhappy that you are claiming Ambrosius' title."

Arthur nodded wearily. "I know."

His smile turning crafty, Leodegrance said, "I have a way to settle the matter, my boy."

Surprised, Arthur blurted, "You do?"

"Yes."

Impatiently, Arthur demanded, "Well, what is it?"

Looking as if he could part the Red Sea, Leodegrance explained, "You bow to the will of the assembled knights and withdraw your claim to be Ambrosius' heir."

"Withdraw . . . ?"

"Hear me out," Leodegrance said, raising both hands. "You withdraw, and throw your support to me."

"You?" Arthur looked stunned.

"Yes, me!" Leodregrance's face was wreathed with self-satisfaction. "You support me as High King. The others will agree, knowing that I am already a king among them."

"But—"

"You will continue to be my Dux Bellorum," Leodegreance want on. "You will marry my only daughter. When I die you will quite naturally inherit my title and powers. You will be High King!"

Leodegrance's smile was full of teeth. Arthur looked perplexed. I could read his mind, almost. All Arthur had wanted was to continue as Dux Bellorum and keep on trying to drive the Saxons and other barbarians out of Britain. Sly Leodegrance was offering him just that—at the price of helping Leodegrance to be named High King. I could see the conflict on Arthur's face. He was asking himself, Can I trust this smiling man? And must I marry his daughter?

6

As before, the evening's deliberations about Ambrosius' heritage settled nothing. The noblemen assembled in Cadbury's great hall were about evenly divided over the idea of naming a new High King. Some of them saw the necessity for unity; others cherished their individual rights and privileges more than anything else.

As Arthur had told me more than once, the curse of the Celts was their stubborn individuality, their inability to unite even in the face of looming catastrophe.

At times the arguments turned into nasty, snarling quarrels, with one knight challenging a rival's right to claim the castle or even to dream of being named High King. Bishop Bron, frail in body though he was, stepped between the angry men and made them back down.

"Civility," the bishop demanded. "This matter will *not* be turned into a brawl."

At length the knights and petty kings retired to their chambers, Arthur frustrated and disconsolate.

"If only Merlin were here," he said to me as he entered his bedroom. "Merlin would know what to do."

I said nothing, knowing that Hades, the Creator who had helped young Arthur as Merlin, probably now agreed with the Golden One that Arthur's usefulness was approaching its end.

I wanted to stay with Arthur, but the squires were quartered in the stables. Even so, that was better than Lancelot and most of Arthur's other knights had to endure, sheltering in flimsy tents against the cold of the winter's night.

"Sleep lightly, my lord," I said to Arthur. "And keep Excalibur close to hand."

He gave me a wry smile. "Would you prefer to sleep here, Orion, so you can guard me?"

Surprised that he took my warning seriously, I blurted. "Yes, my lord, I would."

"Fetch your sleeping roll, then," said Arthur, sounding resigned, regretful. "You can sleep on the floor by the door."

I did so gladly. And once I closed my eyes, I found myself transported to the realm of the Creators once again, to their timeless city of eternal monuments, on the flower-dotted slope beside the bright, calm sea. The sun shone warmly out of a nearly cloudless turquoise sky. Seabirds glided across the waves, hardly a wing's span above the water.

But beneath its shimmering dome of energy the city was empty, lifeless. Its monuments stood mute, the colossal statues staring blankly. Even Phidias' incredible statue of Athena, helmeted and clutching her spear—my Anya—was cold and dead.

I called to her with all my soul, but received no answer. The gods and goddesses are busy at other tasks, I told myself. They have universes and worldlines to tend to. The problems of Arthur and Orion are too insignificant for them to worry about.

"Don't be foolish, my love."

Anya's voice! Speaking in my mind.

"Even though I am far across the sea of stars, Orion, you are in my heart and in my thoughts."

"And you in mine!" I shouted.

"Aten seeks Arthur's destruction," she said. "It would be wise for you to bow to his will."

"Never!"

"Then you must use your wits and your strength to help Arthur to pass this test that faces him."

"Test?" I asked.

"Use your wits and your strength, Orion. Find the way to pass this test."

The scene blanked out. Instead of that warm, sunny hillside I was stretched out in my sleeping roll on the stone floor of the castle chamber, in the cold and dark, an infinity away from the goddess that I loved.

But I knew what I had to do. The question in my mind was, could I do it?

7

A squire could not even raise his voice among the assembled knights, much less offer them a way to settle their dispute. I needed an ally, a mouthpiece.

Lancelot.

In the cold and gray morning I found him in the courtyard, standing alone in a corner, looking disconsolate. Other knights were hacking away at each other merrily, the cracks of their blows and the grunts of their exertions echoing off the courtyard's high stone walls.

"Sir Lancelot," I called to him. "Why so glum, my lord?"

Like an unhappy little boy he confessed, "None of the other knights will face me."

"None?" I asked. "No one at all?"

"They all claim I'm too good. Too eager to win."

I nodded knowingly. Lancelot was faster than any of them, I knew, and obsessed with proving himself, despite his youth. Or perhaps because of it.

"I will practice with you, my lord," I said, "if you will accept a humble squire as your opponent."

He broke into an eager grin. "Gladly!"

So we faced each other with wooden practice swords. I took a shield and helmet from the storeroom at the far end of the courtyard; it would have hurt Lancelot more than a thrust through the heart if I had faced him without a protective shield or helm. My senses went into overdrive automatically, but I deliberately allowed Lancelot to hit me now and then as we danced back and forth along the courtyard's snow-covered ground. Many of the other knights stopped their banging at each other to watch us as we hacked at each other.

By the time he at last cried, "Enough!" we were both puffing steam into the frigid air and our shields were well dented.

As we headed back inside, I said, "My lord, how do you suppose we can get all these others to support Arthur's rightful claim to kingship?"

Lancelot shook his head. "I wish I knew."

He was sincere, I knew. He worshipped Arthur, who had raised him to knighthood.

I began carefully, "I wonder if it would be possible . . ."

By the time the nobles gathered again in the great hall to resume their disputation over Ambrosius' legacy, Lancelot was aflame with the idea I had planted in his thoughts.

"A contest?" King Mark asked, once Lancelot had spoken to the assembled knights and kings. "You mean, like a joust?"

"Nay, my lord," said Lancelot respectfully. "Not a contest of arms, but a contest of God's will."

"God's will?" King Leodegrance's usual smile vanished into a befuddled scowl.

Bishop Bron, wearing a plain black robe this day, looked troubled. "And how do you propose to fathom the will of our Lord and Savior, lad?"

His face beaming with enthusiasm, Lancelot explained, "The old High King's great sword lies upon his grave. Let he who can pull that sword from its scabbard be recognized as God's choice to be High King of the Britons!"

The bishop's parchment-skinned face wrinkled into a suspicious frown. "That sword is riveted to the stone slab covering Ambrosius' grave. It cannot be removed."

"It could be," Lancelot retorted, "by the man God has chosen to be our High King."

"But . . ."

"Nothing is impossible to God, my lord bishop," Lancelot coaxed. "Is that not so?"

The bishop nodded warily, unable to disagree but still unconvinced of Lancelot's plan.

It took nearly two more hours of discussion, of voices raised sometimes to the point of violence, before the bishop finally conceded, "Why not? If it be God's will, which of us can op-pose it?"

Thus the knights and kings gathered in the frost-covered grave-yard around Ambrosius' headstone, staring at the heavy two-handed sword riveted to the stone slab covering the old High King's mortal remains.

One of the castle's blacksmiths was summoned to examine the broadsword and affirm that it was riveted solidly in place.

"It cannot be moved, your grace," the burly blacksmith told the bishop, "without the proper tools . . . and a great deal of sweat."

Satisfied that it was impossible to remove the sword with a man's unaided strength, the bishop raised his hands in prayerful supplication. As the noblemen knelt on the snowy ground, Bishop Bron intoned, "Oh Lord, we humbly beg that Thou showest Thy favor to the one You choose to be King of all the Britons."

A deep chorus of "Amen" answered the bishop's plea.

Then the old man turned to Lancelot. "This is your idea, lad. You try first."

"Me?" Lancelot squeaked with surprise.

"You," said the bishop, with a beatific smile. From where I stood, on the outskirts of the gathered nobles, I thought the bishop's smile masked a subtle humor. He seemed to be saying to Lancelot, You thought up this nonsense, let you be the first one to be humiliated by it.

Glancing warily at Arthur, Lancelot stepped up to the head-stone. Arthur smiled at the young knight, warmly, without malice or any trace of jealousy.

Lancelot placed both his hands on the greatsword's hilt, planted his booted feet firmly on the edge of the stone slab, and pulled with all his might.

The sword did not budge.

One by one, for more than an hour, the knights and self-styled kings trudged up to the sword and tried to pull it out of its scabbard. One by one they strained, red faced and grunting, until they admitted defeat. King Leodegrance accepted his failure with a wry smile. King Mark tugged and huffed until I thought he would pop a hernia.

The sword remained in its scabbard.

The moment was coming for Arthur to try. It was the moment when my test would come.

I had seen Aten and Anya create a stasis, freezing the flow of time to suit their whims. They were Creators, with godlike powers. I was a creature, made by Aten to do his bidding. I had learned how to translate myself from the point in spacetime where I existed to the eternal city of the Creators, far in the future of the place and time where I dwelt. Aten always scoffed at my skill, claiming that he or one of the other Creators had aided me.

But I knew I could translate myself across the worldlines. Now a different task faced me. Could I create a stasis? Unless I could, my plan for Arthur would turn to ashes.

8

Praying silently to Anya for help, I brought up in my memory the times that Aphrodite and Hades had created a stasis, once at the megalithic monument of Stonehenge, and then again when we'd been at Sir Ector's castle at Wroxeter.

Humans think of time as a river that flows in one direction, I recalled. But time is like a vast sea, with currents that surge this way and that, eddies and whirlpools, and great surging waves.

Create a whirlpool, I told myself. You have experienced it before; now use the power of that knowledge to suspend the current of this timeline.

I realized that every time I faced battle, my sense of time slowed, stretched like taffy being pulled into a languid stream. I had that capability, Aten my Creator had built it into me. Now I would use it to create a stasis. Without help from Aten or Anya or any of the Creators. I would do this myself.

I hoped.

I reached out with my mind and sensed the flow of time, the streaming current that was carrying these people through their lives. Closing my eyes, I willed the current to be still, to freeze in place. I did not want a whirlpool, I wanted this timeline to stop where it was.

I opened my eyes. Arthur stood frozen at the edge of the stone slab covering Ambrosius' grave, his hands reaching for the great-sword. Bishop Bron stood near him, his creased parchment face staring intently at Arthur's strong, youthful figure. King Mark, Lancelot, Gawain, King Leodegrance, Bors, and Kay and all the others stood motionless, not breathing, as if encased in invisible ice.

I rushed through the motionless courtyard, past the frozen knights and squires, past Friar Samson, standing at the edge of the crowd and staring sightlessly like a statue made of petrified flesh, and headed for the blacksmith's shop. Not even the air moved; the courtyard was silent and still. Birds hung unmoving in midair.

I rummaged through the blacksmith's tools as the burly smith and his two young apprentices stood stock-still, unblinking, un-breathing. Back to the gravesite I hurried, with a stout pry lever in my hands. Wondering in the back of my mind why I felt this urge to rush, I worked on the rivets that fastened the greatsword inside its scabbard. They popped loose at last, and I bent down to replace their broken ends in their proper holes.

I realized as I raced back to the smithy that I couldn't maintain the stasis indefinitely. Perhaps Anya or another of the Creators could, but I felt in my mind the subtle, insistent power of the time flow gnawing at the edges of my stasis, eroding it like a river wears away solid rock.

By the time I returned to the crowd of noblemen gathered around the grave, the stasis gave way and time resumed its flow. Men breathed and stirred. The chill winter breeze gusted. Birds flapped across the pewter-gray sky.

And Arthur bent down to grasp the hilt of Ambrosius' sword. For an instant it did not budge, but then suddenly the rivets I had broken popped loose and the sword slid easily from its scabbard.

For an instant no one moved, no one spoke. It was if another stasis had frozen the moment in place.

Then Arthur raised the greatsword over his head and every man in the graveyard raised a heartfelt cheer.

"Hail to Arthur," the bishop bellowed, "rightwise King of all the Britons!"

From the back of the crowd, Friar Samson shouted, "Deo lo volt!" God wills it.

Every man dropped to his knees, except Arthur, who still held the sword exultantly in both his raised hands.

High King of all the Britons. Deo lo volt.

CHAPTER NINE

Leodegrance's Wedding Gift

1

Leodegrance appeared to swallow his own ambition and take Arthur's accession to the High Kingship with good grace, knowing that his daughter would become Arthur's queen. The wedding was set for the spring, but before she and her father left Cadbury castle—together with all the other nobles who had assembled there—Arthur had to be formally crowned.

It took a week to plan the coronation, a week in which Bishop Bron held nightly vigils and morning masses, and the high-strung court chamberlain flitted through the castle like a hummingbird darting from flower to flower as he prepared for the coronation feast.

Not one of the noblemen left the castle; none of them wanted to miss the great ceremony. Arthur spent his time, though, huddled with Bors and Kay and his foster father, Sir Ector.

"If the High Kingship is to mean anything," Arthur said to them earnestly, "we must use it to bring peace to the land. We've got to find a way to stop the wars and the constant fighting and allow the people to prosper once more."

We were in Arthur's room, high in the castle's stone keep. I stood by the door; the others were seated around the trestle table near the foot of the bed.

Bors gave Arthur a scowl. "Stop the fighting, eh? Tell that to the Saxons."

"Men will fight for what they want," said Ector, more mildly. Tugging unconsciously at his white beard, he went on, "When men have a dispute between them, an appeal to arms is the natural way to settle it."

Shaking his head, Arthur countered, "That wasn't the way the Romans did it. They had laws."

"And officials with the authority to enforce those laws," said Kay, jabbing a finger in the air to emphasize his point.

"And courts to decide disputes," Ector added.

"Then that's what we must have," Arthur said flatly. "Laws and courts, instead of constant fighting and bloody wars."

Ector shook his head. "I don't see how you can make free and independent men accept such restraints, my son."

With a wry smile, Arthur replied, "Neither do I, Father. Not yet. But that's what we must do."

♋

The day Arthur was to be crowned dawned at last. I had been sleeping in his chamber, wrapped in my bedroll on the floor by the chamber door. As usual, I opened my eyes as the first light of the new day crept through the room's only window.

Arthur was already standing by the window, fully dressed in a crisp new tunic of white emblazoned with the red dragon that was his totem.

As I scrambled to my feet, Arthur turned toward me. "The day is here," he said softly. The expression on his face was pensive, almost sad.

"You're about to take on a great responsibility, my lord," I said as I reached for my clothes, draped across the back of one of the chairs.

"And a wife," he said. "The High King must have a wife, so that he can have a son and heir."

"I meant the responsibility of returning Britain to law and peace."

"Oh, that." He smiled carelessly. "That will take a lot of effort, but it can be done, I'm sure."

"Do you truly believe that you can bring these fractious Celts to a law-abiding society?" I challenged.

"The Romans did."

"They had an army to enforce their laws."

Arthur rubbed his brown-bearded chin. "Well, we have our own army: Bors, Gawain, young Lancelot, and the others. They bested the barbarians, didn't they?"

"But will they fight to turn their own people into law-abiding Britons?"

Arthur broke into a wry grin. "That's the real task, isn't it?"

I suggested, "You'll have to give them some goal to inspire them, something greater than their own individual passions."

"Yes," he agreed. "I wonder what that might be?"

"Whatever it is," I said, "after today you will speak to all the Britons as their High King."

"That's a start, I suppose."

It was a start, I thought. Arthur had the right instincts, and he understood that what the Britons needed more than anything was peace, the stability to allow people to plow their fields without fear of raiders, to grow their grain and animals and market their goods peacefully, to live their lives and raise their families without the terror of blood and fire hanging over them.

Arthur was pondering how he could turn his little army of knights into a dedicated band that would enforce the law and protect the weak against any who would despoil them, whether they were barbarian invaders or British noblemen who thought it their right to take whatever they wanted by force of arms.

I had an additional worry. Which of those armed and independent noblemen would try to strike Arthur down? Which of them would be Aten's assassin?

3

The coronation ceremony took almost the whole day, with a high mass in the stout stone cathedral and a tediously slow procession from the cathedral to the castle's great hall and then a ritual that ended at last with Bishop Bron placing a circlet of gold on Arthur's brow as he knelt at the bishop's feet.

All the knights and petty kings packed the cathedral, together with their ladies, dressed in their finest robes, with furs and sparkling jewels, although many of them looked rather threadbare to me. I recalled the coronation of a self-made emperor many centuries in the future of this time: there was splendor.

Of course, Napoleon snatched the crown from his cardinal's hands and placed it on his own head. Yet the French followed him through decades of war, and even returned him to power when he escaped his exile on the island of Elba. It wasn't until the slaughter at Waterloo that they finally gave up their dreams of imperial glory.

But for this time and place, in the midst of a dark age, Arthur's coronation was splendid enough.

"Rise, Arthur, King of the Britons," the bishop intoned.

And as Arthur solemnly got to his feet every voice in the great hall cried fervently, "Hail to the King! Long live the King! May the King live forever!"

I knew that could not be, but I was ready to give my own life to protect Arthur's.

4

That evening the great hall was filled to bursting as the nobles and their ladies feasted and raised goblets of tart red wine to Arthur's health and success.

But no one swore fealty to the new High King, I noticed.

I stood beside the wire-thin chamberlain through most of the feast, off by the side doorway that led into the steaming, bustling kitchen. His darting eyes took in everything, and he directed the serving men and women with abrupt gestures and whispering hisses. Everyone seated at the long tables ate his or her fill, and drank freely. The chamberlain fretted that the wine would run out, but his fears—thankfully—were unfounded.

Remembering the drunken revels of Philip II's court in ancient Macedonia, I thought that these knights were reasonably well behaved. Perhaps it was because their ladies were with them. Men thought more about their dignity when their women were watching.

At long last, as the candles were guttering and several of the noblemen slouched in their seats, almost dozing, Lancelot got to his feet: young, completely sober, very serious.

Raising his wooden goblet, Lancelot said in a clear voice that carried across the great hall, "I hereby pledge my fealty to Arthur, High King of all the Britons. Command me, my lord, and I will obey."

Before Arthur could say a word, doughty old Bors struggled to his feet. "Aye! You have my loyalty, Arthur. I pledge it so!"

One by one, at first, and then in knots of threes and fours, the knights and kings swore their fealty to their new High King. I thought perhaps the wine had mellowed them or softened their wits, and some of the pledges were clearly reluctant, but the oaths were made. And witnessed. Arthur would have a cadre of dedicated knights to carry out his bidding.

A good beginning, I thought.

5

For the next several days the noblemen who had gathered at Cadbury castle took their leave of Arthur and started off through the gray winter toward their own homes.

At last King Leodegrance came to Arthur in the castle courtyard to tell the High King that he would depart the next day. The weather had cleared; even though the air was still freezing cold, the sky was a perfect blue.

"My daughter," said Leodegrance, with his sly smile, "wishes to take her leave of you this evening. Will you take supper with us?"

Even from a dozen paces away, where I was standing, I could see the alarm on Arthur's face. And I noticed that Leodegrance did not show the deference that was due the High King. As far as he was concerned, he was a father talking to his prospective son-in-law.

"Supper with you and Guinevere?" Arthur said, trying to hide his concern. "Yes, of course."

So that evening Arthur put on his finest tunic and repaired to Leodegrance's chambers in the castle's keep for supper with his future father-in-law and bride.

I waited outside in the drafty stone hall; a mere squire was not allowed to be in the room with the nobility. I watched the serving wenches carefully, together with the chamberlain fussing beside me. He was fretting about each dish, each bottle of wine. I was worried about poison and the chances that one of those wenches hid an assassin's dagger in her skirts.

But the supper went uneventfully. Once the last of the dishes had been brought out and the chamberlain hustled his weary team back down to the kitchen, I expected Arthur to come out into the hall.

He did, with a smiling Guinevere on his arm. Once again I realized how slight she was, and how young. Even with a green fur-trimmed robe draped over her shoulders, she looked small, elfin. She was smiling up at Arthur, her bright brown eyes asparkle—from the wine, perhaps, I thought.

"Orion, we're going out for a walk in the courtyard," Arthur said to me. "Fetch my warmest cloak, please."

I stared hard at Guinevere and saw nothing but a very young woman. She was pretty and possibly even intelligent, but I could find no hint that she was one of the Creators in disguise.

With a quick bow I trotted down the curving stone hallway, up the stairs to Arthur's chamber, then back to them again. I trailed a respectful distance behind the young couple as they went down the winding stairway to the ground floor and out into the frigid night.

The stars glittered like jewels in the dark sky, although my namesake constellation was not visible. Arthur and Guinevere walked slowly along the snow-covered path across the courtyard, lined on either side with growing banks of snow that had hardened into ice. I hoped they would take care to avoid the piles of horse droppings that dotted the path.

I let them stay far enough away from me so that they thought they were out of earshot, but I heard them perfectly well.

"You must be baptized before we can be wed," Arthur said, his voice low, very serious.

"If that is your wish," said Guinevere.

"It's not so much that it's my wish, lady, but the bishop and all the church hierarchy would refuse to marry us if you were still a pagan."

For a few paces Guinevere remained silent. Then she said, "A few drops of water and some incantations in Latin make all that much difference?"

The tone of her voice was teasing, almost mocking.

Arthur remained completely serious. "Baptism is an important Christian rite. Without it you could never enter the kingdom of heaven."

"Have you been baptized, Arthur?"

"So I'm told. I was only a baby; I have no memory of it."

"Will it make you happy if I'm baptized?"

Now Arthur hesitated before answering. "It's not about what makes me happy. I'm the High King now. I must have a wife. And she must be a Christian or half my kingdom will rise up against me."

"What about the other half?" Guinevere asked, her voice more serious.

Arthur sighed. "In time, I suppose, they'll all be converted to Christianity."

"Converted by the sword?"

"Never!" he snapped. "Not while I live. Pagans will come to Christ willingly, I'm sure."

"As I am?"

His voice full of perplexity, Arthur asked, "Well . . . you are doing this willingly, aren't you?"

Slowly, Guinevere replied, "My father told me I must marry you. You tell me I must be baptized. No one has asked me what I want, how I feel about this."

"How do you feel about it?"

"I will marry you, my lord. I will accept baptism. I will stand beside you as your queen. But my heart . . ." She lapsed into silence.

"Your heart?" he prompted.

"I don't know you, Arthur. This evening is the first time we have ever been alone together."

"Well, that's all fitting and proper, isn't it? A man can't simply walk up to a woman and carry her away. That wouldn't be right."

"Perhaps," Guinevere replied. "But a woman wishes for something more . . . more romantic."

Arthur stopped and stared at her, completely tongue-tied.

"I know that this marriage was my father's idea, not yours," said Guinevere. "I get the feeling that you don't really like me."

"I . . . I . . ."

"And there are stories, you know."

"Stories?"

"About you and Lady Morganna."

Even from the distance where I stood, even in the cold winter's darkness, I could see Arthur's face flame red. He stood there facing Guinevere, his breath puffing out in little clouds of steam, like a horse that had been run hard.

At last Arthur said, "What is past is beyond change. I am High King now, and I will act as a king must."

"And a king must be married."

"Just so."

"Very well, my husband-to-be. I shall be your queen. Your Christian queen. No matter what my heart feels." Before Arthur could reply, she added, "And no matter what your heart feels."

6

Leodegrance and Guinevere left Cadbury the next morning, heading back to castle Cameliard.

"I'll return in the spring, Arthur," said Leodegrance cheerfully, "with your bride."

Arthur nodded solemnly.

"But before that," Leodegrance added, smiling brightly, "I'll send you a gift. A gift worthy of the High King!"

With that he climbed into the coach beside his daughter and gave the coachman the order to drive off. The horses trudged slowly across the courtyard, clattered over the cobblestones by the main gate, and thundered out across the drawbridge.

Arthur watched the coach until it disappeared around the first switchback on the road. In truth, he looked very relieved.

7

The winter died slowly. Snow and more snow penned us into Cadbury castle.

One morning, as a brisk cold wind swept the low gray clouds across the sky, Arthur trudged across the courtyard with gruff, battle-scarred Sir Bors.

"At least the weather keeps the Saxons in their villages," Bors said grudgingly as they paced along the shoulder-high banks of snow.

Arthur asked, "Do you think they've heard of my being crowned High King?"

With a slow nod, Bors said, "Yes. They must have, by now. Such news travels fast no matter the weather."

"I want to talk to their leader," Arthur said. "To all the barbarian chiefs."

"D'you think they'll want to talk to you?"

"They will, if they believe it to be to their advantage."

"And what advantage could you dangle before their greedy eyes?" Bors demanded.

"Peace," said Arthur. "A lasting peace between us."

Bors looked dumbfounded.

And I noticed a timid yellow crocus poking up through the snow, nodding in the cold wind. Winter would end, after all. Spring was coming.

That evening, as Arthur prepared for sleep, he said to me, "Orion, I want you to go to the Saxon villages along the coast and seek out their leader."

Surprised, I blurted out, "Me?"

"You will carry a message from me. I want to meet the leaders of the Saxons and the other barbarians. I want to talk with them about creating a lasting peace between our peoples."

"But I'm only a squire," I protested. "Surely you should send one of your knights on such a mission, sire."

"My knights are fighting men, not messengers. The Saxons would be suspicious of them. A squire, on the other hand, might be received and his message listened to."

I nodded acceptance. And if the Saxons kill the messenger from the High King, I thought, Arthur has lost only a lowly squire, not one of his fighting men.

Bors thought Arthur's offer of peace was foolish.

"The barbarians will see it as a sign of weakness," he warned, as Arthur's closest knights sat with him in council in Cadbury castle's great hall.

There were five of them: Bors, Kay, Gawain, Lancelot, and white-bearded Ector, seated at one end of the long table that had held thirty during the coronation feast. Lancelot had been burning with zeal to take on the messenger's mission, but Arthur insisted that the messenger could not be a knight.

Ector said slowly, as if thinking it out while he spoke, "The barbarians might indeed see an offer of peace as a sign of weakness . . ." He hesitated a breath, then went on, "But remember that Arthur and his knights have gutted their tribes of the cream of their fighting power. They might welcome a time of peace."

"While they grow a new crop of warriors," Gawain muttered.

"We will offer them peace," Arthur insisted. "Peace is what we all need."

Gawain looked dubious, Bors downright disgruntled. Kay glanced at his father and said nothing. Lancelot alone seemed unconcerned: whatever Arthur wanted was fine with the hero-worshipping young knight.

"And how do you propose to establish peace among our own people?" Bors asked. "How will you stop the fighting among the Britons?"

Arthur smiled ruefully. "We'll have to find a way to bring the rule of law to the land."

8

On the day before I was to leave for the Saxon territory, King Leodegrance's wedding gift arrived. A heavy cart lumbered through the castle's main gate and a quartet of laborers unloaded a large package swathed in fuzzy wool blankets.

Arthur was eager as a young boy at Christmas. "What could it be?" he asked the knights standing with him in the courtyard, watching the unloading. Warmer weather had turned the courtyard into a sea of slushy mud, so Arthur had the workmen lug the heavy package inside the entrance of the castle's stone keep.

It was taller than a man, taller even than I, who stood several finger widths higher than any of the others. It was also as wide as two men standing together.

Arthur's impatience spread to Gawain and the others as the workers carefully untied the ropes and began peeling back the blankets.

"Let me help!" Lancelot urged, but Arthur held him back with a single shake of his head.

At last the gift was unwrapped and stood before us on the unfurled blankets that had protected it on its journey from Cameliard.

"It's a chair," said Lancelot.

"Nay, lad," said Ector. "It's a *throne*."

Indeed it was: an elaborately carved seat of power, bright sturdy oak inlaid with filigrees of darker wood. Its high straight back bore the emblem of a dragon; its arms ended in the claws of a lion.

"A throne for the High King," said Bors, smiling for once.

But Arthur looked pensive. "It's very elaborate, isn't it?"

"A fitting throne for you, Arthur," said Gawain. "It will impress anyone who sees it."

"I suppose it will," Arthur murmured.

"Carry it into the great hall," Ector commanded the workmen. "The High King will sit in state upon it."

Arthur said nothing. He turned and headed into the castle, the expression on his face pensive, almost worried.

That evening in Arthur's bedroom, as I packed my meager possessions for the journey into Saxon territory, Arthur watched me from his chair by the trestle table, still brooding.

"What's troubling you, sire?" I asked.

His eyes narrowing slightly, Arthur replied, "The throne that my father-in-law has gifted me with."

"It's a splendid gift," I said.

"Too splendid, I think."

"How so?"

Arthur shook his head. "I wish Merlin were here. He would know what I should do."

"Why are you troubled so?" I asked.

"That throne is so . . . so fancy. So elaborate. I have to step up on its footstool to be able to sit upon it."

"It's fitting for the High King, don't you think?"

He shook his head. "It's too much. The other knights will grow jealous of me. Wait and see. I know them, Orion. I know how their Celtic hearts and minds work."

"But—"

"Already they grumble that I'm too young to be High King. They say that pulling Ambrosius' sword was some kind of trick."

"But they all swore fealty to you, sire."

"Yes. When they were filled with wine. Now they wonder if they should truly follow me."

I realized that Arthur was more sensitive to Celtic ways than I.

"Once they see me sitting on that fancy throne . . ." He almost laughed. "They'll think I intend to lord it over them."

"Isn't that what a High King must do?" I asked. Before he could reply I added, "Subtly. With grace and wisdom."

"When we were fighting the barbarians we were a band of brothers," Arthur said. "I was content to be Dux Bellorum. Now I've become their High King . . ."

"If the throne bothers you that much, then don't use it. Tuck it away somewhere in the castle and meet your knights more as equals."

"That would offend my future father-in-law," Arthur said, with a wry smile. "Besides, if I'm to bring peace to this land, I must act as the High King. I can't beg my knights to follow me. I must command."

The vague tendril of a memory tugged at me. "Sire, why not have richly wrought chairs made for your knights? Then, when you sit in assembly with them, each of them will have a fine chair for himself."

Arthur's face brightened.

"Your throne will be only a little more splendid than their chairs," I went on. "Just enough to buttress your position as High King, but not so great as to cause them to become jealous."

"And we could arrange the chairs in a circle!" Arthur said, excited by the idea. "Not with me at the head of the hall and them sitting below! A circle of equals, almost."

"That could work," I said.

"A circle of the finest knights in the land, who meet here at Cadbury and then sally out to protect the weak and correct wrong-doing."

I smiled at him and Arthur smiled warmly back at me. I realized that a legend was being born.

CHAPTER TEN

Among the Saxons

1

I traveled alone from Cadbury castle eastward, toward the Saxon villages along the coast of Britain. As I nosed my mount down the switchback road from the castle's main gate I could hear the sawing and hammering of the castle's carpenters and cabinet-makers, busy building the chairs that would seat Arthur's knights.

Soon enough I was down in the thick forest, where the freshly leafing trees rose on all sides like immense pillars. The weather was warming; spring had come at last. And with spring, I knew, a new season of fighting would begin. As soon as the snows melted and the ground hardened under the climbing sun, the raiding and pillaging would begin again. Unless I could get the barbarian chiefs to talk of peace with Arthur.

I recalled dimly that I had served as a messenger before. Wily Odysseos had sent me into Troy to bargain with King Priam and his sons. General Sheridan had ordered me to speak a message of peace to Sitting Bull even while he prepared to destroy the Sioux nation.

My trek was a lonely one. I passed villages that had been burned and pillaged, fields that had once been filled with golden grain now lying fallow and untended, pitiful graves dug next to the blackened remains of what had once been farmhouses, abandoned villages, whole cities that had been reduced to ghostly wrecks.

One night I camped in the ruins of a fine old Roman villa that had been torn apart, demolished by barbarians or Britons who stole the stones for their own purposes. Graceful statues of Roman gods lay broken into pieces scattered on the burned ground, noses smashed from their faces, fingers broken off.

In the darkening shadows of twilight I recognized one of the mutilated statues: Athena, her shield cracked in two, her spear broken, her beautiful face smashed. Still, I knew who she was and longed for Anya there in the dusk and gloom of this dark, dark age.

I tethered my horse loosely so she could crop the weeds that grew among the broken stones. Placing my sword on the ground next to me, I stretched out and tried to sleep.

And found myself in the infinite featureless realm that I had seen so many times before. No tree, no building, no hill broke the endless horizon. Softly billowing mist covered the ground, ankle deep. I was standing in my tunic, arms and legs bare, weaponless except for the dagger strapped to my thigh. I hadn't transported myself here, I knew. One of the Creators had summoned me.

"*Summoned* is such an unfriendly word, Orion."

Turning, I saw that it was Hades, decked in a midnight-black cloak edged with blood-red tracery. His trimly bearded face showed amusement, almost smirking.

"Why have you called me here, then?" I asked.

"To give you a word of advice," he replied loftily.

"Arthur misses Merlin," I said to him.

"A pity, but the young man will have to find his way without my guidance. That's part of the agreement I made with Aten."

"And the rest of the agreement?"

With a self-satisfied little smile, Hades said, "You'll find out soon enough."

"You're going to help Aten to assassinate Arthur, aren't you?"

He shook his head. "Not I. You'll take care of that when the time comes."

"Never!"

Hades scratched at his trim dark beard. "We'll see."

"Why have you brought me here?" I asked again.

His expression grew serious. "To offer you a friendly warning, Orion. The Saxons kill messengers, if they don't like the message they hear. They kill them slowly and very painfully."

"Are you trying to frighten me?"

"Aten swears that when you die in this placetime he will not bring you back. He has no further use for you."

I felt cold anger seething within me. Not the hot-blooded rage that comes with battle. Not the boiling fury that can drive a man to insane violence. I was totally calm, yet filled with an implacable hatred.

"Tell Aten," I said calmly, "that his threats don't impress me anymore. I know that he doesn't revive me. I know that once I die, he builds another body and implants it with the memories he wants me to have."

Before Hades could respond I continued, "And I know that my powers are growing. I can translate myself to your city of monuments. I can create a time stasis. I am becoming stronger each time he creates a new version of me. That's why Aten won't bring me back from death. He fears me!"

"No, Orion," Hades said, shaking his head. "He hates you. He hates the fact that Anya loves you, a mere creature. He has decided to do away with you once and for all."

"And Anya? What of her?"

"She is too powerful for him to harm. But he will hurt her by destroying you."

"Where is she? Why can't I be with her?"

"Anya is far from here, struggling to maintain the fabric of spacetime, to prevent the collapse of the continuum and the extinction of our very being."

"And somehow Arthur is part of that continuum?"

"A very minor part."

"And Aten wants him removed," I said.

"It is necessary, Orion," Hades replied. "If you love Anya, if you don't want to see the continuum crumble into utter chaos, you must do as Aten commands and allow Arthur to die."

"I don't believe you!"

Hades shrugged. "Just as Aten expected. He asked me to give you this message, because he knew you would not believe his word. He thought that perhaps you would accept the hard truth from me, instead."

"I don't believe you," I repeated. "I can't believe any of you."

Looking somber, weary almost, Hades said in a low tone, "It is the truth, Orion. If Arthur lives, your precious Anya will be destroyed. Everything will be destroyed, the entire universe, Orion! The choice is yours."

Before I could reply I found myself back in the gloomy forest, with the first gray light of dawn breaking in the east and birds chirping in the trees high above as if they hadn't a care in the world.

♍

More than anything I wanted to find Anya, to learn from her own lips if Hades was telling me the truth. But no matter how hard I tried, I could not make contact with her. Aten must be blocking my attempts, I thought. And I hated him all the more for it.

It was several days later when I finally came out of the deep forest and stumbled into a trio of Saxons. They were mounted bareback on emaciated donkeys; I could count the animals' ribs. The men looked slightly ridiculous on the flea-bitten little animals; their bare legs almost reached the ground. They were plodding along a trail that meandered along the edge of the forest. Beyond them I could see a village that looked peaceful enough, smoke rising from cottage chimneys, a fenced-in enclosure that held a dozen or so bleating sheep. And I could smell a salt tang in the air; we were not far from the sea.

The weather had turned decidedly warmer. Spring rains had brought new green shoots among the forest trees, and beyond the village I could see neatly tilled fields of furrowed earth.

The three men pulled their donkeys to a halt and stared at me, their faces hard with suspicion. They were bare to the waist, well muscled, armed with short stabbing swords and heavy-looking throwing axes.

I raised a hand in greeting.

"Who are you?" asked the biggest of the three. He was cleanshaven, his light brown hair pulled back and tied in a single braid that dangled down his spine.

"I am a messenger from Arthur, High King of the Britons," I said.

The fellow laughed at me. "High King, eh? And what's his message?"

"The message I bear is for the chieftain of the Saxons."

He turned toward his two companions, then back to me. "I'll bring your head to our chief. It'll make a nice decoration for the front gate of his fortress."

"Your chief will want to hear Arthur's message," I said.

Grinning broadly, he said, "We'll see if your head can speak once it's lopped off your shoulders."

The three of them seemed eager to fight, thinking that they could easily overcome one man. I knew that I had to convince them otherwise.

As they nosed their gray little donkeys toward me and hefted their axes, I slid off my horse and faced them on foot. My sword hung at my hip, but I made no move to grip it. My senses speeded up as they always do when I face battle. I could see the nostrils of the closest donkey dilate slightly with each breath the beast took, see the men's eyes shifting back and forth as they sized me up.

They spread out slowly as I stood there, ready to fight. But I thought that it would be best not to kill them; I wanted them alive, to show me the way to their chief.

The Saxon directly in front of me kicked his donkey into a trot. I watched the animal come at me in slow motion as the barbarian warrior slowly, slowly lifted his axe over his head and aimed a killing stroke at me.

I easily sidestepped his swing, then grasped his wrist before he could recover and twisted the axe out of his grasp. Out of the corner of my eye I saw his companion on the right hurl his axe at me. It came spinning lazily through the air. I easily parried it with the axe in my hand, then turned to see what the third Saxon was up to.

Just in time. He, too, had thrown his axe at me, and I barely had the time to knock it away from me. It thudded into the ground at the feet of the first one's donkey, frightening the poor animal so much that it reared on its hind legs, throwing the Saxon to the ground with a hard thump.

Hefting the man's axe in one hand, I grinned at the goggle-eyed amazement on their faces.

"Now that you've disarmed yourselves," I said gently, "perhaps you can show me the way to your chieftain."

Their leader climbed slowly to his feet, his eyes fixed on me as he unconsciously rubbed his bruised rump.

"You're no messenger," he muttered.

"Yes, I am." Then, remembering a ruse that crafty Odysseos had once used, I added, "I am a messenger from Arthur, High King of the Britons. If he had sent one of his knights, the three of you would be bleeding corpses by now."

They were clearly impressed. Reluctantly, their leader said, "We will take you to our chief."

As I climbed back into my saddle, the Saxon walked back to his donkey while his two companions picked up their axes—eying me all the while. I let them rearm themselves, then followed them toward the peaceful little village.

3

"I am Gotha, chief of the West Saxons."

He was a big, burly man, heavily muscled despite his graying hair. His eyes were iron gray, too, suspicious and scheming.

Gotha's so-called fortress was nothing more than a long wooden hall with a pitched roof supported by stout timbers. It stood at the far edge of the village, on a low bluff overlooking the gray, churning sea. I could hear the crash of surf against the rocks out there. Its packed-earth floor was empty: no tables, no chairs in sight. Only Gotha sitting before me, with a handful of bare-chested warriors standing on either side of him.

The hall reminded me of another mead-hall I had been in, long ago, at an earlier time, King Hrothgar's feasting hall of Heorot. Dimly I recalled a hero named Beowulf, and monstrous beasts.

Gotha sat at the far end of the strangely empty hall, on a high wooden chair decorated with skulls mounted on poles; their sightless eye sockets seemed to be staring at me as I stood before the chief of the West Saxons.

"I am Orion," I replied, "messenger from Arthur, High King of the Britons."

Gotha rubbed at his gray-bearded chin. "I heard that the lad has made himself High King. Some sort of magic involved, eh?"

I put on a patient smile as I replied, "The only magic, my lord, is his courage and skill in battle."

"Him and his knights," Gotha murmured darkly. Then his eyes shifted beyond me: I heard the tread of several pairs of feet making their way along the hall toward us.

Turning, I saw it was a trio of Saxons, each bearing a long stave. Mounted at the ends of the staves were the heads of the three warriors I had met earlier that day.

I turned back toward Gotha, astonished at such brutality. He merely smiled cruelly at me and said, "Three warriors who together cannot kill a single man have no place in my clan—except as decorations."

And he laughed as his servants fixed the staves in the bare earth behind his throne.

Abruptly his laughter cut off and he grew serious. "Now then, messenger, what does your High King have to say to me?"

Trying not to stare at the three gaping heads, I recited, "Arthur, High King of all the Britons, invites you to his castle at Cadbury, along with the chiefs of the other Saxon bands, as well as the chiefs of the Angles, Jutes, and other tribes."

"To his castle?" Gotha laughed harshly. "Does he think I'm fool enough to go there, where he can murder me in my sleep?"

"My lord," I said, "Arthur wishes to make a lasting peace between the Britons and your invading tribes—"

"Invading?" Gotha roared. "We were *invited* onto this island, messenger. We fought the Picts and Scots for the older Ambrosius. Our reward was to be told to pack up and go back to our own lands."

"Arthur is not asking you to leave Britain. He wants to find a way for you to live here in peace."

"There can be no peace between his people and mine! Our destiny is to drive the Britons into the sea and take possession of this island for ourselves."

I could hear the echo of Aten's scheme in his words. The Golden One was behind all this, I knew.

"My lord, this island is large enough for your people and Arthur's, both. You can live here in peace. Why make war? Why see your young men slaughtered when you can have what you want without bloodshed?"

Gotha stared at me, scowling. For many moments he was silent. At last he seemed to relax slightly and said, "Perhaps we should talk of peace, after all."

The warriors flanking either side of his throne twitched with surprise.

Raising one hand, Gotha said, "Tonight we feast. Then I will send my reply to your High King."

I wanted to heave a sigh of relief, but I knew that Gotha and his fighting men would take that as a sign of weakness, so I said merely, "You are as wise as you are brave, my lord."

As dusk fell across the village, Gotha's hall filled with warriors. Scurrying servants had set up long tables and benches for feasting. A huge fire blazed in a stone-lined pit at the far end of the hall, its smoke rising through a hole in the roof, much as the fire pit of Priam's palace in ancient Troy.

Gotha sat at the head of the hall, in the center of the longest table, sloshing beer out of a golden cup that was decorated with elaborate Celtic designs. Spoils of battle, I realized. The chair to Gotha's right was empty; I wondered why. Had someone failed to show up? Was Gotha waiting for an important guest?

I was led by a servant to a place on the bench at one end of the wooden table. The assembled warriors were dressed in fine tunics and grasped cups and mugs in their strong hands. Servants kept pouring beer for them, while a pair of what looked to me like elks turned slowly on the roasting spit over the cook fire.

Food was piled upon the tables in abundance, everything from pigeons to savory melons, but the warriors paid hardly any attention. They were too busy swilling beer, and getting more uproarious by the moment. I noticed that none of them bore weapons, except for the half-dozen men standing directly behind Gotha's throne. Guards of honor, I thought.

Behind them, in the shadows by the wall, stood the staves with the mounted heads of those three warriors. A reminder, I thought, from Gotha to his men: losers don't live long in this tribe.

The men were getting rowdy, sloshing beer on one another and roaring with laughter. I was splashed more than once, but I stayed at my place on the bench, trying to behave as a messenger from the High King rather than one of these drunken Saxon louts.

At length, though, Gotha raised one hand and the hall quickly fell silent. All the warriors sitting on the long benches looked expectantly toward their chief.

Gotha peered down the length of the table and said in a loud, commanding voice, "Orion! Messenger from the High King. What are you doing down there? Come, sit here beside me." And he indicated the empty chair next to his own.

I rose slowly, made a polite little bow, and replied, "Thank you, my lord. You are most gracious."

The hall was absolutely silent as I made my way along the table to the chair beside Gotha's. I could feel the eyes of more than a hundred flaxen-haired warriors watching me.

I arrived at the chair and made another little bow to Gotha. "With your permission, my lord."

"Of course, of course," he said, with a toothy smile. "Sit down here, as befits a messenger from the High King."

The instant I sat, his six guards grasped my arms and pinned me to the chair. Gotha slipped a long knife from beside his plate and rose to his feet as I struggled uselessly against the strong arms holding me down.

"The reply I send to your High King," Gotha said, loudly enough for everyone in the hall to hear him, "will be your head!"

The Saxon warriors cheered lustily and Gotha came at me with the knife. Someone grabbed me by the hair and yanked my head back. He was going to kill me, and this time Aten had no intention of bring me back from death. I could hear the mocking laughter of the Golden One in my mind.

Gotha pressed the sharp edge of the knife against my throat. I felt it cutting into my flesh and knew I had to translate myself out of this placetime—or die the final death.

Closing my eyes as the Saxon's blade cut deeper into me, I willed myself to the eternal city of the Creators. I had translated myself through spacetime to that nexus before, I would do it again.

I could hear Gotha's sadistic laughter, feel his knife slicing my throat. Then suddenly all sensation ended. I was suspended in the continuum, frozen in cryogenic cold and utter darkness.

I had no eyes with which to see. I had no body to feel pain or joy or love. There was nothing except my consciousness, the central awareness of my own being.

Vainly I tried to translate myself through the continuum to the Creators' city of monuments. I could not reach it, and I realized that Aten was blocking me, keeping me away from it.

Was this the final death? An eternity of nothingness? Oblivion?

And then, like a faint tendril of hope, I felt the warm touch of Anya's presence. But it was weak, delicate as a butterfly's fragile wings, feeble as the last whisper of a dying man.

"I can't help you, my love," she said to me in my mind, her voice filled with despair. "There's nothing I can do to save you."

Interlude

I felt warm summer sunshine on my face. Opening my eyes, I saw that I was sitting on a grassy lawn in a wooden framed sling-back chair, wearing a sky-blue uniform of cotton twill. Several other men in similar uniforms were sitting in a motley set of chairs scattered across the grass.

The sun was just above the distant wooded hills, shining in my face. Lifting a hand to shade my eyes, I saw a half-dozen airplanes parked on the grass, sharp nosed, looking vaguely like sharks. Hurricanes, I somehow knew.

A phone rang. Turning in my chair, I saw that the ringing was coming from a small wooden building, little more than a shack.

A red-faced man stuck his head out the shack's only window and bellowed, "'A' flight! Scramble!"

The men sitting around me leaped to their feet and sprinted toward the fighter planes. As I struggled out of the sling-chair, a broad-shouldered man with gold-flecked brown eyes and a short brown beard grabbed my arm and helped me to my feet.

"Come along, Irishman," he snapped. "Up and at 'em!"

Arthur? I wondered. Here, in this placetime? But he looked older, harder, grimmer.

Hardly knowing what I was doing, I raced alongside him toward the planes. He veered off and I puffed to a halt alongside one of the Hurricanes. I saw a pair of small black crosses painted beneath the rim of the cockpit. Then my eyes went wide as I saw the name painted in flowing script across the nose: *Athena*.

A pair of ground crew men were standing on the plane's wings by the open cockpit, beckoning to me. Engines were coughing to life all around me. *Athena*, I thought, as I sprinted to the fighter. Even though Anya could do nothing to help me escape the final death in Gotha's timbered hall, my plane was dedicated to her.

By instinct I clambered up onto the wing and squeezed into the fighter's cramped cockpit. I recognized a parachute pack on the seat. As I plumped down on it, one of the crewmen flipped its straps over my shoulders while I automatically pulled up the thigh straps and clicked them into place.

"Christ, Irish, you're goin' t'be the last one out," the second crewman yelled in my ear as he handed me a soft fabric helmet.

"Better late than never," I muttered. Like an automaton I whipped through the preflight checklist and started the plane's engine. It was called a Merlin, which made me smile. It came to life with an explosive roar and a burst of gray smoke from its exhaust manifolds.

In less than a minute I was bouncing along the grassy field, the earphones in my helmet crackling with voices and frantic instructions. Most of the flight was already in the air; I saw the plane ahead of me leave the ground and pull up its wheels.

While I pushed the throttle forward and my Hurricane lifted into the blue summer sky, I realized I was in England in the summer of A.D. 1940, by the Christian calendar. Britain was at war against Nazi Germany, facing invasion once again. I was known in this time and place as John O'Ryan, a volunteer from the Irish Free State flying with RAF Fighter Command in the Battle of Britain.

Arthur's Britain was nearly fifteen centuries distant, but I had escaped the final death that Aten had planned for me. Without Anya's help. Without the aid of any of the Creators. I had translated myself across the worldlines on my own!

Once I had cranked up the plane's landing gear and fastened my oxygen mask over my face I concentrated on getting into my assigned position: tail-end Charlie on a vee of three planes. Our flight of nine Hurricanes flew in a vee of vees. I somehow knew that the pilots called the three-plane formations "vics."

"Dorniers at angels twenty-two," I heard the flight controller's calm female voice in my earphones, "heading for Hornchurch."

The formation of Hurricanes angled off to the right, leaving me struggling to catch up with them.

"Close up, you bloody Irishman! You'll be a sitting duck for the bastards!" Arthur's voice, harsh and demanding.

I felt the invisible hand of gravity pushing me down into my seat as I edged the throttle higher and tried to catch up with the rest of my flight.

"I see them! Twelve—no, fourteen flying pencils, two o'clock high."

The Dornier bombers were slim as spears, painted glossy black with German crosses in white on their sides and the crooked swastika against a blood-red stripe on their tails.

"Climb above them."

"Watch out for their fighters."

"Looks clear so far."

"Keep a sharp eye. They're up there someplace, waiting for us."

Our flight curved up and above the Dorniers, which were flying in a long, shallow dive that made their speed almost as high
as our own. But almost wasn't good enough.

"Tally-ho!" came Arthur's voice as he peeled off and dove at
the bombers.

My job, as tail-end Charlie, was to watch out for enemy fighters and protect the two other men in my vic. I twisted around in
the narrow cockpit, trying to look in all directions at once. It was
difficult to see behind me, almost impossible. The sun was beaming brightly back there, and—

A pair of sleek deadly Messerschmitts swooped out of the sun's
glare, guns twinkling as they roared past me.

"Break left!" I screamed into the microphone built into my
oxygen mask. But it was already too late. One of the Hurricanes
was smoking badly, slipping off into a spiraling death dive. The
other snapped into a left turn and I tried desperately to stay
with him.

The Messerschmitts were faster than our Hurricanes and could
turn more tightly. Another pair of them perched on my tail;
heavy caliber machine gun bullets started to rip chunks out of my
wings, my fuselage. I could *feel* slugs slamming into the armor
plate behind my seat.

"Where're the bloody Spits?" Arthur's voice yelled in my earphones. Fighter Command's top squadrons were equipped with
Spitfires, planes that could equal the best fighters the Germans
had, faster and more maneuverable than our Hurricanes.

My shot-up plane was buffeting badly and losing altitude;
pieces of the wings' fabric covering were tearing off. I was trying
to make myself as small as possible, hunching behind the seat's
protective armor plate. The Messerschmitts roared past me, going after Arthur, my flight leader.

There was nothing I could do to help him; I could barely keep my crate in the air. But then a pair of Dorniers slid right in front of me. They almost seemed to be gliding, compared to the swooping charge of the Messerschmitts.

I saw the rear gun on the nearer bomber twinkling; the gunner was firing at me. I rolled my battered Hurricane to the right as I came up on him. The Dornier's fuselage filled my gunsight ring, I was so close.

I pressed my thumb on the red firing button on my control yoke. The Hurricane seemed to stop in midair as the eight machine guns in my wings hammered away.

At first nothing seemed to happen, but then the Dornier abruptly slid off to the left, angled down sharply, and dove steeply toward the ground. Its left wing crumpled and folded back.

And just that abruptly I was alone in the air, flying inverted, hanging by the shoulder straps of my seat harness. I straightened out, realizing I had lost a lot of altitude. Looking up, I saw swirling contrails tracing fine white arcs against the blue summer sky. My plane was buffeting badly and its engine was stuttering, coughing.

I knew I couldn't be far from my home field, but all I could see below me were the checkered green fields of East Anglia sliding past. Dimly I recalled that the land below me was the shire of Essex, a corruption of the term *East Saxons,* just as neighboring Sussex had once been the territory of the South Saxons.

There were trees down there. Lots of big, ancient trees lifting their leafy arms as if they wanted to pull me down. My Hurricane was wobbling, sinking fast. I barely cleared a row of oaks and there before my happily surprised eyes was our airfield. It was nothing more than a grassy meadow with a few unserviceable planes parked at the far end and a cluster of small wooden buildings near another row of trees, but it looked beautiful to me.

Someone fired a white flare, the warning that my landing gear was not deployed. I pumped hard on the lever and hoped that the wheels came down and locked in place. No more flares; the wheels must be down.

I worried that the faltering engine might quit altogether before I touched down, so I came straight in, no circling of the field, no downwind leg. The Hurricane bounced once on the grass; when it touched down again the left wheel collapsed and I was thrown into a grinding, lurching slide across the field. It sounded like a junkyard being dragged across a pasture. One of the propeller's blades snapped off and banged into my windscreen, cracking the bulletproof glass.

The Hurricane finally scraped to a stop, resting on its badly twisted left wing. I tugged frantically at the canopy. It refused to slide back, its frame bent by that errant propeller blade. I smelled aviation fuel and knew that the plane could burst into flames at any instant.

With all the strength in me I grabbed the canopy latch with both my gloved hands and, planting both booted feet on the shattered control panel, pulled as hard as I could. The canopy yielded at last and slid back. I struggled out of the cockpit and jumped to the ground.

A dozen ground crew men were running toward me.

"Get down, you idiots!" I screamed at them. "She's going to blow up!"

They hit the ground and I slammed down in their midst, twisting around to look back at my crashed Hurricane. For eternally long moments we lay there on our bellies, waiting for the Hurricane to burst into flames. Nothing happened. The plane simply lay there, battered and ravaged with bullet holes, the hot metal of its engine ticking slowly.

No explosion. No fire. The ground crew men began to chuckle and whisper to one another.

"Y'think it's all right to get up now, sir?" asked one of them, smirking at me.

I rose slowly to my feet, feeling decidedly embarrassed.

But that was nothing compared to the scorn that Arthur heaped on me once he landed and called me into his spare little office in the wooden frame building that housed our squadron headquarters.

"You stupid Irish oaf," he snarled. "You got Collingswood killed and damned near me along with him!"

His gold-flecked eyes were blazing with anger—and something else, I realized. It wasn't fear. I realized that Arthur was brimming with cold, unreasoning hatred. This war in the air was making him an old, hate-filled man, despite his youthful years.

"Sir," I began, "they came out of the sun—"

"Of course they came out of the sun! How many times have we tried to drill it into you: 'Beware the Hun in the sun!' Your job was to watch out for them and give us warning—in time to keep our necks from being broken!"

He went on for what seemed like an hour, blaming me for the death of his wingman, for all the deaths our group had suffered, for the war and all the evils that it had brought to Britain's shores.

"At least I got a Dornier," I muttered.

"And cracked up your own ship," he snapped.

I stood there seething. He sat behind his wooden desk, the marks of his oxygen mask creasing his cheeks, his brown beard frayed, his hair disheveled. He looked up at me with utter weariness, and a disdain that was little short of contempt.

"Get out of here," he said at last. "Get out of my sight."

I saluted halfheartedly, turned, and left him to himself. I closed his office door very softly.

The orderly sitting at the small desk just outside the door looked up at me, a glum expression on his round, jowly face. He was a sergeant who had served in the First World War, twenty-some years earlier.

"Don't take it too hard, O'Ryan," he said to me, softly, as if afraid the commander would hear him through the closed door. "Old Artie's got a lot of pressure on his shoulders, y'know."

I nodded, too angry to speak, afraid I'd say something I'd regret.

"Collingswood's hit him pretty hard," he went on. "They were schoolmates, y'know."

"I didn't know."

"You're not the only one he's screamed at," the orderly said, with a sad, patient look. "He's done so much yellin' and squallin' these days that th' boys are startin' to call him King Arthur."

"King Arthur was a better man than that," I said, and I walked out of the wooden shack, into the afternoon sunshine.

The rest of the pilots were sitting in the chairs scattered across the grass, some dozing, some trying to read magazines, some just staring blankly at infinity, at an endless succession of flying, fighting, killing, dying.

I found the sling-chair and lowered myself into it.

"Tough morning," said the young pilot sitting in a straight-backed wooden chair next to me.

"Yes," I said wearily.

"I hear you got a Jerry."

"One of the Dorniers."

"Good for you."

"Think they'll be back today?"

"Probably. Better get some rest while you can." His young face eased into an old man's weary smile. "Before Jerry comes over for his matinee appearance."

I smiled back at him and closed my eyes. In an instant I was asleep. But it was not sleep. I wanted to return to Arthur, when he was High King of all the Britons. I had no intention of remaining separated from him.

I had fled Gotha's death trap, but now I had to return to Arthur. Aten still wanted him killed. I still vowed to protect him.

If I could translate myself across the continuum back to Arthur's time and place.

BOOK III

The Death of Arthur

CHAPTER ELEVEN

Castle Tintagel

1

Once again I found myself in utter darkness, disembodied, translating across spacetime. Cold, abyssal cold, with not even a star to break the darkness.

And alone. Totally alone. I sensed no other presence, neither Aten nor Anya nor any of the Creators. I was translating myself across the centuries, striving to get back to Britain in Arthur's time. By myself. Without the help of any of the Creators.

I heard the raucous screech of a gull. Opening my eyes, I climbed slowly to my feet and saw that I was standing on a green, grass-topped bluff at the edge of the sea. Far below me the ocean crashed on gray rocks. Overhead, puffy white clouds sailed past on a gusting summer wind.

I was dressed as I had been at Arthur's castle of Cadbury, in chain mail with a plain tunic draped over it. Boots, but without spurs. A Celtic longsword was belted to my hip, but I had neither shield nor helmet. I felt the comforting presence of the dagger Odysseos had given me at Troy, long ages ago, strapped to my thigh beneath my tunic.

Across an inlet of the sea rose a rock-bound island, topped with a formidable-looking castle. No, not an island, I realized. It was actually a cape, connected to the mainland by a narrow stem of land.

This must be Tintagel, I told myself. King Mark's castle by the sea, in Cornwall. Why am I here, I asked myself, instead of at Cadbury, with Arthur?

On the mainland side of that neck an army was encamped. I could see field tents scattered across the grass, grubby and soiled. They had been there for months, it seemed to me. Some of them were so large they reminded me of the imperial tents of the Mongol khans, where I had met Ogatai, High Khan of the Mongols, son of the magnificent Genghis Khan. Ogatai had befriended me, took me hunting with him. In return, I had murdered him, as Aten had commanded me to. I had saved Europe from Mongol conquest; I had saved my friend Ogatai from the long agony of cancer.

Shaking my head to clear my mind of those memories, I realized that the encamped army must be besieging Tintagel. I studied the castle for a while and saw how truly redoubtable it was. Built of stone, Tintagel sat atop a high, steep hill in the middle of the semi-island. The only access to its high walls was along a narrow road that twisted up the hill laboriously, then ran along the length of the castle's protective wall.

Attackers would have to come up along that road, vulnerable to fire from the wall. And the road was so narrow that only a few men-at-arms could approach the castle's main gate at a time. A handful of men could defend Tintagel against an army, I realized.

Looking back to the camp of the besiegers, I saw large flags planted in front of the biggest tents, each of them bearing the stylized red dragon of the Pendragon clan. Arthur was here! That was why I had materialized here; I willed myself to be near Arthur, and he was at Tintagel, not Cadbury.

But why was Arthur, High King of the Britons, not making war on the barbarian invaders of the island? Why was he besieging a fellow Celt, King Mark of Cornwall, here at Mark's castle of Tintagel?

ʠ

I walked down along the bluff's edge and into the camp of Arthur's army. Instead of attacking high-walled Tintagel, Arthur was apparently content to try to starve King Mark into submission. Discipline was lax. The young men-at-arms lolled before their grimy tents, some honing their weapons, many of them simply sprawling in the sun. Serving wenches were plentiful, their clothes filthy. Disease would soon strike this camp, I knew.

No one challenged me as I walked through the outlying tents, heading toward those banners bearing their red dragons. But there was a trio of armed men standing guard as I approached Arthur's tent, leaning nonchalantly on their spears. Their tunics looked grimy, as if they hadn't been washed in weeks.

"Where d'you think you're going?" their leader challenged me.

"I am King Arthur's squire," I said.

"Squire? I never saw you around here before." He was a tough-looking veteran, his right cheek marked with a livid scar that left a white line across his beard. His eyes were narrowed with suspicion. He bore the red dragon emblem on his tunic.

"I've been away," I said, truthfully. "On a mission for the High King. Arthur will be glad to see me."

"Maybe he will and maybe he won't." The guard was clearly puzzled, unsure of what he should do. His two companions came up and stood on either side of him, gripping their long spears tightly. They were younger than he, mere lads.

"Take me to Sir Bors, then," I said. "He'll recognize me."

"Bors?" the guard exclaimed. "Old Bors has been dead these five years and more."

Five years? How long have I been away from Arthur?

"Sir Kay?" I asked. "Gawain?"

"Kay's too sick to see anybody," said the guard, "and Gawain's over in Brittany seeking vengeance for his brother's killing."

My head spinning, I blurted, "How long has Arthur been High King?"

The guard's suspicious face went even tighter. "How long . . . ? How should I know? He's been High King as long as I can remember. What of it?"

"I was his squire when he was crowned," I tried to explain. "Send word to him. Tell him that Orion has returned."

Clearly distrustful, the guard shook his head. "So I'm supposed to go up to the High King and tell him his squire's come to see him?"

Starting to feel desperate, I said, "Is Lancelot here? He'll know me."

All three of the men burst into mocking laughter.

"Sir Lancelot?" said their chief. "With him as your friend you won't need any enemies!"

"He's the one Gawain's gone after. He killed Gawain's brother."

No, I thought. That couldn't be! Lancelot killed Gawain's brother? And now Gawain is seeking vengeance on him? What happened to the brotherhood of knights that I had known in the old days, when we fought shoulder to shoulder against the barbarian invaders? What have Arthur's knights come to?

"I can't believe it," I said.

"Believe it, stranger. And begone with you. The High King has no time for the likes of you."

I began to grow angry. Arthur's tent was a scant hundred paces in front of me, yet these three oafs would not let me past them.

Drawing myself up to my full height, I told them, "The High King will be glad to see me. And he'll be very unhappy with anyone who prevents me from reaching him."

"How do we know you're not a spy?" said the younger man-at-arms on the guard's left.

"Or an assassin?" said the other, on his right.

I could see they were determined to keep me away from Arthur. Protecting him, they thought. How different this camp was from Amesbury fort, or from the easy camaraderie of Arthur's knights when we fought the length of the land against the Saxons and their barbarian allies.

I decided to act. Swifter than their eyes could follow, I plucked the spear from the chief guard's hands. Before he could react, I used the spear as a quarterstaff and clouted his two younger companions, one-two, and down they went.

The older veteran stared at me, stunned. I pointed the spear's sharp tip at his throat. "Now take me to the High King."

"He'll kill me if I try—"

"I'll kill you right here and now if you don't," I said, my voice cold with fury.

He glanced at his two companions, moaning and stirring faintly on the ground. With real terror in his eyes he turned and led me to Arthur's tent.

It was a trap, of course. Of sorts.

The amazed guard led me reluctantly to the largest tent in the camp. A pair of guards stood at its entrance, well dressed in clean tunics bearing the red dragon. Both of them clutched spears, and eyed our approach with a mixture of curiosity and suspicion as I walked behind the disarmed guard, his spear in my hands, pointed at his kidneys.

As we approached, I called to them, "Orion, squire to the High King, has returned from his mission."

"Better let him in," muttered my disarmed guard.

The two men at the tent's entrance glanced at each other, then the one on the right said, "Go on through, then. But you can't carry that spear into the High King's presence."

With some misgiving, I handed him the spear and stepped through the tent's entrance.

"Seize him!" yelled the guard who was holding my spear, and a half-dozen men-at-arms stationed just inside the entrance grabbed at me.

I had half expected it. My senses snapping into overdrive, I saw their hands reaching for me, slowly, almost as if in a dream. I grasped one of them by the wrist and flung him into several of the others, then side-kicked the one standing nearest me solidly in the chest. As he toppled over backward I ducked beneath the reaching arms of the other two and knocked them both down with a rolling block.

Springing to my feet, I saw nine men sprawled on the carpeting that lined the tent's floor. But they were scrambling to their feet, drawing swords, leveling spears at me.

"What's going on here?" a deep, commanding voice shouted.

Turning, I saw it was Arthur, High King of all the Britons.

3

It truly was Arthur, but he was older, much older than when I had seen him at Cadbury castle. His beard grew halfway down his chest, gray tufts streaking the brown. His face was lined and gaunt, his eyes hard beneath graying brows. Yet his apparel was far richer than anything he had worn when I knew him earlier. A fine robe of dark soft wool was draped across his shoulders. His tunic was trimmed with fur: sable, I thought. His boots of beautifully tooled leather looked brand new: they had never seen a battle or even a hard trek across country.

But those gold-flecked eyes of his widened as he looked at me. "Orion?" he gasped.

I dropped to one knee. "My lord," I said, with bowed head.

He rushed to me and raised me to my feet. With some of his old, youthful vigor he demanded, "Where have you been? What happened to you? Why . . . you haven't changed a whit! It's been more than twenty years and you're still the same!"

Before I could reply he snapped at the guards. "You ignorant louts! How dare you attack this man? Didn't he tell you he was my squire, my friend?"

"Y . . . Your majesty," the chief guard stammered, "we didn't know. We thought—"

Arthur dismissed his guards with an angry wave of his hand, then led me deeper into his tent. Serving wenches scampered to bring us wine in golden cups as we sat in finely wrought chairs of mahogany at a table inlaid with colorful tiles.

"I was told that Gotha the Saxon had murdered you, all those long years ago," Arthur said.

"He tried, sire," I replied, "but I escaped."

"And where have you been these twenty years?"

I hesitated. "On a far journey, sire. But I have returned to serve you, just as I did at Amesbury fort."

Arthur leaned back in his chair, smiling with memories. "Those were the days, weren't they? We beat the Saxons, the Angles, the Jutes . . . all of them."

"Indeed we did, sire."

Then his face clouded and he shook his head. "Yet we could not drive them out of Britain, as I had hoped. Old Gotha united the barbarians and we fought a great battle against them at Badon Hill. We broke their power, but we couldn't drive them completely out of this island."

"They live along the coast," I murmured, recalling the origins of the shires of Wessex, Sussex, and the rest.

"Yes," Arthur agreed. "They've stopped their raiding. They live peacefully enough now. For more than twenty years Britain has been at peace."

"Then you've achieved your goal, sire."

"At a price, Orion. A terrible price. Bors was killed in the fighting. My brother Kay lies sick with the wasting illness. Sir Ector, Peredur, Gareth . . . all gone."

I said, "I was told Sir Gawain was away . . . on a quest."

Arthur shook his head. "Gawain's quests used to involve women, every time. I once told him he'd have to make a pilgrimage to Jerusalem if he wanted to save his soul. But now . . ." His voice faded into silence.

"He seeks vengeance against Lancelot?" I found it hard to believe.

"Yes," Arthur whispered. "Blood vengeance."

An uncomfortable silence fell upon us. At last I said, "But twenty years of peace is a great achievement, sire. You've accomplished a great deal."

"Have I?" Arthur's gray brows knit. "For more than twenty years I've given my people peace. They've grown prosperous and content, knowing that they are safe in their homes. Fat and happy they are. Forests have been cleared for cultivation, villages have grown, even the ancient Roman cities have been rebuilt."

"That's wonderful, sire."

"But the curse of the Celts remains. Each petty lord considers himself a king, even though his kingdom is no more than a patch of land. They all build castles now and hire men-at-arms."

"But they obey the High King, don't they?"

"When it suits them," Arthur replied sourly. "When they see some advantage to themselves in it."

Suddenly he leaped to his feet, nearly knocking over the table. The serving women cowered in the far corner of the tent.

"Ingrates! Fools!" he thundered. "I bring them twenty years of peace and they pay me with disloyalty! Most of them have refused to join my siege of Mark's castle here at Tintagel."

"King Mark rebelled against you?"

"He murdered one of my knights!" Arthur bellowed. "He stabbed Sir Tristan in the back, drove his traitorous dagger through the heart of a fine and noble knight."

"But why?"

His expression twisting, Arthur admitted, "Tristan was in bed with Mark's wife. She said afterward that some witch had given them both a love potion and they couldn't control themselves. But Mark didn't wait for explanations; he foully murdered Sir Tristan!"

"And Mark's wife?"

"He took her back. He accepted her story about the love potion."

"I see."

"Mark must be brought to justice," Arthur insisted. "But the other nobles sit in their castles and refuse to join me. They refuse their High King!"

"There must be—"

"It's treason," Arthur said. "Out-and-out treason. And worse. In the north Modred is gathering an army for himself."

"Modred? Your son?"

Arthur's expression turned withering. "My bastard son by the witch Morganna, yes. My loving son. He will rebel against me as soon as he thinks his army is strong enough. He knows I'll never name him as my heir, so he's determined to seize the High King-ship by force."

"While you're here in Cornwall, besieging Tintagel."

Arthur muttered something too low for me to hear.

"But what of Lancelot?" I asked again. "He's loyal to you, isn't he? He'd be worth a small army all by himself."

"I told you, Orion, don't ask about Lancelot."

I sat there and watched the bitterness etching his face. Arthur returned to his chair and reached for his wine goblet, drained it, then held it up for one of the serving wenches to refill.

"It seems to me, sire," I began slowly, "as if you could use King Mark and his men against the rebels that Modred is assembling. Perhaps you could come to an understanding with Mark . . ."

Arthur raised a dismissive hand. "No, Orion. He murdered Tristan. He must face trial. And punishment."

I had a sudden idea. "Could it be a trial at arms?"

Arthur nodded. "It could."

"You could meet Mark on the field of honor, if he would agree to it."

"He would never agree," said Arthur. "Face me? With Excali-bur in my hand? He'd shit his pants."

I blinked at his crudity. "Then perhaps he might agree to face someone else. Someone he wouldn't fear. A lowly squire, perhaps."

Understanding dawned on Arthur's face. But then he shook his head once again. "He could not face anyone lower than a knight. It would be unseemly. He would never agree to it."

"I suppose not."

Then a crafty look came into his eyes that I had never seen on Arthur's face before. "But I could make you a knight, Orion. I could bring you into the fellowship of the Round Table."

"Me? A knight? But—"

"Silence, Orion. I am High King. I can do anything I want. And I will make you a knight this very day."

4

Thus it was that I was knighted.

The procedure was much more ceremonious than it had been back at the time when Lancelot won his spurs. There was more Christian ritual to it: I had to fast the night before, allowed to ingest nothing more than a few sips of water from sundown onward. As the sun rose the next morning a half-dozen knights— none of whom I knew—roused me from my tent and marched me in procession to the crude wooden hut that served as a chapel for the besieging army.

Summer it might be, but the air was chill and damp with dew that rose up from the ground like ethereal wraiths. I could see our breaths steaming in the crisp air. The crash of surf against the rocks was accompanied by the sighing of a dank wind that came off the water.

Inside the makeshift chapel stood Arthur, draped in a rich

robe trimmed with ermine fur, at the head of the central aisle, in front of the altar. He was flanked by two priests in clean white robes; a teenaged page stood behind them and slightly off to one side.

I glanced around the chapel, wary for danger. But I saw no one else. Nor could I feel the presence of any of the Creators. If Aten intended to assassinate Arthur, would he do it here? I reached out with my mind, but sensed nothing: none of the Creators was here, not even Anya. I smiled inwardly to think of the sensation it would cause if she appeared here as the Lady of the Lake.

My escort of knights and I marched up the central aisle, bowed to the High King, and took seats in the front pew. Arthur turned to the carved wooden throne at one side of the altar and sat slowly, stiffly on it. The priests began to say the ritual of the Christian mass.

All through the mass I strove to make contact with Anya, but it was useless. It was as if I were in a bottle of smooth, impermeable glass. No matter how I tried, I could not contact her. Aten was maintaining his blockade, keeping me from reaching or even contacting her.

Once the mass was finished, the ceremony of knighthood began. Arthur rose slowly, with great dignity, to his feet, and I got up to stand before him. Like the mass, the ceremony was in Latin; it was basically designed to test if I was worthy of knighthood. I answered all the priests' question well enough for Arthur at last to unsheathe Excalibur and order me to kneel before him. Once I did, he tapped me on each shoulder with that matchless blade and pronounced:

"Rise, Sir Orion, and welcome to the fellowship of the Round Table."

One of the priests raised a hand to his lips and murmured, "But, sire, that's a pagan name! He can't—"

Arthur froze the man with a scowl. "It is a Roman name, priest. Your High King tells you so."

The priest's face reddened and he lapsed into silence.

Arthur then turned to the page who had been standing behind him, and took a box of polished sandalwood from the lad's hands. He opened the box, then presented it to me.

Inside were spurs made of gold.

I looked up at him. Arthur was smiling at me. "Remember when you fashioned spurs with your own hands, at Amesbury?"

Something of the old, youthful Arthur shone in his gold-flecked eyes.

"I do, sire," I said. And I recalled how Arthur had given spurs to Lancelot and from that day forward made spurs the symbol of knighthood.

"Many years have passed since then," Arthur said, wistfully.

"Sire," whispered the other priest. "The ceremony—"

"The ceremony is what I make of it, holy one," Arthur snapped. "I created this ceremony before you were even conceived."

Both priests looked shocked, but they dared say nothing. I felt saddened. The smiling vestige of youthful Arthur that I had briefly seen had disappeared. The High King that stood before me was a stern old man who would brook no criticism, not even from a priest.

"Go, Sir Orion," he said in a sonorous voice, "protect the right, defend the weak, and serve your High King with all your heart and strength."

I bowed and replied, "I will, sire."

Then I turned and—once again escorted by the six knights—walked out of the chapel, into the bright morning sunlight. The knights said nothing to me; they merely left me outside the chapel, each of them going their separate ways. How different this was from the old days at Amesbury! I missed Gawain and his good humor, Kay's loud booming voice, even Bors' rough old sour puss.

And Lancelot. What had become of Lancelot?

5

It took several days for Arthur's heralds to arrange the trial at arms with King Mark. Mark was no fool: he suspected a trick of one sort or another when he received the challenge from Arthur's messengers.

Once the heralds returned with Mark's demands for the trial, Arthur imperiously ordered them to tell Mark that he would select the newest knight in his army, a man who only a few days ago had been a mere squire.

"Tell King Mark," he said to his chief herald, "that he need not fear facing an experienced knight of the Round Table. I am so sure of the justice of our cause that I am willing to send a mere fledgling against him."

To this Mark agreed—providing that he could select a champion to represent him. He claimed that he was in ill health, and an old wound in his shoulder was troubling him.

"A champion, eh?" Arthur mused. He had called me into his tent to hear Mark's demand. "What say you, Sir Orion?"

I recalled a time in the distant past of this epoch, when the wily Odysseos had used me in a trial at arms to stop the blood feud that had erupted after he slaughtered his wife's suitors upon his return to Ithaca following the Trojan War. He had posed me as a country bumpkin, trying to convince the families he faced that I was no threat to them. In return they produced a champion—who turned out to be my Creator, Aten, in disguise. We fought a savage duel that ended in our killing each other.

"Well, Orion, will you face Mark's champion?" Arthur prodded, misunderstanding my silence.

"Gladly, sire," I replied. But I feared that I would be facing one of the Creators, rather than an ordinary mortal.

Waving a hand at the chief herald, Arthur commanded, "Tell King Mark that we will face his champion. The loser of this trial will obey the will of the winner. God's justice will be done."

The heralds withdrew from the tent, leaving Arthur and me alone for the moment. I decided to use the opportunity.

"Sire," I began, "what has happened between you and Lancelot? Why is Gawain seeking vengeance against him?"

A troubled frown came over Arthur's bearded face. He glanced about the tent, making certain that no one was there to hear him.

"That lad has been like a son to me," he muttered.

"I know. But why isn't he here, with you?"

"It's Modred's doing."

"Modred?"

"My loving son," Arthur growled.

"I don't understand, sire."

Arthur went to the table where the wine flagon rested and poured himself a goblet of red. Sitting tiredly on one of the chairs, he motioned me to sit beside him.

"Have some wine, Orion," he said.

I poured a little into one of the jewel-encrusted goblets.

"You told me that Modred is gathering an army in the north to march against you," I prompted.

"Yes. And he is clever, devilishly clever. He knows that Lancelot is the finest warrior of all my knights, so he has separated him from me."

"Separated? How?"

His face glowering with anger, Arthur told me, "Modred spread the story that Lancelot loves Guinevere, my wife. And that she loves him in return, rather than me."

I waited for more, remembering how Lancelot had seemed mesmerized by Guinevere when we had first met her, at her father's castle of Cameliard.

When Arthur didn't speak, I asked, in a near whisper, "Is it true?"

"No!" Arthur snapped, pounding his goblet on the table so hard that wine sloshed out of it. Then he looked at me, his eyes full of sadness, and admitted, "Yes, in a way."

"He loves your wife," I said.

"She never loved me," Arthur sighed. "She married me to please her father."

I remembered that Arthur seemed troubled by the idea of marrying Guinevere. Terrified, almost.

"I knew that Lancelot was fascinated by her. I gave it no mind; he was young, he had stars in his eyes."

I nodded.

"But when Modred started circulating his foul lies, I asked Lancelot directly. He told me the truth. Yes, he loves my queen. But no, he had never touched her, never even spoken to her of his love."

"And Guinevere?"

Arthur shook his head. "She's a pagan, at heart. I had her baptized, but it did no good. She would bed any man she took a fancy to. For all I know she slept with Modred himself."

"Your son?"

"I've sent her off to a convent, for her own good. Lancelot has gone back to Brittany and married, from what I hear."

"Then they're apart," I said.

"And they'll stay apart," Arthur swore. "But the rumors persist. They've both been stained, and I've been made to look like a fool, or worse."

"And Lancelot is no longer among your knights," I said.

"No," Arthur replied. "Modred has separated him from me just as effectively as if he'd killed Lancelot."

I could see the grief in his lined, graying face, the remorse. And more: there was anger smoldering in his eyes.

"If I defeat King Mark's champion—"

Arthur cocked a brow at me. "If?"

With a smile, I amended, "When I defeat Mark's champion, what demand will you make of him, sire?"

"Why, I will demand that he confess to the murder of Sir Tristan and do penance."

"Penance, sire?"

His face set in grim determination, Arthur said, "Mark's penance will be to take all his men-at-arms and come north with me, to face Modred."

I nodded. Angry and saddened he might be, but this High King was thinking ahead to his next challenge.

6

The trial at arms was at last arranged. The day dawned clear and bright. Gulls called shrilly as they glided over the waves breaking against the bare stone bluffs. The breeze blew out from the land, warm and moist with the sweet flowery smells of high summer.

Arthur was astride a fine white stallion, looking splendid in chain mail covered with a crisp white tunic emblazoned with his red dragon symbol, a sky-blue cape draped across his shoulders. A squire stood at his stirrup, bearing helmet and shield. Another lad behind him carried a pair of lances.

I nosed my gray charger to Arthur's side. "It's a fine day," I said.

Arthur glanced up at the cloud-flecked sky and replied, "A good day to teach Mark a lesson."

I had acquired a squire, as befitted a knight. He was a beardless youth who carried helmet and shield for me. My shield bore a crude likeness of a hunter dressed in a bearskin and carrying a club. My squire carried no spears, because the heralds had already agreed that this fight would be on foot. Mark's negotiators wanted no part of facing one of Arthur's knights on horseback, charging with a lance in his hands.

"I'll do my best, sire," I said.

As I turned my mount toward the narrow neck of land that connected Tintagel with the mainland, Arthur said to me, "Take your helmet and shield, sir knight."

"They'll only slow me down, sire."

"Take them," Arthur repeated, more firmly. "I don't want Mark to realize his champion is facing a warrior so superior that he doesn't need helm or shield."

For the first time I realized that Arthur had watched me in battle, and understood my superior prowess. More: he wasn't above a bit of trickery. He's grown wily over the years, I thought, telling Mark I was a newly fledged knight, letting him think I was little better than a mere squire, while all along he knew that I was an able fighter.

With some reluctance I accepted the heavy shield and padded helmet from my squire. I had a longsword dangling from my hip.

"Good luck, friend Orion," said Arthur. "May God's will be done."

"Thank you, sire."

As I prodded my mount into an easy trot, I got the impression that Arthur regarded his God's will as his own.

I followed the three white-clad heralds on their mules across the rock-bound neck and onto the grass-covered cape of Tintagel. A cluster of men stood waiting for us: several heralds in white, a dozen men-at-arms, and husky, barrel-chested Mark himself, in chain mail and tunic bearing his totem of a black raven. His pennants snapped noisily in the strong breeze.

The heralds palavered for what seemed like an hour while I scanned the men-at-arms gathered around Mark. None of them seemed especially threatening. They were all in mail and bore ordinary swords.

But then another group of men left the castle's main gate up on the hill and started down the meandering road toward us. As they approached, I saw that one of them stood head and shoulders above the others. A giant with a thick mop of hair the color of golden straw.

Once they reached us, Arthur's chief herald objected, "That man is a Saxon!"

Mark pushed through his men-at-arms and said in a harsh voice, "This man is in service to me. He's my champion. Saxon though he is, he serves me."

He was truly a giant, a full head taller even than I. Bare to the waist, golden hair braided down his brawny chest. Arms bulging with muscle. I wondered if this was Aten in one of his guises, but I saw in the giant's ice-blue eyes no hint of the Creators. He was simply a very large, powerfully built mortal man. A Saxon, no less.

"This is not seemly," the herald complained. "A Saxon barbarian—"

"Seemly or not, he is my champion," replied King Mark, in a tone that brooked no further argument.

The herald turned to me, and I nodded my acceptance. Then two of Mark's retainers carried a pair of huge two-handed broadswords to the clearing between us and rammed them into the ground.

"Since our gracious Lord Mark is the challenged party," King Mark's wizened old herald announced, in a high, piping voice, "he has the choice of weapons." Gesturing to the two blades standing between us, he concluded, "King Mark chooses broadswords."

I slid down from my horse as Mark's Saxon champion pointed to my shield and helmet.

"You have need of those, brave knight?" he jeered. "And chain mail, as well?"

Several scars marked his naked chest and bare arms. I thought that a coat of mail could have saved him some pain in the past, but he was probably proud of his scars. Without speaking a word, I let go of both my shield and helmet and let them fall onto the grass; then I unbuckled the sword at my hip and dropped it beside them.

Mark's herald cleared his throat noisily, then proclaimed, "The combatants will proceed to their weapons. No blow shall be struck until I say, 'Begin.'"

The Saxon sneered at me, and no one could miss his swagger as he advanced to the heavy two-handed sword sticking up out of the ground.

I went to my sword and stood before it. The others backed away, giving us plenty of room to fight.

"Your coat of mail won't protect you," the Saxon said to me, loudly enough for all to hear. "I'll cut through it as if it were butter."

Mark and his men laughed. I said nothing.

The aged herald coughed once, then said, "Ready . . . begin!"

The Saxon yanked his broadsword out of the ground with one hand and twirled it above his golden-haired head as if it were a feather-light reed. I tugged at my sword with both hands. Let this giant-size oaf think he has the advantage over me, I thought.

My senses ramped up, and the world decelerated into dreamy slow motion. I could see the Saxon's cold blue eyes focusing on me, the muscles of his arms and legs bunching as he moved. For all his size, he was light on his feet. And he handled his heavy broadsword as if it were a wand.

He started a mighty, two-handed overhand swing at me, then changed it in midmotion to a sideways slice. I danced away, not willing to try to parry his blow for fear my blade would snap from the force of it.

Grunting, he came at me, swinging his blade back and forth with what he thought was blurring speed. I watched and back-pedaled, waiting for him to tire and change tactics.

"Fight, you coward!" someone yelled. It might have been King Mark, or one of his men.

As if on that cue, I engaged the Saxon's blade with my own, and with a two-handed twist, tore it out of his hands. It went sailing into the crowd of men around Mark. They scattered wildly to avoid being skewered. The sword struck the ground point first and impaled itself in the grass, quivering.

The Saxon stood before me, puffing, amazed, disarmed.

I pointed with my sword. "Pick up your weapon, man. Unless you want to fight me bare-handed."

He looked confused for a moment, then his face hardened and he trotted back to the broadsword and yanked it out of the ground.

Now he advanced on me more slowly, carefully, gripping the sword in both hands, weaving its point back and forth, as if trying to hypnotize me.

I saw the muscles of his shoulders bunch as he pulled the sword back slightly and then aimed a mighty blow at my head. I easily ducked under it and tripped him. He went down on his face with a thunderous crash.

He spun onto his back, sword raised to protect himself. I merely backed away and gave him time to get back on his feet.

His lip was cut and bleeding. Tufts of grass were stuck in his yellow hair. I looked into his face and saw fear. He was puffing, blinking, wondering what he could do to get the best of me and fearing that he couldn't find a way. Fearing that he was going to die. Fearing that I was going to kill him.

And suddenly I was disgusted with the whole business. I, who had been created to be a warrior, an assassin, a killer—I was weary of it all. I saw the faces of other men I had killed, over the ages, from Troy to the interstellar wars, from the Ice Age caves of the Neandertals to the worlds of alien beings. Death and blood. They were my heritage, the reason Aten had created me: over the millennia and parsecs of spacetime, the joy of battle, the blood-lust of killing, had been built into the very fabric of my being.

But now as I faced this frightened flaxen-haired young giant, I saw a terrified youth who was staring at his own death.

Enough! I told myself. He can't harm you; why should you kill him?

I took a step toward the Saxon. He leveled his sword at me, but I could see the tremor of its point as he gripped it in his trembling hands.

I struck his blade with my own. He backed away a step and then swung his mightiest at me. I dodged the blow and let its momentum carry his blade to the ground. Before he could react, I stamped my booted foot on the end of his blade and swung as hard as I could at it, halfway up its length. The sword snapped in two, leaving my sweating, wide-eyed Saxon foe holding the stump of his sword in his two hands.

Before anyone could react I pointed my sword at his throat.

"Yield!" I commanded.

He glanced around toward Mark and his companions, still clutching the useless broken sword.

I touched his throat with the point of my blade. "Yield!" I repeated.

His face utterly miserable, the Saxon dropped his sword and fell to his knees, head bowed abjectly.

"I yield, sir knight," he said.

I turned to King Mark. "Are you satisfied, my lord?"

The look on Mark's face could have etched steel. But he muttered, "God's will be done."

CHAPTER TWELVE

Guinevere and Lancelot

1

With enormous reluctance, King Mark agreed to join Arthur's forces heading north to deal with Modred.

Arthur was pleased with my victory and its results, but he was already looking ahead to the coming struggle.

"If we can get to the northlands soon enough," he told me as we rode together, "we can scatter Modred's forces before they are strong enough to offer us battle."

That was Arthur's hope.

Summer was waning. As we headed north, a miles-long column of knights and squires, churls and workmen, serving women and camp followers, I saw colors of autumn beginning to tinge the trees. The weather was warm and bright by day, but at night it grew chilly.

The land we rode through was peaceful and prosperous, it seemed to me. Neat little villages were dotted among the ripening fields of crops. People gathered at the roadsides as we passed, dropping to their knees as Arthur rode by, preceded by his red dragon banners, calling out blessings upon him. How different this land was from the years when I had first encountered Arthur, when invading barbarians had created a wasteland of death and fear.

"The people love you, sire," I said to Arthur as I rode beside him.

He gave me a wry smile. "They love peace, friend Orion. They love not being attacked, not having their throats cut and their farmsteads burned out. They would praise Satan himself if the Fiend would protect them and let them live in peace."

A strange bitterness, I thought. The years had hardened Arthur. The bright-eyed idealist I had known earlier in his life has turned into a graying cynic. I felt saddened.

We had been on the road for several weeks, buying provisions for men and horses from the local farmers as we progressed northward. We slept in tents most nights, although now and then a local nobleman hosted Arthur at his castle. Most of our army slept outside the castle walls, of course; there were simply too many of us to be housed indoors. Usually, though, Arthur brought me with him as he allowed the local lord to treat us to a feast and a roof over our heads.

Knights and eager, unfledged youths joined our army at each such stop. Arthur accepted them graciously enough, and put experienced knights to training them when we camped each night.

He steered our growing army well clear of Cameliard, I realized, and smiling, cunning Leodegrance, father of Guinevere. The weather turned sharper as we proceeded north; the trees were in high color, already dropping their leaves, which swirled about us on a cutting chill wind. I half expected snow sometime soon.

One night, as the men made camp, Arthur asked me to ride with him through the dark, sinister forest, well away from any listening ears. Once we were well into the trees, we dismounted and led our horses on foot.

"I'm leaving the army for a few days, Orion," he told me. In the shadowy woods, it was difficult to make out the expression on his face, but the tone of his voice was grave, almost dismal.

"Leaving, sire?"

He let out a breath that might have been a sigh. "Call it a pilgrimage. I'll only be away for a few days."

"You're going alone?" Suddenly I was alert to possible treachery. I hadn't forgotten Aten's goal of assassinating Arthur. Even though more than twenty years had passed, the Golden One still held to his objective, I was certain.

"Alone, yes. I'll be back in a few days."

"My lord, let me go with you."

I could hear the smile in his voice. "Faithful friend Orion, still trying to protect me."

"That's what a friend is for, sire."

He shook his head. "No, Orion. There's no need. No one would dare to confront me." He tapped the sword at his hip. "Not with Excalibur in my hand."

"But where are you going, sire? And why?"

"There's no need for you to know," he said, his tone stiffening. "Sir Percival has been taking care of logistics for the army; he'll handle matters until I return."

My brows rose. "You expect Sir Percival to handle King Mark?"

For a moment Arthur did not reply. At last he said, "Mark is busy with his own men. If all goes well, he won't even know I've gone."

I thought that if Mark found out that Arthur had left the army, either he would try to take command of the entire force or he would gather up his own men and head back to Cornwall.

"It will be all right, Orion," Arthur assured me, sensing my doubts.

I was not assured.

Arthur climbed back into his saddle and trotted off, leaving me standing in the moonless forest, my horse tugging at the rein in my hand as he nibbled at the shrubbery at the base of the trees.

I waited until I thought Arthur was far enough away, then swung up onto my mount and began to follow him.

Westward he rode through the entire night, out of the dark forest and into hills that climbed steadily. The moon came out from behind silvered clouds, and I had to hang far back, lest Arthur see me following him. The night grew chill, but he kept heading west, higher up into the hills. I could see him silhouetted against the starry sky, a lone figure doggedly heading toward . . . what?

2

Once the sun came up I had to hang even farther back from Arthur. I lost sight of him entirely, but in the daylight it was easy enough to follow his trail. He never stopped moving west. Now and again he dismounted and let his horse walk unburdened, but he kept moving, like a man on a quest, like a chip of iron being drawn by a magnet.

Is this part of Aten's plan? I wondered. To draw Arthur out into the wilderness and then kill him? A gang of robbers, a marauding band of Saxons, an invading army of Picts or Scots?

"How melodramatic you are, Orion."

I jerked around in my saddle to see the Creator who styled himself Hades riding alongside me. He who had earlier disguised himself as Merlin now was clad in a magnificent cloak of midnight black, etched with fine blood-red traceries. His mount was shiny black, as well, as powerful a steed as I had ever seen.

"What are you doing here?" I demanded of him.

He cocked a brow at me. "You grow insolent, creature."

"What are you doing here?" I repeated.

With a sardonic smile, he said, "Actually, I'm here to give you a message."

"From the Golden One?"

"No. From Anya."

My heart leaped. "From Anya!"

With a slight shake of his head, Hades told me, "She really cares for you, Orion. Even though she is engaged in difficulties that you could never even imagine, she wants you to know that she will do whatever she can to help you."

I felt a flood of overpowering joy rush through me. Anya cares about me! She'll try to help me!

"But I can also tell you this, creature," Hades went on. "You have no need to worry about Arthur at this point in spacetime. He is perfectly safe—for now."

"Meaning that he won't be perfectly safe for long," I growled.

"Until Camlann," said Hades lightly. "That's when Arthur will be killed."

"Not if I can help it," I said.

Hades laughed in my face. And then disappeared as abruptly as a candle flame snuffed out by a gust of wind.

3

Late that afternoon, as the sun dipped toward the jagged horizon of a rugged ridgeline of tumbled bare rocks, I saw where Arthur was heading. Up atop the steepest of the harsh, unforgiving crags stood a stone building. It looked too small to be a castle, and although it was surrounded by a high protective wall, I saw no watchtowers. A monastery, perhaps, I thought.

I pushed my tired horse as hard as I could and just before sunset, as the sky flamed red and a cold wind began to bluster across the bare landscape, I came close enough for him to spot me. Arthur stopped his horse and dismounted, waiting for me. I slid out of my saddle and walked my mount the rest of the way to him.

"Orion," Arthur said as I approached. "I might have known."

I made a little bow to him and explained, "I couldn't let you go alone, sire. My duty is to protect you."

"Your duty is to obey my orders," he said sternly. But then his face softened and he added, "Yet I'm glad to see you, old friend."

He clasped my shoulder and together, side by side, we walked our mounts the rest of the way to the building's main gate. It was a convent, Arthur told me, a place of healing both body and soul, famed throughout the land.

"Gawain lies here," said Arthur, "near death from the wounds he suffered at Lancelot's hand."

"I was told that Lancelot killed Gawain's brother," I said, still finding it hard to believe.

"It's all Modred's doing," Arthur muttered. "He's broken the fellowship of the Round Table, unraveled everything I've worked for twenty years and more to achieve."

As we approached the stout wooden gate, Arthur explained that Modred spread the rumor that Guinevere and Lancelot were lovers. Sir Gareth, Gawain's younger brother, discovered Lancelot in Guinevere's chamber at Cadbury castle. Foolishly, he attacked Lancelot and was killed in the fight. Lancelot escaped and

Modred demanded that Guinevere face trial for adultery. Instead, Arthur banished Guinevere to this remote nunnery.

The white-clothed novice who slid back the peep hole in the convent's main gate went wide-eyed at the sight of the red dragon emblazoned on Arthur's tunic.

"You . . . you come from the High King?" she asked, in a trembling voice.

"Child, I am the High King: I am Arthur, King of the Britons."

Fumbling in her hurry, the lass unbolted the gate and led us directly through empty, silent stone corridors to the abbess, a flinty-looking, rake-thin woman, her face as bleak and unforgiving as the stones on which the convent stood. She wore a tattered gray robe that hung on her bony shoulders like an old sheet thrown over a piece of broken furniture. Her office was as spare and undecorated as she was: cold stone walls, bare except for a crude crucifix over her worn-looking oaken desk, no chairs except her own.

She stood behind her desk as we were ushered into her office, leaning on the chair's back, but it was clear that she was less than awed at the sight of the two of us.

"Your majesty," she said flatly. "I presume you have come to see your wife."

"And Sir Gawain," said Arthur. "I was told he is near death."

"We have sent for a priest to give Sir Gawain the sacrament of extreme unction."

"Then he truly is dying."

"The sacrament sometimes has healing power," said the abbess.

"Kindly take me to him."

"Not your wife?"

"I'll see her later," said Arthur, clear distaste in his tone. "She still has much of life in her."

"Indeed," said the abbess dryly.

In obvious pain, she moved laboriously around her desk and with a whispered, "Follow me," led us, limping, down a dimly lit corridor.

"Sir Gawain has another visitor," she said as we walked along the stone floor. "In fact, he is the man who brought the dying knight here. He hasn't left Sir Gawain's side, night or day."

With that, she opened the creaking door to a cramped bare cell. Gawain lay on a narrow bed, his face as pale as death, his forehead swathed in bloody bandages. The man who had been sitting beside the bed shot to his feet as we stepped into the chamber.

Lancelot.

"You!" Arthur blurted.

"Sire!" said Lancelot, and he dropped to one knee.

"You're the one who brought Gawain here?"

"Yes, sire," said Lancelot, his head bowed.

Arthur's tone hardened. "You came to see Guinevere."

"I didn't know she was here," Lancelot replied. "This convent is known far and wide for its healing powers. I thought . . . perhaps the sisters could work their magic on Gawain."

"First you nearly kill him," Arthur growled, "then you want to heal him."

Climbing to his feet, Lancelot exclaimed, "I didn't want to fight him! I didn't want to fight his brother; Gareth gave me no choice."

"Sir Gareth was defending my honor." Arthur's hand moved to grip Excalibur's jeweled hilt.

Lancelot shook his head sadly. I realized all over again how small he really was, barely as tall as Arthur's shoulder. Yet he was a demon in battle.

"My lord, your honor was never tarnished by me," he said

earnestly. "I had come to Guinevere that evening to tell her that I had taken a wife, back in Brittany, to stop the stories that Modred was spreading. And . . ." Lancelot's voice softened, ". . . and to help me forget her."

"Then you truly did love her."

"Yes," Lancelot answered, in misery. "I do still. But I never touched her. I swear it, sire. We never even held hands."

Arthur's shoulders slumped. He had known Lancelot since he'd been a reckless youth, keen to win glory and honor for his lord.

From his bed, Gawain said weakly, "I forgive you, Lancelot. I forgive you my brother's death. And my own."

Lancelot bent over the bed and clutched Gawain's hand in both of his own, his eyes brimming. "Gawain," he whispered. "Gawain . . ."

But Gawain heard nothing. Those dark eyes that had danced with laughter so often now stared sightlessly into Lancelot's tear-streaked face.

4

Arthur was grim faced as the abbess led us slowly up a flight of steep stone stairs to the chamber where Guinevere was housed. I could almost feel her pain as she toiled arthritically up the stairway.

"Has the queen been made comfortable?" he asked as we climbed.

"As comfortable as we can manage," said the abbess. "She is in the chamber that we keep for visitors. She is more comfortable than any of the sisters, I assure you."

Arthur fell silent as he, Lancelot, and I followed the bone-thin abbess upward. The stone walls seemed to breathe coldly upon us. Through a narrow slit of a window I saw that it was fully night outside, with a crescent moon riding low over the hills. A wolf bayed in the distance, a chilling mournful sound.

A middle-aged nun in gray habit was seated before Guinevere's door, bent over a palm-size breviary, squinting painfully in the dim light of the sputtering candle in the wall sconce above her. She sprang to her feet at the sight of the abbess.

"Open," said the old woman, and the nun fairly leaped to comply.

Turning to the three of us, the abbess commanded, "Wait here." Then she entered Guinevere's chamber. I heard her voice, too low to make out the words, and then a younger, clearer voice replied, "Show them in, by all means."

I had to duck slightly to get through the low stone doorway. There stood Guinevere, looking rather out of place in a richly wrought gown of golden cloth trimmed with dark fur about the neckline and cuffs. She had gained some weight over the years; where before she had looked elf slim, now she was chunkier, fuller. Her face was still quite lovely, even though somewhat rounder.

"My lord and master," she said to Arthur, sarcasm dripping from her words.

"My queen," said Arthur, tightly.

We stood in the middle of the somewhat spacious room, in awkward silence. The chamber looked comfortable enough, with a big canopied bed in one corner and a shuttered window on the other side. A broad table with four cushioned chairs, a chest of drawers, and a commode with a wash basin atop it. The abbess sank stiffly into the straight-backed chair by the open door.

"And Lancelot, how nice," Guinevere went on. "Have you come to comfort me in my solitude?"

Lancelot stood tongue-tied before her.

Arthur did not bother to introduce me, nor did Guinevere ask who I was. To her I was merely one of her husband's men, a nonentity. Yet I realized that she eyed me carefully, with a hint of a smile curving the corners of her mouth.

"Gawain is dead," Arthur said, without preamble.

"So now you must kill Lancelot, here," she replied, her smile growing.

"No," Arthur said wearily. "There's been enough killing."

"How Christian of you, my husband, forgiving your enemy."

Lancelot finally found his voice. "I'm not an enemy, my lady."

Guinevere turned away from him and faced Arthur. "Why have you come here, Arthur? To see Sir Gawain or to see me?"

"Both," he said.

Looking toward me, she asked, "And who is this handsome lout, standing there in silence?"

"This is Sir Orion, newly elevated to knighthood."

She looked me over again, quite boldly, from head to toe. "Have you brought him here to comfort me?"

Arthur's face flamed. "Guinevere!"

"What do you expect of me?" she snapped. "You bundle me away in this . . . this . . . prison full of holy women who speak in whispers and tell me to spend my days in prayer and meditation. Do you expect me to thank you for this?"

Arthur took a deep breath before replying, "If I had kept you at Cadbury you would have been brought to trial for adultery—"

"Sire, it's not true!" Lancelot burst.

Arthur shook his head. "Not with you, lad. But there were others."

"What of it?" Guinevere challenged. "You never loved me."

"I am your husband!" Arthur thundered. "And the High King! You were making a mockery of me and everything I stand for!"

Guinevere scoffed, "And I am the queen, am I not? Why must I obey the same laws that the commoners follow?"

"Because in my domain everyone obeys the law," Arthur said, straining to keep his voice civil. "My kingdom is a kingdom of laws. How do you think we've kept the peace all these years?"

Guinevere turned away and started across the room.

"Don't you understand?" Arthur called after her. "If I hadn't spirited you away to this convent you would have been brought to trial for adultery. You'd have been condemned to the stake!"

"Who would dare to testify against the queen?" she shot back.

"Modred would get a dozen witnesses to testify."

"Your loving son."

"I'm trying to save your life, Guinevere!"

"Why? Because you love me?" Before Arthur could reply she answered her own question. "No. It's to save your throne, isn't it? To save your precious kingdom. To save yourself from looking like a cuckolded fool! That's why I'm locked away in this barren confinement."

For long moments Arthur did not reply. Lancelot stood mute also. Guinevere glared at them both, a mere woman standing before the High King and his bravest warrior, contempt etching hard lines on her face.

At last Arthur said, "I'm taking my host north, to find Modred and do battle against him before he can organize a real army."

Guinevere's lips curled into a sneer. "He's already organized an army. He's waiting for you, up by the Wall, near his mother's domain."

"How do you know this?" Arthur demanded.

"Because Modred has been here to see me," she said, with triumph in her voice. "Because he has told me that once you are dead, he will marry the Queen of the Britons and rule this land."

Arthur looked stunned. Lancelot shook his head and I could fairly hear what he was telling himself: To think that I loved this woman, that I thought she was the most desirable woman in the realm. What a romantic young fool I was!

And then, as if from a vast distance, in my mind I heard the scornful laughter of Aten, the Golden One. "What do you think of your Arthur now, creature?" he jeered at me. "He is already destroyed. Everything he tried to achieve has been turned to dust and ashes. He will die an ignominious death, and soon, Orion, very soon. Nothing remains but to dispose of his body."

5

We were three silent, saddened men as we left the convent. For hours neither Arthur nor Lancelot said a word. At last we descended from the jagged rocks and our horses trotted onto a broad, grassy meadow. A stream gurgled nearby, clear and inviting.

"Deer will come for their evening watering," I said, trying to sound hopeful, hearty. "We can eat venison this night."

Arthur said, "The deer will stay in the forest, Orion. You know that."

"Rabbits, then," I said.

"Squirrels, more likely," said Lancelot.

We made camp within sight of the stream, and as the sun went down I bagged a brace of plump rabbits, hitting them with stones when they approached the water. If either Arthur or Lancelot noticed my prowess as a hunter, neither of them mentioned it as we gnawed at the half-raw meat by our meager campfire.

"Tomorrow we'll rejoin my forces on their way north," Arthur muttered, more as if he were talking to himself than us.

"I must return to Brittany, sire," said Lancelot.

Even in the flickering shadows of evening I could see the disappointment on Arthur's face. "You won't come with me to face Modred?"

Lancelot shook his head sadly. In a tortured voice he replied, "I've had enough of killing, sire. Gawain . . . he was my friend! I never want to fight again."

I knew how he felt. Even though my Creator had built me to be a warrior, a killer, the terrified look on the face of that young Saxon lad at Tintagel had sapped the bloodlust out of me.

"If what Guinevere told us is true," Arthur said slowly, "then Modred already has an army waiting for us. He can choose the place of battle to suit himself."

"I suppose so," Lancelot agreed, in a voice so low I could barely hear him.

Arthur said, "I could use you, sir knight. Your presence at my side would be worth a hundred valiant warriors."

Lancelot shook his head once again. "It cannot be, sire. I just don't have it in me. All I want is to return to my castle in Brittany and try to build a new life with my bride."

Arthur sighed, but said nothing.

The next morning I followed Arthur as he made his way back to his army. Lancelot said a brief farewell and turned his horse eastward, toward the sea.

CHAPTER THIRTEEN

The Lady of the Lake

1

The days grew shorter, the nights colder, as we made our way northward. To the untrained eye we made a considerable sight, an army of knights and squires mounted on fine steeds, followed by wagon after wagon of provisions and arms, with workmen and camp followers trudging along after us. Our host stretched along the roads for miles, so huge that Arthur split us into three separate columns so that the horses and mules could find enough fodder to munch on.

But to me, our host looked like an army trudging unwillingly toward defeat. From Arthur, riding beneath his red dragon pennants, on down to the lowliest churl, the morale of the army was dwindling. Men disappeared every night, deserters slinking away from the coming battle. Reports came from the north that Modred's host was huge, and growing stronger every day. Arthur's army was melting away. Youngsters no longer sought to join us. Instead, the army was shrinking: slowly at first, but each morning there were fewer of us.

It was as if the entire army was gripped with despair, and already knew that fighting against Modred and his forces would be futile—and fatal.

One night, as we huddled by our campfires, I heard a couple of knights whispering, "If Sir Lancelot has abandoned the High King, why should we stay with him? Better to go back home while we still have our whole skins."

Gawain's death and Lancelot's departure had been bitter blows to Arthur, who now seemed to be going through the motions of preparing for combat without hope of victory. It was as if his will to win—his will to live—had been sapped out of his soul.

I stayed at Arthur's side as we traveled along the straight old Roman road heading north, toward Hadrian's Wall. Guinevere had said that Modred was waiting for Arthur there, close by the land of Bernicia, which his mother, Morganna, still ruled. Morganna, who I knew was the Creator who styled herself Aphrodite. How many of the Creators would engage in the coming battle? I wondered.

I decided to try to find out.

That night, as a cold rain turned our camp into a miserable muddy swamp, I left my sleeping blankets on a stretch of slimy wet rocks and walked off beyond the edges of our picket fires, into the dark and rain-soaked forest.

Anya, I called mentally with all the strength in me, Anya, help me. Show me what Arthur is facing. Let me see the reality of the coming battle.

For long hours I tried to make contact with the goddess who I loved. The pelting rain slackened and finally stopped. The clouds broke apart, and through the black limbs of the trees I could see a crescent moon gazing lopsidedly down on the soaked forest. Humans would walk on that dusty, barren world, I knew. They would build cities beneath its battered surface and go outward, across the solar system and to the stars.

But would that timeline actually come to pass? Or was it fore-doomed by my failure to save Arthur?

Of all the Creators, only Anya would deem to help me, I knew. The others played their mad power games, driving the human race to blood and war to satisfy their own overweening egos.

"How little you understand, creature."

I whirled and beheld Aten, the Golden One, standing before me, resplendent in a skintight uniform of glittering metallic fabric, glowing like the sun in the darkness of the dripping, chill forest.

He was smirking at me. "My mad power game, as you put it, will determine the fate of the human race. I am working to save them, pitiful half apes though they are."

"They are your ancestors," I countered. "If they die off, you will be snuffed out of existence."

His sneer diminished, replaced by a more sober expression. "Which is why I won't allow them to be driven into extinction, Orion."

"And Arthur's coming battle? That is part of your plan?"

Now his face became stern, severe. "Arthur would have died long ago if it hadn't been for you and your silly notion of defying me. As it is, all you've done is made his death more bitter. His own son will slay him, at Camlann."

"Not while I live," I said.

"You're a fool, Orion. The next time I make a creature to serve me, I'll have to build more intelligence into his feeble brain."

And with that, Aten disappeared, like a light winking out. I was alone once more in the dank, dark, cold forest.

But not entirely alone. I felt a presence, a pale tendril of another person, glinting weakly, just on the edge of my perception.

"Anya!" I called.

A pale silvery glow appeared before me, like a patch of moonlight in the darkness. It shimmered and took on a faint, flickering shape.

Anya.

She was as insubstantial as a phantom, as fragile as a snowflake, but it was her. My love. She wore a graceful robe of pure white with a garland of flowers crowning her flowing, onyx-black hair. The Lady of the Lake.

"Orion," she whispered, in a voice so weak I could barely hear her. "Orion, I thought I would never see you again. Aten has decided—"

"I know what Aten wants," I said. "Where are you? I can barely see you, hardly hear your voice."

Her fathomless eyes were wide with wonder. "You've broken through the stasis that Aten has placed around your locus! You've reached across millions of light-years to contact me."

"With your help, goddess."

"No, Orion! I did nothing! You summoned me to you. By yourself, without help from me or any of the Creators. Despite Aten's barrier, you broke through."

"But only just barely. You seem as insubstantial as a specter."

"So do you, my darling. But we're in contact, in spite of Aten. And you did it by yourself. Your powers are growing!"

With all my soul I wanted to take her and myself away, back to the Paradise we had known long ages ago, when the paltry few humans on Earth lived in tribal hunting bands and the world was open and free of villages and farms and wars.

But that could not be, I knew. Not yet.

To Anya, I said, "Aten has schemed to destroy Arthur and all he stands for. Even now, Arthur is heading toward a battle against his own son, a battle he fears he cannot win."

She nodded faintly. "Aphrodite has insinuated her poisonous thoughts into Arthur's mind. Aten is using her powers to drain Arthur of his vigor, to bring him to defeat even before the battle begins."

"How can I stop her?"

Anya's image began to waver even more. Her voice became fainter still. "Aten has discovered your link with me!" she said, in a weak, fading sigh.

With all my strength I tried to hold on to Anya's presence, but I could feel her slipping away.

"How can I stop Aphrodite?" I demanded.

"Accept what cannot be changed, Orion. Accept the inevitable." She was fading away, dissolving before my despairing eyes.

"Anya, don't leave me," I pleaded.

"I will return to you, my love," she called, her voice as faint as the distant whisper of a hunting owl's wing.

And I was alone again in the night, surrounded by the dark boles of the trees, glistening wetly in the fading moonlight.

2

Aphrodite was helping Aten, sucking the fighting spirit out of Arthur's mind like some psychic vampire. What could I do about it? How could I free Arthur of her mental thrall? Anya told me I must accept Arthur's fate, but how could I? How could I allow Aten to snuff out this flickering candle of civilization and allow barbarian darkness to engulf Britain—and the whole world?

The morning rose bright and clear, but so cold that the grass was stiff with frost. The men creaked and groaned as they awoke and went through their morning pissing and complaining.

Once we were mounted and clopping along the paving stones of the old Roman road once again, I rode alongside Arthur.

Trying to sound cheerful, I asked him, "How do you feel this bright morning, sire?"

"Old, Orion," he replied, downcast. "I feel old and weary."

I forced a smile. "Let the sun soak into you. That will warm your bones."

But Arthur shook his head. "Gawain, Bors, my foster father Ector, his son Kay . . . all gone. Dead. That's what makes calamity of long life, Orion: all those you hold dear depart from you."

"There are new friends," I rejoined. "Young knights like Sir Percival, Lamorak—"

"Even Lancelot has left me," Arthur muttered.

He was not going to allow himself to be consoled. Morganna/Aphrodite had somehow taken all the fighting spirit from his soul.

"I have dreams," Arthur said, in a low, troubled voice. "Every night I dream of Morganna and the wicked lovemaking we indulged in. The sins of our youth, Orion. The sins of our youth."

So that was how Aphrodite was destroying his courage. Using his feelings of guilt, amplifying his remorse about the past.

"She is truly a witch, sire. You were young and she took advantage of you, tempted you."

"Aye, that she did. And I gave in willingly enough. If it hadn't been for the Lady of the Lake I'd have been killed all those years ago." He sighed heavily. "Maybe it would have been better that way."

"No," I snapped. "You've given Britain more than twenty years of peace." Sweeping the colorful autumnal landscape with my extended arm, I urged him, "Look at the land around you, sire! The farmsteads are safe from barbarian raiders. The harvest has been rich and full. The people are happy, prosperous—"

"And we march to face my son in battle," Arthur countered. "One of us will die on the day we meet."

He seemed inconsolable, staring at a past he regretted, looking forward to a future he dreaded.

All that long, golden autumn day I pondered over how I might break Morganna/Aphrodite's spell over Arthur. By the time we stopped for the night and made camp, I had decided what I must do. The question was, could I do it?

3

That evening, as we made camp at the side of the Roman road, I walked off and left the men unfurling their sleeping rolls on the cold grass. Churls and esnes were putting up the tents for the knights. Arthur's was flanked by his red dragon pennants, but in the deathly calm night they hung limp and spiritless.

A noisy brawl suddenly erupted among the tents. I saw two of the squires tussling with each other in the flickering light of the campfires. Over a woman, I supposed. A trio of knights, swords drawn, quieted them down. I shook my head; discipline was falling apart, and Arthur was doing nothing to reinforce it.

More men would sneak off this night, I knew, deserting Arthur and the coming battle. I was leaving, too, but I intended to return.

Once far enough from the camp I looked up at the harvest moon, grinning lopsidedly at me as it rose full and bright above the wooded hills. I saw my namesake constellation of Orion climbing sideways over the horizon and thought of Anya, somewhere out there among the stars, kept from me by Aten's barrier.

Very well, I thought. If she can't come to me, I will go to her.

I willed myself to the timeless city of the Creators. The moon-bright night of Britain vanished and for a moment I was in total darkness and cryogenic cold. I could sense the geodesics of space-time shifting, bending. To my will.

Abruptly, I was in the city of the Creators. Not on the flower-dotted hillside above the city, but inside the city itself, standing in its central square, surrounded by the immense monuments the Creators had built for themselves over the ages: the Parthenon stood before me, a giant golden recumbent Buddha smiled benefi-cently at me on my right, a steep Aztec pyramid rose on my left. Turning, I saw a massive granite sphinx staring sightlessly at me, with columns and temples stretching into the distance behind it.

I turned back to the Parthenon, and its matchless statue of Athena, armed with shield and spear.

"Anya," I breathed. "Please come to me."

"I am here, my love." She appeared before me, again wearing the robe and flower garland of the Lady of the Lake. Her fathom-less gray eyes were solemn, her matchlessly beautiful face grave.

"We are all here, Orion," came the haughty voice of the Golden One.

And indeed they were. All the Creators: cruelly beautiful Aph-rodite, dark-bearded Zeus, Hades, looking almost amused, Ares with his shock of rust-red hair, his beefy arms folded belligerently across his chest, Hermes, Hera, all of them in flowing robes or skintight uniforms or even sculpted armor.

In his usual sneering manner, Aten said to me, "You grow tiresome, Orion, summoning us here. We do not cross the lightyears of spacetime to please your whims, creature."

"Yet you are here," I said.

"For this one time," said Aten. "For this one *final* time."

Anya stepped to his side. "You mustn't destroy him! After all the services he's done for you—"

"He's always been a nuisance. Now he's becoming—"

"A threat?" I interrupted.

Aten glowered at me. "You're going to die, Orion. And this time there will be no revival."

"You've never revived me after death," I said. "You build clone copies of me, fill their brains with the knowledge you want me to have, and send me out to die for you again."

Zeus smiled tightly. "He's learned quite a bit, Aten."

"This time you die for good," Aten said. Then, his voice rising to an enraged howl, "And I'll destroy the clones, I'll destroy all the cloning equipment, I'll destroy the entire cloning facility!"

I made myself smile at him. "You can't destroy me." Hoping it was true, I added, "You can't control me anymore, my Creator. I've grown too powerful for that."

Aten's face went white. I saw his eyes flick from me to Anya's face, then back again.

But before he could say anything, Zeus asked me coldly, "What is it that you want, creature? Why have you summoned us away from our tasks across the multiverse?"

Sharp-eyed Hermes spoke up. "Every time you bend the spacetime geodesics you make the cosmos unravel more and we have to toil to repair the damage you've caused."

Pointing to Aten, I replied, "He's the one who began sending me across the timelines. He started the unraveling that you're trying to repair."

"Enough bickering," Zeus snapped. "Orion, you have summoned us. Very well, we are here. What do you want?"

I looked into Anya's infinite eyes. What I wanted was to be with her, always and forever, in the sunny glades of Paradise, where we'd been happy for so brief a time. But before that could be, I knew, I had to protect Arthur.

Looking squarely into Aten's angry eyes, I said, "I want to save Arthur from the death you've planned for him."

"He's a mortal," Zeus said to me, not unreasonably. "Mortals die, Orion. You know that."

"I want him to live long enough to protect Britain against the barbarians."

Sullenly, Aten told me, "He's already done that. He's accomplished his goal. The barbarian invaders have turned to peaceful ways; they've learned to live with the Britons. The British Isles will never become subservient to the European mainland."

I stared at him. Had the Golden One given up on his dream of creating a unified empire that stretched from Ireland to Japan's inland sea? A unified empire that worshipped him?

"You've won, Orion," said Anya. "Arthur has brought peace and safety to the Britons."

"But now he must die," Hades added. "He's outlived his usefulness."

"So he's to be thrown away like a tool you no longer need," I said.

"If he lives longer," Aphrodite said, "he will become a stiff, unbending tyrant. The British people will suffer under him. He must die."

I turned to Anya. With sadness etching her lovely face, she agreed. "It's time, Orion. Let Arthur die. Let him be remembered as a hero among his people."

I nodded dumbly. They were all agreed. Even Anya. Arthur's fate was sealed.

But not before he stops Modred, I told myself.

4

It was difficult for me to look Arthur in the face the next morning. The sun rose, pale and lacking warmth, against a pewter-gray sky. The men were breaking camp, loading the carts and pack mules, saddling their horses.

Arthur stood in the midst of the morning bustle, watching his tent being taken down, his pennants furled.

As I came up beside him, he said, "We'll be at the Wall in another two days."

I nodded, unable to bring myself to say anything.

Striding toward his mount, Arthur said, "Remember all those years ago, Orion, when we chased the Picts and crossed Hadrian's Wall. How happy Bors was to be north of the Wall?"

I made a smile for him. "That's when we encountered King Ogier in Bernicia."

"And Morganna," he said, his voice dropping a notch.

"You saved Britain from an invasion by Ogier's Danes," I said, trying to brighten our mood.

Arthur grinned at me, remembering. "As I recall, Orion, it was you who bested Ogier."

"I serve Arthur, High King of the Britons," I said.

"Indeed." He slid his foot into the stirrup and swung up into the saddle. "And you serve him well, Orion."

Not well enough to save your life, I replied silently.

Arthur turned in his saddle and shouted to his mounted knights. "Northward! We go forward to face the enemy!"

They followed him. Reluctantly, I thought. And noticeably fewer than there had been the night before.

CHAPTER FOURTEEN

Morganna and Modred

1

"There they are," said Arthur.

The morning was dank and chill, with a ghostly fog rising from the frosted ground. The sky was gray, low clouds hiding the sun. Across the mist-shrouded ground, at the crest of the ridgeline rising before us, stood the mounted host of Modred's army, waiting for us. Modred had chosen this place for his battle, still a half-day's march from Hadrian's Wall. I wondered how much Aten or one of the other Creators had helped him to make the decision.

Arthur turned slightly in his saddle, surveying the ground and the enemy forces.

"They hold the high ground," he muttered.

Mounted beside him, I nodded agreement. "They've been resting while we've been marching north to meet them."

"Modred's no fool," said Arthur.

He was wearing an old Roman cuirass over his chain mail. It was gilded, but in the dull morning light it gave no glint of splendor. A pair of squires stood at either of his stirrups, one bearing his shield and helmet, the other clutching a double armful of lances and spears.

The air felt chill. Not a breath of breeze blowing. The fog rose from the frozen ground like spirits of the dead, slowly writhing.

Sir Percival rode up and nosed his steed between Arthur and me. He looked almost boyish, with golden hair so light that his beard seemed almost invisible. A stylized lion, in bright red, was emblazoned on his tunic.

"Sire, which one is Modred?" he asked.

Arthur pointed. "He in the black tunic, with the boar's head pennant."

Percival licked his lips nervously. He was young, just as young as Lancelot had been all those years ago at Amesbury. But where Lancelot had been eager to fight, afire with enthusiasm, Percival seemed much more circumspect.

"He's assembled a mighty host, sire. They outnumber us by far."

"So they do," said Arthur, almost wistfully. "So they do."

I said nothing. Arthur seemed downcast, almost defeated even before the battle had begun.

Looking past Sir Percival to me, Arthur said, "Modred expects us to charge uphill toward him."

That would not be wise, I knew. In the years since I'd first met Arthur, all the knights in Britain had learned to use stirrups. If Arthur's men charged uphill, Modred would wait until they were halfway up the rise or more, then have his host charge at us downhill. They would have more than merely the advantage of numbers; they would have momentum, and steeds that were fresh and rested.

"Should we wait him out?" I asked. It was a suggestion, really, but I wanted Arthur to make the decision on his own.

He cocked an eye at me. "You think he would be impatient enough to charge at us?"

"He might," I said, with a shrug. "He's young. Perhaps he's also foolish."

Arthur thought about it for several heartbeats. At last he said, "Let's see."

So we spent the morning sitting in battle array, neither side budging except for the occasional nervous shuffling of the horses. The morning fog slowly dissipated, revealing hillocks and shallow dips in the land, which was covered with dead brown grasses and shrubs wilted by frost.

The sun, pale though it was, climbed higher. By midday Arthur allowed his knights to dismount, a few at a time, so that the churls could bring them food and wine. I could see that Modred did the same.

We were playing a waiting game. Arthur would not be induced into charging uphill against superior numbers; Modred would not take the temptation of charging downhill against us. I wondered how confident Modred was of his men. Arthur had the cream of the Round Table's knights with him, what was left of them. Modred's forces must be composed of lesser men, I thought.

At any rate, Arthur was content to be patient, while Modred was unwilling to attack. The sun sank low in the west, twilight shadows began to creep across the uneven brown land. I could hear the knights behind me muttering. Some sounded impatient, others relieved that there would be no fighting this day.

At last Arthur told his bugler to sound retire. As the first notes rent the air, I heard the same call from Modred's host. There would be no battle until the morrow.

2

It was careless of me to discount the possibility that the Golden One would not wait for the battle, but try to kill Arthur that very night.

The churls pitched tents for the knights, squires took the horses to the roped-off makeshift corral and saw to their feeding. Camp women started cook fires and the men ate boiled meat and cabbages. Arthur gave strict orders about wine: two goblets for each man, no more.

Pickets were placed at the edge of our camp, guarding us against a surprise attack, and more stood at our rear, to prevent deserters from skulking off into the night. It grew pitch dark, with neither moon nor stars showing through the gloomy low clouds. The camp quieted as the men slept on the cold ground, some of them with the grimy women who had accompanied us.

Wondering how many men would try to sneak away in the night, I unrolled my sleeping blanket next to Arthur's tent and sat with my back against a rounded boulder. I willed my body to relax; sleep would be good in preparation for tomorrow's exertions.

As I began to doze, though, I sensed a furtive movement behind me. Worming myself down onto the blanket, I stretched out and pretended to sleep, while straining every nerve to detect what was going on.

There were three of them, quietly slicing at the rear of Arthur's tent, daggers in their hands, swords at the hips. I turned slowly onto my side and reached for my own sword. The three of them cut at the tent's fabric. But they were not infiltrators from Modred's camp; I recognized the three of them. They were knights that Arthur had recruited during the long march north.

Bloody anger filled me. Assassins. Traitors. Men who had sworn fealty to Arthur and now were going to murder him. If I allowed them to.

Leaping to my feet, I roared, "Assassins!" loudly enough to wake the whole camp. The three of them froze for an instant, then reached for their swords as I rushed at them.

The first one had barely pulled his sword halfway from its scabbard when I hacked his arm off. He screamed as blood spurted and the other two backed away from me, wide-eyed with sudden terror. With my senses heightened I easily knocked the sword out of the hand of the killer on my left, then clouted the other one on the head with the pommel of my sword. He went down like a felled oak.

The one I had disarmed was crouching to reach for his sword, on the ground.

"Don't make me kill you," I said.

He froze where he stood, stooped over, his hand stretching toward the sword.

A dozen other knights were rushing toward us in their sleeping shifts, each of them brandishing a sword that glittered in the firelight.

The would-be assassin dropped to his knees and began to sob. "Spare me! Please spare me!"

Arthur came up beside me, Excalibur in his right hand. "What's this?"

I pointed to the kneeling one, then to the one I had knocked unconscious, who was now groaning and writhing on the ground.

"Assassins, my lord. Traitors who had sworn fealty to you but this night intended to slay you."

With a glance at the third one, lying dead next to his severed arm, Arthur said, "You've saved my life, Orion."

I nodded grimly, then returned my attention to the one on his knees. "Who sent you? Why have you tried to murder the High King?"

Visibly trembling, he babbled, "A sorceress, my lord. A powerful sorceress. She appeared to us in the night. She took us to Lord Modred's castle by magic!"

Arthur muttered, "Morganna."

"What did Modred say to you?" I demanded.

The man swallowed, then confessed, "He said that Arthur was prophesied to die and if we fulfilled the prophecy he would reward us with rich lands and castles of our own. He would make us nobles at his court!"

"He would slit your throats," Arthur said.

Throwing himself facedown on the ground, the knight begged, "Have mercy on me, sire. Have mercy!"

"Hang them both," said Arthur. And he turned away.

The other knights grabbed the two of them, the one still pleading for mercy, the other too stunned from my blow to know what was happening to him.

I followed Arthur to the front of his tent.

"Modred is not so certain of victory," I said. "He wanted to make certain that you were dead and unable to lead your army."

Arthur nodded bleakly. "And his mother, the witch Morganna, is using her powers to help him."

I took the opening. "My lord, I think she had been using her powers to undermine your strength, invading your dreams to weaken you."

He looked at me for a long moment, and I saw understanding dawn in his gold-flecked eyes. "Perhaps so, Orion. Perhaps so."

"I am certain of it, sire."

His old grin lit his face. "So what should I do about it, sir knight? Refrain from sleeping?"

"No, my lord. Sleep well and deep," I told him.

I had decided to deal with Morganna/Aphrodite myself.

But how?

3

The night turned cold, but the men built a sizable bonfire to illuminate the hanging of the two would-be assassins. Arthur came out of his mutilated tent, wearing a fresh tunic, to preside over the executions personally.

Knights, squires, even the lowest of the workmen and serving women crowded around, lurid firelight painting their eager faces, while a squad of knights dragged the two bound men to the sturdy oak that had been selected for use as a gallows. They both looked sullen, resigned to the fate they knew they could not escape.

A knight shoved one of the prisoners so hard that he stumbled and fell. The knight aimed a hearty kick at his ribs.

"None of that!" Arthur bellowed, and the knight checked his blow. "This is Britain and we are servants of God," Arthur proclaimed loudly to the throng. "We are not barbarians who torture prisoners for the sinful joy of it."

The crowd murmured unhappily. They were not above watching a pair of helpless prisoners get a beating.

A brown-robed friar stepped up and muttered some words in Latin, then made the sign of the cross in the air. He stepped back, bowed to Arthur, and let the executions proceed.

The knights put rope nooses around the prisoners' necks, pulled them snug, then tossed the lengths of the ropes over the lowest branch of the tree. Two knights on each rope hauled them off their feet. The crowd roared with delight. The men kicked and thrashed about for a few moments, their faces bloating, flushing, and then going blue. They emptied their bladders and their bowels in their struggle and the onlookers laughed. Finally they both gave a final jerk and went still, swinging in the cold night wind. The crowd fell silent.

"May God have mercy on their souls," Arthur said, mechanically.

"Not bloody likely!" came a voice from the throng.

The onlookers dispersed, some laughing. I saw two men exchange a few coins; they had apparently bet on which of the hanged men would die first.

Arthur trudged back to his tent, looking totally untroubled. A pair of miscreants had gotten what they deserved.

And I still faced the problem of how to deal with Morganna.

I went back to my blankets and sat once again against the same rock. The bonfire collapsed with a crackling hiss, spitting embers, but at this distance it gave more light than heat.

I recalled that when I had returned to the Creators' city they had all gathered to face me. If I translated myself there again, probably the same thing will happen. I couldn't fight them all; I needed to get Aphrodite by herself.

I thought of calling on Anya to help me, but she had her own tasks to perform, her own problems to deal with, far away in space and time. No, I told myself, dealing with Morganna is something I must do myself. Without help. Myself against the self-styled witch.

I had to face her here, in this placetime, in her guise as Morganna, at her castle in Bernicia on the other side of Hadrian's Wall.

So there is where I went.

To my surprise, it wasn't that difficult. I pictured the dark and gloomy castle, remembering it from when Arthur and his knights had gone there years earlier. I closed my eyes and felt an instant of bitter cold and sudden weightlessness, as if I were falling from an enormous height.

When I opened my eyes I was standing atop the highest

battlement in Morganna's castle, with a cold wet wind from the nearby sea whistling through my thin tunic.

"How dare you?"

Turning, I saw Morganna standing before me. Aphrodite, really, more alluring than any woman has a right to be. Temptress. Goddess of love and beauty. In this time and place she posed as Morganna, the witch, dressed in a stygian black gown that clung to her figure like a second skin.

"Good evening," I said.

"What are you doing here?" she demanded, her dark eyes blazing. "Who sent you?"

I took a step toward her. Even furious as she obviously was, she was temptation personified.

"No one sent me. I came on my own volition."

"Impossible! A creature? Aten didn't give you such capabilities."

I smiled at her. "I've learned a lot. My powers are growing."

For all her haughty anger, Aphrodite backed away from me. "This is Anya's doing," she spat. "She's working against Aten."

"And you're working for him."

"We all are." Then she amended, "Most of us."

"To kill Arthur."

"He must die. It's inevitable. All mortals die."

"But you Creators are immortal."

"Yes." But there was a quaver of uncertainty in her voice, a hint of doubt.

I chuckled. "Of course. How can you know you're immortal? You'd have to be able to see all of eternity to be certain."

More firmly, she demanded once again, "Why are you here, Orion?"

"To get you out of Arthur's dreams."

"Ha! And how do you propose to accomplish that?"

"It's very simple," I said, stepping so close we were almost touching. "You've assumed human form. All mortals die." And I circled her smooth alabaster throat with my right hand.

Strangely, she smiled. "Mortals enjoy pleasures that not even the Creators may taste, Orion." She melted into my arms. My right hand slid down her back, to her waist.

"Forget your precious Anya for a while, Orion," she whispered into my ear. "I'll leave Arthur alone if it pleases you."

Resisting her was harder than facing the cave bear that had crushed the life out of me in an earlier existence, harder than allowing Philip of Macedon's guards to kill me after he'd been assassinated. My body wanted her and my mind was spinning, falling.

She laughed softly. "It's time for pleasure, Orion. You've toiled so hard; now it's time for your reward."

It was her pleased amusement that broke the spell. She was so sure of herself, so certain that she could control me, any man, with her sexual allure.

I grasped her throat with both hands. "All mortals die, Aphrodite. Once you assume mortal form you take on the risks of mortal life."

Her eyes flashed wide. "You can't! You mustn't!"

"The witch Morganna is going to die," I told her. "Or disappear from this time and place forever."

And that's just what she did: disappeared. One instant her body was pressed against mine and my hands were around her throat. The next I was alone on the windswept battlement of the castle.

Not entirely alone. I sensed a blazing anger, a raging hatred burning across the eons and parsecs of spacetime. Aphrodite was furious that I could resist her, enraged that I could reject her enticements. In her eyes I had been merely a creature that she could toy with; now she was my implacable enemy.

So be it, I thought. She's gone from this placetime. Perhaps she'll return, but this night Arthur will be able to sleep without being troubled by her dreams of guilt and shame.

4

Instead of returning to Arthur's camp, I willed myself to the camp of Modred's army, up at the top of the ridgeline facing Arthur's forces. Modred himself was sleeping in a fine tent, guarded by four men-at-arms, with dogs chained to posts pounded into the ground. The instant I appeared there the hounds snapped out of their slumber, ears perked, growling and alert.

In the light of the guttering campfire in front of the tent's entrance, the guards stiffened with surprise. As they leveled their spears at my belly, the tallest of them demanded, "Who are you?"

"I am Orion, a messenger from the High King."

They glanced uneasily at one another.

"Messenger," snapped one of them. "More likely a spy from the High King."

"The High King?" asked their tall leader. "You mean Arthur?"

"Yes. I wish to speak to your commander, Sir Modred."

They dithered, apparently fearful of waking Modred in the middle of the night. I stretched my senses, searching the camp for some sign of the Creators. Nothing. They were not intervening in the coming battle, I thought. They were content to allow these mortals to slaughter each other without their aid or direction— except for Morganna's insidious undermining of Arthur's spirit.

But now that I'd chased Aphrodite away, I wondered if the Creators would return here to exert their will.

One of the guards eyed me suspiciously and asked, "How did you get this far, into the middle of our camp? Didn't the pickets stop you?"

"They didn't see me," I answered truthfully.

"You made yourself invisible?" gasped the smallest of the quartet, his hand going to an amulet he wore around his neck.

"Not really," I told him.

Their leader, the tall one, said curtly, "Sir Modred is sleeping. We dare not awaken him."

Then I will, I decided. Recalling how the Neandertals could communicate with animals and control them, I reached with my mind into the four shaggy hounds chained at the feet of the guards. Within moments all four of them were howling, baying at the moon, even though it was nothing more than a faint glimmer behind the low, threatening clouds.

The two younger guards tried to hush the dogs, to no avail. Their yowls got stronger, louder. One of the youths started to kick the nearest hound, but I jabbed his shoulder hard enough to push him off balance.

He wheeled at me, pulling his sword. The other three leveled their spears at me once more.

"Stop that infernal noise!" came an angry voice from inside the tent.

Modred stepped out, one hand rubbing at his eyes. "I can't sleep with that damnable racket in my ears!"

I let the dogs stop. In the sudden silence, Modred saw me—a stranger—and the guards confronting me with drawn weapons.

He was a handsome young man, almost beautiful. A slim, nearly ascetic face that showed his lineage from Aphrodite quite clearly, with nothing of Arthur's hearty, more boyish good looks. Ebon dark hair falling to his shoulders and a trim dark beard outlining his jaw. He was shorter than Arthur and far more slender, almost delicate.

"Who's this?" Modred demanded, eying me warily.

"My lord, he says he's a messenger from the High King."

"Take his sword, you idiots."

They unclipped my sword from the belt around my waist. I held my arms outstretched and made no move to stop them. Odysseos' dagger remained hidden beneath my tunic, strapped to my thigh.

Modred stepped up to me, eyes narrowed. He was several finger widths shorter than I.

"Messenger, eh?" he said, in a derisive tone. "You look more like a fighting man to me."

"I am Sir Orion," I replied, "and I serve the High King."

"My loving father," said Modred, dripping acid. Turning to the guards, he said, "Stand alert here. I'll listen to what this . . . messenger has to say." With that, he beckoned me to follow him inside his tent.

The tent's interior was handsomely furnished, with carpets on the ground and a fine table surrounded by four sturdy chairs. A full bed stood in one corner, plush pillows piled high atop it, rich blankets roiled and hanging halfway to the carpeting. Modred liked his luxuries, I realized.

He lit the oil lamp on the table, then turned back to me.

"So what says my loving father? Is he prepared to die?" Before I could reply Modred went on, "Is he enough of a Christian to realize that he'll roast in hell for all eternity?"

I smiled tightly at him. "I expect that Arthur believes he will see heaven."

"With the stain of fornication on his soul? And incest? He raped my mother! His own sister!"

My jaw dropped open. His sister?

"You didn't know that, did you, sir knight? He didn't tell you that one little point, did he?"

"My lord, I was his squire when he first met Morganna," I said. "She bewitched him, enticed him beyond any man's power to resist. And he certainly did not know that she was his sister."

"So he tells you," Modred grumbled.

"Be that as it may," I said, "there is no reason for you to fight the High King. You can settle whatever the differences may be between you—"

"Only death can settle our differences!"

"My lord, surely—"

"He ignored me! He pretended that I didn't exist! Even when I went to his fine castle at Cadbury and asked him—begged him!—to be invested among his knights of the Round Table, he acted as if he wished I'd disappear, as if he wished that I'd never been born!"

Modred's anger was like a physical force. All the years of his life Morganna had filled his ears with this hatred, and now it was implacable.

Suddenly he laughed: a harsh, bitter laugh. "You think we can settle the differences between us, messenger? There's only one point of difference. I want his throne. It's rightfully mine, after he dies, and I'm going to see to it that he dies! He'll never give it to me willingly, even though it's my right by birth. So I'll take it from him. With these two hands."

I could see something close to madness in Modred's blazing dark eyes. An obsession that had been planted in his mind from birth. I had banished Morganna/Aphrodite too late, far too late. Her poison filled Modred. Only death could extinguish it.

"Now go back to your High King and tell him that his son will slay him on the morrow and take his crown for my own. And his wife, in the bargain! Tell him that!"

For an instant I thought that I could kill him with my bare hands. Snap his neck before he knew what was happening. But something stopped me. Perhaps it was Aten's will overpowering me, perhaps it was my own disgust at the thought of committing still another murder.

Whatever, I slowly turned and left Modred's tent, to make my way back to Arthur's camp and the coming battle.

CHAPTER FIFTEEN

The Battle of Camlann

1

The morning dawned thick with fog, worse than the day before. Arthur's knights roused themselves and slowly, reluctantly, donned their chain mail and climbed onto their horses. Once again we stood in battle array at the foot of the slope, barely able to see through the chill, dank fog the army of Modred waiting for us at the crest of the ridge. The air was still, and the tendrils of fog seemed to clutch at us like cold, evil fingers.

Sir Percival was mounted at Arthur's other side, staring gloomily at Modred's host atop the ridge. "Look, sire," he said, pointing. "They're in sunlight up there."

"Mayhap the sun will broil them in their armor," Arthur joked.

Percival was not amused. "They outnumber us by far, sire," he said, just as he had the previous morning.

Arthur turned to him and smiled wryly. "What of it? If we are to die, there's enough of us to make our people mourn our loss. But if we win, the fewer we are, the greater our glory."

Percival looked unconvinced, but he muttered, "I suppose so, sire."

I looked at Arthur's smiling face. "Did you sleep well, sire?" I asked.

"Quite well, Sir Orion," he said happily. "Very well indeed."

Arthur was himself again. Morganna's invasion of his dreams had ended.

Shielding his eyes against the rising sun, Arthur wondered, "Will this everlasting fog burn away?"

"Not for hours, sire," I answered.

"We can't just sit here for another day, Orion. Half my men will pack up and leave if we don't fight this morning."

"But it would be folly to charge uphill against Modred. That's just what he's waiting for."

Arthur shook his head, murmuring, "I wish there was some way to entice him to come down here."

"Perhaps there is, sire," I said, remembering a tactic that the Mongols had used when I'd been among their horde under the leadership of the wily Subotai.

I explained to Arthur the Mongol tactic of the feigned withdrawal. Often Subotai, when faced with a force that outnumbered his, would have his mounted warriors pretend to retreat, inviting the enemy to charge after them. The Mongol horsemen bent their line into an arc, like a bow, with the middle retreating faster than their wings. The enemy usually charged into the center of the retreating line, thinking that the Mongols were fleeing.

At a given signal, the Mongols wheeled about to face their pursuers. Before they realized they'd been tricked, the enemy found themselves attacked on both their flanks, while the center of the Mongol line stood firm and faced the enemy's charge. Hemmed in on both sides, the enemy's numbers became a liability instead of an asset; they were too crowded to fight effectively.

It was a tactic the Mongols had devised from the great hunts they undertook every autumn in their homeland by the Gobi. Subotai perfected the trick and used it to slaughter armies from the Gobi to the Danube River.

"Pretend to retreat?" Arthur asked, uncertainly.

"Let the center of our line move the fastest, and the wings more slowly," I said.

"It sounds complicated."

"Explain it to the leaders of your knights. And have the churls pack up the wagons, or at least move them out of the way."

He scratched at his beard.

I urged, "Modred will think you're retreating, running away. He'll charge down from his hilltop position to chase you. Your knights can surround him and chop his men to pieces."

His face furrowed with deliberation, Arthur at last nodded and smiled at me. "It's worth trying," he said.

The fog did not burn away, even though the morning sun climbed higher in the sky. Arthur called his leaders together and explained what must be done. The workmen were sent scampering to pack up the wagons and start them down the road we had taken to get here.

"Modred can't see the wagons through this damnable fog," Arthur complained.

"But he'll see your knights when they begin to retreat, sire," I said.

"Yes, he will, won't he?"

"And he'll come charging down the slope to catch you in retreat."

Nodding doubtfully, Arthur muttered, "More men are slain in retreat than when they face the enemy bravely, that's true."

It would work, I was certain. We'll trick Modred into racing down here and face him on this level.

It was nearly high noon before Arthur gave the order to begin the retreat. Despite the sun shining high above, the fog still lingered, chill and dank, like an evil omen. Arthur gave the word at last; as the bugles blared, he turned his steed and, with a glance over his shoulder, began leading his troops away from Modred's waiting army.

It almost worked.

2

I should have realized that these Celtic knights, who gloried in single combat, were not able to match the well-drilled maneuvers of Subotai's veteran army of hardened Mongol horsemen. The retreat began well enough, although it was clear that Arthur's men thought their High King was showing cowardice to run away from the enemy. That was all to the good, as far as I was concerned: perhaps Modred, watching us from up on the ridgeline, would also think Arthur had lost his nerve.

Slowly we plodded through the fog, which seemed as thick as ever. I could not see more than a few dozen knights on either side of me. Turning in my saddle, I looked back at Modred, still sitting in the clear sunshine, unmoving beneath his black boar pennant.

The feigned retreat depends on careful training and strict obedience to the commander's orders. The Celtic knights had precious little of this kind of training in coordinated maneuvers, and hardly any of the iron discipline that had made the Mongols conquerors of most of the world. Practically born in the saddle, the Mongol warriors were drilled mercilessly in the kinds of maneuvers that confounded the enemies they faced. Subotai's men swept across the breadth of Asia and crushed the armies of Europe's Christian kings because they rode as one mailed fist: thousands of hardened warriors fighting as a single entity, controlled by one mind.

This kind of discipline was unknown to the Celts. These knights had little knowledge of tactics beyond the headlong charge into their enemy's midst. After that, their battles broke down into individual fights, man-on-man, little better than the vainglorious Achaean warriors who spent years on the plain of Ilium because they had no idea of how to surmount Troy's high walls.

So Arthur's knights slowly, unwillingly retreated into the fog. Even in the little I could see clearly, instead of moving in a smooth unbroken line they were already clumping together, a few knights riding close to each other, leaving gaps in their line.

"Sire," I said to Arthur, "the men should keep an even separation from one another. If there are breaks in our line, the enemy can take advantage of them."

Arthur nodded. "Ride up and down the line, Orion, and tell them what they must do. Tell them their High King commands it."

"Yes, sire," I said.

But as I spurred my horse to begin giving Arthur's orders, the air was rent by the blast of bugles. Looking up, I saw that Mo-dred's host was at last charging down the slope toward us, lances leveled, pennants flying.

"Ah-ah!" Arthur shouted, relieved, as squires went racing among our knights, handing out helmets and shields, heavy thrusting lances and lighter throwing spears.

Arthur's face was smiling, buoyant, as he lifted his helmet over his head. The battle was about to begin and he was in his element. Mongol tactics were not for him, even though he understood the value of them. The enemy was charging at him, and he was eager to countercharge straight into their midst, lance in hand, Excalibur at his side.

I pulled on my helmet and spurred my mount. The whole army was aroar, charging now pell-mell into the enemy, all thought of tactics and discipline blown away in their sudden relief. This they could understand. Face your enemy and smite him with heavy blows. Battle at its most brutally elemental.

Through the swirling fog we charged, lances in hand, horses racing at full gallop. Once again my senses went into overdrive; I saw Modred's knights charging at us as if the world had slowed to dreamy languor. Even as I spurred my steed onward I could see the bulging eyes of the horses approaching us, spittle dripping from their bared teeth.

With their helmets hiding their faces and their heavy shields in front of their bodies, the enemy knights looked more like robots than humans. I could not see their faces. I tried to tell myself that they were intent on killing me, and worse, killing Arthur.

Yet the old primitive excitement that I once felt in the heat of battle was no longer in me. I tried to tell myself that these faceless warriors charging toward me were machines, toys, inhuman killing machines. Yet I knew that inside those helmets and suits of chain mail were men, human beings who lived and hoped and feared and did not want to die.

No matter. They were upon us and the two armies clashed into each other with a roar and clang of metal against metal. Lances splintered. Knights were lifted out of their saddles. Men and horses went down. The swirling fog was filled with shouts and curses, screams of agony and blood-chilling war cries.

In an instant the battle lost all semblance of order. We were not two armies fighting against one another but a wild tangle of men slashing and thrusting in individual combats.

Charging alongside Arthur, I smashed into the first knight I could reach, my lance cracking through his shield and knocking him out of his saddle. He crashed to the ground as I drove past him and took on another knight. His lance thrust screeched along my shield and passed me harmlessly while I feinted toward his helmeted head and then dug my lance into his middle, beneath his raised shield. He screamed in agony and fell off his charging horse.

A sudden blow from behind dazed me. Turning, I saw a knight in heavy body armor, swinging a studded metal ball at the end of a short chain. Off balance from his first strike, I raised my shield to ward off his next, but he cannily changed the direction of his blow and struck my horse hard on the neck. The poor animal reared and buckled on his hind legs, taking me to the ground, one leg pinned beneath the thrashing steed.

My mace-wielding foe wheeled about and came at me again, swinging that studded metal ball over his head and yelling a piercing battle cry. Watching him in slow motion, I tugged at my leg, pinned beneath the bleeding horse, and ducked his blow as he rode past.

My horse scrambled to his feet and trotted away unsteadily, bleeding from the wound in his neck. I pulled out my sword as I slowly got to my feet. My leg felt numb but there was no time to test its strength. The knight was charging me again; I could see wisps of fog swirling about him as he came galloping in slow motion toward me.

I threw my shield at him edgewise, like an oversize discus. It struck him a glancing blow, but it was enough of a distraction for me to ram my sword into his side as he rode past. I felt the point grate on bone. He howled and rode off, slumping in his saddle as he disappeared into the fog.

I yanked the heavy helmet off my head; it restricted my vision too much. Glancing around, I saw that the battle had broken down into a wild melee, a tangle of individual fights. Knights ahorse and on foot were battering each other in the swirling mist. The fog was still chill, but we were hot with rage and bloodlust.

Where is Arthur? I wondered. I had been at his side when we first charged against Modred's host, but now he was nowhere to be seen. I started off afoot to seek him, without helmet, without shield, sword in hand.

A mounted knight came charging at me, crouching behind his shield, his lance pointed at my heart. I froze, watching the point of his lance as it bobbed slowly in rhythm to his horse's pounding hooves. At the last instant I dodged sideways, and as he rode past me I hacked at his extended arm. He howled and dropped his lance, his arm almost severed just above the elbow.

Two more men in chain mail advanced upon me on foot behind their heavy shields, one bearing the emblem of a bear, the other a stooping hawk. Both of them carried long Celtic blades.

"Yield, sir knight," called one of them from inside his helmet, "or we will slay you."

"Yield yourselves, gentlemen," I shouted back at them, "and save your lives."

That ended our conversation. They ran at me, spreading slightly to come at me from two different angles. I sprang at the one on my right, diving into a rolling block that knocked his legs out from under him. Leaping to my feet, I drove my sword into his ribs before he could get up, then recovered just in time to block the vicious swing his companion aimed at me.

I backed away from the dying man on the ground while his

companion advanced upon me, shield in front of him, held up to the eye slits of his helmet. Slowly he came at me, confident that a man without shield or helm had no chance against him. I retreated slowly, feeling my way across the uneven ground, littered with fallen men and broken weapons.

I knew that it is impossible to thrust at an opponent and defend yourself at the same time. A winning fighter must be fast enough to switch from offense to defense almost instantaneously. But with my hyperspeeded senses, almost instantaneously was not good enough.

My attacker aimed a mighty blow at me. I saw him cock his right arm over his shoulder, plant his feet, and swing his sword at my bare head. His blow came at me as if it were swinging through a thick invisible goo, languorously slow, so leisurely that I had plenty of time to dance back and avoid it, then thrust forward and slice his forearm from wrist to elbow with the point of my sword.

He bellowed with pain as his sword fell to the ground. For a moment we faced each other, his mouth hanging open, his face twisted in agony. He awkwardly fumbled off his shield so that he could grip his bleeding arm with his left hand. I pointed my dripping sword at his throat.

He dropped to his knees and beseeched, "Spare me!"

I nodded and stepped past him, looking for Arthur. And felt a searing pain in my back, just above the kidney. The treacherous dog had stabbed me with his dagger. I swung round and took his head off with a swipe of my sword. Then I sank to my knees, bleeding hard. I reached around and yanked out the bloody dagger, then willed my blood vessels to clamp down and stanch the bleeding. The pain was monumental, but I commanded my brain to ignore the flaming signals my nervous system was flashing.

Still, the world wavered before my eyes and I toppled face-first onto the cold bare ground and slipped into unconsciousness.

3

How long I was down I don't know, but it couldn't have been more than a few minutes. When I opened my eyes men were still hacking at each other in the swirling fog, screaming and cursing in victory or in pain; riderless horses trotted by, their eyes wide with fear as their masters killed and maimed one another. The broken, rocky ground became slippery with blood. Bodies of the dead and wounded littered the field.

But where was Arthur? I had to find him.

I saw Sir Percival, down on one knee, crouching behind his battered shield that bore his red lion emblem. He was bleeding heavily from a gash on his shoulder. Three mounted knights surrounded him, and it was clear that they were offering him no quarter.

Stiffly, I got to my feet. The wound in my back was already clotting; the pain was only a distant throbbing ache. Picking up a spear from the littered ground, I hurled it at the horsemen surrounding Percival. It sailed past them harmlessly, but it served its purpose. They turned their attention to me.

As they spurred their horses, I charged toward them and jabbed my sword toward the eyes of the nearest horse. It whinnied in fright and reared on its hind legs, nearly throwing the knight out of his saddle. Running past him, I slashed at the exposed leg of the second of them before he could lower his shield enough to protect himself.

Percival staggered to his feet and hurled himself at the third, dragging him out of his saddle to thump painfully on the ground. In an instant all three of them were dead, and I saw that Percival was bleeding from several wounds and gasping heavily. His shield was badly dented; even his helmet was cracked.

"Get away while you can," I told him.

"Not while there are enemies to fight," he answered bravely.

"Then find yourself a horse."

Nodding, he added, "And a lance."

"Where is the High King?" I asked him.

Percival pointed into the fog. "He went after Sir Modred."

I started off in the direction he pointed to, limping slightly, my leg weak and my back twinging.

It wasn't a battle now, the fight had turned into nothing more than a jumble of separate brawls, men slashing at each other with swords and maces, spears and knives, even bare hands, intent on slaughtering each other. Blood and pain and red-hot fury filled the cold gray fog. Men were killing each other for the mindless urge to kill, to batter, to destroy their enemy.

The Creators had built that bloodlust into the human psyche, I knew. They had made us killers, haters, beasts who slaughtered not merely to survive but to revel in the power and passion of killing.

I hated them for it. All of them, especially Aten. All of them, except Anya.

And then I saw Arthur. With Modred. It was a sight I will never forget.

They were up on a little rise in the ground, two dark figures in the gray fog, silhouetted against the silvery, clouded sky. Both of them had lost their helmets. Neither of them bore his shield.

Arthur had transfixed Modred on his lance, gripping the lance with both his hands, his teeth gritted, the expression on his face awful as he stared at his spitted son.

And Modred was crawling up the length of the lance, even as his entrails slithered out of him, dragging himself inch by agonizing inch, the lance penetrating completely through him, dripping blood, pulling himself along with one hand while his other gripped a heavy sword. Modred's once-handsome face was grimacing with agony—and something more: sheer hatred, unadulterated malevolence—his delicate features were twisted into the countenance of a demon from hell.

I was more than a hundred paces from them, but I tried my best to reach them, hobbling slightly from my wounds.

Modred was spitted on Arthur's lance, but Arthur himself was also transfixed, wide-eyed, as he watched his son crawling toward him, sword raised high to strike.

It was a horrific nightmare. In sluggish slow motion I watched Modred creeping nearer to his father, while Arthur did nothing but stand there, gripping the lance in both hands, staring at his approaching doom.

I wanted to scream at them. I wanted to tell Arthur to drop the bloody lance and get away. Modred was as good as dead, save yourself, I wanted to say. But no words came out of my mouth. In desperation I hurled my sword at Modred, but it sailed past him unheeded.

I knew I was running as fast as I could but it wasn't fast enough. Modred, his teeth bared, his eyes blazing hate, struck at Arthur's bare head. I saw the blade smash into Arthur's light brown hair. His knees buckled and he dropped the lance at last as he sank to the ground, bleeding. Modred fell, too, writhing for a few moments before his body finally stiffened into death.

"It's finished, creature." I heard Aten's arrogant voice in my mind. "Your precious Arthur is dying."

"He's not dead yet," I muttered as I stumbled toward the fallen High King.

Arthur's scalp was streaming blood, his amber eyes were half closed, yet still he recognized me. "Orion . . ." he gasped. "Orion . . ."

"Come, sire," I said, sliding an arm beneath his shoulders. "I'll help you."

He groaned with pain as I lifted him to a sitting position. "No use, sir knight. I am slain."

"You're not dead yet, sire," I said, wishing I knew what to do, how to help him.

"Excalibur," he murmured. "What will become of Excalibur?"

"That's not important now, sire. We must get you to safety, to a healer."

"Merlin could heal me. He could do anything." Arthur's voice was growing fainter. He was dying.

I glanced around us. The fog was thinning at last, and the battle seemed to have ended. At least I could see no one near, hear no sounds of battle, no shouts or screams or even moans of pain. Nothing but deadly silence. The very air had become absolutely still.

Arthur was sinking fast. His voice barely a whisper, he said to me, "I want you to take Excalibur, Orion. Return it to the Lady of the Lake, with my eternal thanks."

"I will, sire." Then the idea struck me. "And you with it."

4

Grasping him carefully, tenderly, I picked up Excalibur in one hand and then rose to my feet with Arthur in my arms. The pain from the knife wound in my back nearly made me collapse. But I fought it down and willed us to the distant lake far to the south where Anya had first appeared to him in her guise as the Lady of the Lake and given Arthur his Excalibur. One instant we were on the blood-soaked battlefield of Camlann, wispy tendrils of fog clinging to us, the next we were at the shore of the lake, in the silver moonlight of a calm, warm evening.

And Anya was standing at the shore, the little wavelets lapping at the hem of her long white robe, her lustrous onyx hair garlanded with flowers. Her beautiful face was framed in moonlight, her lustrous eyes wide, startled.

"Orion!" She gaped at me. "How did you bring me here?"

"I?" I asked, just as surprised as she looked. "I thought you came of your own power."

Anya shook her head. "I was halfway across the galaxy, Orion. Now, suddenly, I'm here with you."

"One of the other Creators . . . ?" I wondered.

With a slow smile of understanding, she said, "No, Orion. It was you. You summoned me. You translated me across eons and light-years."

I started to shake my head. "I don't possess that kind of power. Aten never built that capability into me."

"You've learned how to do it, Orion. You're gaining the powers of the Creators themselves."

The realization stunned me. I stood there with the dying Arthur in my arms, staring at Anya, who smiled back at me knowingly. I am gaining the powers of the Creators themselves, I thought. Yet I felt no different than before. But wait: the wound in my back was healed. I was no longer in pain; I felt strong, powerful.

A groan from Arthur snapped me back to my senses. Strong and powerful I may be, but Arthur was dying in my arms.

"I failed, Orion," he said, his voice weak, faint. "I tried to bring them peace, tried to protect them from the barbarians, and it all came to naught."

"Not so, sire," I said, as I laid him gently on the moonlit grass. "The Saxons and other invaders have turned to peaceful ways, because of you. You and your knights have brought peace and stability to Britain, while the rest of Europe has sunk into savagery and despair."

"I killed my own son," he sobbed.

Kneeling beside him, I said, "He gave you no alternative. He was intent on killing you and ending all you stood for."

With a painful sigh, he said, "Modred has succeeded, then. All that I stood for is lost."

"It's not lost, Arthur. Britain will never sink into the barbarism that would have engulfed it if you had not lived. Over the coming years, the coming centuries, Britain will remain free, strong, a haven against the tides of barbarians that will sweep the continent."

He almost smiled. "The Channel . . . our moat defensive, to protect us against barbarian invasions."

"Not merely the Channel, sire. That's just a band of water. It will be the men on this side of the Channel, the men who remember Arthur and his knights of the Round Table, who remember that you fought for the right, to protect the weak, to keep human decency alive on this island."

"It would be pretty if it were true," he whispered.

"Believe it, sire. Britain will be a beacon of freedom and hope for ages to come. The memory of you and your knights will shine across the world."

He actually did smile. And closed his eyes.

Anya touched my shoulder. "Let him rest, Orion. Let him die in peace."

Getting to my feet, I looked down at Arthur. His face was covered with blood from his terrible wound, but it looked peaceful, content. I placed Excalibur in his folded hands.

My eye caught a faint glimmering in among the trees that ringed the lake. As I watched, it grew into a bright golden glow and I knew that Aten, the self-styled Golden One, had come to join us.

Once, his presence would have paralyzed me, left me helpless with awe, unable to move a muscle. But no longer, not now.

He stepped out from the trees, a stunning figure resplendent in a skintight uniform of metallic gold. He smiled coldly at Anya, then turned his gaze to me. I stood before him, unmoving, unmoved.

"Your work here is finished, Orion," said the Golden One, glancing down at Arthur's body.

"Not yet," I said. "Not yet."

5

Almost before I myself knew what I intended to do, Aten snarled at me, "You dare?"

"I dare," I replied.

"I'll destroy you forever!"

Anya held up a restraining hand. "No, Aten. You can't. Orion has learned far too much to buckle to your will."

"You defy me, too?"

She gave him a serene smile. "Let Orion do what he wishes. In fact, I don't think you can stop him. He's almost our equal now."

"Equal?" The Golden One sputtered with rage. "A creature, my equal?"

"You built him too well, Aten," said Anya. "He is learning how to be a god."

"Never!"

"See for yourself," Anya said. Then she turned to me. "Go ahead, Orion. Save Arthur if you can."

I looked down at Arthur's dying body. Closing my eyes and focusing all my energies, I translated him through time. In a swirl of centuries I sent Arthur through the spacetime vortex, across the continuum, to appear in Britain whenever he was needed.

In a wild kaleidoscope of shifting time I was with him as we led townsmen who battled the brutal Viking invaders bringing fire and death to Britain in their longships.

I was part of Arthur's crew in the fireboat as we sailed across the choppy waters of the Channel to defend Britain against the Spanish Armada.

On the deck of a man-of-war, slippery with crewmen's blood, together we fired our cannon at the French ships off Trafalgar, loaded, and fired again, as we desperately held Napoleon's invasion forces at bay.

I flew alongside Arthur in the Battle of Britain as we few, we band of brothers, hurled our Hurricanes and Spitfires against the Nazis who were trying to invade and conquer Britain.

And I stood at the edge of the moonlit lake, facing the smiling Anya and the enraged Aten. Arthur's body was gone, translated through spacetime, leading his people whenever they were threatened with invasion.

"He isn't dead," I said to Aten. "He will never be dead, not as long as Britain needs him."

Blazing with fury, Aten roared at me, "You fool! You ignorant, arrogant fool! Do you realize what you've done? Do you understand that every change you make in the continuum unravels the fabric of spacetime? You've forced us to spend eternity trying to repair the damage you've caused!"

"So be it," I replied. "You began the unraveling by your tinkering with the fate of the human race."

"We *created* the human race!" Aten bellowed.

"And the human race evolved into us," said Anya, coolly. She seemed almost amused.

Steaming, Aten swore, "I'll destroy you, Orion. Once and for all, I'll erase your existence."

Anya shook her head. "I doubt that you have that power, Aten. Orion is too strong for you now."

He glared at her. "We'll see," he snapped. And with that he disappeared as abruptly as a light switched off.

Anya stretched out her hand to me. "You're in great danger, dearest. He's a deadly enemy now."

"You're in danger, too," I said, clasping her soft warm hand in mine.

She laughed lightly. "Both of us, then. Together."

Epilogue: Paradise

We lay side by side on our bellies in the high grass. We had been tracking the boar all morning. The sun burned hot above, but beneath the shade of the broad-leafed trees the air was cool with the breeze blowing in from the nearby sea.

Anya didn't look much like a goddess. She wore an animal pelt, arms and legs bare, her lovely face smudged with dirt, her flowing onyx hair wildly tangled.

She smiled at me, and her beauty shone through all the stains and smears of this existence. We were in Paradise, the broad, beautiful, game-filled forest that stretched across the northern rim of Africa. The basin that would one day be known as the Mediterranean Sea was filling from the enormous waterfall spilling in from the Atlantic Ocean where the Pillars of Hercules stood. Every day the sea grew, bringing fresh rains to nourish the broad, green forest.

North of the filling basin the land that would become Europe was almost completely covered by a two-mile-thick ice sheet that stretched all the way to the North Pole. An Ice Age gripped much of the world, and the human race—scattered across Africa for the most part, in tiny bands of nomadic hunters—had yet to invent agriculture or build villages.

Paradise. A hunting ground teeming with game and freedom. Anya and I were happy here. Who wouldn't be? There were no chiefs here among the meager human tribes, no kings or vassals, no cities to confine us, no wars to bring slaughter and misery.

What would one day become the island of Britain was still attached to the mainland of Europe, buried beneath the glaciers that would not melt for another thousand centuries.

Silently, Anya tapped me on the shoulder. I could not see the boar through the high grass, but I heard it snuffling. We were upwind of the beast, yet it still sounded wary, dangerous.

Inching along slowly on our bellies, we followed the boar's grumbles. I moved slightly ahead of Anya. Like her, I was gripping a wooden spear in one hand, its tip hardened by fire.

With the tip of the spear I slowly, carefully parted the tufts of grass obscuring my vision. There was the boar, rooting in the ground with its curved tusks, unaware of our presence and its impending death. It was a big animal, enough meat to feed our little band of hunters for many days. If we could kill it. If it didn't kill us first.

Anya tapped my shoulder again and made a circling motion with her free hand. I nodded, and she slithered off to my right as silently as a snake. I smiled at my huntress. In later ages she would be worshipped as Athena, warrior and giver of wisdom. In this era she was a Neolithic hunter, happy and free.

I worried that she might move too far in her ploy to attack the boar from two sides. If the breeze changed even a little the beast would sniff us out and bolt away. Or charge at her with those powerful, sharp tusks.

And that is just what happened. Almost.

The boar's head suddenly snapped up. It grunted, much like an old man suddenly disturbed in his slumber. My senses went into overdrive. I saw the boar's muscles tense beneath its shaggy coat. If it charged at Anya while she was still inching along the ground, prone, it could rip her apart before she could use her spear to defend herself.

I leaped to my feet and bellowed at the animal. It froze for an instant, then turned toward me, its narrow little eyes blinking. For a moment I thought it would scamper away, and our whole morning's stalk would be wasted. Instead it bunched its muscles, lowered its head, and charged straight at me.

I gripped my spear in both hands, ready to impale the beast when it got close enough. But then Anya burst out of the foliage to my right and nailed the animal through its ribs with her spear. The boar growled and twisted, yanking the spear from Anya's hands. Slathering, spouting blood, it turned on her.

I raced forward and rammed my spear through its hindquarters, nailing it to the ground. It screeched horribly as it thrashed about, trying to work itself loose. I held on to my spear, keeping the beast pinned.

Anya jumped lightly to the boar's side, yanked her spear out, then jammed it in again at the base of the animal's skull. It collapsed and went silent.

"Well done," I said, puffing.

She laughed. "Well done yourself, Orion."

By the time we finished quartering the carcass we were both grimy and splattered with the boar's blood and entrails. I grinned at her. Anya didn't look like a goddess now—unless perhaps she was Artemis, goddess of the hunt.

As we toted the meat through the forest, back to the clearing where our band had made its little camp, Anya said happily, "We'll feast tonight."

"And tomorrow," I said. "Several tomorrows."

Her cheerful smile faded. "How many tomorrows do we have, Orion?"

I knew what she meant. "As many as we desire, dear one."

But she shook her head sadly. "Aten is scheming to destroy you, darling. You know that."

"Let him scheme. We can stay here in Paradise as long as we want to."

"I wish that were true."

"Why not?" I demanded.

She caught me with those infinite gray eyes of her. "Aten must be plotting with others of the Creators to eliminate you, erase you from the continuum as if you never existed."

"He can try," I growled.

"He *is* trying! I can sense it."

"We're safe enough here."

"For how long? A week? A year?"

Shaking my head, I admitted, "I still don't understand how you can travel through time and yet still be bound by it."

"The point is, Orion," she said, very seriously, "that the longer we stay here in Paradise the longer Aten has to plan your destruction."

"Maybe I should destroy him, then."

Her eyes widened. "Destroy a Creator?"

"He'd destroy me if he could. Why shouldn't I fight back?"

"But . . . destroy a Creator?" The idea seemed to shock her.

I stopped and let the bloody chunk of the boar slide from my shoulders to the ground. "We've got to do something. You're right about that."

"What do you have in mind?" she asked.

"I don't know. Not yet." I felt a weight far heavier than the boar settling on my shoulders. "But I've got to do something, don't I?"

"*We* have to do something, my darling. You and I, together."

I lifted the bloody meat off her shoulder and took her in my arms and kissed her. Two Neolithic hunters, covered with grime and gore, who loved each other through all the eons and light-years of the continuum. We would face Aten and the other Creators together, for all eternity if need be.